Praise for *Road Maps*

"Youngers has written an exceptional book that delves into human relationships with the insights of someone who has done their own inner work. It is touching without being maudlin, emotional without being overwrought, and touches one to the core. This is a top-tier book and a must-read."

— **U.S. Review of Books**

Praise for Angela Youngers's other novel *Another Dance*

"Skillfully written...Youngers artfully tells two different love stories, juxtaposing past and present romance, both with exquisite sweetness and poignant heartache."

— U.S. Review of Books

"*Another Dance* unfolds a warm series of revelations that are revealing, dramatic, educational, and alluring, all in one."

— Midwest Book Review

Road Maps

Road Maps

ANGELA YOUNGERS

BookPress
publishing

Published in Des Moines, Iowa, by:

Bookpress Publishing
P.O. Box 71532
Des Moines, IA 50325

www.BookpressPublishing.com

Publisher's Cataloging-in-Publication Data

Names: Youngers, Angela, author.
Title: Road maps / Angela Youngers.
Description: Des Moines, IA: Bookpress Publishing, 2025.
Identifiers: LCCN: 2025916049 | ISBN: 9781960259431
Subjects: LCSH Authors--Fiction. | Iowa--Fiction. | Travel--Fiction. | Family--Fiction. | Man-woman relationships--Fiction. | Romance fiction. | BISAC FICTION / Women | FICTION / Romance / Small Town & Rural | FICTION / Travel & Vacation
Classification: LCC PS3625 .O86 R63 2025 | DDC 813.6--dc23

First Edition

Printed in the United States of America

10 9 8 7 6 5 4 3 2 1

To my sister, Gina.
The greatest gift
our dad ever gave us
was each other.

Road Maps is a work of fiction that contains discussion of terminal illness, grief, mental health, infertility, and miscarriage.

PROLOGUE

Excerpt from *Iowa Nice* by Logan Sterling

Rows of youthful green corn whiz past me as I speed down the rural highway. I look over to my dad in the passenger seat where he leans his head back, his eyes closed tight with pain. It's one of his bad days. I should be grateful that we've had so many good ones, that I've even been able to have any *days with him, but it still feels unfair.*

There's always been an expiration date on this journey, but now, looking at his weathered form, I realize it's almost over. I've been a child about this whole thing, naively thinking there was room for more. More time together, more roads traveled, more boxes checked.

My hands cling to the steering wheel, my knuckles white as I silently pray that he recovers from this particular bout of infirmity. But his illness won't end—not until he does. Suddenly, I feel a finger brush against my bare arm, and I turn to see my dad smiling at me through a strained wince.

"Logie Bear, I think it's time to go home." He says this as an apology, as a diagnosis, as a final decree.

I gag on my sob. I don't want him to see me fall apart, not after so many years of cold resolve, but witnessing my father weakening as his illness takes hold, I must bend to the realization that death is finally coming to make good on its threat to take him away from me. And I just got him back.

1

We humans are always trying to calculate the worth of something, trying to ascertain what value an action will add to our lives, how we will be compensated after the initial investment. I, for one, think we are obsessed with trying to answer the question, "Was it worth it?"

Was it worth it for a teenager to be caught sneaking home after curfew, damaging their parents' trust and their own freedom, just to enjoy a few more moments of unsupervised bliss?

Was it worth it for an eager entrepreneur to destroy their life savings, relationships, and morals while trying to prove themselves an economical champion?

Was it worth it for a partner to have an affair, blowing up their entire life and forever changing the lives of others?

The simple answer: No. But life isn't simple.

There are so many times we humans act before we think, and, in the end, we almost always have to answer for our impulsiveness.

So why do we do it? Why do we veer off the known path and make decisions that we will later regret?

Because we're human, and we're predisposed to failure. At least, that's how I've come to justify my own catalog of ill-advised doings.

I've been predisposed to failure since birth, sentenced to suffer the consequences of my progenitor's sins. There's always collateral damage.

I am the collateral damage of my father's many choices in life, the first being my name.

"My dad always wanted a boy" has become a knee-jerk response whenever a new acquaintance pauses to contemplate my first name. When the blunt comment first flees my mouth, I can see them freeze, their eyes dilating with fear, jaw muscle twitching as they try to work out a proper reaction. It's only then that I lift up the left side of my mouth and raise my eyebrows in jest, instantly releasing my conversational partner from their social paralysis with an awkward, yet relieved laugh. I'm generous that way, giving them a fun little bonding moment and a way to remember my name the next time we meet.

But I'm also a liar. Because it's not fun, and it's not a joke. My dad did want a boy, a son he could mold into a shiny plastic model of himself. A replica that would play sports, attend West Point as a top student and athlete, serve his country, and eventually step into a noteworthy profession of law or medicine. Then First Sergeant Malcolm McClarnon could announce to every Tom, Dick, and Harry with a proud twinkle in his eye, "That's my boy. That's my son. That's my everything." And then he could die happy.

Instead, he had me: Logan Sterling. Unathletic. Uninterested in physical labor or discipline. Permanent civilian. Chooser of impractical professions and partners. Source of paternal disappointment.

That's okay. I didn't get everything I wanted in life either. That, too, is a side effect of being human.

To say my dad's and my history is rocky is an understatement. We've been through All. The. Shit. All due to his life choices:

→ Divorcing my mother when I was five

- → Replacing his previous family with a new wife and two stepdaughters
- → Living multiple states away throughout previous daughter's formative years
- → Trying to exert control over rebellious teenage daughter from across said multiple states
- → Attempting to reconcile with daughter after second divorce and relocation to nearby city
- → Recognizing strong personality differences exaggerated by years of absence
- → Dropping the ball when daughter's mom dies her senior year of high school

And that's only the first eighteen years. I'm now thirty-two and about to have a movie made from the book I wrote detailing the events of the other fourteen years.

I'm overflowing with disbelief. I'm buzzing with excitement. I'm festering with disgust. I. Am. All. The. Things.

And I'm wrestling with the potential fallout. Will it be worth it? Will this finally make me happy? Should I be allowed to be happy?

I can't keep worrying myself with all these conflicting emotions though because I'm about to meet a bona fide movie star, and from what I've heard, movie stars don't appreciate others' messy emotions. Their own messy emotions, for sure, but definitely not the loud, demanding ones that are currently duking it out in my overactive brain.

How sad is it that even amid the cacophony of my emotional battlefield, the pathetic voice wondering "Would Dad finally be proud of me?" still cuts through all the noise.

Unfortunately, I'll never know. Dad has been dead for five years. And his death is to thank for my current success.

"Mr. Sterling?" A young woman in a pressed pencil skirt and

white blouse with tightly pulled back hair and perfectly drawn eyebrows appears in the waiting room.

I inhale sharply at the redundant routine of having my gender misidentified. Luckily, the circus routine of explaining my name will not be happening today as my literary agent Niya Sanghvi answers for me.

"It's Ms. Sterling. She's a bestselling author, for fuck's sake. Do your research and be better," Niya says from her seat next to me, her eyes never leaving her phone as she messages clients about other life-changing deals while my own life-changing deal waits for me in the next room.

The assistant's face instantly reddens, a stain of crimson seeping through her flawless foundation. "I'm so sorry. Mr. Price is just finishing up a call, then he'll be right with you." Without making eye contact, she bows her head and retreats to the empty desk across from us to hide her face behind a computer screen.

"You didn't have to be so mean," I whisper, leaning close to Niya while trying to be discreet. Though I may have similar thoughts, I tend to bury my snideness beneath Midwestern politeness. Niya, on the other hand, is pure urban snark.

"Of course I did. It's Hollywood. It's like the official brand. Mean and desperate," Niya responds while making no attempt at a hushed tone. "You'd better get used to it, Logan. We're not in Iowa anymore."

I exhale loudly and continue bouncing my knee while running my mind through calisthenics of worrying and wondering.

The fact that my life-changing deal wears the face of a Hollywood Adonis only increases my anxiety. Thomas Price came to prominence as a teen drama heartthrob, eventually going on to star in numerous action movies, a handful of romantic comedies, and my personal dreams. As a teenager, his face was the last image I saw before falling asleep in my Tommy Price poster-adorned bedroom in

Ottumwa, Iowa. I lost hours of time daydreaming of randomly meeting him during Oktoberfest, or possibly running into him at the Iowa State Fair. Our eyes would meet, and he would instantly realize that we belonged together.

I know, chances are a million-to-one that I would have run into a movie star in America's fly-over country, but there were actually better odds in my case because Thomas Price is also a homegrown product of Iowa. Sure, he's from a different city, but people run into each other in Iowa all the time, and they usually say hello out of polite obligation.

So how does a simple Iowa boy end up one of the biggest television and movie stars of our time? By being drop-dead gorgeous, for starters. He became a model after being spotted at a college football game; his natural charisma, strong work ethic, and overall likeability took over from there.

So how does a simple Iowa girl end up in a production studio about to meet her adolescent crush?

For years, I struggled to find my creative voice, whether writing songs, essays, fan fiction, or emails for the mundane jobs I held (and hated) in order to pay the bills. But I finally found the magic sauce when I put to pen the story of a dying dad and his doting daughter going on an end-of-life road trip through their home state. People just ate that up. Its designation as a true story only added to the marketing frenzy, and after months of translation deals, book signings, and clandestine meetings about movie rights, I've found myself in sunny California about to meet many Americans' relationship hall pass. It's been tough for me because I'm not really one for the spotlight and the book has become bigger than I ever imagined—or even wanted—but Niya's worked so hard, and I could use the money, so I guess I am now ready to sign a deal. Unless I say something stupid. Or inappropriate. Or too real.

"Stop it," Niya snaps, tucking her phone into her Prada mini bag and swiveling her crossed legs to point accusingly my way.

My body flinches in response. Even though I've known Niya for four years, she still catches me off guard with her beauty and competence. Today, she is nothing short of fierce. Her dark hair is pulled back into a sleek ponytail, her trim body accentuated by a fashionable charcoal business suit. Her large brown eyes narrow as she waits for my puny response.

"Stop what?" I squeak out unconvincingly. I uncross and recross my legs, fixing the hem of my blue pleated skirt.

"Stop doubting yourself. There's nothing to worry about. He wants this. Badly. And I think he's the best man for the job. Seriously, this is it. The fun is about to begin." She settles back into her seat, her phone back in her hands, her attention already onto the next task.

I wish I had Niya's confidence. I wish I had Niya's everything. Her looks, her income, her large family. But even if I can't have her life, at least I get to have her in my life. Ever since I signed with her, we've curated the perfect good cop/bad cop dynamic. Her sharp features, fashion, and wit is the yang to my rounder, meeker yin. I bring the sweet and she brings the "shut the fuck up unless you have a good deal for me" vibe. She scares me…but I love her.

"I suppose," I answer, though she's already moved on from the conversation. I occupy myself by looking around the modest waiting room, trying to catch the assistant's eye so I can give her a reassuring smile, but her eyes are laser-focused on her screen. I shift my gaze, taking in the gray walls, the dark-gray carpet, and the light-gray furniture. It's a gray aesthetic assault.

Niya filled me in earlier on how Thomas rents this very gray office for all sorts of movie-making deals. He runs his own production company, Price Pictures, as most successful actors do now, often bankrolling movies in which he also stars. That's why I'm so nervous about this meeting. Not because I have had countless sex dreams about him, many of which occurred before I even knew what sex really entailed, but because I don't really know what he wants with my story. There's no role for him. It's either me or my dad, and Thomas Price cannot play my dying father. That would definitely put a damper on my nocturnal fantasies.

The office door opens and Niya stands up, so I follow, stumbling on my heels as I do so. Thomas Price stands in front of me in all his six-foot-two, broad-chested, lean glory. His dark-brown hair is tousled and pushed back, giving my eyes full access to his blue orbs and perfect nose. And that mouth. That mouth is quirked into a shy smile; the same shy smile he's been known for since his first television show, *Rocky Mountain High*, in which he played the football star/secret genius/all-time heartthrob Jackson Rove. That grin brought several female characters into his bed, and if the rumors are correct, many real-life starlets into his real-life bed. I gulp and try to stand without swaying on my pinching high heels.

"Hello, ladies. Tom Price," Thomas greets us. He sticks out his hand and I go numb. I'm sure I shake it, but I can't look away. Niya is in complete control as always, handling the introductions while discretely poking me in the ribs. *Get yourself together*, says the sting of her perfectly manicured nails.

Thomas leads us into his office decorated in (surprise) more gray and gestures to two empty chairs in front of his desk. "This is my business manager, Landon Becker. He'll be joining us today." He nods to the handsome man in a blue suit perched on the edge of the desk like a catalog model. Seriously, is everyone in LA in perma-pose here? Landon leans over to shake our hands as Thomas moves to his own seat across from us. He's all casual comfort and classic good looks in a soft-cream henley shirt and dark tailored jeans. I hold my hands in my lap, my face frozen in a forced smile while Niya looks between both men, already bored with this game. Thomas cracks a smile at Landon and suddenly slaps both hands on the desk, making me visibly jump while Niya barely blinks. "I want to make your book into a movie."

"Yes, of course. That's why we're here," Niya answers stoically.

"Yes, but *I* want to make it. I want to produce *and* direct it." A childish look of glee illuminates his entire face, and he balls his hands up into excited fists as Niya and I wait for the punchline.

Thomas Price is known for his connections and friendly relationships with many revered directors. One of the reasons Niya and I were so confident in this match was due to his ability to network. But it sounds like that network may be null to us now.

I can no longer stand Niya's cold corporate stare down, so I start talking. "Mr. Price, have you ever directed before?"

"It's Tom," he says, glancing at me quickly before bringing his attention to Landon. "And no, I haven't. But I've been in a lot of movies and I've learned from some of the best. I'm ready for my turn." Landon nods his head in approval, but Niya jumps in.

"And what makes you think my client's first movie deal of what we hope to be many should be your turn to see if you have any directing chops?" Tom and Landon slide their focus to Niya, a lioness calmly waiting out her prey.

Landon stands up. "Ms. Sanghvi, you must know how many book-to-movie rights get purchased then tossed in the bottom of a storage closet never to see the light of day. Tom is giving Ms. Sterling's book an actual chance at life."

"I understand the business, Mr. Becker. I've been doing this for a decade. But I also know my client's story and I know that there are other production companies that could find seasoned directors who could do her story justice."

"I don't want to just do it justice. I want to make it memorable.

I want to touch every cold, shriveled heart in Hollywood with a bit of movie magic and make each grow three times bigger like the fucking Grinch. I want to make a goddamn masterpiece."

The three of us all stare at Tom blankly, shocked by his passionate interjection. Under the pressure of our wide-eyed stares, he stands up and moves around his desk, coming to squat between Niya and me. I slowly turn to meet his gaze as he looks up at me, my nose picking up his scent of citrus and sandalwood. When he reaches up to grab my hand in his, the hairs on my arm stand at attention.

"Ms. Sterling?"

"Logan," I manage to mumble, unable to look away from the ocean pools of his eyes.

"Logan." He smiles, knowing he has me. "I want to make this movie because I think you deserve someone that sees the true heart of your story. To have gone on this journey across your home state, *our* home state, with your dad before he passed must have been the experience of a lifetime. It's probably a memory that crosses your mind every day. You did something meaningful, something memorable. And now, I want to make it magical. I want every audience member to feel that magic, to know that they, too, can still make amends and heal their own wounds. And I want to do it while featuring some of the greatest, most underappreciated countryside in the whole United States. I want to make this movie for you, Logan. I know it means the world to you, and I promise I will make it my world, too. Please, let me do this."

Thomas Price, esteemed actor and gorgeous male specimen, is going to make my book into a movie. I lose myself in his sharply cut jaw, perfectly symmetrical features, and long-lashed, jeweled eyes as I nod my head and seal the deal. I'm so swept up in the beauty of it all that I don't even stop to think of all the reasons I shouldn't.

Excerpt from *Iowa Nice*

OMAHA

"You came." My dad stands in the doorway of his modest home on Grover Street, his face shrouded in shadow. I'm still unable to see how time and illness have changed him, but I can't escape the very real truth that we are in the same physical space for the first time in eight years.

It takes a moment to find my voice, years of restrained anger blocking my airway. When I speak, the words claw upwards, leaving my throat feeling bloody and raw. "You asked. And you're dying. Of course I came. I'm not a monster."

First Sergeant Malcolm McClarnon releases a breathy chuckle as he opens the storm door, stepping into the light and back into my life.

He's a shell of himself. His once-compact athletic build is now soft and puffy, drooping with exhaustion. The usual summer tan, often dark in contrast to my paler skin, is now pallid and yellow.

A once-lush oasis of thick hair is nothing more than a bald landscape, the past remnants of a trimmed brown beard now spotty and gray. A soldier's straight spine is replaced by the weary bend of a cancer patient. This is my dad. My body recognizes him, wanting to throw myself into his open arms and be consoled, a decade of hurt longing to be soothed by a father's assured whispers. But I'm also hesitant, afraid to harm him with an enthusiastic squeeze. And worried of hurting myself by accepting him too readily without apology.

But he did apologize. He apologized on the phone when he called me one week ago. The number and contact lighting up my phone was surprising; even more surprising was my willingness to answer. Seeing "Dad" scroll across my screen ignited a moment of clarity that I can only attribute to a higher power. Once I answered with a questioning hello, he took over the conversation, telling me of his terminal diagnosis, apologizing for years of silence, and requesting a final chance to reconnect. He asked me to join him on a trip across our home state, to give us a chance to see the hidden jewels Iowa has to offer while remedying our relationship and reaching closure for his milieu of mistakes.

I didn't want to come. I wanted to stay holed up in my one-bedroom apartment in downtown Des Moines, vacillating between the two polars of my professional endeavors: composing poetry and short stories that feed my creative soul versus constructing mortgage contracts that feed my actual body. Working for a monolithic bank has allowed me to work from home while successfully avoiding social interactions. But it's also left me socially isolated, emotionally scarred, and deeply depressed; in other words, it's made me a prime traveling partner, for sure.

"You packed?" I ask, stepping back to signal our departure.

"Uh, yeah. I just need to grab a few things. Do you want to come in?" His gaze locks with mine, twin pairs of choppy-water irises con-

necting with their kin. I quickly turn, descending the small set of stairs to the sidewalk.

"Nah, I'll wait in the car." My breathing becomes faster and shallower as my heart starts to pound against my chest. I make it into the driver's seat before a sob rips through me. The torrent of emotions wracks my body with a tempestuous wind. I'm angry my dad is dying, angry he had the nerve to drag me here to see it, and angry he didn't call me sooner.

I let the rage spew from me rapidly in hopes it will dissipate before my dad takes his place in the passenger seat. It was his dying wish that we make this trip together, and I'm going to prove I'm more reliable as a daughter than he ever proved to be as a father.

I snort the last sniffle away as he pulls open the door of my Toyota Corolla. We look at each other, and I know he sees it in my face: splotchy cheeks, red nose, watery eyes. To his credit, he doesn't mention it, just presses his mouth into a thin line and puts on his seatbelt.

"Shall we?" he asks. I take a deep breath, turn the ignition, and pull away from the drive, headed toward our first daddy-daughter destination. No phones, no distractions, no buffers. Just a marked roadmap, a cramped car, and each other.

2

I'm not a Michelin-starred restaurant kind of gal. Meaning, I've never been to a Michelin-starred restaurant. My only knowledge before Googling was that these restaurants are pricey. That knowledge was further solidified by my search, but I also learned about the award criteria, so bravo to me for becoming more worldly every day.

I'll actually get to pop my Michelin cherry tonight, as Niya and I are meeting up with Thomas and Landon to discuss script ideas and finally sign on the dotted line. It'll be just enough time for me to exchange my life's work for a wad of cash before going back to Iowa. I call Niya from my hotel room, certain I'm having a panic attack.

"What are we even going to talk about at this meeting?" I ask, wondering if I can manage to get a free pass. Any woman in America would switch places with me in a second if it meant getting to breathe within the radius of Thomas Price. And while I'm not immune to the same contagion that is Tommy Price fever, I don't trust myself in a super formal setting. I say one wrong thing, and he could back out of the whole deal. Then I'd retreat back to Des Moines with my tail between my legs and a resume at the ready because there's no longer a job for me back home. When I asked about taking off time to come to LA and broker these deals, my request was denied. So I quit. And now, I'm nervous I won't make my rent without this contract. I give air to my worries, telling Niya I'm not immune to putting my foot in my mouth.

"That's why you pay me the big bucks," Niya states.

"I don't pay you unless I get paid."

"Exactly. So toss aside your overalls, slather on some mascara, and hoist those titties up. That way, even if you say something embarrassing—which you won't—pretty boy and his lackey will be too distracted by your corn-fed cleavage to even notice. I'll see you at the restaurant in a few hours."

"I don't have overalls—" I retort as Niya hangs up. I finish my thought to a dead line. "With me." I don't even blink at her blatant objectification of my breasts. Niya taught me to use everything I have to contend in a male-dominated business. She's the reason I started buying more expensive bras, and I can't deny that the perks of perky boobs are very real.

I follow orders and manage to zip myself into a curve-hugging bodycon dress I bought for the occasion. The black satin hem hits high on my thighs, and the corseted bodice accentuates my chest while contouring my waist. But two hours later, I'm regretting my choice of black heels as I clamber out of the Uber and walk toward the frosted-glass doorway of Foam.

I stumble, my heel twisting just steps away from the entrance. I holler out, "Ope!" and prepare myself for an unceremonious landing on the concrete before I am suddenly caught around my waist and pulled upward.

Thomas Price holds me against him, and I look up only to become lost in those ocean depths, the waves of blue that are currently focused on me in my folded disarray. I remain hovering in his arms, a damsel in distress supported by a debonair hero, a character trope Tom has portrayed not once, but four times: Medieval knight Griffin Largo, Secret Service agent John Branden, small-town sheriff Beau Buford, and Unnamed Knight Who Catches Lady in Waiting in his first on-screen role. (My fangirl knowledge goes deep).

I utter a monosyllabic "Wow" as I stare up at him. I see Thomas's lips move, but my ability to hear is completely overridden by the visual and tactile sensation of being pressed against him. His lips move again, more persistently. *Oh my gosh, is he going to kiss me?* But then he shakes me, undoubtedly concerned by my muteness, and I redirect my senses enough to hear him ask, "Are you okay? Can you stand?"

"Oh, uh yes. Yes, I can stand," I fumble while pulling down the hem of my dress from its unfortunate position above my ass. Thank goodness for shapewear. Once I'm assured I won't be arrested for indecent exposure, I look up and manage to squeak out my gratitude. "Thank you for the grand gesture."

"Grand gesture?" he asks as we move toward the side of the walk.

"You know, the grand gesture of saving me." I stare in awe at a group of fancily clad diners entering the restaurant. "Was that a Kardashian?"

"Probably." He glances quickly at the glittering patrons before focusing back on me. "And let's be clear: I don't consider what I did a grand gesture, just basic human decency."

I turn to meet his gaze, suddenly aware of the vision that stands before me; a perfectly tailored black suit paired with a crisp white shirt on a body that knows how to hang a jacket beats a Kardashian sighting any day. After my not-so-subtle once-over of his body, my eyes meet his and a knowing smile brings me back to my manners. "So what do you consider a grand gesture?"

He hums lightly and taps his chin with elegant fingers as he directs me toward the entrance. "Hmm, I'm not sure. But if I make one, you'll definitely know it."

His eyes flick to mine, and I'm pretty sure I black out only to come around to the sound of my own voice rambling on. "Oh, that's uh…yeah. Anyway, it's not my fault that I stumbled. I'm not used to high heels. Or tight dresses. Or fancy restaurants. I figured I should try to fit in, but I still feel like I'm playing a part with a flashing marquee that says 'Not From Here' over my head."

"Yeah, that never really goes away. I've been out here for almost twenty years, and I still think someone is going to send me on the first flight back to the farm." He opens the door and guides me in, a light hand at the small of my back. I stammer a response as we head toward the host.

"What? No! Not you. You're Thomas Price—"

"Tom," he interjects, then he turns on that megawatt smile as he greets the beautiful woman in a black suit. "Reservations for four. They should be under Thomas Price." The woman smiles demurely, her eyes darting from the celebrity A-lister to the anonymous blonde teetering next to him. She instructs us to follow as she shows us to our booth in the dimly lit restaurant.

I continue our conversation while trying not to trip again. "If anything, they're just looking at you because you're so gorgeous… I mean…uh, yeah. You know it. Of course you know it. That's your job, right?" We sit across from each other at a dark walnut table set between buttery black leather booths with diamond tufting. I sink backward, almost falling into the deep end cap, and freeze when I notice Tom frowning.

"What? To look pretty?"

The hurt in his voice catches me off guard. This is a man that's made a living off of his face, but my incredible discomfort with conflict urges me to explain. "No. Well, kinda—but it helps that you're so attractive. People want to watch you on-screen because of it."

"You know, there's more to me than a pretty face."

"Oh. Yeah. For sure. I didn't mean that, I just—" *Shit.* And I thought I was going to be the one getting objectified tonight. I shift in my seat, trying to lean into my own feminine wiles. What was it Niya said? Tits up?

He sighs and leans back against the cushion, his arms crossing his chest. I can't help but notice the pull of fabric against his biceps. *Down girl, down.* "It's fine. I know what you mean. But that's the problem. Everyone sees me for my looks. I have a lot of substance, too."

An awkward pause is thankfully interrupted by our server bringing water. We go ahead and order drinks while we wait for Niya and Landon. Once alone again, I ask, "Is that why you want to direct the movie? To prove you have substance?"

"Yes and no." He leans forward with his elbows on the table, his hands tented beneath his chin. "I do want to prove myself. But I also want to be challenged. I don't want to be stagnant. The only way to survive in this business is to adapt. I'm nearing forty, and I have to accept that there may be a time when no one's going to cast me as a romantic lead. Maybe I get too gray, too fat, too jowly—"

"I don't believe it. Never gonna happen." I'm met with another smile.

"Whatever it is, I want to have other ways to exist. And when I read your book, I knew. This is it. Your story is the one I need to tell in order to move onto the next chapter in my own story. Reading your book changed my life, Logan. It made me want to be a better version of myself, to put the past behind me and move forward with grace and confidence. I'll forever be grateful to you for that."

Wow. How does one even respond to that? How I do it is by looking down and pretending to get distracted by the row of numerous utensils, suddenly overwhelmed by both Tom's comment and the future task of eating. "Oh my gosh, you're going to need to help me. Unless there's a manual, I'm going to mess up."

"Don't worry about that. No one here is judging you." When I finally get the nerve to look up, I'm met with a gaze that blankets me in warmth and acceptance. I can't look away, his magnetizing stare only broken when he looks down to fiddle with the fork furthest to the right. "Anyway, it's easy. Just start on the outside and work your way in."

It's unfathomable that I'm here alone with The Thomas Price, aka the man of my teenage dreams, and that our conversation feels so natural. Maybe it's the softened lighting; maybe it's the rich aura of a Michelin restaurant; or maybe it's just the intoxicating pull of his shoulders, hairs, eyes, mouth…ahem. I've gotten distracted, so I blurt out a question, trying to keep the easy exchange going while hiding my drifting focus. "How did you do it? Make the shift from Iowa to California so easily?"

"Who said it was easy?" He gives me a lopsided grin and I have to stifle a giggle.

"Well, you've been here long enough. And you know the right fork order. Sounds like a successful transition to me," I manage to say, proud of myself for the average ability of stringing words together.

"I learn fast. I can memorize really quickly. And I have a great skin care regimen." I laugh just as our server sets our drinks in front of us. I take a sip of my martini, grateful for the ability to pause and catch my breath. We share a moment of silence as we both take a drink, and I find my words again.

"I have to admit, I was a bit surprised you weren't late. Isn't that the LA way?" The fact that Niya and Landon are each now ten minutes past our reservation time goes unmentioned but hangs in the air between us.

He leans back, relaxing into the conversation. "Yes, but I'm not from LA. I'm an Iowa boy. Ten years of waking up at five in the morning to milk cows taught me the value of staying on schedule. It's never fun to have pissed off cows with sore udders."

Tom grew up on a farm outside of Iowa City. I remember reading a feature about him at his family farm, complete with interviews with his mom, dad, and older sister. "What does a pissed off cow do besides moo louder?" I ask, genuinely curious.

"Kick." His perfunctory answer makes us both laugh, and I start to feel as if we exist in a bubble, an ecosystem separate from the dining room of Foam. He must feel it, too, evidenced when he leans forward and says, "It's nice getting to talk to another Iowan. Sometimes I feel like a hick out here when I start talking about the farm—"

"Cow tipping?"

"Or dirt biking."

"How about detasseling?"

"The worst summer job ever!" Our burst of laughter earns us a few awkward glances from other patrons, but it doesn't matter. Our bubble is impenetrable. Tom stops laughing, and his gaze centers on me, his eyes steady, warm, inviting. "I'm really excited about your movie, Logan."

I take a gulp, still disbelieving that such a famous person would even spend time with me, let alone be so kind and encouraging. "It's going to be your movie, Tom"

He leans forward, shifting into business mode. "Well, that's what I wanted to talk to you about—" Just then, our bubble bursts with the arrival of Landon and Niya. The hostess glides away just as smoothly as she appeared when showing them to the table, and we all exchange greetings as they settle into their seats. Niya slides in next to me, her glance quickly shifting to my chest and back up with an approving raise of her eyebrows.

"So sorry. Traffic was a bitch," Niya states to the table at large.

"What are we drinking?" Landon asks, and we all start discussing the exorbitantly priced menu. Luckily, Tom is financing tonight.

***

Five courses, three martinis, and two hours later, we are all enjoying an after-dinner coffee. I don't know how I'm ever going to fall asleep after a ten o'clock espresso, but I didn't want to look inexperienced in the ways of formal dining. Even though Tom said no one would judge me, I'm still hyperconscious of being an outsider.

"Before the evening ends, let's get the paperwork signed." Landon whips out his phone and starts tapping. A notification pings on my own phone. "I just sent you the Docusign." Part of me was hoping for a ceremonial signing of an actual paper contract, but I guess everything is boring and electronic now.

"Hey, before you do that, I want to run something by you," Tom interrupts, placing a hand on Landon's shoulder. Landon looks like he wants to interject, but Tom ignores him and focuses on me. "I know you thought we were just going to buy the rights to your story and you would be rid of us, but I have a proposition for you."

"Oh really?" Niya settles back, her eyes narrowed with suspicion. She was not briefed on this, and I can tell she is uncomfortable with the unknown plot twist. She looks between Tom and Landon as if she's a tiger backed into a corner.

Landon's dark-brown eyes drink her in as he smiles coyly, stating in a calm voice, "Claws in, Ms. Sanghvi. Just hear him out."

Niya's nostrils flare as she completes her own assessing scan of Landon, but her focus coolly shifts to Tom when he begins explaining.

"I know this is my first time directing, and I promise I'm going to do everything possible to keep true to the heart of your story. But I don't want some random screenwriter adapting your book. I want you to write the screenplay."

I almost spit out my coffee, but a small miracle enables me to keep my lips sealed and instead just slightly choke as the liquid goes down the wrong pipe. After an interlude of unladylike hacking, I'm able to gasp out, "What? Are you crazy? I've never written a screenplay!"

"And I've never directed a movie! See, we'll make a great team!" He claps his hands together gleefully, his face lit up with the epitome of a movie star smile. I wouldn't be surprised to see a shiny twinkle appear at the corner of his mouth scored by a tinkling sound effect.

"Why didn't you mention this earlier today, or even during dinner?" I feel put on the spot, without the proper amount of time or soberness needed to think this through.

"What can I say? I love a grand gesture." Tom winks at me, and my need to think through anything quickly vanishes.

Niya steps in, allowing me to break free of his photographic pull. "So how would this work? Would she get paid more? Is this another contract? Does she earn residuals?"

"Yes. Yes. And yes. I'll set her up with an experienced screenwriter that can mentor her and help her through the process, but I feel very strongly that Logan should write the screenplay." He turns his attention from Niya so he's looking solely at me. "And I want you with me—with the cast and crew—while we film." He pauses, and I feel my chest rising up and down with labored breathing. He adds, "You know, in case of rewrites and to make sure we don't mess it up." It sounds like an excuse, but my brain is so muddled, I can only stumble forward clumsily with my answer.

"I don't know what to say," is the most unoriginal utterance I could ever respond with. It's not a good sign for someone being asked to write a screenplay, but it's all I have. Tom continues looking at me, his eyes shining with hope and opportunity. I register that Niya and Landon are also awaiting my answer. I wish I could talk to Niya privately, discuss whether this is a good idea, and ask if I should focus on writing a new book, which was the original plan. But part of me can't help but gush over the idea that Thomas Price wants me on his team. It's not like I have another job waiting for me. It's not like I have *anything* or *anyone* waiting for me. I might as well take this opportunity while it's being handed to me on a golden platter from Hollywood's golden boy. So with another cliche line that should probably never see ink on the page, I answer with, "When do I start?"

from: Logan Sterling <lasterling@gmail.com>

to: Thomas Price <tprice@pricepictures.com>

Hello Mr. Price,

Once again, thank you for giving me this opportunity. I am beyond excited to be part of the process of turning my book into a movie, but I do have some reservations about the scriptwriter you've recommended. To put it frankly, he is mean. And not mean like my agent Niya who is doing it because it makes her better at her job. His meanness is personal, having insulted my writing ability, vocabulary, hair color, gender, and intelligence. Is there any way that we could bring another experienced screenwriter onto the project? Preferably one that will not make me cry and doubt my overall worth as a person every night?

Thank you for considering,

Logan Sterling

from: Thomas Price <tprice@pricepictures.com>

to: Logan Sterling <lasterling@gmail.com>

Hey Logan,

I'm sorry to hear that Abe's unconventional methods have led to any personal crises. I've worked with Abe several times, and while I do wholeheartedly agree with you that he can be very mean, he is an amazing screenwriter and there is much you can learn from him. Maybe if you imagine him as Walter Matthau from *Grumpy Old Men*, you can envision his potential. That's how I have survived his curmudgeonly ways. In this business, there are certainly some people that we excuse for their uncouth ways because of their untouched talent. I'm not saying it's right, but it is a sad reality of the business. Another sad reality is that he owes me a favor and is doing this free of charge. Please blame all of his passive-aggressiveness on me and my cashing in on a decade-long debt.

Please reach out if you want to discuss this further,

Tom

from: Logan Sterling <lasterling@gmail.com>

to: Thomas Price <tprice@pricepictures.com>

Mr. Price,

First of all, I would much rather deal with Walter Matthau from *Dennis the Menace* over Walter Matthau from *Grumpy Old Men*. Forgive me, but I try not to picture geriatric lovemaking, which is most of my association with that movie. So thanks for the reminder.

Secondly, it is very difficult for me to learn while being insulted. I have always performed best with praise rather than punishment. Harsh words make me want to crawl under the floorboards and wait until the danger subsides (I believe I may be part opossum).

Thirdly, Abe is not passive-aggressive. He is fully aggressive. Seriously, the man has a loose wire in that amazing brain of his. And therein lies the problem. You were correct. He is immensely talented, and I hate myself for having to admit to that truth.

Fourthly and finally, I am impressed with your strong use of diction. And here I thought you were only a pretty face. (Ha ha, that's payback for pairing me with this monster of a mentor.)

I hope I survive this assignment long enough to read your reply.

Logan Sterling

from: Thomas Price <tprice@pricepictures.com>

to: Logan Sterling <lasterling@gmail.com>

Logan,

I'm sorry, I really am. But as I said (and as you have conceded) Abe is one of the best, and I only want the best for our movie. I believe in this project, and I believe in you. If anything, maybe you two could discuss your grievances and start anew? The Abe I know and love…okay, that's stretching it…the Abe I know and tolerate has never been insidious with his annoyance. I wonder what's going on. Would you like me to reach out to him and ask him to take it easy on you? This more-than-a-pretty-face awaits your response.

Tom

PS: Please stop calling me Mr. Price. We're working together. We've shared comical insights and poignant observations. Niceties be damned.
PPS: I suggest you keep your distaste for geriatric lovemaking on the down-low. With the current cancel culture and general fondness and nostalgia for Walter Matthau, we wouldn't want you staining the reputation of our movie, now would we? Old people like sex, too.

from: Logan Sterling <lasterling@gmail.com>

to: Thomas Price <tprice@pricepictures.com>

Thomas Price,

Please DO NOT "reach out" to Abe about me. That will only make me look weaker. No. I will handle it.

Thanks, but no thanks,

Logan Sterling

PS: Please refrain from discussing old people sex in our future emails. That's a hard boundary for me.

from: Thomas Price <tprice@pricepictures.com>

to: Logan Sterling <lasterling@gmail.com>

Logan,

Sorry, I never meant to impose. I just wanted to help you out. And I'll make sure to respect your hard boundaries about old people sex from now on.

Tom

PS: Aren't you proud of me for not making an ironic joke about the use of "hard" and "old people sex"? I am.

from: Logan Sterling <lasterling@gmail.com>

to: Thomas Price <tprice@pricepictures.com>

Thomas,

Did you know that Abe recently went through a very messy divorce and that his ex-wife is now "diddling the pool boy that looks like a glorious cross between Brad Pitt and Antonio Banderas"? (His words, not mine). Well, I do. I now know more about his personal life than I ever wanted to because I said I would handle it. After asking him what his problem with me was, he divulged ALL of his problems: Abe apparently had a very unstable childhood, felt unappreciated in the traditional academic setting, and had been searching for unconditional love long before his first wife left him for his writing partner thirty years ago.

I've created a monster. So thank you again for this glorious union…not. However, he now respects me and even texts me pictures of Brad Pitt after I shared my verbal appreciation of Missouri's finest. And I do get why you asked him to mentor me. He is inexplicably gifted, but now I worry I may never shake him (even though he says I remind him of his ex-wife, minus the boob job).

Your hesitant screenwriter,

Logan Sterling

from: Thomas Price <tprice@pricepictures.com>

to: Logan Sterling <lasterling@gmail.com>

Logan,

I knew you could do it! You've thawed the frozen heart of Abraham Weiss. I can't wait to see what you two create together. Please keep me posted! If your screenplay is half as entertaining as your emails, then I think we have a true gem in our future.

Call me Tom. Or Iowa's Finest. Your choice.

PS: Good job and good luck with Abe. But try not to fall in love. Workplace romances can be rough on production.

from: Logan Sterling <lasterling@gmail.com>

to: Thomas Price <tprice@pricepictures.com>

Tom,

No. Just no.

Logan

3

I hate parking at airports. Omaha's Eppley Airfield is not to be excluded. Sure, I may have brought some of the chaos on myself, but I'm still letting OMA take the brunt of the blame. The cast and crew of *Iowa Nice: Working Title* is supposed to arrive in Omaha by nine. Instead of being smart and getting a hotel last night, I made the drive from Des Moines this morning. Yesterday, I picked up my rental car funded by Price Pictures and was all packed and ready to leave by six, but then my alarm malfunctioned. Okay, actually the power went out at some point last night (yes, I still use an alarm clock radio), so I woke up thirty minutes behind schedule. I literally threw my bags into the car and booked it down Interstate 80. Good and frazzled by the time I reached the parking lot, I then had to take time to read the signs directing me to the proper area for short-term parking. I'm an intelligent woman—I mean, I wrote a book for God's sake—but add in an unknown parking situation and a fast-approaching deadline, and I'm as panicked as a cat with a piece of tape on its tail.

Okay, that's not the only reason I'm panicking. Today I'm meeting the cast of the movie. Phil Grant is an accomplished stage and film actor, having starred in numerous action and detective movies. He also starred in my dad's all-time favorite television series for twelve years. He's a legend and he's playing the role of my father. Megan Marks is playing the role of the daughter, which I guess means she's playing me. It's quite laughable because she and I seem nothing alike, but I guess that's what an actor is supposed to do: successfully pose as someone they're not. They are planning to dye her signature brunette locks to match the blonde Iowa-girl aesthetic, but that might be the only way Megan will resemble me. She's tiny, probably four inches shorter than me at five one; her skin is flawless, more than likely enriched by a skin cream that contains mermaid tears from the Fountain of Youth; and she's fiery, having tiptoed the line of cultural cancellation for standing up for what she believes in…and showing too much cleavage on the red carpet. She's also Tom's ex, having starred in *Rocky Mountain High* with him for the entirety of the show's run. And, yes, they had multiple love scenes throughout the years and were admiringly able to remain close friends even though they broke up three seasons in.

The idea that Tom and Megan are going to be reunited in close quarters leaves me feeling a bit uneasy, which is ridiculous because I have absolutely no claim to him. But after working on the script and corresponding with him over the past six months, I definitely am familiar enough to have caught feelings. For sure.

After overcoming the slight road bump that was Abe, Tom and I continued emailing regularly, and it became the most thrilling part of my day to see his name in my inbox. I'd like to think that he enjoyed our digital banter as much as I did, but it could have just been his natural charisma. Either way, I'm nervous to see him in person for the first time since our Hollywood dinner. Nervous that it'll feel awkward to see him, nervous that our comfort over email won't translate, and nervous that I imagined the easy camaraderie created by a flashing cursor.

Now here I am, just a girl, standing in front of an escalator, waiting for a film crew to arrive and start filming my movie. I started out thinking about it as Tom's movie, but after writing the book, then the screenplay, and fully birthing all aspects of it, I really do see it as mine. Well, Tom's and mine. So that makes us parents together, right? *Stop it, Logan.* The last thing I need is to have a crush on my boss. That would be unprofessional, messy…and incredibly hot. *No!* I will not succumb to sexy feelings toward Thomas Price. There's too much to lose. I chide myself and continue waiting.

A peek of black attire appears at the top of the escalator, then the crew and cast emerge, pouring into the lobby, a river of Hollywood chill and business fervor.

Tom gave me a rundown of the crew, sending me a list of names and roles, but seeing the arrival of bodies is much more overwhelming than reading those names on a piece of paper. I'm hoping we do a proper meet and greet so I can connect names with faces; maybe I'll make flash cards. I don't want to insult anyone by not remembering their names.

My palms are sweating as I try to work up my nerve to walk toward the gathering of film set professionals, but it's then that I see Tom appear amid the crew. He's wearing a Hawkeye baseball cap and Ray-Ban sunglasses in an attempt to hide his movie star status. It's a futile attempt; the air shimmers around him, and his smile radiates pure specialness. Drawn to his light, I wave my sopping hand, but drop it when I see him turn backward and lean down to whisper into the ear of one remarkable specimen of a woman.

I've seen Megan Marks on-screen several times, but seeing her in person without makeup and realizing how stunning she naturally is hits me like a sledgehammer of truth. How is she ever supposed to pass for me? Of course Tom would be enamored with her. I would be, too. In fact, looking upon her from afar, I *am* enamored. I want to hate her, but realize that'll be impossible as she jogs in front of Tom and rushes at me, enveloping me in a tight petite grip of steel.

"I'm so excited to meet you! Tom has told me so much!" she exclaims, her face buried in my shoulder.

"Oh. I'm excited to meet you, too. I've seen you…well, everywhere. Movies, TV, social media…" I ramble. Is this flattering or is this insensitive to her celebrity status?

"Oh my gosh, aren't you just the sweetest thing!" She releases me from her vise-like grip and takes a step back to stand beside Tom. He looks down at me with a small smile.

"Hey Logan, it's so nice to see you in person." He leans over, reaches around me with his free hand, and places a peck on my cheek. It's friendly, it's polite…it's extremely professional. The disappointment in me is irrational. Of course, he wouldn't wrap me in his arms and swear his undying devotion to me. We've been corresponding because of the script. That's all this is, a work relationship. And I need to reign in my wandering feelings and start focusing on why we're all here.

"It's nice to see you, too." Parroting others' greetings seems to be my basic function. To kickstart my personality and ability to form original thoughts, I clap my hands together and look around at the surrounding semicircle. "It's nice to meet all of you!"

"This is Logan Sterling, everyone. The author, screenwriter, and script supervisor." Tom moves to stand next to me while facing his team. I wave, a smile plastered on my face as I scan the details of the entourage while Tom makes introductions. It's a hurricane of names, faces, and small tastes of personalities yet to be discovered. My brain, recently drowning in everything screenwriting, registers this flood of information in a familiar structure:

INT. EPPLEY AIRFIELD LOBBY - MORNING

LOGAN stands frozen in mental overload as TOM introduces a line of crew members. Tom first points to a brunette with chunky red glasses. She waves, a smile on her lips but tension in her shoulders.

TOM

This is Marnie. She's my first assistant director and will be helping you with script supervision.

Tom continues, directing Logan's attention to a tall, sturdy man with a pile of locs twisted in a bun at the top of his head.

TOM

Jasper is the director of photography. He's amazing. Was supposed to be working on the next Scorsese project, but he chose me over Marty.

JASPER

The Scorsese film got pushed back two months, Tom. It just all worked out.

JASPER'S voice is velvet, surely used to his advantage in many situations.

TOM

I'm going to stick with my story.

Tom smiles and turns to a smaller man with brown skin, dark-brown eyes, and the most beautiful lashes to ever grace a human face.

TOM

Bruno is his first assistant.

BRUNO tips his ball cap in greeting, his smile revealing two perfectly symmetrical and melt-worthy dimples.

TOM

(pointing to a slight young woman with a curtain of dark hair)

Kalina is our production assistant. Best to get on her good side. She knows everybody and everything. Keeps it all running smoothly, right Kalina?

KALINA shakes her head with a terse smile.

TOM

Leroy and Cole are our lighting crew. Great guys, but don't ever play poker with them.

(Warning with a hint of jest as he points to two identical men with curly brown hair, thick beards, and Dodger jerseys which, fortunately, are not identical.)

LOGAN

I don't know how to play poker anyway.

COLE

We can teach you.

TOM

Just don't start placing bets. They'll empty your pockets and leave you stranded without shoes.

LEROY

It was one time.

Tom glares at him for a silent moment then looks toward a petite blonde woman and a taller blond boy.

TOM

Moving on. Pam is the sound engineer, and her son Dawson is the boom operator. We got a discount. Two for the price of one.

PAM

Dawson is learning the business. And is super excited to be exploring Iowa during his gap year, aren't you, sweetheart? (reaches up to pinch Dawson's cheek playfully. Dawson flinches out of reach, a wince of acceptance evident in his smile of greeting.)

TOM

Rene and Deedee are our amazing hair-and-makeup team. They've mastered making me look presentable for a number of productions.

A partnership that at first looks as different as night and day rushes up to smother Logan with air kisses. RENE is tall, buxom, and bold. Her hair is a mass of dark-brown curls streaked with slasher red and Barbie pink. A southern drawl oozes with the warmth of pecan pie as she introduces herself. DEEDEE is quieter, a sleek black bob accentuating flawless porcelain skin, red matte lips, and wide green eyes. Her hello is a shared secret, her head bowed close, her slanted smile promising more secrets to be shared.

RENE

And what a task that was! It's nice to meet you, Logan. Congrats on the book and script, honey.

The whirlwind reaches an end as Tom sweeps his arm toward the last crew member.

TOM

And last but certainly not least is Atlas. She's our wardrobe and set designer.

ATLAS towers next to Tom in sky-high platforms, a mass of mermaid-colored hair, and knife-sharp cheekbones. She waves enthusiastically in greeting.

All introductions made, the cast and crew stand looking at Logan until she realizes that they are waiting for her to greet them formally.

I am suddenly thrust back into reality as I blurt out a greeting. "Wow. There's a lot of you. This is all…so…real now." I scan the group, trying my best to absorb all the details that will help me through the next two months.

Tom leans closer, his voice quieter with a message just for me. "Of course it is. I told you. This movie is going to be magical. And these are our magicians."

Our gathering of magicians suddenly parts as if revealing a master illusionist. An older gentleman with a brown blazer, orange rollneck, and flat cap ambles through to the core of our nest.

"Logan, I'm sure you know who this is, but let me formally introduce you to Phil Grant. He'll be playing your dad."

I'm speechless. I knew I was going to be meeting him, but seeing Captain Smith Altide of *The First Order of Flight* is a transcendent experience for which I could never have prepared. Past, present, and future all smash together to meet at the apex of this man's wrinkled yet square jaw, softer yet dimpled cheeks, and smaller yet still sparkling blue eyes.

"Does anyone know where the goddamned bathroom is? I need to take a piss like my life depends on it." Even his voice is resonant, sending me back to when I was four years old, sitting on the floor in front of the television, watching him command a battleship as he fought an oncoming slew of intergalactic foes.

I stammer as Phil comes up to me, hand out dutifully while his eyes search the perimeter of the lobby for a bathroom.

"It's such a pleasure to meet you, sir. My dad was a huge fan. The biggest fan. I'm sure you hear that all the time, but really. He had a ton of *First Order* memorabilia and made me watch it with him when I was a kid." I'm pushing air out of my lungs and words are coming out, though I'm not really conscious of what I am saying.

He pumps my hand vigorously, reaches over to pat my shoulder with his left hand, then releases me. "That's great, dear. Just great. Sorry, but I need to take care of this or my prostate is going to pop out of my ass." He stalks off to a nearby restroom, relief surging across his face as his strides tighten with anticipation.

I stand there shocked that I've met Phil Grant, that he's spoken to me about his prostate, and that he has left the scene with as much cinematic flair with which he entered. Huh. Perhaps the saying is true: maybe we shouldn't meet our heroes.

"He warms up eventually. Traveling just makes him grumpy," Tom says quietly. He squeezes my shoulder in the same place Phil just patted and directs his voice to the crew. "All right, team! Let's make a movie!"

***

I wish it were that simple—that we would start making a movie right away, but there are so many logistics to figure out, especially traveling with fifteen people and a buttload of equipment. We'll start filming in Council Bluffs in a couple of days, so we're going to stay in downtown Omaha while we prep, test, and organize. At least, that's what I know from the first assistant director Marnie's email. We can't yet check into our hotel rooms at the Embassy Suites, but Kalina, production assistant extraordinaire, has secured us a meeting room where we all gather around a rectangular table and report on our individual visions to combine into one harmonious plan.

Easier said than done. Three hours later, my head hurts, my eyes are strained, and my jaw is stiff from having uttered no more than five words during our logistical meeting. When Tom announces a break, a collective groan of relief makes him smile with bewilderment.

"What, did I go on too long?" He looks over at Megan and me, and we turn toward each other before cracking up with exhausted giggles. "Excuse me for being passionate." Tom gets up, mumbling something about wishing we'd all take him more seriously, but his smile lets us know he's only jesting.

I stand to stretch, and Megan stands with me. She's decided to attach herself to my side, watching me constantly, undoubtedly trying to catalog my movements and mannerisms as she prepares to dive into her character. It's weird but also flattering to be the object of a famous person's attention. The other famous actor (besides Tom) has essentially ignored everyone, holing up in the corner and even blatantly snoring at one point. Phil Grant has so far been a disappointment, which I guess is on point as he's playing my dad. It's funny when art imitates life.

"So I was hoping you and I could hang out, maybe talk about your life, your relationship with your dad, the trip, you know, anything to help me do your character and story justice." I almost laugh at her tense expression, but her doe eyes indicate that her concern is real.

"Megan, you're an amazing actress. I have no doubt you'll do the story justice. Please do not stress."

"Okay, yes, I've done some good work, but it's because I stress that I do well." She starts chewing on the cuticle of her thumb, and I soften my own expression.

"I get that. I overstress, too. See, you're perfect for the role."

"But I've never played a real person before. And even though you are super friendly, it's still intimidating to have you here while filming."

"Oh. I didn't think about that." Doubt colors my response. Sure, I always question my self-worth and certainly did when agreeing to work on the movie, but I didn't even think about how my presence could impact the process.

"No, it's fine! It's great! And it's what Tom wants. What we all want," she rushes to explain, but part of me still wonders if there's a fissure between what Tom wants and what the others want. Marnie and I have already scheduled time this evening to go over our script supervisor duties, but so far, I've felt like a superfluous addition to the team who's not really earning my keep. So if Megan needs me to help her, who am I to deny her?

"You know what, let's mark out some time tomorrow afternoon while they're prepping locations. Maybe you and I can go get coffee or something and talk." Her face lights up, a dazzling beacon that makes it easy to see why she is a screen starlet. She nods her head, excited to have a future heart-to-heart scheduled. She bounds out of the room, leaving me to have my first moment by myself since the airport. I instantly prepare for an internal battle. I'm here for all the wrong reasons, trying to further my own career and fabricate some connection with Thomas Price while potentially curtailing the productivity of the other fourteen people who actually know what they're doing.

I'm a fraud. I'm sure of that.

The only question is, who's going to be the next person to find out and alert everyone else to that harsh fact?

With Megan attaching herself to me so intricately, she'd be my best guess. But if I watch my step, maybe I can prolong the inevitable and perhaps salvage this film and my career without derailing everyone else's.

***

Omaha's Old Market has quickly caught on to our presence here. Okay, not my presence, rather the presence of my famous coworkers. Our group of fifteen wandered out of the hotel to explore the downtown scene, take in the quirky emporiums, and hear the carriage horses clop down the historic brick road; our relaxed roaming was short-lived, however, because of the appearance of Phil Grant, Thomas Price, and Megan Marks, along with the possibility of a romantic reconciliation.

After that, we were followed around by a gathering of tourists and locals wanting pictures, sometimes hollering out their undying devotion. If we can't make it one day without being spotted, how are these next sixty days going to be productive at all?

We took refuge in a quaint restaurant where Kalina had arranged reservations, and I once again found myself gathered around a table, silent while everyone else talks over each other.

"Oh baby, you need a drink." Rene of hair and makeup plops down in the seat next to me, a bottle of wine in her hand. "Here, let Mama help you." She empties my water glass into the pitcher and replaces the contents with more than the recommended serving size of red wine.

"Oh my," is all I can say as I stare at the large gulp of alcohol.

"You do drink, right?" Rene's voice drops.

"If you don't, that's okay. A majority of LA is sober…or at least pretends to be." Deedee appears so quietly next to me that I visibly startle at her words.

"No, I drink. But usually I keep it to one glass of wine, not a full carafe."

Atlas sidles up across from me, her long rainbow hair already a messy mane of debauchery. "Where's the fun in that?"

Rene and Deedee exchange looks over my head and start laughing. All three take their own full-size drinking glasses and clink them across the table, erupting in tipsy giggles. They turn to me with imploring eyes.

"Well, what are you waiting for? It's the first night of your book becoming a movie! Celebrate! Drink! Be merry!" Rene's jovial tidings are tempting, but I'm unsure of letting loose. I look around the room and see everyone relaxing, carrying on conversations, and enjoying themselves. Even Phil is in a tense poker game with Leroy and Cole. My gaze then catches on Tom, Megan, and Marnie who are sequestered in a booth. Megan clings to Tom's arm, leaning in to lay her head on his shoulder. The three laugh as Marnie holds up her phone to take a picture. Megan turns and kisses Tom on the cheek as he smiles at the camera.

And so it begins. The on-set romance, the public displays of affection, and the social media fervor. I don't know if I can take it. And tomorrow I'll have to sit down with Megan and hear all about it. I want her to like me, and I get why someone would fall under her spell so quickly, but we haven't even begun filming and she's already sleeping with the director?

I'll learn to deal with it. But tonight, I'll just drink.

I lift the glass to my lips and drain half the contents. The dry red burns my throat, but a flame of courage suddenly ignites in my belly. When I return my glass to the table, I look at three sets of eyes widened in shocked appreciation.

"Damn, girl. You get it!"

We all burst into laughter and clink our glasses. I drain the rest of the wine and hold it out for a refill. I'll be with these people for two months; I might as well figure out a way to survive whether that's through making friends, learning my place, or pretending I'm something I'm not. But I'll worry about that tomorrow. Tonight, I'll just celebrate my success, try to keep up with the LA scene, and drown my implausible romantic disappointment in wine.

Excerpt from *Iowa Nice*

COUNCIL BLUFFS

"Why is it called the Squirrel Cage Jail?" I ask my dad while parallel parked next to the historic brick building a block from the unofficial town square of Council Bluffs.

He looks to the driver's side and says in a deadpan tone, "I heard it's because the inmates all went nuts." My eyes widen with disbelief before rolling in annoyance, and his seriousness drops as he starts laughing at his own joke. "Sorry, I guess you're not ready for dad jokes." Nodding toward the building, he finally answers my question. "I'm not exactly sure. Let's find out."

After paying admission we enter the rotary jail, all concrete floor, pie-wedged cells, and corroding metal slats. The aged musty smell blankets us as we stare up at the levels of the circular steel cage.

Dad reads from the provided pamphlet, "'The Squirrel Cage Jail gets its name from its unique design that looks as if it could house small animals. The name is a further nod to the prominent presence of the black squirrels here in Council Bluffs.' Huh, well there you go. I still think they should have included a nut pun somewhere." He sifts through the hefty pamphlet as if searching for more answers, but I can't look away from the stacked cells. One jailer could manage the three levels of stacked triangular cells by turning a single crank. In theory this would make it difficult to escape. However, it also resulted in numerous broken limbs and injuries, many of them purposeful, allowing inmates to visit the infirmary and attempt a breakout. Even though it hasn't been active since 1969, it still holds a deep sense of foreboding desperation.

We head down a tight hall and end up at a barred hole. The sign for solitary confinement indicates the cell is six feet tall with a base of two feet by one foot.

"So the prisoner barely had room to sit?"

Dad looks up to mirror my viewing of the displayed cell. "Well, solitary confinement is meant as a punishment. They must have done something pretty bad to get put in here."

"But ten days?" I whisper, reading the posted facts. Of course I've heard of inhumane treatment of prisoners and patients throughout time, but it's different to see it, to actually feel it like an injection of cold entering my veins. I shiver, amazed and appalled that this once existed in working order.

"Prison isn't supposed to be pleasant. The whole point is to make someone suffer, pay for their wrongs." He turns and backs out of the shallow passage, continuing to read some of the plaques and captioned pictures on the walls of the bullpen. I follow, still in my head.

"It just seems unfair. To be stuck in such a depressing place. Who wants to better themselves if they're already in hell?" I slowly approach him and we meander through the exhibit.

"Not all prisons are made of steel bars," he says, not noticing my sudden halt, managing to walk ahead ten feet before turning

around in surprise. "What's wrong?"

"What do you mean by that?" I take a step forward in offense.

He seems to realize his mistake. "I just meant that people are in situations every day that feel like prison. Like jobs, school—"

"Families?" There, I said it. He pulls back as if I've slapped him, though we're still standing far apart. The quiet of the museum crowds us with its heaviness.

"I didn't say that."

"Yeah, but that's why you left. Because your life with Mom and me felt like a prison, right? And once you had your chance to escape, you took it." I didn't mean to do this so early in our trip, definitely not the first day, but here I am, piling all my repressed anger onto my dad despite his vulnerable state.

"It wasn't a good relationship for either of us, Logie Bear."

"Don't call me that. I'm a grown woman."

He recoils at my snapping, but he still utters a mournful explanation. "Your mom and I were both unhappy."

"But what about me? I was happy...until you left." It's pitiful, but I need to remind him that I was there, too. That I was the collateral damage in my parents' failed marriage.

"I'm sorry about that, and I wish I could take it back. Do better. But I can't. But at least we're together now, right? At least I'm learning...even though I'm almost out of time." He looks at me with a mix of hope and sorrow, his eyes crinkled with deep crow's feet. For a moment, I try to imagine how difficult it was for him to walk away. But he could have always come back. It didn't need to take twenty years for a return trip.

I sigh loudly. We have the whole state of Iowa to get through. I should ration out my angst before we run out of things to talk about. "Okay. So maybe not a family, but would you say marriage can be like a prison?"

"Well, I think my zero-to-two record speaks for itself. Guess I didn't learn my lesson. What's your verdict?"

"In the 'is marriage like prison' debate?"

"Yeah, was your marriage a prison or something else?"

"I don't want to talk about it, Dad." I pick up my pace, already anxious to exit the staleness of this place and breathe in some fresh air even though we still have two more floors to view.

"Logan, I wasn't accusing you. I just thought we could talk about it." Dad tries to catch up, but his illness has taken a toll on his stamina. As soon as we break out of the gift shop entrance, hurried thank-you's thrown at the curator as we exit, I spin around to see him gasping for air.

"Sit down, Dad," I demand in exasperation, pointing to a bench facing the museum. "I can't have you dying on our first day. It'll look bad. They might even throw me in one of those torture cages."

He doesn't argue, which is a sure sign that he needs to rest, but he does manage to lift the corner of his mouth in a small smile. He plops down heavily, his head hanging between his knees. I stand in front of him, my arms crossed over my chest with indignation. A black squirrel scurries up the trunk of an ash tree, chittering its disapproval at our invasion of its space. I match its beady glare until Dad is satiated with proper oxygen. He looks up at me and says, "I just want to be able to talk about your life. Please. I missed so much."

My body wants to retreat, but I resist, dropping next to him on the bench instead. It seems like every argument is going to end with the dying-dad card. "It wasn't a prison. It just wasn't what I wanted it to be."

"Yeah, I know how that goes. So who broke it off?"

"I'm not sure. I was long gone before I actually moved out."

"Oh. So what was it that you wanted?"

"I don't really know. It's not like I had an example of a good

marriage to model it after."

"Hey, it wasn't all terrible. It's not like your mother and I ever fought around you."

"No, you didn't fight. But you also didn't show me what love looks like either."

"Oh."

We sit there in silence, both looking at the road as the occasional car rambles by. When I'm no longer able to stand squinting into the sun, I rise and hold out my hand. "Come on. We've got more to see today, don't we?"

He grabs my hand and I pull him up to make our way back to the car. We haven't found our way back to each other, but we're working on it, slowly and painfully as we wade through the memories and the weight of past mistakes.

4

Wine headaches are the worst. Throbbing, bright headaches to match the throbbing, bright vibes of the previous night. Ugh, the previous night. I'm haunted by blurs of loud laughing, secret talent divulging, and losing $50 in…solitaire? I vaguely remember telling Atlas, Rene, and Deedee about my fangirl crush on Tom, which makes me cringe at the adolescent energy. This information was unveiled at the hotel bar, where a good chunk of us continued the party after dinner. Tom, Megan, and Phil were part of the small group that smartly chose to tuck in early, whereas the rest of us stayed out until the bar closed. Fortunately, the hotel bar closed at eleven, creating a gracious end to my moderately self-revealing night. Unfortunately, I can't sleep away the pain or the shame because I am a perpetual early riser.

Malcolm McClarnon passed on many things to his only daughter: blue eyes, a duck-shaped birthmark (his on his arm while mine is on my back), a pointed chin, a lack of a round butt, extreme stubbornness, and consistently waking up at the first sign of sunlight. It's a curse, like many of the things I inherited from my father. If only I could be one of those people that can doze the day away then emerge from their bedroom like a sleep-cursed princess, fully rested and renewed in spirit without a hair out of place. But no. I'm destined to always be tired unless I go to bed at an early hour which, with this crew, may be a tough task for the duration of filming.

After lying in bed long enough to know there is absolutely zero hope of falling back asleep, I drag myself out; I pull on some jeans, a T-shirt, and a sweatshirt, and I start making plans to become a functioning adult today. I start by heading to the front desk and purchasing Tylenol, then swinging by the breakfast counter and ordering lemon water and a waffle. The lemon water is a hack my ex taught me, a way to clean out the body after too much imbibing the night before. Though the sight of food makes my stomach flip, the waffle is meant to soak up the alcohol, and I know I will feel better once I choke enough of it down.

All of this takes less than half an hour; I then find myself bored and alone because it is still ungodly early. I meander over to the atrium to sit in a modern deco chair where I can stare at the lush green foliage, art sculptures, and room balconies with the calming soundtrack of an indoor waterfall. This might not be as good as sleep, but I can find some sort of solace in these surroundings. I close my eyes and lean back, waiting for the medicine and food to kick in and relieve me of all my previous night's pain.

"Logan?"

My eyes pop open and Thomas Price is all I see. He stands in front of me, hair damp, eyes sparkling, in gray sweatpants and a purple Lakers hoodie. I almost believe I am having a wine-induced hallucination until he plops down in the chair across from me and continues speaking.

"You have a hard time sleeping in, too?"

I have to visibly shake myself into responding, my hangover

daze causing me to stare awkwardly. "Uh, yeah. I never sleep late. Even when I stay up way past my bedtime, as I did last night."

He chuckles and settles farther into the leather chair. "Did the Trendy Trifecta do their best to break you in?"

"'Trendy Trifecta'?"

"Atlas, Rene, and Deedee. They deemed themselves the 'Trendy Trifecta' a few years back when they were overserving me."

"Was it red wine for you, too?"

"Long Island Iced Teas."

I wince and gag at the same time. "That sucks for you."

"It certainly did. I could not remember my lines the next day and had to have a trash can on hand. The director finally had enough and sent me home. I've never forgiven the Trendy Trifecta for that embarrassing smear on my resume." His words are harsh in contrast to his relaxed smile.

"Yet you brought them on for your movie?" I raise an eyebrow in a playful challenge.

"Well, yeah. They're a blast. Plus, they're all crazy talented. In this business, if you find people good at their jobs and fun to be around, you never let them go." His gaze lingers on me, making me shift uncomfortably in my seat. The leather makes an unbecoming fart sound, and I sigh with the cruel injustice of my life. Tom just laughs, so I do my best with damage control and redirection.

"First of all, that wasn't me. Let's be clear, that was the chair. Second, what are you doing up so early? Nothing is on the itinerary until ten, right?"

"Right. But I like my alone time before all the craziness of the day."

"Oh, do you want to be alone?" I start to make my way out of the chair, emitting even more fart sounds. Seriously, couldn't the hotel invest in some more polite furniture? Tom must find it amusing watching me struggle to get up, a large grin slapped across his face. Before I can actually lift my ass off the offensive leather structure that will forever haunt my dreams, Tom gestures for me to remain seated.

"No, silly. I interrupted you, remember? Anyway, I can be alone with you here. It's nice." He smiles, and if I had to get up and walk away, I'm fairly certain I would fall over. He shifts his body and the conversation back on track. "I went for a swim, got dressed, had some breakfast, and now here we are."

"Here we are." I exhale and dive in. "Is Megan an early riser, too?"

"I don't think so. She won't ever be late, but she's always just made call time. I'm sure she'll take advantage of as much beauty sleep as she can get." He nods, his gaze drifting off for the first time since sitting down.

"Well, she doesn't need it. She's stunning," I almost whisper, a concession that she would be a prize for any hopeful suitor…or director. Last night, between drinks four and five, the Trendy Trifecta explained to me the intricacies of film set romances. Apparently, hotel rooms and set trailers get cold during long production hours, so many choose to share their bed with someone, even if it's just for the duration of the filming. Atlas tried convincing me that I should hook up with Jasper, who kept smiling at me from the other end of the bar. He's attractive and seems nice, but my heart still beats faster when I'm around Tom, even if it is unrequited. Maybe it'll be following a different rhythm in a few weeks, but for now, I need to make smart decisions and not awkwardly hook up with all the single straight men on set.

"Yeah, she is beautiful. Great on-screen." Tom continues staring in front of him, his long fingers idly tapping the arm rest. Something seems to be off, so I try to lighten the mood.

"You might have to tone her down a bit for the movie, make her look more plain if she's going to be convincing as me." I offer a crooked grin but am met with a frown.

"Why do you do that?" he asks.

"What?"

"Insult yourself like that?" He pins me with an inquisitive stare, and I shift beneath his accurate accusation.

"I didn't—"

He interrupts my futile attempt to explain my self-degradation away. "No more. You're a beautiful woman, Logan. Don't let yourself or others make you feel otherwise."

I go to open my mouth, but nothing comes out. Thomas Price just called me beautiful. I don't believe it, but I don't ever want to forget it either.

"Hey, do you want to go for a walk?" A gracious change in the conversation allows us both to relax again.

"Uh, sure." The waffle and Tylenol have begun to work their magic, and I think I can walk at a normal pace, so why not get some fresh air?

"Come on, let's go." He stands up and holds out his hand.

Is it worth it? Spending time with Tom and getting to know him? Part of me wishes I could logically think through this dilemma, but the part of me that wins in this moment doesn't care. I take his hand, allowing him to pull me up out of the torturous chair, relishing in the dry warmth and strong grip of his palm, and it's then that I know I'd let this man lead me anywhere, even if it is down a path of heartache and disappointment.

***

The sunlight sparkles off the Missouri River as Tom and I match strides while walking across the Farnam Pier. It feels as if we've been swallowed and spit out by a whale as we emerge from the ribcage-like architecture to peer down at the water.

Tom's spoken for most of the walk, divulging the travel plans and scene work that he envisions for the movie, though a few times we've been content to stroll in silence. Now, he clutches the safety fence and turns to me with a serious look.

"Tell me the truth. Why do you seem so morose? Is it because you did in fact fall in love with Abe and you are missing him dearly?" I squint at him, his form backlit by the morning sun, hiding his face and any clue to his earnest words in shadow.

"What? In love with Abraham Weiss? Absolutely not. And what do you mean by 'morose'? I don't look morose. This is just how I look." *With a hangover, no shower, no makeup, and no preparation.*

"Really? You and Abe didn't even make it the run of the film?" My unamused glare stops his bit, and he barks with laughter. "I'm sorry. I had to bring him up. We haven't talked about him since our emails, and I was starting to think I imagined those."

"What do you mean by that?"

"Well, you haven't really given me the time of day since I arrived." His previous light tone fades, revealing a rawness that affects me more than it should. I rush to defend myself.

"I have too! I've talked to you! I'm talking to you right now!"

"Yeah, only because I approached you. Otherwise, I think you would have hidden in that fart-chair forever." I look down at my feet, my cheeks hot. He's not wrong, and his accurate observations leave me feeling too visible, too seen. Thankfully, he picks up on my regret and brings some levity back into the mix. "So did all those shared observations about life, love, and geriatric sex mean nothing to you?"

A grin breaks through my shame, and I look back up at his beautiful silhouette. "I clearly remember telling you not to bring up geriatric sex."

"In emails. Face-to-face is free game. No paper trail." Our conversation pauses as we let the closeness of our digital relationship begin to seep into reality. I realize I need to see him clearly to further solidify this transition, so I walk to his other side, and he angles to match me. I lean back against the fence and set my hand on the safety rail next to his. My breath catches as his pinkie lifts and grazes my own, and I must be imagining a hint of longing in his voice when he says, "I don't know. I just thought my pen pal would be happy to see me."

A jolt of electric energy rushes through my body at his words, causing me to jump and remove my hand from the fence as I step safely away from the bright light that is Thomas Price. Like a moth, I could easily get burned. I rush to fill the awkward physical moment, suddenly blurting out, "'Pen pal'? I'm pretty sure the word you're looking for is 'employee.'" He laughs, giving me the courage to continue. "And who says I'm not happy to see you? It just so happens you're the most important person on the team. Anytime I would try to give you the time of day, you'd have a line a mile long of people wanting to talk to you, take your picture, get your opinion, or ask your permission. You're never alone!"

"So you've been waiting to get me alone?" I swear a touch of flirtation curls the edge of his words, but I choose to proceed on the side of caution in the name of self-preservation.

"Well, not really. I just don't like to intrude when you're talking to others. I want to make sure I'm not getting in the way."

"Logan, you're never in the way and you certainly aren't intruding if you join in on a conversation. Remember, we're all here because of you. It's your story that has brought us all together. In my humble opinion, *you're* the most important person here." My heart is racing with the compliment, and since receiving a compliment is a Midwesterner's kryptonite, I scrabble for clearance, trying to shift the conversation away from me.

"Well, wouldn't you say Megan is pretty important? As you warned me with Abe, aren't workplace romances a bit problematic on set?" Tom cocks his head, and I wonder if I've gone too far. It's not my place to warn him with his own advice, but I am curious what is going on with them. Call me masochistic, but knowing for certain would be a hell of a lot more merciful than this unsure ache every time I'm near him.

"What are you implying?"

"Well, she and I are meeting this afternoon. She wants to get to know me better, pick my brain for character work, and it would be helpful if I knew what is and isn't off-limits. What's safe to talk about, what I can say about you…" I'm rambling beneath his stare, which has run the gamut from warm and playful to analytical and cold. Oh great, Logan, you've been alone with the man less than an hour and have already self-sabotaged. I'm going to have to start skimming the Help Wanted listings at this rate.

"Say whatever you want about me. I don't care. I don't have any secrets." His voice is stripped of the carefree lilt I was getting used to. I hate that I'm the one who ruined the moment. All because of my nosiness about his love life.

"Oh, okay." I think maybe I should apologize, or at the very least explain what I mean, but it's then that Tom's phone starts chirping. He answers it and indicates with a nod for us to start walking back. I fall in-step beside him as he discusses space rental with Kalina, but even when he hangs up, we never get back to the place we were before I brought Megan Marks into the conversation.

Boy, now I can't wait to be alone with her for two hours this afternoon.

***

"I've been so excited all day to be alone with you and pick your brain!" Megan squeals. She's wearing an oversize, buttery-soft cream sweatshirt that probably costs more than my entire wardrobe, and I'm in jeans and a T-shirt adorned with a kitten holding a laser gun. We make quite the pair seated on a two-person sofa (damned leather, again) in her two-room suite. We decided it would be better than trying to meet in public and deal with adoring fans, and it's much better than teetering on the edge of the bed in my one-person hotel room meant for us commoners. (Though I suspect she might have liked poking around my suitcase for clues into my true nature.)

"Me too!" I force through clenched teeth. I can't let on that I've been dreading these two hours: having to talk about myself, my past, and my habits is my special brand of nightmare. The irony is I wrote a book including all of that in intimate detail. But the difference is the medium. Behind a computer, I could separate myself from the subject as I typed the words, almost experiencing a release from the hold of those phrases as I handed them off to the world. In conversation, I'm claiming ownership, letting the words exit my mouth, only to hang around the empty space of my heart before they settle back into my soul with the renewed bite of fresh air and revelation.

But Megan's success is my success and all that, so I guess I'm ready to push play on all the painful memories.

"Your dad left your mom when you were five?"

Oh, God. Here we go. "Yep. That is correct."

"What was that like? Like, what did you do for holidays, did you talk to your dad on the phone, were there planned visits?" Megan continues with her prompts, looking at me with expectation, her body cradled around a notebook as she prepares to write down observations. I know from past interviews that she grew up in a loving family, the youngest daughter of three who starred in all the school plays, won all the solos and talent shows, and was crowned homecoming and prom queen. When she left her small Colorado community, she had the strength and confidence needed to succeed due to the support of her entire town. *Rocky Mountain High* was her first audition, and her star only rose from there. As I go through the messy interactions and feelings tied to being a child of divorce, and further, a young girl abandoned by her father, it's tough to not resent Megan and others like her who believed in themselves enough to go after their dreams. It makes me wonder what my life would have been like if I'd had my dad around. What I could have accomplished if my mom were still alive. Who I would have been if I knew what real love was before having to lose time and time again.

"Your mom died when you were eighteen. What was she like?

My body softens with a topic I'm actually fond of talking about. Sure, I miss Mom, but I would much rather remember her than pack her ghost away in the crowded attic of my mind. I feel my lips settle into a smile as I recall the woman who raised me. "She was awesome. Tough, snarky. I don't think she was always that way. When she and my dad first got together, she was pretty meek, very traditional, you know, like staying at home, keeping up the house, making sure supper was waiting. But she started breaking out of that mold after I was born. We were used to moving with my dad being in the military, but when we returned to the States after living in South Korea, she changed. Something happened there that made her done with traveling, done with putting up with my dad's late nights and thin excuses. They tried to work it out for a few more years, but she finally had it when he met Sandra in D.C. She was a single mom working on the same base as Dad, and they ended up getting married shortly after Mom and I moved back to Iowa."

"Wait, so you have a stepmom and siblings?"

"Uh, no. I only met them a handful of times. Sandra seemed nice enough, but she already had two daughters. Didn't need another one."

"Oh. Do you still keep in contact with any of them?"

"Absolutely not."

"Oh." Megan jots down something poignant in her notebook, her tongue caught between her teeth in concentration. She looks back up. "What else about your mom? What was her name?"

"Her name was Rose Marie. Everyone called her Rosie." My heart blooms with the memory of people in town calling out her name, her cheeks pink like her namesake.

"Did she ever get remarried?"

"Nope. Said she had her fill of marriage, never wanted to be tied to a man again. She just focused on me and work." Mom had made a hard shift from doting wife to stern divorcée and even though it hadn't worked out for her, she still had hopes that I would find love and have a happy marriage and family. It's too bad she couldn't ever see that for me. And it's too bad that I tried to force it.

"What did she do?" The question hooks me, steering me back from my journey down Regret Lane.

"Oh. She worked at Discount Depot." She had worked her ass off for little pay. But she did it for me, so I never wanted for anything.

"For how long?" Megan's writing furiously, asking questions while her eyes dart between my face and the paper in front of her.

"Um, until she was too sick." She stops suddenly and looks up.

"What was it?" she asks gently.

"Breast cancer. They caught it too late. She didn't have the best insurance so wasn't going in for routine checkups, even though her own mom died from it. They tried surgery and chemo, but it spread too fast." My voice is robotic, careful to tiptoe over the land mines of unresolved grief.

"I'm sorry, Logan. That must have been awful."

"Yeah, worst year of my life. And that's saying something."

Megan's brow creases, but I carry on, ready to end this part of the story. "So Mom dies, Discount Depot awards me a hefty scholarship so I can attend college, and life goes on."

"What about your dad? Did he come help you?"

"Uh, he tried. But we had some major disagreements."

"About your marriage?" I wince with Megan's strong journalistic skills. Girl has certainly done her homework and read the book.

"Yep."

"How long were you married?"

"Too long."

She visibly reacts to my succinct answer. "You know, Tom was married."

"Yes, I know. I've used the internet before." She ignores my snide comment and continues.

"I remember hanging out with him and Julia at the Golden Globes, and I just thought they looked so perfect together. Just goes to show you that if you slap pretty clothes on a disaster, it might mask the truth for a bit, but eventually the clothes have to come off and the naked mess is all that's left."

"Whoa, that got a bit sexual, Megan."

"Yeah, I didn't mean to, but I still stand by it." We exchange a soft smile. Even though she's a movie star, she still gets it. Which makes it hard to hate her. Plus, as she dives into the character of me, hating her is like hating myself; while it's what I'm good at, I need to start practicing more forgiveness toward myself and others. At least, that's what my affirmation calendar at home says.

"Does it bother you that Tom was married?"

"Oh, not at all! It's actually fairly common in this business. Everyone dabbles in marriage and divorce. Honestly, it's like a badge of honor. Once you've survived a marriage scandal, you've made the big time. You probably know this, but I was engaged. Twice."

"Yeah, I remember. So what happened?"

"Oh, I like shiny things and was dazzled by the glamor of it all. Broken engagements are a dime a dozen in Hollywood, just like narcissists. And it just so happens that I found two dimes back-to-back." I laugh with appreciation at her joke, and her face lights up with recognition. I can see myself relaxing into this friendship, a friendship I know she wants so badly, but I'm still unsure I can fully invest when I'm harboring this secret affection for her boyfriend.

"So how are you and Tom doing? What's it like working with him on this film?"

"Oh, Tom's great! I remember he directed an episode of *Rocky Mountain High*, and he was so conscientious about the actors' needs, well, because he is an actor. And so far he's been nothing but a dream to work for." She's not offering up the details like I thought, so I change my tactics from discrete to blatant.

"What's it like dating on set?" I try to ask nonchalantly, but my voice is still tinged with the need to know. Forget all this bright-side stuff. Give me the nitty gritty.

Megan leans forward with conspiratorial glee. "Oh, do you have your eye on someone? Tell me, tell me!" I'm caught off guard by the turn of the spotlight (man, this girl is good), but I'm saved by the knock of someone announcing their arrival at Megan's suite door.

"Oops, sorry. I forgot that Deedee wanted to go over hair color options. Can we put a pause on this conversation?"

"Uh, sure."

"Just a pause. I want to know all about your secret crush. Or crushes. There's a few tasty morsels on set." She waggles her eyebrows as she gets up to let Deedee in.

"Hey, Logan," Deedee greets me warmly.

I say my goodbyes, but not before Megan wraps me in her arms and whispers, "Thank you so much for your honesty. I'm so glad we're friends."

Well, it's official. I'm friends with a movie star, crushing on my famous boss, and struggling to stay afloat in unknown waters. And this is the calm before the storm. Filming starts tomorrow, and I still need to figure out what a script supervisor does.

Excerpt from *Iowa Nice*

SIOUX CITY

"Remember that vacation to Virginia Beach? Where we all went out on a sailboat and a seagull crapped on your stepmom?" My dad turns to me from his side of the bench as we watch the Missouri River rush by.

"I wasn't on that trip. I've never been to Virginia Beach," I say robotically. The previous day and evening have been filled with correcting Dad's memories, removing myself from his recollections. In most, I'm an apparition, floating in the margins of storylines, summoned by his own guilt about his absence in my life. So on this morning walk after breakfast, he's decided to sift through the entire catalog of his mind until he finds an accurate telling.

It's been a long morning.

It was a long night to begin with. Sharing a hotel room with a father I haven't seen in eight years was going to be awkward at best, but even from the sanctuary of my own bed, the symphony of his sleeping sounds sent me back to a time when my father wasn't such a foreign figure in my life. Snores, snorts, and shifts would carry me away to when I was four and sneaking into my parents' room because I had a nightmare. Or remind me of evenings when he would fall asleep in his favorite recliner, the news program barely audible above his own percussive audio.

Last night was a therapy session in live action, enduring the memories as a multitude of emotions washed over me instead of the sweet release of sleep. It's as if I traveled through the five stages of grief while my body rested heavily on the hotel mattress, the grating sound of the air conditioner a soundtrack to my insomnia.

Dad woke up rested and ready to attack the day. I woke up even more tired and irritable than I was the previous day. But two cups of coffee and a greasy diner breakfast has me feeling, while not entirely rejuvenated, at least energized enough to carry on with our journey.

"Lake George! You were on that trip, I know it! It was just you and me, right?"

His face lights up, ready to be congratulated on his ability to finally recall a memory in which he spent time with me. When I signal my agreement with a nod, he takes off, his voice enthusiastic as he brings up the restaurants where we ate, the activities we did, and the views we took in.

I let him have this. I let him remember the Italian restaurant as a bonding experience, rather than the actuality of my sitting silently, slurping my spaghetti as he shared military experiences with another veteran sitting at the next table. I let him remember that he took me to The Patriot, a gift shop and museum filled with military artifacts, leaving out the detail of his constant nagging not to touch anything. I let him remember that I went parasailing over the lake, soaring through the air, my legs dipping into the cool water as the boat brought me down; in reality, he wasn't even on the boat, tied instead to the phone after his wife called with an emergency at home. No, I went parasailing on my own, a girl of ten tagging along with a family of four who probably pitied me for my loneliness.

There were breathtaking views on that trip. And there were stories, laughs, and time spent with my dad. But he doesn't remember the abandonment, the distance, and the tension that permeate a majority of my memories with him. And maybe that's for the best. Because I do remember, and it's hard to see the good when the bad runs through it all, like water seeping into the cracks of a foundation, eventually eroding it from the bottom up.

However, we've been given a second chance, a last chance, to remedy these memories and take a final trip together. So I watch the swirling water of the Missouri as I keep my mouth shut and let my dad enjoy this moment, another falsity to add to his growing collection of distorted memories.

5

Making a movie is like chewing a piece of gum. That first moment of actual filming is full of excitement as the transformation from script to screen begins, just like popping a stick of gum in the mouth, bursting with flavor as it releases the juices and changes form. But as filming goes on, it loses its vibrance until chewing it becomes a redundant chore, a repetitive motion that delivers nothing new.

This is my educated evaluation of the first day of filming.

It's still exciting, but the start was clunky. We were late getting out of the hotel for a plethora of reasons:

→ The sound equipment wasn't working, the drop-off of our official film vehicle (a trusty Toyota Corolla, of course) was late, and the official film vehicle was the wrong color (white, please—not red. We're not filming *Fast & Furious: Midwest Edition*)

→ Phil was nowhere to be found (eventually, he was discovered drinking coffee in the corner of the lobby)

→ Rene and Deedee took longer with hair and makeup than

anticipated (though Megan does look remarkably average yet captivating—those two are miracle workers)

- → Gathering the whole production team was like corralling cats, with Tom holding the reins as our overwhelmed wrangler

Despite all that, we did manage to film two major scenes: the Omaha pickup and the Squirrel Cage Jail.

As we travel along the highway, our modest caravan of five desperately trying to stay together like ducks in a storm, Tom hops from car to car, overseeing all aspects of the process while Bruno and Jasper film driving and landscape scenes. While most of our filming will be in order due to the nature of the story, there are some scenes that will need rearranging. That's my job as script supervisor. I have to keep notes on the organization of the scenes; monitor the continuity of the wardrobe, actions, and props; and follow along to make sure my script is being delivered as intended. With such a small cast and limited production aspects, it's not too hard to catch on, and by the end of the day, I'm starting to feel like I can actually do this.

And even though there have been strained moments while filming, Megan and Phil are magic. Their talent sneaks up on me, an awe-inducing surprise amid all of the chaos. I hadn't seen any of their screen tests and only knew them from previous works and our interactions so far. And with Phil, the interactions had been few and far between, with him choosing to float on the perimeter of the crew while keeping to himself, the majority of his words consisting of questions of need or statements of complaint. But when the cameras start rolling, he is magnetizing, as if natural charisma was brewing under his skin, only requiring the pull of the lens to surface and morph him into a shiny specimen.

Unfortunately, his ability to remember lines is not as shiny nor at all magnetic.

He is in his late sixties, but still. Maybe it's because the script is so heavy with his lines, but it's a struggle to get through filming. We all become privy to some of his favorite interjections of frustration:

- → "God dang it to hell!"
- → "What the fuck is wrong with me?"
- → "Son of a bitch tits!"
- → Just a throaty growl of irritation
- → And my personal favorite: "Oh, fuck balls!"

He's a colorful sort. There's shock, amusement, and eventual exasperation over Phil's inability to deliver lines as intended, along with all the craziness of a first day. We haven't adapted yet, haven't broken in our filming shoes, and we are all feeling weary and blistered by the time we enter the Embassy Suites for the last time. We're staying here one more night, then we move onto Sioux City for a day, stay the night, then cover most of the northwestern Iowa route the following day. At least, that's what Marnie's itinerary indicates. There was a preproduction discussion about whether to stay at hotels or bring campers, but Tom was adamant we keep our traveling experience as close to the book as possible. He may not be a method actor, but I'm starting to wonder if method directing is a real thing.

I've barely made it inside my room, face-planting on the bed and laying there in numbing exhaustion, when I hear a knock on my door.

"Just a second," I mumble into the comforter, wondering how I am ever going to will my body back into a vertical position. Another persistent knock instills enough motivation in my limbs to push me up, and I trudge to the door. I'm assuming it's Megan wanting notes on her accurate depiction of me, or maybe the Trifecta wanting to gossip about the day. "I'm really tired. Can we do this another time?" I whine as I pull the door open, my words cut off as I see Tom leaning up against the door jamb, his head in his hand, fingers clenching his messy nest of hair.

"Sorry, I know you're tired, but I just need to vent." His eyes search my face with hope. Of course I step back and open the door wider. A chance to have Thomas Price alone in my room? Yes, please.

He stalks in, looks around my small room, then plops himself down on my bed, his limbs spread wide as he stares up at the ceiling. He blubbers a giant exhale then says, "That was a fucking disaster."

I make my way over to the bed and perch lightly on the edge. "It was only the first day. I'm sure it will get better."

"It goddamn better or we are royally screwed." He covers his face with his hands, trying to hide the crumpling of his spirit that shadows his features.

I don't know what to do. Yeah, we were pen pals, and we shared some witty correspondence, but we haven't really talked since our walk yesterday. I can tell he needs comforting, but I'm not sure how to do that while still operating within the realms of professionalism, especially while he's strewn across my bed. I reach out and pat his knee, a supposedly innocent gesture that still leaves my belly tingling with unprofessional desire. "It wasn't that bad, Tom. We got what we needed. Phil's just easing his way in."

"Easing his way in like a virgin on prom night." He heaves himself up and his face is right next to mine, his head bowed down. I pull my hand back quickly, the distance between knee and crotch shortening with his seated position. "Sorry, I shouldn't bother you with this, but I needed someone I could be real with, someone who's just as invested as I am."

"I get it."

He looks up and locks his gaze with mine. We're so close I can see the tiny swirls of dark blue swimming in his irises. Silver screen eyes that have seduced millions of viewers are currently roving up and down my face, pleading for consolation. "I just want this to be a success. I want to do right by you, Logan."

My hand lifts cautiously, hovering in the air next to his cheek before gently settling on his shoulder. He looks down at my touch, and I think about sliding my palm up his neck, cradling his stubbled cheek, and running my hand through his hair, but that would definitely be crossing HR lines. (Do we even have an HR department?) So instead, I leave my hand safely on his shoulder and say, "It's going to be great. Today was just the first day. Phil will get his character, he always does. He wouldn't be so successful if he didn't."

"But he hasn't worked in a few years, and I'm starting to see why."

I gulp, not having known that small detail, but continue on. "Well, he's just warming up then. Probably a little rusty."

"Yeah, but I worry it's my fault. Like I should have been focusing on his performance more."

"You were laying the foundation, figuring out how all the parts work, giving every crew member equal time. I think you did a fantastic job." He looks up and we stare at each other in silence, and the distance suddenly seems too small, like if I leaned slightly forward my lips would collide with his. I go to pull my hand away, but he reaches up to cover it with his own, his fingers laying delicately over mine.

"Thank you. I'm sorry for intruding like this, for putting this on you." He weaves his fingers between my own as he lifts our hands between us.

"It's okay. I get it," I say, hoping the shakiness in my voice isn't too apparent as he brings our hands to rest lightly on his chest, pulling me even closer.

"I just feel like it's different. Like I can be myself with you." His gaze drops to my mouth, and my chest clenches with the conflict of desire versus decorum.

"What about Megan?" I blurt out, untangling my hand from his. I drop my hands heavily into my lap, keeping them safe to avoid the temptation to touch him again.

With glazed eyes, Tom looks me up and down, confused by my sudden shift. "What about Megan?"

"Can't you talk to her?" It comes out more accusatory than planned, but I'm now the frustrated one: frustrated he's put me in this position and frustrated in physical ways that can't be satisfied.

"Well, yeah. But she doesn't get the big picture. Sure, she's doing a good job, but she's not invested like me. Or you." His eyes are starting to regain focus, his words struggling to match the new cadence of the conversation.

"Okay," I reply dumbly, and I sit silently, not knowing what else to say or do. Tom leans back, and looks around the room, as if just now realizing the inappropriateness of this whole scenario. He scoots off the bed and stands, his arm lifting for a moment before being jammed into his pocket.

"Well, I should get some rest. It's going to be another long day tomorrow. Thanks for letting me vent."

"Of course."

He turns with a sudden jerk of his hips, as if he is forcing his body to go, and we say goodnight.

As soon as the door clicks shut, I release all the air in my lungs. Working on a film set is so much more than I imagined, and I'm starting to see how the drama can leak from the screen into the real world. I don't know what I can do about it or how I'm going to resist. This was only the first day. I have so many more to go and I'm not sure my resolve can withstand it.

***

The second day has its stumbles, but we seem to have found our stride by the last shot. Spirits seem high as we all gather in a private party room at the Hard Rock Hotel & Casino. The lighting twins, Leroy and Cole, scarf down their food, eager to hit the roulette table. Others are planning to try their luck at the slot machines, but I've turned down all invitations. This gal doesn't have a guaranteed source of income beyond this gig, so I need to watch my finances.

Atlas and Deedee have already left, their target set on a *Simpsons*-themed slot machine that is more likely a novelty than a payout—definitely a luxury a girl on a budget can't afford. Rene sits across from me, draining the last of her rum and Coke, red lipstick staining the rim of the glass. She's never afraid to leave her mark, always willing to be noticed and celebrated. I wish I could be that bold, that confident in myself. Along with the thought, my gaze drifts to the end of the table where Tom sits between Megan and Phil. I'm sure they're discussing notes from today's filming, but I can't help noticing how Megan leans in, how she rests her hand on Tom's arm, the sleeves of his button-up shirt rolled up to reveal strong, tan forearms speckled with golden-brown hair. Just last night, that was me leaning close, touching his shoulder, thinking it could easily lead to more. It makes me wonder if it's all in my head, this magnetic pull between Tom and me, or is that his superpower, able to attract anyone close and make them feel special? And who am I to believe I'm special enough to deserve the attention of The Thomas Price? Despite this cold dose of logic, envy still fogs my reason as Megan throws her head back with laughter in response to something Tom just said, and he and Phil exchange bemused smiles. How lovely it is to be the focus of his smile. I sigh, remembering the glitter in his eyes, the feel of his hand, the faint smell of spice as he leaned in…

"Baby girl, you got it bad," Rene declares.

"What are you talking about?" I ask, hoping I've successfully feigned ignorance.

"Just your mooning over Tommy Boy over there." My silence serves my answer on an open platter. "Oh honey, welcome to your first film set crush."

"I don't have a crush. I'm a grown woman," I grumble.

"I'm older than you and I have crushes all the time! Of course, I also have a man in Reno, so my crushes can only play out with friendly banter. I can look, and look I do, but I don't touch." She lifts her empty glass, this time catching the ice cubes in her mouth and crunching loudly.

"You have a boyfriend? You never told me that!"

"Sweetie, we've known each other for four days and I've been alive for forty-five years! Of course I haven't told you everything. You gotta start hanging with me and Dee more during hair-and-makeup call. That's where you'll get all the deets."

"So you're saying a film set crush is normal?"

"For sure! Days of hard work leading to nights of forced proximity and partying? It's a breeding ground for the feels. Location filming makes it even more likely, with hotels and isolation from home making it even easier to bed-hop at night."

"I don't want to bed-hop—"

"So you're telling me you wouldn't curl up like a cat on that man's lap and purr like a goddamn Porsche if you had the chance?"

My look of shock elicits a loud bark of laughter, and my eyes widen with the worry that we'll attract unwanted attention. "Rene! He's right over there."

"Oh, he doesn't know we're talking about him. We could be talking about any of the other handsome men on set. What, you think I didn't notice all these beefy boys rarin' for a bite?"

"Are you the one with the crush, Rene?"

She sighs. "No, just appreciating the view. But Benji's the one for me. So I keep my hands to myself, but my eyes are always wide open. I see *everything*." She smirks and winks knowingly.

"Good for you. Able to enjoy the sights but still remain loyal. In my world, that's a trait that's hard to come by. And that's why this crush can't be anything more." I roll my eyes at her pointed look. "Yes, I admit, I have a crush. Now just let me suffer in silence."

She scoots her chair closer and leans across the table, her sleeves no doubt soaking up some of the spilled liquid and food smears on the surface. But nothing can stand between Rene and some good gossip.

"So you have a crush. What's the problem? You're single. He's single—"

"*That's* the problem, I don't think he's single."

Rene leans back with a raised eyebrow. "Sweetie, we've only been here for three nights. That man's been working like a mule. Where in God's name do you think he's found time for a clandestine hookup?" Just then Megan rises, squeezing Tom's shoulder as she makes her way to the casino. He flashes her a quick smile before returning his attention fully to Phil. Rene whistles with understanding, crossing her arms across her heaving cleavage. "Here's the deal, Logan. Emotions run high on a film set and everyone's looking for something to distract them from missing home. The traveling, late hours, and the creative spirit have a way of connecting people quickly and dramatically. It's okay to have a little fun, but it rarely lasts. Do you know how many broken hearts I've nursed on set, including my own, over the years? That being said, relationships are also pretty casual. Even if Tom and Megan are together again, I doubt it's serious or even exclusive. I don't see a ring on his finger."

"I would never want to break a couple up—"

"I'm not saying that. What I am saying is don't get all caught up in assumptions, but don't hold yourself to one opportunity, either.

Have some fun, but don't get too attached. Just know that most set relationships are frivolous in nature, however that sways your affections or actions."

"So what I am hearing is that it's a bad idea to get involved with anyone on set because it doesn't last?"

"Rarely. I said it *rarely* lasts," she offers with a sympathetic smile.

"Oh, okay, much better." I look down at my empty glass, swirling the melting cubes at the bottom. "Well, I'm used to things not lasting, so at least that tracks," I mumble, unable to hide my bitterness.

"You could just ask him if he and Megan are together. Could help you settle some of those unsettled feelings."

"I've brought her up a few times when we've been alone, but we always end up getting interrupted."

Rene slaps the table loudly, drawing attention from others in the room. My widened eyes scold her and she responds in a harsh whisper. "You've been alone with that man? What are you keeping from me?"

I bring my voice down to match hers. "Nothing, we just went for a walk the other day, then he came to my room last night—"

"Wait a second, you didn't tell me any of that! Well, damn girl! Maybe you do have reason to be crushing. The man is giving you clear signals. Sounds like his lap is prime real estate for making biscuits," she announces rather loudly, and I almost choke on my spit. I look around nervously. The mother-son sound duo of Pam and Dawson, who's too young to gamble or drink, looks up from their hand of cards, and Tom looks over to catch my eye, his ear still tuned to Phil as the older man continues on with a story.

"No, like you said, it's a bad idea to hook up on set."

"I said that before you told me he's been visiting you in your room—"

"Rene, stop! You were supposed to get my mind off him, remember?"

"I've changed my tune. Instead of getting your mind off him, my task is to get your body on him." I nearly upset an entire table of dirty dishes trying to cover her mouth with my hands. I'm so distracted with cleaning up my mess and shushing Rene that I don't even notice when Tom is standing right above me. He says my name, and I freeze, turning my head in slow motion until I meet his gaze.

"Hey, Tom. Great job today," I throw out, hoping to cover up any overheard objectification of his body.

"Rene, sorry to interrupt, but can I steal Logan away for a bit?"

Rene's face melts into the biggest grin as she rises. "Sure thing, boss. I'm going to get my gamble on anyway. I'll see you tomorrow, Logan. Have a nice night." The emphasis on her last sentence causes daggers to fly out of my eyes in her direction, but she backs away, smiling smugly, and leaves.

Tom surveys the remaining stragglers, then asks, "Can we go outside? I need some fresh air."

"Oh, uh…sure." I gather myself while Tom waves goodnight to those still hanging out. His hand settles at my lower back as he leads me through the door, and we weave our way through the maze of smoke, neon words, and flashing lights until we find ourselves outside on the sidewalk of Fourth Street. "What's up?" I ask, eager to figure out what Tom needs to discuss. If it's my termination, I have Rene's big mouth to thank.

"I just spoke with Megan and Phil, and they're having trouble with some of the lines. Phil especially is having trouble finding the rhythm. I'm okay if he ad-libs a bit, as long as he keeps the spirit of the lines intact—but I wanted to check with you before I give them free rein. I wouldn't want to disrespect your father's words, or your recollection of them." He looks over at me with his hands in his pockets as we pass a few bars and turn right down the next block.

I relax at the subject matter. So this is a work conversation. Makes sense. But the part of me Rene appealed to is achingly disappointed. “Uh, of course. I don’t mind.”

“It’s okay if you do. I want you to be honest with me.”

“No, it’s fine. If it helps Phil, then I’m all for it.”

“Okay, good. Thanks.”

We walk in silence a few beats. “There’s something else.”

“Oh yeah? About Phil?”

“No, about your book. Your dad specifically. Sometimes I don’t understand him. How he just asked you out of the blue to join him on a trip after so many years. How he could assume you would just drop everything. I just can’t fathom having that level of arrogance about a jilted daughter.”

“Well, he was dying—” I try to interject, but Tom is still active in his analysis of my life story. He stops, causing me to halt my stride as well.

“But what’s even more impressive is how you went. Most people I know would never be able to forgive someone like that. It really stands as a testament to your character.” He’s staring at me and I shiver beneath his gaze. It’s late August, but even in the summer night heat, goosebumps still pop up on my arms. “Oh, are you cold? Here.” He’s not wearing a jacket, but he does have a white shirt under his button-up, which he undoes and hands to me. My limbs are stiff as I push my arms through the sleeves, and I’m suddenly wrapped in the intoxicating scent of citrus and spice that routinely floats around Tom.

“Thanks. For the coat. And the compliment.” I don’t really know what else to say. So Tom likes a woman that is forgiving and gracious. Good to know. I don’t know Megan too well yet, but she does seem like a good person worthy of Tom’s affections. “Can, uh, we turn back? I don't really want to get lost in Sioux City."

Tom laughs. "What, you don't like off-roading it?"

"Uh, no. I'm more of a follow-the-map gal."

"Noted." Tom's voice softens as we turn around and walk back the way we came.

My stomach drops, realizing Tom probably likes adventurous and spontaneous women, but whenever I've traipsed into unmarked territory, I've ended up taking it too far. Better to stay safely on the designated path. I do just that as I look down at the sidewalk, my feet pulling my body forward. That's where I should be looking. Forward toward what I am going to do after this movie. Toward how I am going to continue working for myself after this is all over. Toward a life completely on my own.

Because that's how it always ends. Completely on my own. I need to remind myself of that more often lest I get my hopes up too high.

"So Logan—"

I stop abruptly, interrupting whatever he was going to say. I came here to make a movie and work on my career, not get sidetracked by schoolgirl longings for my boss. "Tom, I really appreciate this opportunity. I just want you to know I'm all in. I want to do whatever we can to make this movie a success. That's my main focus. So whenever you need to talk to me about work or whatever you need me to do, I'll do it. I'm here to work, and I'm not going to let anything distract me." There, that should send the message. Even if he's not with Megan, now he knows that I'm not in the market for film set hookups. I have to be steady and follow the rules. No more mooning over my unattainable boss. I've got my eye on the prize, and that prize is not Thomas Price in my bed. Once I convince myself of that fact, I can start devoting all my energy completely to the task at hand: ensuring I have a lucrative future beyond this movie.

He seems to have picked up on my meaning, his eyes searching my face, his brows pinched together in thought. "Okay, message received. I'll make sure I'm including you more, giving you even more responsibilities. You're here to work? Well, I'll work you then."

I turn away and start walking forward before he can see my wide eyes and red cheeks. Though surely it was unintended, Tom just blew up my attempt to quell my spicy fantasies about him, and I'm pretty sure I just agreed to spend even more time with him. *Shit, this may have backfired.*

Tom catches up with me, and he begins rambling about tomorrow's schedule. He lets me know he'll be the first person I talk to in the morning and the last person I see at night so we can go over plans and performances. He talks with an excited fervor, the passionate pace set by a man motivated by the goal of leaving a legacy. There's no flirting this time, no reveal of feelings, no accidental lingering touches. Nope, he's all business this time. And I'm worried I've just taken a sharp detour bringing me ever closer to falling head over heels.

Excerpt from *Iowa Nice*

LE MARS

"You didn't know I was lactose intolerant?" I ask as Dad and I wait in line at the Blue Bunny Ice Cream Parlor. Walls of purple, green, and blue are adorned with historical ads and clocks plastered with a smiling suit-clad bunny mocking us from his various mountings. Other patrons are scattered throughout the dining room, happily enjoying their creamy treats. We've been fighting all day and are now stuck in a long queue waiting to order, which for me will then be followed by abdominal cramps, flatulence, and diarrhea.

"Well, as you keep reminding me, I haven't been there for a majority of your life, so, no. I didn't know you were lactose intolerant. Do you want to leave?" Dad's voice teeters between consideration and irritation.

"Of course not, I love ice cream." I continue looking at the grand staircase, dark wooden paneling, teal metal chairs, copper ceiling tiles, and various promo materials and informational write-ups. I feel

Dad's eyeroll more than I see it, which gives me an odd curl of satisfaction in my chest.

He moves in front of me to block my casual viewing. "Okay. While we're waiting, what else do I not know about you?" My jaw drops at the challenge, impressed that he's willing to meet the issue head-on. He takes my silence as resistance rather than the quiet sifting through of my mental inventory. "Come on, tell me. You have things you want me to know about you? Well, now's the time."

"Okay, you ready?"

"Hit me."

I start stacking facts, incidents, regrets, dreams, fears, and accomplishments on top of my father like a pile of rubble.

"When I was six, my favorite stuffed animal was a Care Bear. Cheer Bear with the rainbow on her belly. But when I saw an episode of the cartoon, it freaked me out that the Care Bears talked, so I threw Cheer Bear outside in the trash. However, I regretted it a week later, tried to retrieve her, and then learned the harsh truth of weekly trash pickup. Cried myself to sleep for a month after that.

"I hate frogs. In every sense. Alive, dead, cooked. They look like aliens and what is with being able to breathe both above and underwater? That's some weird shit.

"I lost my best friend in third grade when we voted for opposing candidates in our mock presidential election."

Dad interjects at this. "Well, that's just good sense."

"I voted Democrat."

My dad grumbles as we move forward in line and along the trajectory of my life.

"The day before sixth grade school pictures, I scraped my face on the pavement after I fell from my bike. Mom still made me sit for the picture, but let me do retakes when she thought I looked like a trampled opossum."

We finally make it to the counter, place our orders, and then take our sundaes up to the quieter second floor where we settle in at a small round table. The formation of my identity is a boulder rolling faster and faster down a slope as I continue.

"I started my period when I was thirteen. By that time, almost every other girl in my grade had, too. So the next day in homeroom, I announced it as a triumph. Everyone laughed at me, and the boys started calling me Bloody Mary. That was a fun year.

"In ninth grade, I won a writing contest. I got to miss school and go to a college campus and read my story out loud. I invited you, you know. But I guess you were too busy.

"I had my heart broken for the first time my sophomore year. Matt Miller cheated on me with the most popular junior girl, and I was the last one to know. I swore I was done with dating...but then I started dating Paul Bleeker three weeks later.

"I tried to keep a diary all through high school. You know, to document all the crazy drama I was apparently part of. But I would forget to write then remember all of a sudden, so my entries were always weeks apart. It made me wonder if I could ever be an actual writer.

"I would like to be a writer. Like actually make a living from selling my stories and novels, but I don't know if I'm good enough."

Our sundaes sit untouched in front of us, both of us unable to enjoy the sweet treat as I go through the more bitter details of my youth.

"When Mom first got sick, I tried to call you. Three times it went to voicemail. So I gave up. Decided I was meant to deal on my own.

"When Mom died, I wished it were you."

I pause and look up. My dad is studying me intensely, his face pulled down by the emotional weight being transferred from me to him. The sting of tears sharpens my breathing, making me feel as if

I'm going to sneeze, but I have to get the rest out. It might be a lot to unload on him, but it was a lot for me to bear as a child. It's only fair that he feels some of the pain I felt for so many years.

"When you came back after Mom died, I resented you for taking interest in me finally. But you already know that.

"When I got married, I knew it was a mistake. And when you told me it was a mistake, I hated you for being right."

We sit in silence, our ice cream melting, mirroring the deflated sadness permeating the space between father and daughter.

"I've spent a lot of my life hating you." I end my spiel of trauma dumping and stare into his eyes, challenging him to look away. But he doesn't. He's right here with me, and this time, he's not going anywhere.

"I know. And I'm sorry," he says. And I believe him.

I raise my hand and lift the spoon from my Monster Peanut Butter Cup sundae, bringing a small bite of chocolate, peanut butter, and whipped cream to my mouth. It's so good I could cry, or maybe that's just the conversation's doing. I set the spoon down and lock softened eyes with my dad's once again. "I don't want to hate you anymore. I just want to know you. Who you really are. And I want you to know me. For who I really am."

He reaches forward for his own spoon, taking a taste of his turtle sundae. Caramel sauce clings to his chin as he says, "That's what we're here for." He smiles and takes another bite. "Is yours good?" I take another spoonful and nod. "It's gigantic. So how does this work with you being lactose intolerant?"

"We'll have to drive with the windows down for the rest of the day." I pin him with a serious gaze, but crack up at the concern washing over his face. I dig back into the sundae, and with a mouth full of peanut butter, I say, "This is delicious, but I'm not going to be able to finish. You want to try?" I point at the frozen monstrosity with

my spoon, and my dad lights up at the offer.

"Sure." He leans over, scoops up a bite, then closes his eyes with pleasure. "Now that's a good sundae." We exchange smiles across the table, eating our ice cream in silence. Halfway through our dishes, my dad says, "Thank you, Logan. For giving me the opportunity to get to know you."

"You're welcome, Dad."

6

“I want scenes with as many of these ice cream cone statues as possible,” Tom projects loud enough so his voice doesn’t disappear into the thick humidity settling over downtown Le Mars. Dark underarm creases and sweat-dampened spots on shirts broadcast the heat as we all crowd on the sidewalk of Main Street, surrounded by idyllic brick storefronts and bright-orange barricades separating us from a gathering of fans and curious citizens.

Phil and Megan stand in a clearing, a circle of crew members protecting them from the admirers. The two already did their diplomatic duty, shaking hands and signing autographs. With Tom too busy planning shots to work the crowd, people linger and intermittently call his name, but he’s too in the zone to care. He’s solely focused on completing filming in Le Mars by two o’clock so we can end our day farther north at the Wayside Chapel, then retreat to our next hotel in Sioux Center. Kalina has already booked rooms in all our intended locations for the duration of filming, so Tom is anxious about staying on schedule. Some might call it obsessive, but he prefers the label “in control.” I know all of this because he and I met this morning, being the only early risers of the crew, and he divulged all of his plans as well as his intentions for me.

Professional intentions, that is.

A week of filming has essentially become a master class in filmmaking. Even if I don't know what I'm doing, I somehow figure it out, and Tom keeps throwing more at me. He's even started bringing me into production meetings where he and Marnie wage polite battles over artistic endeavors and practical implementation. It's interesting to see how he talks to the specific crew heads and how he listens to their ideas and actually applies the feedback. He's a competent and fair leader, and it only makes me like him more.

Phil and Megan are in their places, ready for the next scene, when my phone starts blasting an electronic tune at full volume. Tom finds the source of the sound, frowning in my direction as I mouth an apology and back away from the filming. I answer the call, Niya's information flashing on the screen, and continue walking past the barricade and down the block until I round the corner.

I can't even greet my agent before she is raging on the other side of the call. "Logan Sterling! It has been over a week and you have not called me with any updates! How am I supposed to represent you appropriately in this new phase of your career if I can't even talk to you!"

"Uh, hi Niya. It's nice of you to return my call. You see, I did call you on two different days, but you sent my call to voicemail." I frown into the phone, waiting to hear what her excuse will be.

A pause fills the line briefly, but then Niya's commanding tone is back. "Oh, I see. Well, sorry. I must have been speaking with another client."

I'm not going to let her get away with her attempted chastisement so easily. "I did invite you to come join us, but you said something about being allergic to fresh air."

"That's a very real diagnosis. Especially when the fresh air smells like pig manure. I've been to your state before, Logan. It reeks."

"You know what people in Iowa say when it smells like poop?" I pause briefly, but continue before my agent can ask or ignore me. "'Smells like money.'"

I laugh, imagining the horror that must be settling on Niya's face, but her sense of logic overcomes any disgust when she parries with, "Well, I do appreciate a good marketing plan. Iowa–one, Niya–zero. All right, enough with this riveting conversation. How's everything going out there in that giant cornfield you call home?"

"It's going great. We're in Le Mars right now—"

"I have no idea where that is."

"Ice Cream Capital of the World up in northwest Iowa?"

"Dairy and a whole bunch of white people? That sounds like the definition of hell to me." I hear paper shuffling, and I suspect Niya is multitasking, working on something else while listening. It's not my favorite thing about her, but I get it; she's a busy woman. I go ahead and give her the progress report.

"Anyway, we are in Le Mars and about to head to Sioux Center—" I offer an explanation before we get sucked into the previous cycle. "Even farther north and even more white." My lips curl at Niya's appreciative murmuring. "We are going to film the Wayside Chapel scene."

"On schedule then?"

"Yep, Tom's running a tight ship."

"How about the talent? They're not butchering your creative work, are they? Because I could spin that in our favor."

"No, no butchering. No need for spinning. They're great. Megan is a burst of sunshine, but she's able to tone it down and bring the moodiness for the screen. She and I have spent some time together, and I'm fairly certain she spies on me during meal breaks."

"Not creepy at all."

"Phil had a shaky start with lines, but once I gave the green light for him to improvise a bit, it's been a lot better. His performance is more fluid, and we don't have to cut so frequently."

"Wait a second. He's improvising? Like changing the words? Did we include that in the contract?" Niya is fully dialed in now, her radar scanning meticulously for any hints of legal obstruction against the written word.

"It's fine. Tom and I talked about it. If I need to sign something, send it my way, but it's working. Plus, it's nothing major. Just helps Phil be more natural in the character."

"Okay, but I don't want Tom convincing you to change your story just to appease him. I know how those handsome Hollywood types go about their day. Flashing their perfect smiles and swinging their big dicks to get whatever they want."

I recoil at Niya's crassness, but a surge of protectiveness propels my next words. "It's not like that with him. Tom and I are friends. He's easy to talk to, and he's giving me more responsibility, letting me in on all the production meetings, prepping the schedule each morning, going over dailies each day after shooting…"

"You're spending a lot of time with him?"

"Well, yeah."

"A lot of one-on-one time?"

"Yeah?"

"Just be careful, Logan. I know how you can be. I mean this with the utmost respect, but you are sort of a people pleaser." I wince at her labeling, but don't disagree. "I just want to make sure you're not being taken advantage of. Do the work you were hired for, but don't overextend yourself, and don't sacrifice what you've created for Tom's vision."

"Okay, I hear you."

"You're my sweet Iowa lamb in a pack of California wolves."

"You lost me there."

"You know what I mean. People from LA are different. They know how to manipulate others, how to get what they want."

"Tom's not from LA. He's from Iowa City."

"He's from LA, Logan. Once you hit double digits in years, you officially transfer your origin card."

I don't agree, but I have no time to refute her theory; Kalina rounds the corner, her eyes landing on me with urgency as she beckons me to follow. "Hey Niya, I gotta go. Thanks for finally returning my call."

"That's why you pay me the big bucks."

"I wouldn't say big bucks. Maybe moderate bucks."

"Keep working and keep writing, and we'll get there. By the way, have you thought any more about your next book?"

"Oh, I really have to go! I'll talk to you later. Bye!" It's not like I hang up on her, but it's the closest I've ever come to doing just that. I figured she would soon start asking about my next steps, but I've been so busy with filming that I haven't had the creative capacity to even think about my next book.

There's been pressure from my publisher for my sophomore attempt, and since *Iowa Nice* is a memoir, they're wanting me to write in the same vein. But I don't really have any story worth expanding on from my life, and I already suffer from imposter syndrome, which together create the perfect potion for a stubborn bout of writer's block. Maybe I should start looking for inspiration on this trip, but this book's already been written, so I'm not sure what new material will appear. Niya will undoubtedly ask again, so I make a mental note to be more cognizant of potential stories. If I know anything about myself, it's if I give myself a task, I will complete it.

Sure, I might cry, bitch, and moan, but it will get done.

I catch up to the crew as light and sound are tucking their equipment into their respective SUVs. Tom appears at my side and grabs my arm. "Ride with me. I want to pick your brain about an additional scene." His words speak of work, but his touch still sends more-than-friendly tremors across my skin. Yet, even as I follow him to one of the rented cars, a warning flares up in the back of my mind, incited by Niya's words of caution. He wouldn't be buttering me up just to get what he wants for the movie, would he?

I try to push the intrusive thought from my mind as I climb into the backseat next to my fearless leader, hoping his friendly countenance isn't a deliberate mask. And I woefully wonder if I have what it takes to protect my intellectual property, while also protecting my heart.

Excerpt from *Iowa Nice*

SIOUX CENTER

"Why are we at a church? I never took you to be a religious man." I take in the tiny church in front of me, a small white box of a building with a singular pointed spire topped with a cross reaching toward the heavens. The summer wind whips around us, unbridled and relentless out here in flat farmland. On the breeze, whiffs of livestock and manure assault my senses, stinging my nose and making my eyes water.

"A church doesn't have to be about the religion it preaches. It can be more about the memories it houses."

I slowly turn my head to look at my traveling-partner-turned-philosopher. "Okay, Socrates. Way to go poignant on me." He doesn't answer, responding only with a smile that settles on his thin lips as his eyes drink in the petite form of the Wayside Chapel.

"Hey, Dad. I'm not trying to rush whatever lesson in theology you're trying to make, but it really stinks out here."

He turns, a gleam of amusement twinkling in his cloudy-sky eyes, and inhales deeply. "Smells like money. Smells like home."

Sudden amusement slices through my irritation and I crack a smile. "Okay, Dad. Can we at least go in?"

He chuckles as he leads me inside the small structure and begins narrating the tiny tour. "This is actually where my great-grandparents were married. That'd be your Great-Great-Grandma and Grandpa Klein," he says, diving into the family history that northwestern Iowa contains for him and him alone.

"Really?" I reply with genuine interest. I never spent much time here, except for one visit to see my grandma when she was in a nursing home. Other than that, my paternal lineage is a mystery. Information about Dad's family was previously a stoppered spigot, and any trickles tease my thirst for ancestral knowledge.

"Yep. They both emigrated from Germany and met in Sheldon." He takes a seat in one of the six wooden chairs facing the modest wooden pulpit, lowering himself with a grunt. A Bible lays open on the surface, a cross hanging above it the main focal point of the room. Rectangles of stained glass bedeck the walls, making the space seem larger and grander than it is.

"Where does the Irish come in?" I sit next to him and we both stare forward at the cross as if it's a requirement of being in the sacred space.

"Well, you see, that would be my grandpa, your Great-Grandpa Cormac. Swept Grandma Alice off her feet with his rolling r's." He adds a flourish to his story by lowering his voice and rolling his tongue, making me grin at his silly re-creation. "Her parents weren't thrilled with her cavorting with an Irishman, but she couldn't resist. She was in love. As a consequence, she went many years without speaking to her parents, even though they lived in the same county." He pauses, a realization of similar circumstances emerging in both

of our minds. "You're actually named for her, you know. That's where I got your middle name."

"Did she ever reunite with her parents?" I ask, my whisper filling the space.

"Eventually. But it was never the same." We settle into the silence, and it's undeniable that we are both thinking of our interchangeable pasts. A repeated instance of filial angst and separation tumbling through generations. You would think we would have learned from their mistakes.

I angle my body sharply to the side so I can look at my dad as I ask, "Why have I never heard any of this?"

He looks down as if to mess with the hem of his shorts. "I guess I didn't think you wanted to. Didn't think you were interested."

"I think if you had told me anything, I would have wanted to know everything." My dad raises his head to meet my gaze, and our eyes lock, the stormy skies rushing to fill the space between us. The rain is at bay, but if I blink, I fear the clouds will open up and douse the carefully tended drought of my emotional field regarding my dad. Every day, I'm finding my heart is relaxing, opening up to his affection, his desire to connect before the end of his story. But the more time I spend with him, the more I fear the flood of pain that will inevitably follow. I blink, and a single tear escapes, trailing down my cheek. Dad reaches out and brushes the tear away with the pad of his thumb, his hand hovering next to my face, before dropping back to his lap. Finally, he says, "Well, I'm not dead yet. What do you want to know?"

We sit in that chapel for hours as he regales me with stories passed down through the years. It is a history lesson of heart, bone, and blood. My body responds to the tales as if in recognition, and when we leave, moved by the rumblings of our hungry stomachs and the arrival of another set of roadside travelers, my limbs feel lighter.

It's as if the weight I have been carrying around is now scattered among the years, the burden of ignorance alleviated by truth, and the heaviness of a broken heart lightened by the only thing it's ever longed for: time with my dad.

7

"It's really the difference between 'a true story' and 'based on a true story.' I don't want you to feel pressured into this, but Landon, Marnie, and I think it just needs a bit more...drama...to hook a theatrical audience." Tom and Marnie sit across from me in my hotel room, Marnie in the stuffed high-back and Tom in the rolling desk chair, while Landon's face looks out from the screen of the computer set on the desk. I scan the three of them from my cross-legged spot on the bed, reading their faces: Marnie's hurried anticipation, Tom's hopeful mediation, and Landon's tempered annoyance. A day off from filming was meant to give the crew a day of rest while the heads of production went over all the dailies to see how our week's worth of material is coming together. Apparently, there's something lacking, since the three bombarded me in my hotel room with an emergency meeting over the script.

"So what you're saying is, my story isn't interesting enough?" I ask slowly. It's not that I'm particularly offended or surprised, but after Tom went on and on about how much he loves my book, it's a bit of a head spinner for him to now request we change it.

"That's not what we're saying at all. In the written word, it's perfect. It captures the emotion and weight of your relationship with the prose, but the pacing can be a bit redundant on-screen. We just need a few…roadblocks to create a bit more conflict, a bit more excitement," Tom rushes in, at the ready with all the right words to win me over.

"It's perfectly normal to add in scenes during filming, to massage the script a bit. Don't take it as an insult, just be glad you're still getting paid." Landon's words are less polished, but I understand. I should be pleased that so much of my plotline is being kept, that I've been given such a large amount of creative control and production input. But even as I tell myself this, I still feel like a failure, like my original story and my subsequent script weren't enough. However, so goes the life of a professional writer, a career title synonymous with perpetual self-critic.

"It's fine. I get it. Whatever is best for the movie," I offer easily.

"Are you sure? Like I said, I don't want to push you into anything you don't want." Tom leans forward, his elbows resting on his knees, his hands interlocked in a nervous fist. Marnie and Landon show less concern. To them, this is routine, the necessary changing of a purchased product for the greater good. And I agree with them. I smile and try to put an end to Tom's fears.

"Really, I'm good. So what were you thinking?"

"Well, as the on-set screenwriter, we were hoping you could think of something," Landon chirps from the computer, his face glitching at the end of the sentence, leaving him frozen in time and potentially unable to see the drip of disdain that instantly pulls at my jaw.

"Tom and I will help, of course, but it is your story. We want you to maintain your mark on it," Marnie adds, softening the sense of obligation in Landon's previous comment.

"I mean…I guess I could come up with something."

"That's the spirit!" Tom exclaims, startling me from the gears of creative necessity already running in my head.

"Can I not involve Abe on this, though? I'm not sure I can handle all his…Abe-ness."

"Whatever works best for you," Tom answers quickly.

"When do you need the additions?" I ask.

Three voices reply chorally, "Tomorrow morning."

My jaw drops. I glance over at the digital alarm clock on the end table, my stomach plummeting. "It's already six o'clock. How am I supposed to rewrite a script by morning?"

"Haven't you ever pulled an all-nighter?" I'm over Landon's tone, and it takes all the polite restraint within me not to get up and close the laptop.

"Don't worry. We'll do it together. Let's order dinner, freshen up, then reconvene here in an hour with food and fresh ideas," Tom directs, standing and clapping his hands in the way I've come to know as his personal form of motivation.

I swallow the urge to ask Landon if he's planning to help, hoping he'll catch my drift that his help is unwanted and unneeded, but he thankfully wishes us good luck and exits out of the Zoom call. Marnie and Tom rise from their seats, their bodies stiff with the duration and tension of the meeting, and promise to send me a link for a food order. When they leave, all I can do is remain seated, wracking my brain for ideas. When I first wrote the book, I was writing it for me. Now, I'm having to write the screenplay for others. And unfortunately, I'm not always the best at doing what others like or want, even though it's what I so desperately desire.

I fall back on the bed and stare at the textured ceiling, hoping the random patterns of swirls and spatters will somehow spark some idea in my currently overwhelmed brain. Some people work well with a deadline. Me, I shut down. I can't wait for Tom and Marnie to see me at my worst.

***

It's not as bad as I thought it would be. Tom showed up at my door one hour ago with four sushi rolls and Marnie's apologies that she had to deal with another emergency. Not only was I surprised by Sioux Center having an actual sushi restaurant, but I was also secretly pleased to be working alone with Tom. No offense to Marnie, but I'm just more comfortable with Tom. And he's definitely more of a treat for the eyes, sprawled across my bed in jeans and a soft T-shirt as we both lie on our stomachs, a notebook and my laptop open in front of us as we work on my script. We've been tossing ideas back and forth, the sheer volume and our fading mental capacity driving us to the edge of hilarity. Now we're in a lull—bellies full and brains drowsy.

"I think there needs to be a hint of romantic possibility," Tom shoves a piece of sushi roll in his mouth, his cheeks bloated with the oversize bite.

"Oh really? For whom? Dad's character or mine? Because they both feel pretty outlandish to me."

"Owladish? Whaw are you tawing abouw?" he garbles out through rice and raw fish. I burst out laughing at the cartoonish slant of his usually handsome features. "Wha?" he asks, kernels of rice escaping from his mouth, and we both erupt in laughter, our bodies shaking from the silliness of exhausted brainstorming. Tom swallows and swipes his hands through the air, clearing the slate of our previous lack of productivity. "Okay. For real, though. What's so crazy about you having a romantic tryst while on the road?"

"Oh, you were talking about me? Well in that case, that's not crazy. That's certifiably insane. My dad's character hooking up for a last-chance fling would be much more believable."

"So you're not the kind to hook up on the road, get a little wild, have a one-night stand?" He asks innocently enough, but my cheeks still burn from the intimate nature of the question. He must notice my embarrassment, and he sits up, apologizing. “Sorry, I’m not trying to be a creep. Just wondering what would be realistic for the movie. You know, since it is you, we have to keep in character, but we do also need a bit more…you know, enhancement.”

“Enhanced Logan?” I smile softly.

“Exactly.”

Tom waits for me to speak, and I finally break the silence, though still keeping my gaze on the stitching of the comforter. “I’m not what you would call a rule-breaker. Sure, I’ve been careless, made some bad decisions, made some fun decisions, but I’ve also seen what happens when I stumble my way through life, and I wish I could have tread more carefully. Less lives ruined and all that.” I pause, bringing up my gaze to see Tom watching me intently. I force a smile, hoping to shift the mood. It’s gotten a bit too real a bit too quickly. “But I’m sure Enhanced Logan can bend the rules a bit. She already looks like Megan Marks. Might as well take even more creative liberty and make her more fun, too.”

“Hey! That’s not what I mean. You’re fun, and you’re beautiful.” The previous heat of my cheeks dials up to an inferno.

I’m not great at taking compliments, so I do what I normally do: deny, deny, deny. “I am not. You’re just being nice.”

“I’m not being nice, Logan. I’m being honest. I don’t know why you’re always selling yourself short.”

“I guess that’s what we commoners do to maintain our practical sense of self. We can’t all be gorgeous and talented movie stars that are adored worldwide.” My lips twitch at his resulting smile.

“You, Logan Sterling, are not a commoner. You are a best-selling author. You are a goddamned screenwriter. You just need to shush with that kind of talk,” Tom playfully admonishes me, reaching over to the takeout tray, grabbing the last maki, and shoving it into my mouth.

I sit up quickly and sputter at the unexpected force-feeding, spewing sushi all over my comforter. "Tom! What are you doing?!" He laughs and starts to help me clean up as I try to recover from the potential choking combined with the pure shock of Tom shoving something into my mouth. *Not the something I would have wished for*, I think, instantly blushing at my risqué thought.

"Sorry, that was uncalled for. Just figured we needed to lighten the mood a bit." His voice flattens with seriousness and he raises a napkin to my chin, gently wiping at whatever food debris has clung to my skin during my hacking. "However, I do think we should include a romantic interest. Maybe a bar hookup. Doesn't have to be a full-blown sex scene, but a kiss would be nice. Give the character of Logan a little pick-me-up while dealing with her dying dad."

I stare at him as he continues to wipe at my face. *Shouldn't it be clean by now?* I wonder, and he catches himself, pausing in his cleansing efforts to meet my gaze. "Don't you think that would be nice?" he asks, and I continue staring, studying the shadow of stubble on his jawline, admiring the smooth dip of the bridge of his nose, picturing the soft curve of his lips on mine…

"Logan?" My gaze jumps up to meet his and I startle backward. His hands move as if to pull me forward, but I steady myself, refusing any more of his touch lest it sends me back to daydream land.

"I'm fine. Just this wobbly mattress," I spit out, hoping he'll buy the excuse and ignore the fact that I was willing my face onto his. "So give Logan an on-screen kiss? Sure. That sounds reasonable. We could easily write in a scene. Maybe after the argument in Winterset, or even the hotel in Dubuque."

"Or it could be in your hometown of Ottumwa?"

A rock drops to the bottom of my stomach, and I instantly recoil. "Uh, that seems too close for comfort." The fact that we are even going back to Ottumwa is daunting, but to create a romantic interest there is too much.

Tom must see the wildness in my eyes, the desire to retreat like a scared animal. "Oh, I just figured the more realistic the smoother it would fit into your actual story."

I can't run away. I'm an adult and this is my job, so I compose myself even though the rock is still trying to pull me down. "I suppose…I just…I don't know if I want to go there." I have enough past entanglements in my hometown; I don't need to fabricate another one for a movie.

"Oh, okay. Well, I'm open to options." Tom sits up straighter and curls his legs under his body and I take the opportunity to do the same, hoping the shift in position will shift the tone of conversation, as well.

"So we'll have Enhanced Logan meet a stranger…a handsome stranger, I hope—"

"Of course," Tom answers, quickly following my lead back to our casual back-and-forth banter.

"It'll happen not in Ottumwa—"

"Exactly. Not your hometown."

"And it'll be tasteful. Chaste, even."

"As you wish."

"Who are we going to get to play the romantic interest? Some local and hope he takes direction well?" My brain starts concocting the messy logistics of auditioning and hiring some townie who will have to keep his pants flat while kissing Megan Marks. A tall order.

"I was actually thinking it could be me."

"You?" My head cranks to the side to stare at Tom. It makes sense. He's a good actor, a damned good actor. He's already on set. His cameo will add even more anticipation for viewers.

"Yeah, me. I might as well step in for a scene. It's not like Megan and I will have any trouble with chemistry—"

"Of course not." And it gives them some on set face-sucking time. Cameo Tom and Enhanced Logan make sense, but it also makes me jealous of my literary likeness.

"What? Do you not like that idea?" Tom's eyes search mine as he expertly treads the line between tact and influence. It's become a habit of mine to want to please him, to bend to his charismatic will, which I've already fallen victim to so many times. It's what made me agree to sell him the movie rights, what convinced me to join as a screenwriter, and it's what will persuade me to create a character just for him, a place in my story where he can shine and dazzle, as he's already done for me.

"No. I think it's perfect. Of course it should be you," I answer, and Tom carries on, spreading back out on the bed, oblivious to the heaviness settling on my chest.

"What's another element we could add?" He rolls over onto his back, eyes toward the ceiling, and starts ticking off ideas. "Car trouble, health scare, picking up a hitchhiker—"

"Isn't that illegal?" I interrupt, and Tom swings his head to pin me with a teasing gaze.

"Remember: Enhanced Logan breaks rules."

"Yeah, but Enhanced Logan isn't an idiot. Hitchhiker idea vetoed."

He chuckles at my ruling, then goes back to his brainstorming. My thoughts center on the idea of Enhanced Logan and how we are creating someone that fits the world of the movie better than I fit in my own story. It takes a gentle shoulder shake from Tom to realize he is asking for my opinion.

"How about a health scare with your dad? Or maybe a really bad storm. Would either of those be realistic enough to include?"

"Yeah, I mean either of those would work." I'm distant in my response, still stuck on what I'm supposed to be and what I actually am, and how what I actually am could destroy all I've worked for. But here we are, still working on what I've created, so I can't run away now.

"I want to preserve the integrity of your original script," Tom offers.

"I know. I trust you." And I do, which is scary enough because why would I trust a Hollywood bigwig, an actor adored for his ability to become different people, to successfully wear masks of deceit? But I do trust him, so I sit back and let him take the lead on the next portion of our brainstorm session.

"Okay, well, production-wise, a health scare would be cheaper to include. That way we don't have to worry about CGI or hope for inclement weather. Would it have made sense that your dad would have had a setback, maybe a hospital stay or an ER visit?"

"Sure. We can work that in somehow."

"Great. We finally have a place to start. Let's get writing!" Tom's body bounces on the bed in anxious anticipation for the next step. He slides the laptop in front of me and takes the helm at my side, ready to copilot whenever needed.

"Great," I answer robotically as the bright screen of my laptop sears into my pupils.

Before I can start typing, my hand is covered by Tom's, his fingers curling around my palm. I turn my head, our noses almost touching with his nearness. I study his face as his eyes fill with… admiration? Gratitude? Fondness? "Logan, I just want you to know how much I appreciate your willingness to do this with me. And I promise it's still your story. I would never try to take that away from you." The softness of his voice licks down my spine and I can feel nothing but the weight of his hand or see anything but his widening pupils. I try to respond, but all I can do is open my mouth dumbly then bring my lips back together. I see Tom's eyes dip down to my mouth and it would be so easy to fall into him, to wrap myself up in his arms, and forget all my doubts and fears for a fleeting moment, but he lifts his hand from mine and breaks our gaze to turn to the computer screen. I see him swallow and let myself bask in my imagination for one more brief second before I, too, turn toward our pressing task.

My heart is not in it, but we write for the next two hours until we are both struggling to keep our eyes open against the glow of the computer. We are able to smoothly incorporate the two new scenes, and we're both proud of the final product. By midnight, I succumb to the heavy lull of sleep, and I wake up the next morning with the comforter pulled over my shoulders. Tom is gone, having snuck back to his room after tucking me in. He's now in the script, as a character and a co-writer, an indelible part of my story. And now, he's even further under my skin, pushed beneath the surface with all the other secrets, hopes, regrets, and lies that keep threatening to breach the barriers I've so diligently put up.

I fear this movie is going to break me, or at least destroy the persona I've created to survive. And if that happens, I'll have nothing left.

But today is another day of filming, so I gather up the contents of Logan Sterling and make my way to the hotel lobby where I bottle everything in and hope I can hold it together as we continue our way across the state that made me who I am.

Excerpt from *Iowa Nice*

IDA GROVE

"You refused treatment?" I'm hot on Dad's heels as he strolls up to the castle bridge, the entrance flanked by stone knights who guard the passage onto the drawbridge-like structure.

"What a quirky town, huh? You ever been here before?" Dad is doing his best to ignore me, looking up in feigned wonder as he steps under the arched entrance, the castle turrets rising on either side.

"No," I answer perfunctorily, still following him as he walks on the suspension bridge, stopping in the middle to gaze down at the Odebolt Creek. "Was that true? What you said to that guy?" We've been attempting a game of golf at the Ida Grove Golf & Country Club, mainly because it's the only way to see the golf course castle, but of course, Dad quickly found himself in a jovial conversation of nostalgia when he ran into another veteran. While practicing my putting, I overheard him say that his doctor had suggested another round of radiation for his liver cancer, and I nearly fell over. "You

told me it was terminal!"

"Whimsical, that's what it is." Dad leans against the steel railing, his hand drifting out to pluck the suspension cables as if strumming a harp.

"Dad! Why would you do that?" My voice carries out across the stillness, waves of anger washing over me like the rippled surface of the creek below.

He finally answers me, but continues staring at the water. "Did you know that I underwent treatment for two years before I contacted you? Two years where I hoped to get my life back, fought to survive for the promise of more years? In those two years, I wasted even more time, and it wasn't until I seriously considered dying that I actually started living."

"Why didn't you call me while you were getting treatment?"

"You know, I dabbled with the idea of contacting you, making amends, but I didn't want you to think that I was only calling because I needed help. That I needed you to take care of me. That wouldn't have been right, especially after what you went through with your mother. And I knew I didn't deserve your help, since I was rarely there to take care of you throughout your life. No, I had to do it on my own." He turns to look at me. He still needs to brace himself with a hand on the railing, his body weakening from the time on his feet, but the discipline and pride of a soldier still make him pull his shoulders back and straighten his spine. He may be dying, but he's still here, taking up space and using his voice.

"Logan, I spent my entire life playing by the rules: stay active, eat healthy, don't smoke, limit alcohol intake. I arrived at work on time, paid my dues as a citizen and a soldier, and kept my nose clean. Those rules I could follow. But when it came down to family and fatherhood, I faltered. I ran. And I failed. I failed your mother, I failed your stepmom and stepsisters, and I failed you. Accepting the fact

that I'm going to die from cancer helped me realize it wasn't the life I had led that was important, it was the life I had run from. Family and fatherhood were supposed to be the parts of my life that I looked back on, that I gained comfort from. But there was no comfort there. Only regret."

"Dad—"

"No, I need to say this. I'm sorry for not being around. I'm sorry for making you feel like you were unwanted, like you were nothing more than a casualty of my marriage to your mother. I'm sorry I wasn't a better husband...both times. And I'm sorry I was so blockheaded about your marriage and life decisions. I'm sorry that we went so long without talking, that I missed out on so much, that I wasn't there for you when you needed me. But I'm not sorry for refusing treatment. Because it was that decision to welcome the end of my life that gave me the courage to bring you back into it."

This is what I've always wanted, to hear my dad apologize, but not at the cost of his life. I've been granted my wish, but I feel lost, like there's a hole in my chest where I've been storing my resentment and anger. My eyes are watering, tears beginning to trail down my sunburned cheeks, but I can't move. I don't run into his arms, music swelling during a climactic scene in a movie. I don't tell him that he's forgiven while I look up into his shining eyes, nor do I follow up with a heartfelt speech of my own. No, all I do is silently cry, my eyes squinting against the bright sun, a brittle husk incapable of expanding or swelling with love, and say, "Should we finish the game?"

He chuckles softly to himself and walks over to me, patting me on the back as we make our way to the golf cart. He may have been ready to show his cards, to apologize for his wrongdoings as a father, but I'm not ready. Not ready to accept, not ready to reveal my secrets, and not ready to let him go, especially as I cling to what we could have had and what we lost instead.

8

I wake up with a racing heart, jarred from my sleep by something or someone niggling at my brain, taunting me with the knowledge that could break my heart and ruin my life. I take a huge gasp of air and loudly exhale, my mind beginning to clear as I hear my phone repeat its insistent song. It's just a call. I continue breathing, trying to calm myself as I clumsily grab my phone and slide it to answer.

"What the fuck, Logan? You're changing your story for him?"

"Good morning, Niya."

"Yeah, yeah. Good morning. Seriously, what the fuck? Landon said you agreed to add in new scenes."

"Well, yeah, for the good of the movie."

"This is a true story, Logan! Your true story! This could impact marketing—"

"Tom said it was the difference between 'a true story' and 'based on a true story,'" I lazily interrupt, not prepared for a wake-up attack. I sit up, trying to prime my body and brain for the sparring match.

"Oh, 'Tom said?' Has Tom curated your image and worked with you over the past four years? Does Tom know how easily this could all disappear for you? Does Tom even care that this is your one shot at leaving a literary legacy?"

"Jesus, Niya. Did you harvest the entire field of hyperbolic reactions this morning? I think you're blowing this way out of proportion. Authors massage details all the time, and it's even more common with film adaptations. *The Glass Castle*, *Catch Me if You Can*, *October Sky*, *Eat Pray Love*, all of them added in some dramatic elements."

"Are you just regurgitating what Tom and Landon fed you?"

"No." It's not regurgitating, it's referencing.

"You're supposed to include me in all of these decisions, Logan! You should have had me Zoom in like Landon. I could have protected you and your creative property." She's still berating me, but the venom has evaporated, the initial bite of the phone call containing the highest dose of poison. It's the relaxing of her tone that causes me to question her source.

"How do you know so much about the meeting?"

"Landon told me." I picture her shuffling papers or looking at a coffee menu or even fiddling with her nails, anything that would divert her full attention away from my question.

"Wait, what?"

"We speak every day about the project. Don't make it something it isn't," she snaps. She continues on with her business of trying to fix my missteps. "It's fine. As much as it annoys me to admit, they are right. I figured you'd need to add in a little spice, but I also figured you were smart enough to bring me in on those conversations. So what did you decide?"

I ignore the insult to my intelligence and answer obediently. "We're adding in a health scare for Phil and an attractive man at a bar for Megan."

"Who's playing the attractive man?"

"Tom."

"That tracks. Actually a damn good idea, too. Okay, I approve."

"Well, thank goodness. We were all anxiously awaiting your verdict."

"What I don't approve of is your weakness concerning these changes. You have to stand up for your intellectual property, and if you won't, at least let me." Her chastisement digs deep, and all I can do is mumble an apology. Niya sighs. "Everything else going well?"

There's a list of things I could talk about, but my shame at being called weak essentially works as a gag that holds my words back. I can also tell she has already moved on with her day, so I say no and release her from her duties.

"But seriously, another emergency production meeting and I'd better be on the call, hear me?"

"Yes, ma'am." She hangs up, leaving me to flop back down against my pillow. I gaze around at the hotel room, just another on the list of similarly decorated spaces we've been hopping through since Omaha. It takes me a minute to remember what city we are in and what we are doing today. And when I do, I groan and cover my face with my pillow.

We have a crowd scene planned today. Yesterday, Kalina and Marnie hired locals to be background actors, and we're going to be filming around Clear Lake, including the Surf Ballroom and the Buddy Holly crash site. We've deviated a bit from the book's route, having opted to remain in town and travel to nearby destinations so we can stay at the Lakeview Inn for a week and give everyone a break from the constant bed-hopping.

Well, some of us. According to the whispers on set, there's already been a few film set hookups. Atlas and Bruno were seen canoodling during complimentary breakfast, Kalina has apparently been won over by one of the twins (was it Cole, Leroy, or maybe both?), and there is even talk of Marnie sneaking in an overnight visitor after hours.

I know it's none of my business, but the whole team takes such glee in dishing on who's sleeping with whom, it's difficult not to get caught up in the giddiness of it. Occasionally, however, nauseating swirls of envy launch an attack on my core and conscience.

It's fine. I'm fine. I've made peace with the idea of Tom being off-limits. Whether he's with Megan or just the fact that he's my boss, I can't go there. But he's made it so damn difficult. We've spent countless hours together during the past week, whether for professional purposes or friendly companionship. We normally meet for coffee and morning walks, preparing ourselves for the day ahead while absorbing the local flavor. For meal breaks, Tom appears at my elbow with a carton of my favorite food, ready to debrief the previous filming session. And in the evening, his knock on my hotel door has become the music I hum to myself throughout the day, anticipating the actual rendition when he appears in my doorway and comes in to relax. Sometimes we talk about the shoot or about our lives, and sometimes we just lean back and watch television. A few times, I've woken up in the middle of the night, my comforter pulled up to my chin and Tom nowhere to be found. Falling asleep with him in the room has become a guilty pleasure, a lullaby, but the song always ends before the morning. He's become a good friend, and a perfect gentleman. Ergo, no hopping beds for me.

I register the time as seven thirty and drag myself out of bed. I took a shower last night, so I pull on shorts and a white tank, prepared for a day of blazing heat. I grab a sweatshirt and make my way to the lakeside patio.

As I close my door and head down the hall, the scrape of another door opening draws my attention. I'm taken aback to see Megan, her attention focused on the quiet closing of the heavy door.

"Hey, Megan," I say from a few rooms down, and she visibly startles, losing her hold on the door, which clicks loudly into place. "What are you up to?" I ask, making sure my tone is more curious than accusatory. My brain registers the room as belonging to Deedee, and I cock my head in question.

"Oh, morning, Logan!" she says brightly. "Just had a quick color check. Figured we'd get going early. You know, big day and all." She smiles, her fingers rubbing her knuckles as I approach.

"Cool. Do you want to join me for coffee?" Megan and I have talked since our character heart-to-heart, but we haven't spent much time alone. It'd be nice to see how she feels about our progress, but it looks like I won't find out today as she waves me off, saying she needs to shower. "Okay, I'll see you in a few hours for call time then." She smiles her perfect white smile and rushes down the hallway toward the suites.

The patio is shrouded in cool shadow, the rising sun still peeking from behind the hotel. Shards of orange and pink sunlight burst around the perimeter of the lake, the colors shimmering in an abstract canvas of nautical life. The air carries the crisp bite of a morning breeze and the faint smell of algae and fish. I feel rejuvenated by it all, as if my pores are soaking in the freshness and energizing me for the upcoming long day.

My heart clenches as I see Tom's silhouette facing the lake. He's wearing a ball cap, shorts, and a flannel shirt as he drinks in the calming view before the busy bustle of the day.

"Good morning," I say, disturbing his silent respite as I take the metal patio chair opposite him. His answering smile is brilliant, one endearing dimple drawing my attention as he returns my greeting. He lifts his mug of coffee.

"Did you get one yet?"

He starts to rise, presumably to order me one, but I put my hand out. “No, it’s fine. I can wait for a server.”

We sit there in silence, drinking in the beauty of the lake. The sounds of gulls, lapping water, and the occasional slurp of Tom’s coffee are the soundtrack of the morning. Eventually, a server comes by and I order a cappuccino.

“It’s really beautiful out here, huh?” Tom says as soon as the server leaves. I murmur my agreement, both of us still looking out over the glittering water. He continues, “There’s beautiful pockets in California, too, but nothing has ever felt as beautiful as Iowa to me. Every time I come back out here, it’s like my body finally feels at peace.”

“How often do you get to visit? You know, normally, like when you aren’t making a movie?”

“I try to visit my family every year, but missed a few in the past when I was filming on location.”

“What are some of your favorite places you’ve been?”

“Well, I always enjoy London. I’m a sucker for a hot order of fish and chips and a warm ale.” He flashes that smile at me and my stomach flips. “Dubai is absolutely out of this world. The architecture and design make it feel like you’re in a sci-fi film, which I suppose worked since that is what we were filming. But I think New Zealand is my favorite. The people there are really nice, and there’s a lot of undeveloped countryside. It reminds me of being back on the farm.”

“How long has it been since you’ve been back home?”

“Almost two years. But don’t worry, we’re going to take a detour and stay with my family for a few days. My mom is already planning meals to feed the whole crew. She’s excited to meet everyone, especially you.”

“Me?”

“Yeah. You wrote her favorite book. She’s the one who passed it on to me, and to be honest, it was her idea that I direct the movie.”

"Really?"

"Yeah, she knew I'd been wanting to try my hand at it, and she said this would be the perfect story. She might have seen the chance to rope me into a visit too. Hence, the upcoming stay at Casa de Price."

"Well, I'm excited to meet her. She must be pretty great to have raised such a level-headed movie star." He smiles, but there's a downward tug to it. "What's wrong?"

"You always bring up the movie star thing." He looks up, squinting against the reflection of the sun off the surface of the lake. "There's more to me than that, you know?"

"Of course I know that. I wouldn't be spending so much time with you if I didn't." His smile returns in full force, filling his face with gleeful mischief.

"So you're saying that you like me, you really like me?" His impression of Sally Field disarms me, and I find myself unable to catch my breath, my laughter all-consuming.

Our server returns with my cappuccino amid my bout of merriment, then holds an envelope out toward Tom. "Uh, I have a message for a Mr. Sterling?" Tom's eyes go wide, and he nods in my direction. He grabs the envelope from the server and thanks him.

"He knows who you are, right?" *Who in Iowa—no, who in the country—doesn't know Thomas Price?*

"He probably figured I was using an alias," he answers, examining the missive. "Mr. Sterling, huh? I kinda like the ring to that."

"You shouldn't. That's my ex-husband's name."

He hands over the envelope. "Logan Sterling Room 28" is scrawled across the front, no male prefix to be found. The gendered assumptions continue, and I sigh as I open the letter.

A handwritten memo on the front desk's Lakeview Inn stationery reads, "I'm disappointed by what you did. Make sure it doesn't happen again." My stomach plummets, until I see the message is from Niya (misspelled as "Neeah" by the front desk attendant), and realize this is one of her dramatic ploys to accompany the accusatory call from this morning. I grumble as I continue the drama by ripping up the letter and using the scraps of paper as a coaster.

"Everything okay?"

I nod and respond with a quick, "Just my agent's idea of a joke."

"Oh, I get that. Landon is one for histrionics, as well. I always tell him to just be up-front with me, which he is, but he always likes to punctuate his messages with a cynical encore. But I appreciate the honesty. It's definitely my favorite thing about him."

"Honesty is important to you?"

"Definitely. It's the most important. In this business, I get so tired of the fakeness, the lying, the buttering up. It's exhausting. I think the world would be a much better place if we were all just honest with each other."

I look out at the water, at seagulls swooping down to catch their breakfasts, and I don't know how to respond. Luckily, Tom fills the silence when he asks, "What's with the Mr. Sterling bit? It didn't seem to catch you off guard."

"Oh, it's the name. Most people assume I'm a boy. It's my dad's gift to me, or rather the curse that keeps on giving, even after his death."

"He named you?"

"Yeah. My mom was supposed to name me if I was a girl, and my dad if I was a boy, but he guilt-tripped my mom after I was born. It was a pretty traumatic delivery, one that left her unable to have any more children, so it was his only chance to name a child. At least, that's the story I was told."

"It was her only chance, too."

"Yeah, but he didn't think of that. Just thought of what he wanted without considering the consequences. He was good at that." My voice trails off, the not-so-glittery memories of my dad always gripping my chest like a vise. Since he died, I feel bad rehashing his wrongdoings, as if I'm dishonoring the dead, but just because he passed away doesn't erase all of the hurt he caused.

"Well, I like your name." Tom's smile is a life preserver, pulling me back to shore after drifting off with the currents of past indiscretions. "It's original, it's cute. Who cares if people think you're a boy? The minute they look at you, they realize their mistake."

"So you're saying I don't look like a man."

"Far from it, Logan." His eyes settle on me, scanning me with a heat that cuts through the cool of the lakeside breeze. I break away from his gaze, a weakness coursing through my limbs. He must be unaware of his impact on my center of gravity as he continues without a beat. "Anyway, can I tell you a secret? Something that will make you feel better, but you can't share with anyone. Not even Landon."

"Why would I share anything with Landon?"

"True. So promise? No telling?"

"Of course."

Tom holds out his pinkie, and I laugh as I curl my own around it in a sworn-to-secrecy gesture as old as the spoken word.

"My full name is Thomas Sydney Price."

"Okay?"

"Sydney? It's totally a girl's name."

"Maybe. But it's your middle name. Who cares? And there's famous men named Sydney, like Sidney Poitier, Sydney Pollack..."

"Fine. You've made your point. I have absolutely nothing to complain about. Your pain is greater than mine, Logan Alice Sterling."

"You remember my full name?"

"Of course I do. I've done my homework, read your book multiple times. I'm nothing if not a dutiful student."

I gulp, overwhelmed by the feeling of being studied and known. "Well, you deserve an A-plus…and all the gold stars."

"Can I ask why you published under your married name instead of using McClarnon?"

"Oh. Um…" The question actually surprises me. It's a simple question; it should have a simple answer, but all I can do is sputter out a bunch of nonsense about Sterling sounding better than McClarnon, my wanting to keep my pen name the same as my legal name, and the unnecessary hassle and expense of taking back my maiden name. I force a smile, then turn to take a long look out at the lake, hoping Tom has lost interest during my ramble.

Thankfully, he notices the time on his watch and starts rising from his seat. "We gotta get going. I have to meet with Jasper and Bruno, then make sure Phil and Megan are awake."

"Megan's awake. She was meeting with Deedee this morning for a color check," I repeat her story.

"Oh? Okay. Well, good." He holds out his hand, and I take a last gulp of my coffee then let him help me up. The warmth of his grasp lingers on my own as he releases his grip, and my mind travels back to our conversation about keeping things professional. Oh, how I regret that conversation. I might have started out this trip with a crush, but now I've fallen into a full-blown friendship, knowing the man for who he is and not for what the media portrays. The more time I spend with the man versus the movie star, the more I know and fear the toll it could take on my heart. The pull of the film set is too much to deny, and we keep coming together. Eventually, I won't be strong enough to resist, and really, why would I want to? Except for the small fact that I could lose everything if I let him get too close. But it might already be too late.

Excerpt from *Iowa Nice*

FORT DODGE

"Let's do something different."

"Like what? Wasn't the whole point of this trip to see all the hokey Iowa roadside stops we can?"

"Yeah, but after today, I feel like we're in the negative." Dad turns to me, a look of utter defeat on his face, a face I've noticed is looking more pale and gaunt despite the time spent in the sun, traipsing across the Iowa terrain. Today was definitely not worth the traipsing. Our hopes of seeing the Cardiff Giant, an Iowa replica of a famous money-grabbing hoax, were dashed when we arrived at the Fort Museum only to be greeted by a sign announcing the museum's closure for the day due to a planned all-staff training. We are now sitting in my car, staring at the log cabin facade and the bright white banner advertising the location of our desired stop, trying to figure out what to do.

"We can come back tomorrow and hit it up in the morning. I

know it's important for you to see."

Every time we've arrived at one of our attractions, Dad's ballooned up with interest, native pride, and personal accomplishment. Now, he exhales, emitting a deflated, "Yeah, I suppose. But what do you want to do in the meantime?"

I stare at my dad as I clench the steering wheel, my brain hopscotching through childhood desires and broken promises. "Well, you always promised to take me to Disney World. Think we can make it before closing?"

He glares at me, a soft quirk of the lips revealing his amusement. But he's tired and disappointed, and for some reason, I want to fix this for him. I need to fix this, to make this day worthwhile as his number of days left dwindles. An idea sparks, and I can't hide the glee that sneaks into my cheeks, muscles tight with a barely restrained smile.

I turn the ignition and start pulling out of the parking lot. "I know what we can do."

An hour and one trip to Discount Depot's sporting section later, we arrive at a small pond equipped with two fishing licenses, two fishing rods, a package of red and white bobbers, and a Styrofoam container of earthworms.

"Are you sure I never took you fishing?" Dad asks from the folding chair I also purchased at Discount Depot, squinting against the sunlight from under his baseball cap.

"I'm sure. I've never been fishing in my life. First time, so tell me what to do." I hold the rod out like I'm a knight preparing for battle, and Dad chuckles as he beckons me over to kneel next to him.

I let him bait my worm, its body pleading for escape with its wiggles and stretches. I feel bad for it, but the circle of life must carry on. Dad then takes me through the hold and release of the button while casting and how to swing the rod elegantly through the air. My first few attempts are choppy and a bit life-threatening for all nearby, but by the fourth time, I've mastered the graceful arc. Soon, we are both staring out at the water, watching our red bobbers sit on the glassy surface.

When Dad speaks, it's with a hushed tone, loud voices banned from the holy ritual of fishing, or at least that's what he said when discussing the rules on our drive here. "First time fishing, huh? What's-his-name never took you?"

"No, he isn't really an outdoorsy type of guy."

Dad grunts with disapproval, and I resist the urge to defend my ex.

"Do you still speak with him?"

"Not really."

"Can I ask what went wrong?" I'm thankful we are both still staring at the water, for I don't think I could handle this conversation if his eyes were on me, assessing every reaction. I close my eyes and sigh, knowing this was going to come up on our journey. Of course it was. It was the reason we stopped talking in the first place.

"You can ask, but I don't know if I want to answer." A moment passes with Dad allowing me to sit in my obstinance, but I eventually cave. If I don't tell him now, I may never get a chance. "Fine. I guess it's what you suspect. We were too young when we married. And I think we married for all the wrong reasons. I had an idea of what our life would be, and when it didn't turn out like that, I started to resent him. It's not that he was a bad husband. He didn't mistreat me or anything. I just wasn't happy anymore. And the less happy I was, the worse of a wife I became. I'm honestly shocked he didn't make the first move to split, but when I told him it was what I wanted, he didn't seem surprised. So yeah. Pretty clean break. No kids, he kept the house, and I got the car and my freedom. Which I've done oh-so-much with." I suddenly realize how much I've been talking, and

clamp my mouth shut. Fishing has stealthily lured me into a reveal-all, the water acting as my diary with my words dropping into it like blots of ink.

"You're not a failure because your marriage didn't work out, Logan." It's an olive branch, a gesture of a truce my Dad offers, but it's not enough to wipe clean my deep-seated shame. He doesn't know everything, and I'm still not ready to reveal the punchline. The reason I've been such a failure as a wife, a failure as a woman. I don't know if I'll ever be ready.

I'm about to ask Dad about his own divorces, how he coped and what he regrets, but I feel an insistent tug on my line. I look out to see my red bobber bouncing up and down, almost carried beneath the surface before rising back up sharply. "Uh, Dad?"

He stands up from his chair and exclaims loudly, breaking the whisper rule. "You've got a bite! Reel it in, Logan! Reel it in!"

"I don't know how! What do I do?" I've regressed, a child in the throes of crisis, and my dad comes to save me. He stands behind me and shows me how to tug backward and reel in, repeating the motion until green metallic scales and rubbery ridged fins slice through the water to reveal my catch.

"It's a largemouth bass! A big one, too. What a beauty! Well, there you go, kiddo. You caught your first fish!" He pats me on the back and stiffly sits, working on releasing the hook and throwing the fish back into the water to be caught another day.

It's not Disney World, but it's still a day I will never forget.

TOM: Did you see that cow we just passed?

LOGAN: Uh, yes.

TOM: It was huge!

LOGAN: Yes, cows are big.

TOM: God, I miss cows.

LOGAN: You are a complex mind, Thomas Sydney Price.

TOM: 🙂

TOM: I'm rethinking the bar scene.

LOGAN: What? Why?

TOM: Would a stranger really approach you when your dad is there?

LOGAN: Would a stranger really approach me at all?

TOM: Stop it. 🙄 No, I think you should be on your own. Maybe go to a bar after an argument.

LOGAN: Okay, boss. Sounds like an easy fix.

TOM: Good.

LOGAN: You have a piece of food stuck in your teeth. I can see it from here. 😬🥦

TOM: 😉

TOM: Did that guy really ask for your number?

LOGAN: Yeah! That was crazy!

TOM: He's a good-looking guy.

LOGAN: He's a widowed farmer that lives in the remote tundra of northern Iowa.

LOGAN: It's never going to happen.
Felt nice to be hit on though.

TOM: I'm sure you get hit on all the time.

LOGAN: Absolutely not.

TOM: I remember that dress you were wearing at that first dinner in LA. I would have hit on you in that dress 😉🔥

LOGAN: Do I need to contact HR? 🤔😊

TOM: Please don't. I've put my life's savings into this movie.

LOGAN: For real?

LOGAN: Tom!

LOGAN: Seriously?

LOGAN: Megan looked beautiful in that scene. I mean, she always does. But breathtaking today. Good job.

TOM: Yeah, I'm pleased with it. Everyone did good work today.

LOGAN: Is it nice being with Megan again?

TOM: ?

LOGAN: You know, after dating when you were younger, now working together.

TOM: Yeah, she's great.

LOGAN: And...

TOM: What?

LOGAN: Someone so beautiful is never single for long.

TOM: ?

LOGAN: I just didn't know if Megan was seeing anyone.

TOM: Are you interested in Megan?

LOGAN: That's not what I meant.

TOM: Cuz you know, I could put in a good word.

LOGAN: Never mind. I didn't mean anything by it.

TOM: You know, you can be honest with me. About anything. I'm a great listener. And texter. And advice-giver.

LOGAN: Are you trying to say you're multitalented?

TOM: Remember, I'm more than my good looks and extreme talent.

LOGAN: Oh, I forgot. You also like cows.

TOM: Cows are awesome.

TOM: Hey, are you still up?

LOGAN: Sorry, I fell asleep. Did you need something?

TOM: Nope. I figured it out. Want me to grab you coffee?

LOGAN: Yes please!

TOM: That was a good day.

LOGAN: Yes. Good job, boss.

TOM: I think the crew needs a break tomorrow.

LOGAN: Oh yeah? I'm sure they'd like that. A day of rest and relaxation.

TOM: Not exactly…

LOGAN: What?

TOM: I may have rented two pontoons for the day.

LOGAN: Oh.

TOM: You have a swimsuit, right?

9

"Girl, you are too white for Iowa, and that's saying something. Aren't you supposed to have a farmer's tan or something?" Rene studies me from behind her oversize sunglasses, judgment fanning from beneath her batting lashes, as we wait on Lakeview Inn's dock.

"Not every person from Iowa is a farmer. And I can't help that I'm naturally pale. It's my Northern European roots."

"European roots? More like Casper's kin." Atlas and Rene erupt in giggles as Deedee looks at me with pity while handing me a tube of sunscreen. I've just removed the protection of my T-shirt, already uncomfortable in the too-small bikini borrowed from Deedee, but now I'm also insecure. Uncomfortable and insecure, the perfect title for my future autobiography.

"Girl, your body's bomb, but your skin is translucent."

"You'd better slather this sunscreen on fast or the chef at Lakeview is going to throw you in a pot of boiling water and serve you with melted butter."

"Oh, 'cause I'll be a lobster. I get it." I roll my eyes, pulling at a wedgie before squirting sunscreen into my hand and rubbing it across my exposed skin. And boy, is there a lot of it.

"Of course, with sunscreen on, you might end any potential war between America and extraterrestrials. From space, they'll think we hoisted a white flag in surrender."

"This is great. Keep 'em coming. I'll only cry myself to sleep tonight, no biggie." I feign feeling hurt, but I'm actually enjoying the friendly trash talking, even if I am the target. It's my own fault. I'm not an outdoorsy gal, so I never developed a base tan this summer. I also only own one bathing suit, a conservative one piece, which is currently balled up at the bottom of my dresser in Des Moines. Deedee, who brought three swimsuits, offered me this bikini, which fit just barely since I have a curvier body type compared to her lithesome figure. About two cup sizes curvier. One small misstep and I could earn this film an R rating.

The pontoons chug into sight, Tom at the helm of a double-decker with a slide and Jasper steering the standard one-level.

"If you use that slide, be sure to hold those boobies down, or you and anyone in the vicinity are likely to get black eyes," Rene chortles, managing to land one last dig before moving on to the careful act of preparing to board while loading coolers, towels, and other lake day necessities.

"You're one to talk, Rene. The *Titanic* could sink and we could all fit on your flotation devices," I reply, instantly met with a raucous chorus of laughter.

"Thatta girl! Now you got it!" Rene squeezes me from the side, and it feels good to be included, to be celebrated. This film crew is starting to feel like family, making the work days tick away quickly. Unfortunately, that means the end is also fast approaching, something that manages to cast a shadow on this sunny day.

The shadow is short-lived as I see Tom's gleaming smile. He's in total boat mode: dark aviator sunglasses, hair sticking up and windblown, tropical bathing trunks sitting deliciously low on his hips, enough that I can see the hard lines of his pelvic muscles, almost as tempting as the sculpt of his torso. I've seen his body on display in movies before, but the real thing is even more jaw drop-inducing.

"I see you found a bathing suit," he calls out as he steers the pontoon flush with the dock.

"Deedee had a spare." I shift awkwardly under his stare, unable to see the movement of his eyes, but all too aware of the direction of his gaze.

"You coming, Logan?" Deedee holds her hand out from the standard pontoon on the opposite side of the dock. I look longingly at Tom's boat but decide to follow the Trendy Trifecta.

Jasper gives us an appreciative raised eyebrow as we board. "Looking good, ladies," he says smoothly, followed by a silky, "Hey, Logan." Butterflies rise in my stomach, and Jasper smiles before turning his attention to steering us away and out on the lake.

Due to Atlas's extracurricular activities with Bruno, she's learned and revealed that Jasper thinks I'm hot. Atlas has done her best to convince me to take him for a joyride, even asked me on a double date to a local watering hole one day after filming. But I was busy discussing the script with Tom…and maybe discussing other stuff, too. Atlas either knows I'm nursing a major crush on Tom and is trying to pull me in another, less problematic direction, or she thinks I'm a workaholic who needs to lighten up. Whichever it is, she's not wrong. But even though I've ignored Jasper's advances, I can still sit back and appreciate his sculpted back and arms as our party boat moseys its way through the water.

We've separated into two groups: me, the Trendy Trifecta, Jasper, and Bruno are in the one-level pontoon. Tom's double-decker holds everyone else excluding Phil, who opted for a day of rest indoors. After a windblown turn around the lake, the boats float side by side in an isolated cove as we drink, sunbathe, and swim. Cole and Leroy have placed bets on who can land the longest distance from the slide, and Dawson has begrudgingly accepted the role of referee. It's a beautiful day to be on the water, and I'm having a blast, but the desire to hang out with Tom looms over my happiness.

Atlas and Bruno sit side by side, their legs intertwined, Bruno's arm slung over Atlas's shoulders. Rene sits gazing at something far off, her third can of premixed margarita beginning to take hypnotic effect. Deedee's attention is split between our conversation about television favorites from our childhood and her phone, and I'm stretched across a bench seat at the back of the boat, carefully shielding myself from too much sun beneath the awning when Jasper sidles up to me.

"May I?" He bends, lifts my legs, and sits down, draping my legs back over his lap. It's a good move, and I'm taken aback by his effortlessness and my body's apparent pleasure at his touch. He throws an arm over the back of the bench and swivels to turn his full attention on me. His dark eyes glitter with approval, and his lips curve upward in easy flirtation.

"Are you having a good time today, Logan?"

I'm flustered, but still find my voice, answering with a shaky, "Of course. Are you having a good time, Captain?"

His smile widens, delighted with the assigned moniker. "For sure. Especially with such a good view." He stares at me, hard, and I swear, if one could be impregnated by a look, I'd be having triplets in nine months. I try not to squirm beneath his gaze, but my legs are starting to sweat as they lay atop his lap and apparently all of my friends have vacated the back of the boat. I've been set up. "So tell me about yourself. All I know is that you're a talented writer and you're from Iowa."

I pull out some random facts about myself, and Jasper listens attentively, his hands drifting to my ankle. He begins to tell me about growing up in New Orleans, and I try to relax into it, I really do. I try to entertain the possibility of seeing where this could go, of enjoying a night in his hotel room, because I'm sure it would be physically enjoyable, but I just feel distant, like I'm trying too hard to play a part.

Suddenly, hands rise from the water to grip the deck and Tom bursts from the lake's surface. He pulls himself up onto the boat and slides his hands down his body in an attempt to slick off the water before letting himself in the gate and standing above us as he says, "Hey, guys. How's the party over here?"

Jasper releases my ankle and leans back into the bench. "It's good. We're just chilling." The three of us exchange stiff smiles until Jasper gives in and asks him, "Can I get you a drink?"

"Sure! That'd be great. Thanks, man."

Jasper carefully sets my legs down as I adjust to a seated position and gets up, his movements slow with resistance. He catches my gaze, raises his eyebrows and purses his lips, then goes off to locate one of the coolers. Tom takes the spot next to me and leans back, groaning loudly as he settles down.

"The sun is starting to make me drowsy," he says simply, and I stare at him in wonderment. "What?"

"What are you doing over here? Aren't you supposed to be manning the other boat?"

"Nah, I put Dawson in charge. Made the kid's day."

"Who's overseeing the twins' competition, then?"

"Pam. And she likes to fuck with them, give them silly challenges that they just can't refuse. It's hilarious." Jasper returns with a can of beer and hands it to Tom then retreats back to the helm.

"Tom!"

"What?"

"You completely interrupted us. The poor guy was trying to

make a move, and you totally cockblocked him."

His smile drops and his face pinches up as he stares at me. "What, are you into him?"

"I don't know."

Since I haven't been able to get a straight answer about whether or not he is back with Megan (although I haven't had the guts to come right out and ask), I've been stuck in this limbo of attraction and restriction. For all I know, Tom could secretly be with Megan, throwing me off his scent, playing dumb so he doesn't get called out for sleeping with her. Or maybe I've been entirely wrong about him and Megan. He doesn't really have any spare time on set, and if he does, I'm usually with him. But if he thinks I am interested in Megan …and now Jasper…maybe I've placed him permanently in the friendzone. And then there are moments where I feel the pressure of his attention, as if he can see through my usual barriers and into the real me. It all makes me feel awkward, giddy, and downright perplexed. I'm currently feeling all three especially strongly as I shift beneath his gaze and try to readjust my top without drawing too much attention to my overflowing breasts. It doesn't work; I see Tom's eyes quickly flick down before returning to mine.

"So what? You interested in Jasper?"

I want to tell him yes, to see if the hint of jealousy shining in his eyes is merely my imagination, but I worry that it could push him away. And honestly, I've been waiting all day to hang out with him, so I tell him the truth. "No, not really. He's super nice. Easy to talk to. And attractive." Tom clears his throat. "But I'm not really into him that way. Everyone keeps telling me I need to have more fun, though."

"Who's everyone?"

"Rene and Atlas."

He scoffs, looking off in their direction. "That's hardly everyone.

Besides, we are having fun! We're making a movie. What's more fun than that?"

My mind drifts off to some of my recent vivid dreams and the type of fun Tom and I have in them, but all I respond with is a deadpan, "Nothing. Nothing's more fun than work, Tom."

He takes a long swig of his drink, stands, and holds out his hand. "Fine. Let's go have some fun."

I stare at his fingers, still pruned from the water, and slowly grab his hand. His grip is shockingly cold from holding the cooled can, and a shiver slides down my spine. From the chill—obviously. It's definitely not from the assured way his hand completely engulfs mine as he pulls me up. "What did you have in mind?"

He grins and opens the gate, pulling us to the back of the boat.

"Tom?"

"Let's swim."

I'm not a strong swimmer, a fact I include among my many excuses as Tom continues pulling me closer to the water: I still have my sunglasses on. It'll be cold. I'm scared of fish. There's too much pee in there.

He turns to face me and takes both of my hands in his, weaving our fingers together. "Logan, come swim with me. Please."

"But what if the current drags me down?" We both look out at the placid surface of the water. I glance back at him and wince when he pins me with an exasperated glare.

His face softens as he registers the genuine concern in my ask, and he says quietly, "I won't let that happen, I promise. I've got you."

I can feel eyes on us, but when I turn to look, everyone is staring off at random points in the distance, so I turn back and let myself see only Tom's gaze, steady with reassurance. I surrender.

"Okay."

"Okay?"

I nod and we turn toward the water, hands still intertwined, and jump.

The water's not unpleasant, and Tom's every bit the gentleman, looking away as I reposition Deedee's bikini from around my neck back to its precarious position on my breasts.

We splash around in the water and I'm shocked at how fast time goes while swimming. I'm breathless from dog-paddling (as I said, not a strong swimmer) and laughing as Tom tries to impress me with a myriad of water acrobatics. Eventually, a whole crew of us are in the water, floating on inflatable lounge chairs, splashing, and holding drink koozies above the surface, though lake water inevitably sneaks into our cans and our bellies.

Cole and Leroy start back up with the slide, bringing others into the contest. Money bets are banned, though, and we laugh at the twins' disappointment; their disappointment shifts quickly to relief though when Dawson gets the most air and distance by multiple feet.

"Logan, try the slide," Tom says eagerly, a child pleading for a cooperative playmate.

"No, thanks. I'll watch you, though." I laugh as I tread water, spitting out a mouthful when I bob too low. I'm sure I've ingested a bucketload of urine already.

"Please? Please please please?" he begs.

"Why do you want me to go down the slide so much?"

"Because I want you to have fun. Take a cue from Enhanced Logan and let loose for once."

"I let loose. I've had like two Bud Light Lime-a-ritas today." His cringe at my answer makes me look away in embarrassment. "Fine. I'll go down the stupid slide—but only once. Then it's back to sunbathing."

I hoist myself up onto the boat, climb to the upper deck and sit at the top of the slide. I look down at the gathering of friends circling the end of the slide, my eyes latching onto Tom as he grins from the water. I push myself off, hold my breath, and cross my arms over my chest.

It's fun and exhilarating, even though I still lose my bikini top. Bruno fishes it out from the water and throws it over to me, and I duck beneath the surface to regain my dignity and hide my severe flush of embarrassment.

"See, wasn't that fun?" Tom asks when I spin around in the water. His enthusiasm is endearing, and I can't help but nod in agreement. We spend the rest of the afternoon in the cove, feasting on cold-cut sandwiches, chips, and fruit; drinking a fraternity-sized load of alcohol; and alternating between lazy sunbathing and playful swimming. I even go down the slide two more times, though I secure myself in a life jacket to avoid any more wardrobe malfunctions.

By the end of the day, a happy weariness has settled in my bones and my legs feel rubbery as I regain my footing on land. I turn back to the pontoons, Dawson now in charge of the one-level while Tom helms the double-decker again, and I shield my eyes against the setting sun. Tom waves as he backs up from the dock, and my heart swells. It's been one of the best days I've had in a while and I'm sad to see it end.

I turn away and walk back to the hotel, everyone in our group trudging slowly with heavy limbs. I can't wait to collapse onto my bed, but I also need to rub some aloe on my skin, because I'm no longer glaringly white. No, I'm red—lobster red. Guess I really am too white for Iowa.

Excerpt from *Iowa Nice*

CLEAR LAKE

"What in God's name are we listening to?" my dad grumbles from his seat. He's been grouchy all morning, but for what reason, I'm unsure. My first instinct was to ask what's wrong and my second was to try and stay quiet so as not to bother him; my third and current method of dealing with his grumpiness is to go about my business as usual and sing along to my music.

"It's 'Buddy Holly' by Weezer. Don't you like it?" I bob my head and shoulders to the music as I continue steering down the highway, looking for our gravel turnoff.

I expect a throaty disapproval, but instead he just mumbles, "I'm not sure."

"I thought it would be appropriate for our destination."

"What would be appropriate would be listening to actual Buddy Holly songs." The curmudgeonly clip returns to his voice and I know he's still in his fog.

"I don't know if I've actually heard a Buddy Holly song."

Dad suddenly explodes in motion, turning toward me in shock. "Of course you have! 'Peggy Sue,' 'It's So Easy,' 'Early in the Morning'..." I shake my head, each title still a mystery to me, which seems to energize my dad even more. "Okay, how about 'That'll Be the Day'? You must have heard that."

"I'm not sure. Can you sing it for me?" I turn the music down and listen to him jumble up notes and lyrics, scrambling for the tune. He notices my sly smile and realizes my ploy. He deflates farther into his seat and crosses his arms across his chest, muttering something about trickster daughters. "Of course I know 'That'll Be the Day,' but I'm not sure about the others. Want to sing those for me, too?"

He growls with irritation. "Who the heck let you go your whole life not knowing Buddy Holly?"

I bark out a laugh. "Uh, ding ding ding. Sitting right there, Daddio." But there's no accusation in my voice. We've been together long enough on this trip that it's just common knowledge, an agreed upon fact that has stopped bleeding every time we pick at the scab.

Instead of responding to my flippant jab, he returns to his gloomy cloud. "Can you watch your speed, please? The last thing we need is for you to get a ticket."

"Why? I have a great driving record."

"I just want to get to the crash site, see what we came to see, then check into our hotel."

His utilitarian plan irks me. We've been making progress and starting to slide into a comfortable rhythm, enjoying each other's company and remedying past hurts and misunderstandings. Now, all he wants to do is robotically check off items on our list? And here I thought it was all about spending time with me. "Sounds like a great day, Dad. Drive, see, leave. Rinse, wash, repeat. Wham, bam, thank you, ma'am."

"Now, Logan. Don't get all sensitive. I didn't mean it that way."

"Oh, you didn't mean that all you care about is charging through your custom bucket list? Do you even want me here, or did you just need a chauffeur?"

"Come on—"

"I was starting to think you really wanted to spend time with me. But you've put Oscar the Grouch to shame all day with your whining."

"Of course, I want—"

"Wah! You're driving too fast! Waaah! The air conditioner is too cold. Waaaah! The trees are too green. What else do you want to complain about this morning, Dad? What else is wrong with this day?"

Our back tire suddenly explodes, the rear of the car rising in the air as if one-fourth of the vehicle has launched like a rocket. I holler out as my trusty Corolla swerves sharply to the right and careens into a grassy ditch, jerking with a sudden stop that robs my chest of oxygen. We sit in silence except for our heavy breaths as we both try to regain control of our lung capacity and assess the livelihood of our extremities. We look at each other, nod in silent confirmation of our lack of bodily harm, and turn back to stare through the windshield, our view now entirely composed of unbridled green growth.

"Your stepmom won't accept any of my calls."

"Huh?" I slowly turn to look at him, his face a pallid canvas of shock and release.

"I called her again this morning."

"Oh."

"She wouldn't answer. I've left numerous messages, so she should have an idea it was me from an unknown number." His voice trails off.

"What were you hoping would happen?"

"Well, I certainly didn't think she would answer with a tear in

her eye and a tune in her heart."

"No, I should think not after how your divorce went." Unlike his divorce with Mom, his second wife took him for all he was worth. She went for the whole shebang: alimony, the house, and the dog. Dad didn't move back to the Midwest to be closer to me, he did so to escape the wrath of a scorned second wife. And she forever cursed his name and forbade his entrance back into her or her daughters' lives. I wasn't even a second thought. Just another thread snipped to clean up his frayed past.

"I don't want anything from her. I just want to apologize." Apparently Dad's acceptance of the looming end of his life has inspired him to sweep clean all the dusty roads of his past relationships. I should have anticipated this, but I can't help but feel like our reunion means a little less with him trying to do the same with others. I guess I'm not special.

"She probably doesn't need an apology. Didn't she remarry? Sounds like her life moved forward just fine. People only need an apology if the past messed them up enough to impact their future." Another pause as I start looking outside my various windows, surveying the damage without leaving my seat.

"Is that why you accepted my apology? Because I messed you up?"

The question hangs in the air, heavy with honesty. I bow my head and speak into my lap—one word that holds power over both of us: "Probably."

"I know I've said this already, but I'm sorry."

I look up to see him gazing at me. I thought the cut from past hurt was healing up, but it's still there, a faint white line forever marking me with my childhood issues. What I didn't expect is that he would have his own scars from his part on the other side of the knife.

"I just wanted a chance for her to see me as a better person.

Especially since I never got the chance with your mom."

And that's what he's doing. Rewriting his role, re-creating his character, and renewing a legacy. Making peace with me and others from his past is helping him make peace with his fate. So I decide to grant him this pass and help him continue down the path of acceptance. "It happens. And I forgive you."

"No, it doesn't just happen. You're thinking of accidents, like this one. Speaking of which, let's see what we're dealing with."

As my dad pushes open the door and climbs stiffly from the car, I feel a shift in the air, a lightening of the previous cold front that was his mood. Maybe he just needed to apologize to someone, anyone, even someone he's already apologized to, in order to shave off the guilt that grows daily like a rough stubble on his skin.

After we locate my spare and Dad teaches me how to change a blown tire (another life skill I missed out on due to his absence) we eventually make it to the Buddy Holly crash site. We see the collection of sunglasses hanging off the roadside memorial shaped like Buddy Holly's signature spectacles, trudge through the field to where more varied offerings hang off a steel guitar sculpture, and feel the way grief, respect, and acceptance mingle here to create a cesspool of messy emotions. I remind myself that Dad is struggling with that same cesspool. Some days the muck is knee-deep, other days it licks at his neck. So I forgive him for his bad mood and his need to memorialize himself in a brighter light as we stare at the famed music memorial of the Midwest, our hearts heavy with the power of remembrance and the desire to be good enough to be remembered ourselves.

10

"Everyone thinks we're sleeping together," I announce as I enter Tom's room the next morning, my phone having blown up the previous evening with a string of interrogative texts from the Trendy Trifecta, first separately, then in a group message. I charge in as Tom holds the door open, talking instantly as I pace in front of the bed.

"Just because we're friends?" I hear the door click shut and feel Tom step closer.

"I don't know." If I'm being honest with myself, I do know. While I might try and rationalize that Tom's and my interactions were nothing but innocent, I still spent the previous night overanalyzing the entire day: Tom interrupting Jasper, holding my hand, finding any excuse to touch me. Is that friendship, or something more? And why does any answer make me feel like I'm going to throw up?

"Does that bother you?"

"I don't know," I repeat. It bothers me that the crew would think I am being unprofessional and sleeping with my boss, but it also bothers me that we aren't more than friends. It bothers me that others are apparently taking so much notice of our interactions, a spotlight having somehow found me. And it bothers me that Tom can't manage to see what is right in front of him. Conflicting sources of agitation swirl within my stomach, increasing my nausea.

"Do you want to spend less time together?" A hand reaches out and clamps onto my forearm. I stop my pacing, and my gaze travels from the hand up a blazing red arm to settle on Tom's concerned and very sunburned face. My mouth opens in shock and all I can do is stare at the white band of skin across his eyes. His sunglasses have branded him a reverse-raccoon and the whites of his eyes are bloodshot with the indulgence of the previous lake day.

"Oh my God, Tom! Did you not put on any sunblock?" Megan, having set timers to reapply her own sunscreen and make sure she didn't burn or tan for the sake of her role, kept reminding all of us to do the same, but we must have gotten too caught up in the fun.

"I did…in the morning, before we got on the boat." He releases his hold on my arm and sits gingerly on the edge of the bed. His movements are stiff and painful, without his usual swift sense of ease and control. I sit next to him, our skin close enough that I can feel waves of heat roll off him.

"Have you put anything on this? Wait, do you have a fever?" I place the back of my hand against his forehead, and he closes his eyes against my touch. "I can't tell if it's a fever or just your skin. I have some aloe in my room. Let me go get it."

"Just wait." He drops a scorching hand on my leg, which is also pink from the sun, but dramatically reduced in intensity since I applied said miracle aloe before bed. Our skin seen side by side is the difference between an Andy Warhol and a Monet. One bold and bright, the other muted and soft. I'm staring at the placement of his palm as he continues speaking. "First, let's finish this."

I jerk my head up, unsure of his meaning.

"Do you want to spend less time together?"

It takes a moment for me to remember why I barged in, all worked up over others' childish teasing and observations. I feel guilty for putting my emotional discomfort on Tom when he's suffering with actual physical pain, and his question instantly clarifies the situation for me. Of course I don't want to spend less time with him. Spending time with him is why I rise so quickly from bed in the morning, why I look forward to his call breaks during filming, why I lay down with a smile on my lips at night. Instead of revealing all of this, I just answer with a simple, "Not really."

He closes his eyes and exhales as if he had been anticipating a more gruesome outcome. "Well, okay then. It shouldn't matter what others think. We know what's going on. We're not sleeping together, we're just friends. That's settled. Crisis over."

"Well, maybe that crisis. What about this crisis?" I gesture up and down at his entire body.

"Oh, this? This is nothing. It'll be fine. We don't film my scene for a few weeks."

"That's not what I meant. You could get an infection or get really sick."

He winces as he leans back to lie on the bed, his hand still on my leg, but now resting at the hem of my loose athletic shorts. His touch sends a jolt of heat through me, and I'm not oblivious enough to think it's simply the sunburn. I gently slide off the bed and stand.

"I'll be right back." A weak hand raise is all I get in response as I make my way out of his room, leaving him reclined in a moment of shameless wallowing. He's still in the same position when I return, and I wonder if he's asleep until I sit next to him and he groans as he rises up onto his elbows. "Hey, I brought some aloe gel. I put this on last night and it helped a lot. I'm going to need you to take off your shirt."

Tom's lips attempt to lift in a pained smile as he says, "Be careful. This is how rumors start."

"Ha ha. Just take it off." He grimaces as he pulls his T-shirt over his head, and I crawl across the mattress to sit cross-legged behind him. His back is bloody red, and I have to mute my gasp so as not to alarm him.

"Is it bad?"

"Uh…You are definitely going to peel. Might have a few blisters." *Or fifty*, I think to myself. I squirt aloe on my palm and place my hands on his heated skin. At first he flinches, but then he sighs as I continue sliding my hands across his back, thickly spreading the sticky gel over his injured skin.

"You know, I would really hate it if you had said yes." I feel his voice vibrate low in his back as I focus on the ridge of his shoulders.

"To your burn being bad? 'Cause it is. Don't get me wrong. It's going to hurt."

"No. To wanting to spend less time together."

I pause for a moment. "Oh." I reapply aloe to my hand, trying to cover up the real reason for the lack of action.

"I really value your friendship. And I like spending time with you, both on set and off. We make a good team." He speaks with the quiet calm only possible when your back is turned and there's no way of making eye contact.

"We do." But while he can't see me, he's all I can see.

"I would never want to do anything to jeopardize that. So if you want me to speak to everyone, set the record straight, I can do that."

"There's no need. I'm sure they'll move on. Start gossiping about some other couple tomorrow."

"Some other couple?"

"You know what I mean." We've eased into a familiar back-and-forth, and my hesitance to initially touch him is gone. Now I let my hands travel over the hard muscles of his shoulders and upper arms, wrap around his sturdy rib cage, and dip to his waist and lower back. His soft moan of pleasure causes my heart to flutter, and I jump up on my knees, startled out of my shameless exploration. "You're going to need to do your front."

"Can you do it?" He swivels his head back to look at me, eyes wide with pleading, mouth stuck out in a playful pout. I inhale sharply through my nose and nod hesitantly, moving to kneel next to him. He turns his body around, his eyes closed and his head tipped back as I reach out and spread the aloe on his chest.

His body is compact beneath the swollen redness of his skin. I keep my pressure light and am careful not to scratch him as my fingers and palms travel across the contours of his pecs and abs. When my hands wrap around the sharp lines of his waist, his whole body twitches, and I pull back, afraid I hurt him. "Sorry."

"No, it's fine." He opens his eyes, and I suddenly realize how close I am. My knees are pressed against his outer thigh, my body hovering over his lap, threatening to fall onto him if I were to relax my posture. The blue of his eyes stands out dramatically against the red palette of his face, and I am hypnotized, sucked in closer as if I am swirling around a drain, ready to be pulled under. My eyes dip to his lips as he says my name, and I feel an electric pull propelling me forward—

An insistent knock on the door sends us both retreating. Tom shuffles to find his shirt and pull it over his head as I shoot up to stand next to the bed, my hands held out awkwardly, still slathered with the sticky aloe.

Kalina's voice rings out from the other side of the door. "Tom, the reporter you invited to set today is in the lobby."

"Shit. I completely forgot. Come on in." Kalina opens the door and sticks her head in. I see the brief surprise register on her face when she sees me standing there, but her surprise is replaced by horror when she takes in the blood-red vision that is our director.

"Sweet baby Jesus, Tom! You're really red!"

"Oh, you noticed that, huh?" Tom chortles, then instantly winces from the movement of his shoulders.

"Are you okay to speak to her?"

"Who, the reporter? Of course, as long as she doesn't take any pictures in color." He laughs at his own observation, earning himself another doubled-over grimace.

Kalina swings her attention back to me, her eyes zeroing in on my hands. "Logan, what are you doing right now?"

"Um, I was just…I went back to my room to get…you see, I got burned, too…uh…aloe." If my face wasn't already red from my own sunburn, it's surely now blazing from my embarrassment. Not only am I acting like I've just been caught literally red-handed, I also have apparently lost the ability to string simple words together into a cohesive sentence. Too bad I make my living by doing just that.

"We were going to have you speak to the reporter, too. We might as well have you do it together. Maybe if you're seated next to each other, Tom's burn won't look as severe."

"Oh, okay. Yeah. Sure." At least there was a semblance of properly placed punctuation in that statement. But inside, I am screaming. I hate interviews, hate having to talk about myself, and hate having to talk about my book. Definitely an occupational hazard I need to overcome.

I don't have time to dwell on my insecurities as I soon find myself squished next to Tom on a sticky leather couch, heat radiating from his body and my face as a sharply dressed young woman with voluminous blonde hair, large green eyes, and impeccable makeup stares at us from her chair, her professional decorum keeping her from dwelling on our ridiculous state beyond a friendly, "Oh, I see you enjoyed some time on the lake recently."

The three of us share a laugh and Tom gives her the highlights of our pontoon party. "Yeah, the water has a way of bending time.

You're hardly the first victims of the Clear Lake sunburn. Well, let's get to it. I'm Jacqueline Melbourne from the *Clear Lake Review*. Thank you so much for arranging this interview, Mr. Price."

"Please, call me Tom."

"And Ms. Sterling. May I call you Logan?"

"Sure."

"I'm a huge fan of both of you. Tom, I binged all five seasons of *Rocky Mountain High* during my senior year of college. It helped me get through finals and a nasty breakup."

"Oh, I'm glad to hear that. That you're a fan. Not about the breakup."

She responds with a tinny laugh that ignites a jealous flame in my belly. Tom laughs airily along with her, the previous stiffness of his body replaced by a practiced ease. I, on the other hand, am not a natural at doing interviews, and my shoulders tense at the threat of being asked a direct question beyond my name.

"I'd love to hear how the filming of *Iowa Nice* is unfolding, as well as ask a few questions about your growing up in Iowa. And Logan, I have a few questions about the writing of your book, as well."

Tom answers with a smooth, "That sounds perfect, Jacqueline." I just nod, the tightness in my back and shoulders beginning to knot. I've done press for the book before but was given adequate preparation time, and if I messed up, I was the only person impacted. Well, me and Niya, but she's good enough at her job I'm never too worried about her. I feel like I'm being blindsided, afraid I'll say something wrong or do something to endanger the success of the movie. It's not just me anymore.

I look over at Tom, my brow creased in worry. He catches me in a quick glance, winks, and opens with a terrifying phrase: "What would you like to know, Jacqueline?"

Clear Lake Review

COMING HOME:

Iowa Natives Bring Book to Life with Movie Magic

Jacqueline Melbourne, Feature Writer

CLEAR LAKE, Iowa – Film star, producer, and Iowa native Thomas Price returns to his roots as he engages in a cross-state journey during the filming of *Iowa Nice*, based on the national best-selling memoir by Logan Sterling composed of musings and memories from a road trip across Iowa taken with her previously estranged father as he succumbs to a terminal illness.

Thomas, or Tom as he prefers to be called, has chosen this film adaptation to serve as his directorial debut. Logan wrote the screenplay and functions as script supervisor. The two met with me during a brief reprieve at Clear Lake, both with sunburns evident of a time well spent in our beloved town.

Melbourne: Tom, you're known as a teen heartthrob, an action star, and a romantic lead. What made you want to add director to the list?

Price: Well, the simplest reason is that in the business of filmmaking, it's almost a form of survival or job security. I'm nearing forty, and some day, I might not get those high-quality job offers. If I can choose and be in the movies I make, then I have more control over my fate. But the biggest reason is that I love the process of filmmaking, and I wanted to be a part of every single step. To create more than just the character. Filmmaking is magic in how it all comes together, and I guess I'm greedy and wanted more of that magic.

Melbourne: And what made you choose *Iowa Nice* as your directorial debut?

Price: I knew it was going to be made into a movie no matter what; the book was making the rounds between production companies, and

I couldn't let someone else take it. The lead characters are a father and daughter, but another character is the state of Iowa, a state that is often overlooked despite its beauty and history. I wanted to protect and showcase that part of the story, as well as showcase the powerful emotional journey Logan and her father undertake together.

Melbourne: Logan, what made you choose Tom over all the other offers?

Sterling: Well, his being from Iowa was a plus. There were other producers that wanted to change the location for financial reasons.

Melbourne: Oh really? Like where?

Sterling: There was talk about moving it to California, keeping more filming in a studio versus on location. Atlanta and New Orleans were discussed, but the terrain would have been all wrong. The entire story would have been changed. Tom promised to keep the heart of the story where it belongs, he managed to round up an amazing crew willing to come and live nomadically for a few months, and he even agreed to keep me involved in the entire process.

Melbourne: How is it, seeing the book come to life, essentially reliving this journey you made with your father?

Sterling: It's unreal.

Melbourne: Megan Marks plays you, and Phil Grant plays your father, First Sergeant Malcolm McClarnon. Are there any similarities between the actors and their real-life counterparts?

Sterling: If you've ever seen Megan Marks and me, then you would probably say no. But she's an amazing actress and she's doing justice to the words and emotions.

Melbourne: What about Phil Grant?

Sterling: He's Phil Grant. He brings his own flavor to the set and role, that's for sure. Again, he's doing his job, playing the part of the patriarch well. The two of them together capture the spirit of the story beautifully.

Melbourne: Is it emotional for you to watch the end of your father's life be re-created? How are you feeling as you relive this journey again?

Sterling: There are moments I will watch Phil in a scene and get emotional because he is just so good. But there's a bit of a disconnect because I still see him as Phil. And because I wrote the book and the screenplay, I've already worked out a lot of those feelings. Plus, Tom keeps me busy with other aspects of the filmmaking process, so there's really no time to fall apart.

Melbourne: Is there anything you wish you could have done differently on the initial road trip, now that you can see it through a literary lens?

Sterling: Maybe the ending?

Price: Logan's book is so detailed, so poignant, that there hasn't been much need for change. We added a couple of scenes, but nothing that will take away from the heart of the story.

Melbourne: I know you're still working on this story, but what are some future projects for you both?

Price: I'm so focused on this movie, I haven't had time to think beyond this month. Postproduction will take a lot of time and energy. Ask me that question again after the movie releases.

Sterling: I'm not sure.

Melbourne: You've written fictional short stories before the success of your memoir. Do you think you'll dive more into fiction or stick with memoirs?

Sterling: Well, I'd have to have something big happen to write about if I just stick with memoirs.

Price: Hey, having your book turned into a movie is big.

Sterling: Well, yes, I suppose you're right.

Price: Logan is also a talented screenwriter and she's doing a fantastic job on set. I could see a future for her on any path she chooses.

Melbourne: So what has been your favorite location to film in so far?

Price: Clear Lake, for sure. And I don't say that to pander. It's beautiful, and we enjoyed an amazing day on the lake, as you can probably tell from my severe sunburn. It's just been a great experience to be here with my amazing team.

Melbourne: Where are you off to next?

Price: We head south soon, going through Des Moines and locations around there. Eventually, we'll jog over to the east side of the state.

Melbourne: Logan, you currently live in Des Moines, correct?

Sterling: Yes.

Melbourne: And you'll be visiting your hometown of Ottumwa eventually, right?

Sterling: Yes.

Melbourne: How do you feel about that?

Sterling: How does anyone feel about returning home? My mother died there. My ex still lives there. It's complicated. But it's also the place that formed me into the person I am, for better or for worse.

Melbourne: So Tom, does traveling across our state make you want to come back home?

Price: I've always wanted to come back home. That's why this movie is such a dream for me. I get to do what I love and be where I love to be. It's a win-win.

Melbourne: Well, I wish you all the best on your travels and can't wait to see the finished product.

The movie version of *Iowa Nice* will be released early next year. Logan Sterling's *Iowa Nice* is available at most major book retailers.

Excerpt from *Iowa Nice*

WEST BEND

Religion has always been a nebulous concept for me. There are too many options for me to choose just one. It's like an ice-cream counter, and I'm being handed tiny spoon samples of each. But I'm afraid if I commit to one and get a larger scoop, there's going to be some part of it I don't like, an ingredient that didn't make its way into the sample. Or maybe I'll get sick of the taste before I finish, overwhelmed by too much of a supposedly good thing.

My eyes are bigger than my stomach when gazing upon the spiritual smorgasbord of life, and I am worried I'll be left with a horrendous stomachache if I actually start to fill my plate.

But it's difficult not to dive into the buffet of belief when surrounded by such unique beauty while traversing the path through the artistic, geologic wonder that is the Shrine of the Grotto of the Redemption. I've lost sight of Dad, having given him some space after realizing he was in one of his moods again: reflective, quiet, and testy. The frequency of these moods has only increased. We've started renting separate hotel rooms when available, not because we necessarily need the space from one another, but because Dad's sleep is interrupted and fitful. He exists in a perpetual state of exhaustion and insomnia, desiring nothing more than rest, but unable to drift away into slumber when given the chance. He's taken to napping in the passenger seat more, which has given me loads of quiet time while driving.

I loathe it.

Quiet time means dealing with the demons of my past: my mistakes, failings, and regrets. Things that might be aided by some grasp on theology, but alas, I'm still empty-handed. Being here, however, in this meticulously made structure of stone, minerals, and petrified wood, it's easy to see how people gain solace from religious structures.

I stop on the path, surrounded by the Stations of the Cross, a passageway constructed of fourteen scenes depicting Jesus's journey from when he was condemned to death to when he finally met his fate. To know one is dying is both a curse and a blessing. And though Malcom McClarnon is no Christlike figure, I am aware of the tangential similarities between the grotto's story and that of anyone diagnosed with a terminal illness.

That's what my dad is doing, marching through his own stations, and though I am on this journey with him currently, eventually he'll be on his own. And so will I.

Almost makes one want to find religion.

I reach out to touch the walls, a jagged compilation of earthly materials. They are rough, sharp, and biting to the touch. I think of all the people who have visited here, perhaps touched this very spot. Maybe they were devout Catholics, seeing God's hand in every action. Maybe appreciative agnostics who saw the stories as nondenominational metaphors meant to guide rather than prosecute.

Perhaps they were pagan, seeing Mother Earth in everything, even a structure of institutionalized worship. Or maybe they were atheist, the beauty of the present enough to satisfy any questions they had about existence after life.

I tally the pros and cons of the different divinities, wondering which would be more likely to help me navigate the ensuing experience of losing my father all over again. And then, as I turn to seek out Dad's whereabouts, a sign is bestowed upon me.

Karma.

I wince as I stub my toe on a jutting stone, censoring my desire to cuss while in a house of God. I give myself a moment to assess the damage. No bleeding, thankfully, and I hobble away to find my dad, making sure never to play the wheel of religions game again.

11

The lake day was advertised as a reward for all of our hard work, but it reads more like a preemptive apology as we buckle down the next week without hardly any time for rest or play. We've jogged across the central northern locations, spending days in West Bend, Fort Dodge, and on the surrounding roadways, returning to the Lakeview Inn only to pass out and wake up early to do it all over again.

Tom's sunburn has healed, and now his body shimmers with the bronze of a Greek god. I've returned to my pasty pallor, but my thoughts have not regained firm footing since the day of aloe and almost-kissing. Because that is what was going to happen. We were going to kiss. All that talk about staying professional and valuing friendship flew out the window when I found myself pressed up against him, his mouth so close I could feel the warmth of his breath on my skin. Ever since, I've been imagining what that breath would feel like tickling the hollow of my neck, how soft and insistent his lips would be trailing up and down my skin, how it would feel to slide my hands down his back and over his chest while he hovers above me.

I got it bad.

Which is why I've been spending my free time on set hanging with the Trendy Trifecta rather than longing for a man I shouldn't want and cannot possibly have. But even surrounded by laughter and playful jibing, I can't halt my thoughts from sliding to Tom.

"Should we start drinking now, or wait until the rest of the crew arrives?" Rene asks. We have a closed off area of the restaurant dock tonight as we'll be heading south early tomorrow morning. The four of us were sent back, our work done for the day, but the rest are still out filming since Tom wanted to get some car internals while driving and a few establishing long shots.

"I think we should start the party. They can't be too long now. The sun's pretty much down. What do we all want? Margaritas? Martinis? Mojitos?" Atlas ticks off on her fingers, her long hot-pink nails catching the gleam of the dock lights.

"Does it have to start with an *m*?" I ask, a teasing smile raising the corner of my lips.

"No, but nothing's as fun as making the Mmmmm sound," Atlas purrs suggestively, sticking her tongue out at me and laughing at her own joke.

"Speaking of sensual sounds, I haven't heard any from your room in a while, Atlas. Are you and Bruno not vibing anymore?" Rene asks.

Atlas focuses on her nail bed while answering. "Eh, it's kind of burned out. It was fun for a while, but with our busy schedule this past week, I just wanted some alone time. I'm not banning him from my boudoir, but it definitely has a limited shelf life."

Rene clicks her tongue in a knowing tsk tsk. "As I've said before, film set hookups rarely last."

Atlas rolls her eyes and waves over a server. "Yes, we all are familiar with your prophetic preaching on film set romance. Some of us just aren't so fortunate to have a big, burly man waiting to dote on us at home."

"God, I miss Benji. Phone sex just isn't doing it for me anymore. I'm getting all twirly." Rene squirms in her seat, shaking her chest, and we all burst out laughing.

Deedee speaks up, saying, "Well, I think it's nice to have someone on set. And I commend Atlas for putting herself out there. It's better to have the experience than the lonely wondering about what could have been."

"Easy for you to say. You've barely slept alone since we've arrived in this state!" Atlas accuses Deedee, who smiles and looks down into her lap, her straight hair shielding her like a curtain.

"What are you talking about?" I ask. I haven't noticed Deedee hanging around any of the guys and certainly haven't seen any flirtation. The only people I see Deedee with are the three of us, and maybe Megan when she has early morning color checks…which seem to be almost every morning. "Ohhhh!" I say as I suddenly connect the dots. "You and Megan?"

"Duh!" Atlas dramatically facepalms, almost upsetting the large margarita that a server has just delivered.

"Now she gets it!"

"But I thought Megan was into Tom." Or at least, that's what I've convinced myself of to justify why I shouldn't have lusty feelings for him or believe anything could or should ever happen between us.

"Nope, just friends."

"Baby girl, just because you're head over heels doesn't mean everybody else here is."

"Like you haven't drooled over Tom shirtless before," Atlas snarks, causing Deedee to snort into her drink.

"Sure, the man is a tasty treat of eye candy, but I've waxed his nose hair many times. Sort of kills the attraction," Rene retorts, dignified as she sticks up her pinky and slurps her margarita.

"That's a lie. We know you and Benji go nuts with the hot wax." Rene merely raises her brow and takes another slurp, silently conceding to Atlas's accusation.

"Wait! Back to the part where Deedee and Megan are together. Are you two together? *Together* together?" I ask, my words tripping over one another as I try to complete this puzzle. Deedee nods with a demure smile. "How did I not know?"

"Well, Megan's not completely out. Her publicist told her to lay low, so we've been discreet."

"But I think you're the last one on set to find out," Rene adds in a jab to my already thin ego.

"But why? Did you not trust me? Did you think I would judge you?" I'm hurt I was so out of the know and ashamed if I ever acted unsympathetic. Surely that wasn't the case?

Deedee leans over and grabs my hand. "Of course not! We didn't announce anything. People just figured it out. I think you've just been preoccupied."

"Preoccupied! With what?"

"Uh, starts with a *t*, ends with an *-ice*. Brings you a cup of coffee every morning and walks you to your door every night," Atlas sings, punctuating her statement with an obnoxiously loud slurp.

"He doesn't walk me to my door every night," I mumble, but I see what they're all getting at. I've been so focused on my time with Tom that I never even considered Megan's morning walks down the hall as anything but work-related. Realization suddenly strikes. "Oh God, that's why Tom wondered if I was interested in Megan! I kept asking about her…trying to get him to admit they were together. And now he probably thinks…" I drop my head on the table, eliciting protests from the others as I almost upend their drinks. I feel dumb and blind to all the blatant signs.

However, I don't want my current self-loathing to make me a bad friend, so I pick my head up, ask Deedee to give me the details, and tuck into my drink. By the time the cast and crew arrive, I've learned about Deedee and Megan's year-long friendship that began with a hair-and-makeup test, playful texts, and ended with Megan's specific request to hire Deedee for the movie once she signed onto the project. Apparently, Tom's known about Megan's sexual orientation longer than most, leaning into the tabloid coverage at times in order to give her privacy. And that's what her life has been for the past few years: fake dates with leading men and carefully crafted cover stories. When I ask why Megan doesn't come out, Deedee just shrugs sadly. But her face lights up when Megan arrives, and my heart swells as Deedee runs up to her, grabs her hand, and walks her to the bar.

"Can I join you?" I look up to see Tom standing behind me, a bottle of beer sweating in his grasp. I smile and nod my chin toward Deedee's vacated seat, then do my best to avoid the pointed stares of Rene and Atlas. Tom seems tired but in good spirits as he informs me of all the crew accomplished in the past few hours. I nod along, encouraging him with raised brows and appropriately timed "Mm-hmm's," but I'm also having a conversation in my own head.

Even with her daring image and reputation for rocking the boat, Megan Marks still has her secrets. It makes me wonder what others are swimming around the set, how many supposed secrets are actually well-known by all, and which one will be next on the full-disclosure list.

Excerpt from *Iowa Nice*

STORY CITY

I'm nearing thirty years old and I'm distraught over the seasonal closing of a carousel. However, it's not just any carousel. It's Story City's antique carousel, which doesn't open for another week.

"I don't think there's any waiting this one out," my dad mumbles as we look at the shuttered octagonal structure painted in red, yellow, cream, and gray.

I loudly curse into the morning calm and look around, worried that I've poisoned some poor child's mind.

"It's fine," Dad says, resignation draining his body of the previous lightness he exuded in anticipation of a ride on the century-old amusement.

He's been getting more lethargic, more crestfallen, and I can't bear it. Before this journey and our reconciliation, I may have taken pleasure in seeing my dad not get what he wants, in seeing him be disappointed, as I spent so much of my childhood in the same state.

But after being with him these past few weeks, it hurts me to see him hurt.

"Just hang tight, Dad. I'm going to fix this." I begin scanning the beautiful North Park scenery, frantic in my focus to find anything or anyone that can help us. Dad deposits himself onto a picnic bench beneath a large linden tree, and I begin circling the building. I don't know what I am looking for: a phone number, a calendar that will announce a special opening later today or tomorrow, maybe a crack in the wood that will let me pry open a window or door so we can at least view the wooden figures inside. I don't want to get arrested for trespassing or vandalism, but I very much want this for my dad.

"Can I help you?" I see a woman trekking down the sidewalk from the adjacent parking lot. She has short white hair and a pink T-shirt with Story City Antique Carousel printed across the front, her face scrunched up with concern. My heart leaps at the possibility she represents, and I rush toward the woman. She flinches backward, justifiably startled by my aggressive approach, and I begin rambling.

"Oh my gosh! Yes! Do you know if there is any way to see inside the carousel? I know it's not open to the public for a week...I guess we didn't do our homework on that small detail...but, you see, my dad is dying. And we're going on this trip across Iowa, seeing as many of the roadside attractions and places of note as we can before he can no longer travel. And we hadn't talked in eight years, but then he called me, and, as I said, he's dying. We're only halfway through our journey, but he really wanted to see the carousel. Said he rode it once as a kid, and I would just love for him to see it if possible." I pause, registering the woman's shell-shocked look, then quietly ask, "Can you help us?"

The woman stares at me, then looks past to where Dad sits, his spirit and body visibly withered in the shade. I see the set of her shoulders soften, and she turns back with an apologetic smile. "The carousel isn't quite ready to run. There's a mechanic coming later today. But I can let you inside and you can at least sit on it. Would that work?"

I inhale sharply, my chest expanding with relief at this woman's kindness. I forget to answer, and she has to repeat herself. "Yes, yes! That would be wonderful! Thank you!" I turn to get my dad, nearly skipping with happiness as I tell him the good news.

12

"Dad! Dad! This gentleman is going to let us into the carousel. We can't ride it…something about drive chains and wheel bearings… anyway, he's going to let us in at least. That's something, right?" Megan exclaims while leaning on the picnic bench.

Phil takes a deep breath and forces himself to stand, doing his best impression of having joints achy with travel and terminal illness. "Well, I'll be damned, kiddo. You did it." He extricates his legs from the park bench and approaches a white-haired gentleman donning a Story City Antique Carousel T-shirt. "Thank you, sir. This really means a lot to me. And to my daughter, apparently." Phil looks back at Megan, a small smile on his lips and a twinkle in his eyes. The carousel attendant begins to lead them to the closed doors of the carousel, walking them out of frame.

"And, cut!" Tom's voice rings out from his position behind the camera next to Bruno and Jasper. I watch from my seat, the script crinkled in my lap as I follow along with the action. Rene and Deedee swarm Phil and Megan, freshening up their faces and fixing any stray hairs. Atlas stands farther back, arms crossed over her chest, assessing any costume or set design needs. Everyone is busy with the various needs of the filmmaking process. Everyone has a purpose. Everyone has direction.

"Wow, this is a fascinating process. So many moving parts and all." I turn to see the local playing the carousel attendant standing at my shoulder. "So what's your job?"

I smile in greeting at the man with heavy grandpa vibes, warmed by his small-town Iowa habit of engaging any stranger in jovial conversation. "I'm the script supervisor. I follow along with the script and make note of any dialogue or scene changes for continuity's sake."

"Neat. So you have to know the script pretty well, don't you?"

"Well, yeah. It helps that I wrote it. And the book."

"Oh, dang! You're Logan Sterling?" The man practically slaps his knee at the reveal of my identity, and I can't help but blush. He reaches out to shake my hand. I take it, his strong handshake nearly rocking my whole body. "It's such a pleasure to meet you. My wife and I love your book, and we love what it's doing for the state of Iowa. Certainly brought in more tourists to our little town here. But don't worry, we like it. More tourists means more money."

"Oh, good."

"Hey, did you ever happen to catch the name of the woman that helped you when you and your dad visited?"

"Oh…um, no. I don't believe I did."

"Yeah, just makes me wonder who you spoke with. I've been volunteering with the carousel for the last ten years, so I'm sure I would know her. Maybe Bonnie, or it could have been Colleen…" He stands there, rubbing his chin in thought, going through the archives of the mystery woman's possible identity. I squirm in my seat, feeling awkward about not being able to answer. "Well, either way, I'm glad you got to show your dad. I know I may be partial, but it's one of my favorite chapters in the book." He winks. "And now, it's going to be my favorite scene."

I sigh, relieved to have moved on in the conversation.

"So you've never actually ridden the carousel?" His face is incredulous, his eyes shining with disbelief.

"Sadly, no."

"Well, we need to fix that. Soon." He smiles, but turns suddenly at the sound of Tom's voice calling for places. "That's my cue. It was nice talking to you, Ms. Sterling. Oh, and I'm sorry about the loss of your dad." He marches toward the carousel, prepped to be opened and revealed to Megan and Phil. My chest clenches at his kind words and the heaviness that always accompanies condolences for my father's death.

We continue on with the scene, Jasper stopping to get a myriad of angles and shots to display the opening of the carousel. As the actors and camera move inside, I catch glimpses of shiny animal figurines, golden poles, and muraled panels. I listen to the actors in my headphones as they give life to the words I wrote and am surprised when a singular tear slides down my cheek. I brush it away nonchalantly, hoping no one has seen, and will myself to focus on the lines printed in front of me rather than the swirls of unease and sadness inside.

***

Tom pulls into the back parking lot of the Roland-Story High School and turns off the engine.

"What are we doing here?" I ask, my eyes squinted in Tom's direction with suspicion.

After we finished filming at the carousel, the cast and crew had dinner at a local Mexican restaurant then retreated to the hotel for showers and rest before our continued trip down Interstate 35 tomorrow morning. I had just showered and was dressed for bed in a pair of lounge shorts and an old T-shirt (a personal favorite with a pirate riding a unicorn) when a knock on the door interrupted my channel surfing.

I wasn't all that surprised to find Tom on the other side, freshly showered and wearing a clean set of jeans and a soft heather-gray T-shirt. I was surprised when he announced that I needed to accompany him immediately, that we had overlooked a few details for tomorrow and needed to settle them tonight. I threw on a pair of actual jean shorts and reluctantly abandoned my plans of falling asleep to reruns of *Friends*, my hair still damp and the soles of my feet sore and protesting.

My hair is now a little less damp, but my confusion is even more prevalent.

Tom glances my way quickly before unbuckling. "Let's go," is all he says, and he gets out of the car, shutting the door before I can ask again.

We make our way down the darkened sidewalk, and the carousel shelter looms ahead of us, spotlighted by the surrounding security lights. A shadowed figure stands near the door, and as we approach, he pushes off the wall and reveals himself in the light.

"I told you we needed to get you a ride on the carousel." The local actor from earlier today smiles widely as he gestures for us to follow him.

"Rick told me you'd never actually ridden the carousel before. Suggested we rectify that immediately," Tom bumps my shoulder with his as we step inside. I'm unable to speak, unable to look at Tom, unable to comprehend that this has been coordinated especially for me.

Nighttime has transformed the carousel into a magical wonder. Vintage light bulbs illuminate the interior, twinkles of light reflect off the golden poles, and glossy figures fill the space with whimsical nostalgia.

"Which one do you want?" Tom asks, his voice respectfully quiet in the shrine of childhood amazement.

I take in the options: dogs with outstretched legs as if running through a field; toothy-grinned pigs rearing their heads up mischievously toward a potential rider; chickens that capture a realistic look of concern and hurry; and the classic horses, nostrils flared and mouths open with spirited abandon. I step up to a cream-colored horse with a red saddle, sliding my hands over the smooth veneer then upward to trace the divots of the carved mane.

"Hop on!" Tom places his hand at the small of my back as I mount the horse. He then climbs atop the one next to me and signals Rick to push the button, the carousel coasting to life.

The carousel moves around as the figures dip up and down, my stomach experiencing the slightest flip from the repetitive motion. We're moving in a circle, resigned to a perpetual path of redundancy, but I feel truly free, as if I were riding an actual horse out in a field, the wind whipping my face and all worries leaving my body. The circus music manages to capture every happy memory from childhood and bottle it up inside the bright, jaunty notes pouring from the antique Wurlitzer organ, an attached drum pounding out the beat. My once-tight grip on the pole loosens as I relax into the motion, and my face is nearly split in half with my grin. I finally turn to take in Tom, expecting to see him looking forward, experiencing his own midlife rejuvenation, but instead he's staring at me, his face mirroring my delight. He leans over the aisle and asks loudly, "So you like it?"

All I can do is nod vigorously, and I turn forward to close my eyes and enjoy the rest of the ride.

We ride four more times. I want to experience it from the back of every carved species. Rick and Tom can't help but laugh at my enthusiasm as I skip between the figures. Eventually, Rick informs us that he needs to get home or else his wife will start watching their shows without him. He shakes our hands, bids us goodbye, and disappears into the night, my magical bringer of kindness and fun.

Instead of walking back to the car, we sit on a bench facing out into the darkened park grounds, both sighing with appreciation for a well-spent evening. Tom finally bumps my knee with his and asks, "Was it worth the lie?"

My mind goes blank for a minute, my smile dropping from my face. "What?"

"The lie. To get you out here to the carousel. It was worth it, right?" His eyes shine in the dark, catching the illumination from the security lights, and I laugh with relief.

"Yes, it was definitely worth it. Thank you." I shift in my seat so I can look directly at him, my knee digging into his thigh. His gaze wanders down to our touching skin, then drifts back up to lock with mine. "You didn't have to do that. It was incredibly gracious of you. I know you have so much to do, so little time. You could have been working in your room tonight—"

"Logan, it was worth it for me, too." He continues staring at my face, his eyes following the curve of my cheek and neck. I'm losing this battle within myself, this fight against wanting more with this man who should be unattainable, so far above my level of reality. But he keeps showing up, continues to prove his constancy and his friendship with small acts of kindness. And then he has to go and orchestrate some huge gesture…Wait.

"Tom, is this a grand gesture?"

Instead of answering, he just smiles, his head tipping down to mine, and it would be so easy to punctuate this endearing gesture of friendship with a kiss. But that's all this can be—friendship. Anything more is too dangerous.

"I'm sorry…I can't. The movie…my job…our friendship…" I

blurt, continuing to ramble.

Tom pulls up short. "Of course, you're right. I'm sorry to assume..." His voice trails off as I pull my gaze away and readjust my seat so I'm staring back toward the park, my heated back pressed flush against the cool concrete of the bench. The magnetic pull still lingers in the space between us, but I lean away from it, trying to convince myself it's what's best for the movie, best for my career, and best for Tom.

I hear Tom click his tongue, hear his mouth move as if to address the awkwardness between us, but I rush to fill the space. "Are you ready to be immersed in Cyclone country tomorrow?" I cringe at my clunky attempt to change the direction of our tension-infused moment, but Tom, ever the talented thespian, seamlessly picks up his cue.

He groans loudly, but a smile still touches his lips. "Not really. My family might disown me. We're Hawkeyes, you know.

"Oh, I know. I've seen your hat. And shirts. And foam finger."

"Where've you seen my foam finger?"

"Plastered all over the internet when you attend Iowa games. I know about your traitor blood," I accuse playfully, and he grins.

"Don't worry. I always play nice. Though, I can't say the same for the Hawkeyes when they whip Iowa State's ass this weekend."

I reach out and pretend to punch his shoulder, but he catches my hand with his own and brings it down to settle between us. My breath catches as his eyes stare into mine. "Friends?"

My heart is beating fast. I just shut this down, but Tom is making it so difficult. Somehow I still manage to nod while stiffly answering. "Friends. Of course."

"Even if you did include Ames in your book just to torture me."

Our hands are still intertwined, but his levity loosens up the tightness in my chest. However, my voice is still shaky when I parry back with, "Exactly. I preemptively planned to highlight Iowa State

University in my book just to irritate Thomas Sydney Price—"

"Hey, now."

"Who I knew was going to buy my movie rights and direct the film adaptation. I am that much of a mastermind." I smile, sadness inevitably creeping in whenever I think about my alma mater. "I regret not finishing my degree there."

"What happened?"

"I went there for a semester then transferred to be closer to Caleb."

"The ex-husband?"

"Yeah." I untangle my grip from his and bring my hands together between my legs, trying to calm myself as we dip our toes in murkier waters.

"How did you meet him?"

I wince at this next detail, knowing the trite nature of it. "He was in a band. I saw him playing and was instantly obsessed."

"Ah, lust at first sight." Tom swivels with comical swiftness. "Let me guess, bass player?"

I turn to meet his barely bitten back smile. "No, lead singer and guitar. Plus, he wrote most of the band's songs."

Tom whistles. "Whoa, I'm impressed."

"Why?"

"I guess…I didn't see you chasing after the leading man. You're more of the quiet, bookish type." His words make me prickle with indignation.

"I'm not always quiet. And who says I was the one chasing?"

He erupts in laughter at that, but I'm peeved, a fact he can apparently read on my face as he sobers up from his outburst to explain himself, hands raised in surrender. "Okay, okay. I get it. You, Logan Sterling, are a wild child that gets what she wants and who she wants. I'm sorry I ever doubted you."

"That's more like it." I grin, smug from his concession, and settle back into my seat. "My God, he was hot on that stage, though. I can still remember the first time I saw him."

"So you were together for…?" His voice drops off waiting for my answer.

"Nine years."

"What happened?"

"The short answer: we grew up and grew apart."

"What's the long answer?" I look over to see that he's staring at me intently, urging me to open up. He says gently, "I don't have anywhere else to be tonight."

I sigh loudly, resigned to telling the tale that I've worked so hard to move past. But Tom seems genuinely interested, and this is what friends do, share intimate details of each other's pasts. So here goes. "Okay. So…my mom died my senior year of high school. Instead of moving to Omaha with my dad, I finished out my senior year in Ottumwa and lived with my friend Lilah's family. She's married with three kids now…How crazy…Anyway, I saw Caleb playing at a local club right before graduation, and we had a whirlwind romance that summer. We officially broke up when I moved to Ames, but continued talking—and sleeping together—whenever I was in town… which was almost every weekend. Sort of made it difficult to fully commit to college life. So I transferred. Moved back to Ottumwa, earned my associate's from Indian Hills Community College, my bachelor's in business and communication from Buena Vista, and lived happily ever after." I slap a fake smile on my face to accompany my facetiously bright fairy tale.

"Except…"

I drop the smile and ironic tone. "Except we didn't. He didn't do anything wrong really. We both just changed. We were supposed to write music together, get a record deal, live the dream. But Caleb seemed satisfied with our life in Ottumwa, playing in bars on the weekends, working at a car dealership to pay the bills. He spent most of his time with friends rather than being at home with me. And I… I just wanted more." I stare off into the distance, feeling the loneliness of those years creep back into my bones, a phantom pain that never really disappears, just hides in the dark corners until light happens to flit across.

"Like a national bestseller and the chance to work with Thomas Sydney Price?" Tom offers the jest softly, giving me a way out of the shadows, but I'm in it now.

"More like a purpose. A family, maybe." I release the words into the night, letting them be carried off by the summer breeze. "A reason to come home every night. A place to be valued, to be enough. I've never felt like enough. I still don't. If I were enough, people would stick around." My breaths are becoming shallow and I feel the sting of tears beginning to pool in the corner of my eyes.

Tom's hand slides to my lap and pulls my hand into his. "Logan, you are enough." I look up to meet his gaze, and a tear escapes. He reaches up with his free hand and brushes it away. "You know, I've been married before. Twice." He winces at the admission, and a small laugh escapes me, amused by his comical exaggeration.

"I do know that, Tom. Everyone in America knows that, possibly everyone on the planet."

"Even in Antarctica?"

"As long as they have cell service."

We share a laugh, and he continues on. "The first one was actually annulled. We were young and impulsive and in Vegas and very, very drunk. She was a good sport about it, though."

"Didn't you have to pay her a large sum of money?" I search my memory for tabloid headlines and story details.

"Shhhh." Tom places his finger over his lips, quirked in a coy smile. The smile drops as he adds, "Yeah, there were some false accusations flying around in the aftermath. Definitely makes a guy choose carefully who he marries."

"Oh, because he wasn't before?"

He narrows his eyes at me, "Hey now, I was young. And I thought I was in love. But I'm more cautious now. And I'm very particular about who I choose to spend time with. Honesty, integrity, those are important to me." I nod stiffly in agreement and he continues with his life story. "Anyhoo…the second one, I really thought it was going to work. Sure, Julia was older than me, but I was smitten. Here was a teenage crush of mine, an actress whose posters had hung on the walls of my bedroom, and she actually wanted to marry me."

"She is a fox, that's for sure."

"Yes, she's always been a beautiful woman."

"So what happened there? I read the theories, some rumors about property disputes, prenup arguments—"

"Don't believe everything you read." A raised eyebrow causes me to look down at my lap.

"So what's the real story?" I ask, chancing a side glance.

It's his turn to sigh loudly. "We were at different places in life. She was over all the Hollywood glitz and glamor, and I was still intoxicated by it. She was done having kids and I still wanted a family of my own. Still do." His voice softens as he says, "Eventually, we realized we couldn't compromise. But just because those marriages didn't work out, doesn't mean I regret them or that I consider them mistakes…well, maybe the first one. But I learned a lot about myself through those experiences. About what kind of man I want to be, what I want from the world. I realized that if I want something, I need to make it happen for myself, not wait for it to drop in my lap. So that's what I've been doing. Making it happen. Like this movie. I wanted to start directing, so I sought out a project I knew would be right for me."

"Good for you. You're a master in manifestation." I tilt my gaze in his direction and notice a hungry look in his eye, as if he is imagining all the world has to offer him. I am flooded with the familiar longing for the confidence and drive to go after my desires. But one of those desires is still a bad idea, no matter how attractive and nice and real he is. I tell myself this as I force the topic back to safer waters.

"Too bad you can't manifest a win for Iowa." I narrow my eyes and lift my chin in challenge.

"Oh, ho, ho. Is that how it's going to be? Need I share with you that Iowa has won almost double the games? Iowa State doesn't stand a chance Saturday." His eyes are alight with the tongue-in-cheek trash talk, and I can't help being sucked into his playful pull.

"Okay, movie star. Let's make a wager then. A bet on who will win the game this weekend."

"I'm intrigued. What do you have in mind?"

"I don't know yet, but I'm sure we'll figure something out."

Tom gives me one of his signature dazzling smiles, then stands, pulling me up with him. "Come on, it's getting late. We'll talk conditions on the way back to the hotel." I start to walk alongside him, and my gaze catches on our still intertwined hands. It all felt so natural, I completely forgot we were even holding hands.

I stop, tugging Tom back for a moment. He looks at me, a hint of concern wrinkling the edges of his eyes, but the concern melts into contentment as I say, "Thank you for tonight, Tom. Really. I'll never forget it."

"Of course. That's what friends do." He looks down at our hands, then reluctantly releases his grip, backing away as he taunts, "That and gloriously gloat when their team wins the Cy-Hawk trophy."

I glare with mock anger as he ducks out of my reach, and we make our way to the car, impishly exchanging burns and back talk.

That night, I go to bed with a smile on my lips and a lightness in my heart. I'm warmed by his words that still linger in my thoughts, the idea that I might be enough for someone. But I'm also confused by the near-kiss and terrified that I'm going to give in eventually. That I'm going to let him down when he realizes that I'm not who he thinks I am.

Excerpt from *Iowa Nice*

MADRID

"Do you think anyone has ever thought about jumping off this bridge?" Dad asks, looking over the edge of the rust-colored steel railing at the Des Moines River below.

"Wow. Morbid, much?" I reply as I peer down along with him, my stomach tightening at the height. Being thirteen stories above the water has me clinging to the edge, my feet firmly planted behind the concrete lip, while my head dares to lean forward away from my body and any steady support.

"Life is morbid," Dad continues staring down, his whole body pressed against the railing, the fear of death nonexistent to him in his terminal state.

"Oh, good comeback," I grumble and drift back toward the safety of the bridge entrance. "I'm sure someone has, but it's not like they're going to erect a plaque revealing the stats. Doesn't seem to match the desired aesthetic here."

The High Trestle Trail Bridge links the twenty-five-mile trail across the metro's namesake waterway, a dizzying spiral of sculptural beams turning the former railroad bridge into a functional work of art. But, as humans tend to do, I'm sure some have sneered at the beauty, instead focusing on the functionality of it in bringing someone to their own end.

Anything in life, no matter how beautiful, can be a tool for death.

Dad turns to look at me, his nose and brow scrunched up with questions. "Logan, are you afraid of heights?"

"Of course I am! I've always been afraid of heights!" I exclaim. The volume of my voice makes me feel like I'm losing my footing, so I instantly clamp my mouth shut and put my hands out to steady my stance.

Surprise and doubt color his response. "I took you to the top of the Washington Monument and you were fine." He has the audacity to lean his back against the railing and casually cross his arms over his chest. Just watching him makes my palms sweat.

"Oh, was I? Because what I recall from that little journey is nearly peeing my pants, crying, and following you down the stairs, sobbing as you marched ahead of me in anger."

He takes a moment, considering. "Huh. Really? I don't recall that."

"Whatever. Yes, I'm scared of heights. So what? Everyone has something they're scared of."

"I'm not scared of anything. Not anymore." His declaration stills the air and my own indignation.

"Is that a line they fed you in basic training?" I ask, sarcasm dripping from my retort.

He pushes off the railing and starts walking farther down the bridge. "No. In fact, military training stresses the importance of logical fear. A healthy dose of fear will help a soldier or anyone in a tenuous situation survive. It's the illogical fear that will get to you."

"Like what?" I holler, still unmoved and unwilling to venture too far from the decorative pillars marking the bridge's connective tissue to land.

He stops and turns to assess me. "Well, like your fear of heights. There's no reason for you to be afraid of this bridge. You should be fine."

"Should be?"

"Well, you could get hit by a bicycle, but that's hardly a height-based fear, is it?" I scowl at his reasoning, but he is undeterred. "Even if you lean up against this railing, as I was doing, it's very unlikely that any harm will come to you."

"Very unlikely isn't a guarantee."

"Nothing in life is a guarantee."

"Yes, but doesn't a fear of heights come from our biological evolution? 'Human can't fly. Human no want to die. Human no like heights.'" The corner of Dad's mouth lifts in amusement at my impression, and he starts strolling back my way.

"Okay, I see your Neanderthal logic and raise you innovator logic. Haven't humans been enthusiastically defying natural instincts and odds for the majority of our recent history? Cars, planes, space travel. We as a species work tirelessly to conquer our fears while eliminating the need for them at all."

"And why do you think we do that?"

"Because we're scared of what we don't understand. So if we understand how everything works, understand how to bypass the original impetus of danger, there's nothing to fear." He now stands right in front of me, his eyes the same color as the sky on this clouded evening.

"Is this you telling me that there is 'nothing to fear but fear itself'?" I ask with a sneer.

"No. It's me telling you that no matter what we as humans do to control our environment, there will still be things we can't master, things we can't possibly understand, so why waste time fearing them when we could be experiencing them? What if your fear of heights keeps you from enjoying this breathtaking view? What if a person's fear of flying keeps them from visiting other countries? What if a person's fear of water keeps them from knowing what it's like to have ocean waves break against their legs?"

"Okay, okay, I get your point—"

"No, you don't. Because you're still standing like you just felt an earthquake. You're still worried that you're going to keel over the edge and cease to exist. You still think I wouldn't do everything in my power to keep you grounded." He holds out his hand, palm up, his eyes filled with hope and expectation. "You don't need to be afraid here, Logie Bear."

I go to rebut the childish nickname, but instead swallow my instinct and take his hand. He pulls me in, tucking my grip around his arm as he leads me across the bridge. "So you're really not scared of anything?" I ask.

There's a beat before he answers, "I was. I was scared I was never going to talk to you again. That you would never forgive me. That we would never have moments like this. But now, the fear is gone. Because you're here."

We continue walking arm in arm through the spiraled vortex of the steel beams, a portal through the elevated passage, conquering our fears, controlling our fate, and cherishing each other's company. And I'm no longer afraid.

13

Classic rock pumps through the speakers, only broken by the occasional cheer or jeer brought on by the pregame proceedings playing on the hanging televisions. The Sports Scene Bar and Grill in Winterset is embellished in red and gold while brave pockets of black and yellow dot the scene. Fans cluster around high-top tables and tuck into worn leather booths awaiting the big game.

The cast and crew have hit this day hard, excited to experience the Iowa vs. Iowa State rivalry for themselves, as well as see the outcome of my bet with Tom. We've all been drinking since late morning, having set up camp in this local watering hole hours before the three-thirty kickoff at Jack Trice Stadium in Ames. It's a well-deserved day of excess as the past few days flew by with a number of filmed sights and scenes captured around the greater metro. But now, we're all ready to play.

A hush falls over the bar as all heads turn toward the televisions. The coin is tossed, Iowa wins the flip, and the game commences with the first kickoff.

"Are you ready to wear some black and gold today?" Tom teases, his mouth tickling my ear as he leans close, our barstools pressed tightly together at the bar.

"I'm feeling a storm coming our way today. Dare I say, a Cyclone?" I scrunch my nose up and stick out my tongue, cringing at my own bad joke, and we both take another drink.

Most of our crew is gathered around the corner of the bar, but we've secured a few tables nearby so we can essentially mix and mingle without fear of losing our spots. Kalina, Marnie, Pam, and Dawson are at one table, entertaining themselves with a deck of cards. Megan sits with Deedee, Rene, and Phil at the other table, a basket of picked-clean Buffalo wings serving as a makeshift centerpiece. There was a moment of crowd upheaval when the three famous faces entered the bar, but once the slew of selfies were requested and graciously granted and we all settled in with a clear intention of viewing the game, the other patrons turned their attention to today's main attraction: college football.

At the bar, pitchers of golden ale hold court, but Atlas clings tightly to her cosmopolitan. Jasper, Bruno, and the twins have purchased a bottle of whiskey from the bar, sipping and chasing it with a gulp of beer. Tom and I stick to our light beer, knowing better to pace ourselves.

Or so I thought. By halftime, Iowa State has been performing below par, and I've downed more alcohol than I planned to deal with their disappointing plays.

"I don't get it! Our team has a better offensive lineup. Our quarterback is ranked in the top ten! How do you keep scoring?" I slap my palms on the bar, exasperated with Iowa's third touchdown which ends the first half at nine to twenty-one.

"It's called manifestation, baby," Tom drawls. While I've been stress-drinking, his rushed imbibing has been celebratory in nature. But the effect is still the same. We are both certifiably drunk.

"Well, stop it, Tom. Can't you just for once fail at something in your life?" I whine. Tom's resulting smile lets me know he catches on to my jest, and he leans over to bump my shoulder.

"So tell us the stipulations of this bet again," Cole shouts over the music that has loudly replaced the game commentary during halftime. Thankfully, Tom pointed out that Cole is wearing black today, while Leroy is donning red. They've chosen their sides and undoubtedly have a bet of their own going, though no one knows the resulting payout quite yet.

"Whoever's team loses has to wear the winning team's shirt while they sing the winner's fight song in this bar for all to see and hear. So Logan here will be all decked out in black and gold, crooning Iowa's anthem."

"Whatever. Iowa State could come back," I grumble and finish my drink. Bruno dutifully fills my glass, emptying our I-lost-count-of-what-number pitcher.

"I don't think so, sweetheart. I've got the song already queued on my phone. There's no way to 'fight, fight, fight' your way out of this one." Tom's smile stretches across his reddened face, his adorable dimple taunting me with his assuredness. I want to reach out and place my finger on that dimple, but I realize that's the alcohol talking and manage to restrain myself. For now.

"Joke's on you. Because the Iowa State song also has 'fight, fight, fight' in it. So that taunt just landed flat." My comeback game is performing at Iowa State-level, and I hide my resulting wince with another drink. But I swallow quickly, beer dripping from my lips as I blurt out, "And what's with all the pet names today? Do you always turn into a creepy uncle when you drink?"

"Just when my team is wiping the floor with yours."

"Hardy har har," I sing dryly.

We pause in our trash talk to order more food, and Atlas

impresses us all with her knowledge of college football history until the third quarter starts.

Roars of celebration shake the bar as Iowa State scores a touchdown in the first two minutes of the quarter. By the end of the third quarter, Iowa State has secured another touchdown while Iowa has only made one field goal.

"Twenty-three to twenty-four! We're coming back, baby!" I stress the endearment, using it as a weapon as I wiggle a finger in Tom's stony face. "I bet you look good in red!" I shout over the increasing raucousness of the crowd.

"I look good in every color, *darling*."

Megan suddenly pops her head between us, a jubilant smile on her flushed face as she joins in our playful banter. "I don't know, Tom. I've always thought red brings out the mopey-ness in your face."

"This face has never been mopey."

"How about when Rachel Beckett turned you down?" Megan reaches out and grabs Tom's chin affectionately.

"Rachel Beckett turned Thomas Price down? Oh, please tell."

"Nothing to tell. I asked her out a month into filming *Rocky Mountain*. She said no. A year later, she asked me out, and I'd moved on." He punctuates his story with a well-timed gulp of beer.

"Yeah, but by that time, you'd proven yourself to be a teen heartthrob and she was all about the image. She was so pissed when you denied her. The tension on set was thick that day, and not in a good way," Megan narrates while ordering a drink from the harried bartender, being sure to grant him her most sparkling smile in gratitude.

"So this started out as a story razzing on Tom, but ended up making him look even better? Megan, I don't think you get the point of trash talk," I slur, my inebriation impossible to conceal anymore.

"Oops, sorry. I'll just leave you to it then." She grins, returning to her table and leaving Tom staring at me dopily.

"Just watch the game, Hollywood," I sneer, moaning with disappointment as Iowa intercepts the ball.

Another touchdown for Iowa State with only a few minutes left in the game slides them into the lead at thirty to twenty-four. "Where're your Hawks now, Iowa boy?" I shout over the hoots and hollers of the bar. Tom sits tensely, elbows on the table and his hands interlaced under his chin. Iowa State fans are rejoicing at a sure win when all of a sudden the bar goes quiet and all eyes latch onto the screen. The Iowa quarterback breaks through the Cyclones' defensive line and makes a run for it.

Tom jumps up from his seat, fists pumping the air as he yells, "Go! Go! Goooo!" and the Hawkeye fans burst out in chorused jubilation as Iowa achieves a touchdown, makes the field goal, and wins the game thirty-one to thirty in the last ten seconds. Tom continues clapping while looking at the screen, but his voice carries to me.

"Good game, Logan, but in the end, we all bleed black and gold."

"That doesn't even make sense," I pout, disappointed that my beloved Cyclones were bested by such an amazing last play.

"Yeah, well I've been drinking all day and that's all I got." He sits back down on his stool and angles toward me.

Despite my disgust at losing, I can't help but giggle at his nonsensical musing. Of course, it could be anxious giggling in anticipation of what's to come. I've never been one for the stage, and now I'm being thrust onto it while wearing the skin of my enemy. I hazily register Tom catching someone's eye at the end of the bar and tipping his chin. I swerve my head over to see Cole grabbing a rolled piece of yellow fabric and heading around the bar. He hands it over to Tom, who unfurls it triumphantly.

"I made sure to secure you a shirt, so get ready to pay up," he announces, loud enough for most of the bar to hear. The bartenders, who have been regaled with tales of our bet all day, stand behind the bar, one a Hawkeye fan clapping enthusiastically, and the other booing in Cyclone solidarity. Our crew is all alight with anticipation, their eyes blazing as they prepare to watch the human sacrifice to come.

I sigh and roll my eyes, sliding off my barstool and reaching for the hem of my Cyclone T-shirt. I'm just going to have to get through this like a bad hookup: get undressed quickly, pray it's over fast, and then move on with my life and hope I forget it ever happened.

"Logan, you can just wear it—" I lift my shirt off and stand in my bra and jeans. "Over your other shirt. Aaaand, never mind. Too late." I hold my hand out for the atrocious apparel branded with the crest of my enemy, and Tom obliges. I shake out the shirt and force my head and arms through, my skin feeling as if it's burning from the blasphemous act.

"You got my music ready?" I ask with disdain, and Tom just continues staring at me, his eyes glazed and his face slack with shock as I climb up onto the bar and face the crowd.

"Excuse me, everyone!" I shout, a throng of confused faces swiveling my way. "I'm so sorry to have to do this, but believe me when I say this hurts me more than it hurts you. Hit it, maestro."

Tom cues the song on his phone and the music is barely audible as I shout out the "Iowa Fight Song," most of the words correct, but some distorted due to my lack of knowledge combined with my extreme drunkenness. I punch the air and play to all sides of my audience, my face contorted into a fierce battle cry. If I'm going to do this, I might as well commit. Can't have Tom saying I didn't give it my all.

The crowd, no matter their team affiliation, applauds as I end with a flourish, my arms outstretched as if I'm conducting an orchestra. The recognition is almost as intoxicating as the keg of beer I've ingested throughout the day. I attempt a bow, but end up twisting my ankle, losing my footing, and then I'm falling, ready to meet my maker if my head hits the unforgiving bar floor. I just hope I don't land next to the glop of chili Leroy dropped earlier.

Before I can pray to my god of choice, I find myself snug in Tom's arms, his eyes wide with concern. His body is warm as my limbs wrap around him, and I throw my head back to laugh at the ridiculousness of this whole night. He relaxes into his own sounds of merriment, his body shaking us both with his laughter as he gingerly sets me down, still holding me around the waist as I steady my legs beneath me. We stare at each other with dopey grins.

"That was worth every dollar spent," he exclaims over the music that has been turned back on after my impromptu performance.

"Every dollar?" I shout back.

"Well, I did buy the T-shirt. And the food. And the beer." He gestures around as if weighing his investments. "This was a very expensive bet."

"Oh yeah. Well, thanks. It's been nice doing business with you." The strong desire to touch his dimple from earlier returns, and I can't help but give in to my urge, placing my index finger on his cheek and twirling it back and forth.

"The pleasure is all mine," Tom says as he rears his head back to escape my motherly ministrations.

Just then, Megan pops up between us, draping her arms across both our shoulders. "The bar owner's going to fire up the karaoke machine! Who wants to duet with me?"

I give a melodramatic groan. "I think I've had my fill of stardom today. But you two are more than welcome to take the stage."

"Sure. I'll sing with you, Megs," Tom concedes, his gaze flicking to mine as Megan whoops with glee and grabs his hand.

"Let's figure out our song!" she exclaims as she drags him away to find the karaoke binder.

I stumble off to sit with Rene and Deedee, making sure to have a good view of the karaoke stage, which I didn't notice existed until this moment. It would have been much more scrupulous than the bar, but I guess there's something to be said for showmanship.

The rest of the night is a blur of karaoke, crowd singing, fried food, and more drinking. Hours later, I look around with bleary eyes only to realize that most of our group has retired for the night. Cole, Leroy, and Jasper play blackjack at a high-top table while Tom and I sit next to each other in a booth, legs pressed together, as we visit with Megan and Deedee. The two secret lovebirds are not so secretive anymore, having lost their discretion incrementally throughout the day, an even correlation with the amount of alcohol they've consumed. Deedee sits against the wall, playing with Megan's hair as the starlet leans back into Deedee's side. Their affection and enthusiasm is contagious; I've had a blast hearing stories from the three, spanning the various corners of Hollywood, and my face hurts from laughing so much. Definitely a day well spent.

I'm surprised and disappointed when the lights flicker on, the signal for last call at two in the morning. The harsh light sobers me up enough to realize I have to actually drag my weary body to my hotel room. I complain as Tom pulls me from the booth, and the remaining seven of us head to our home for the night, an odd caravan of satiated partiers.

In the parking lot, I groan, my steps dragging, and Tom squats down in front of me. "Here, hop on," he instructs, and I follow his directions, enjoying my piggy-back ride, my chest pressed into Tom's back and my arms wrapped around his neck. My head is bent down, my nose buried in his neck, and I breathe in the stale, sweet smell of sweat and bar. Maybe it's my imagination, but I swear I feel him shudder beneath me.

Tom gallops across the parking lot and through the hallways, and

I wave goodbye to everyone as we all peel off to our respective rooms.

"Take me to my castle, brave steed!" I shout, and Tom tries to shush me as he laughs along. I drop unceremoniously once we reach my door, my body dragging across his back. My hands are still on his shoulders as he turns around, our faces close. "Thank you for the ride," I say, trying to keep my voice down this time.

"Anytime." His eyes scan my body as I remain anchored to him, his pupils large, dark pools of uninhibited desire. His chest rises against mine, and my breath catches. I've been with this man all day, have experienced public humiliation at the hands of his win, and I still want more. I'm done fighting, done making excuses for why I shouldn't take what I want. All that matters in this moment is that he is here, skin warm beneath my touch, lips teasing me with their fullness, upturned slightly, daring me to come closer.

I take the dare, close my eyes, and lean forward. My forceful lips meet the soft set of his. But then I realize he is pulling away, his hands gently guiding my waist farther from the hard line of his hips. He's pushing me away.

Oh no, what have I done?

"Logan, this isn't right—"

My body bursts into motion, a caged animal frantic in my escape of his rejection. "Nope, of course. What was I thinking? I wasn't thinking. I was thoughtless. Completely void of thoughts. Please just forget this," I ramble as I fumble with the key card. Tom tries to interject, but I finally manage the lock and slip inside, shutting the door on his beautiful face, a look of pity the last thing I see before I throw the deadbolt.

I stumble into the room and sit on the bed, wanting nothing more than to cry. But instead of tears, I feel a roiling within my gut, a desperate need igniting my body and sending me rushing into the bathroom where I empty the contents of my stomach. It's messy, violent, and painful. Everything I deserve.

I throw up until there's nothing left but dry heaves. Eventually, I drag myself back to the bed and crawl beneath the sheets, fully clothed and sweating. I pass out, my brain fuzzy as I drift into a hole of blackness, hoping the memories of this evening follow suit and I can somehow face Tom with some semblance of dignity when I emerge from my cave of humiliation.

Excerpt from *Iowa Nice*

WINTERSET

Bold swaths of red, white, and blue whip in the wind as we drive into Winterset's town square all adorned for Memorial Day weekend, as well as the birthday celebration of John Wayne. License plates from all over the country bedeck the back of luxury SUVs and super-charged pickup trucks as fans of The Duke come to gather and celebrate the birthplace of Hollywood royalty.

"All of this for an actor who died over forty years ago?" I mumble as I brake abruptly to avoid hitting a Chevy Equinox pulling out of the courthouse parking lot. The vehicles of choice are largely American, a point not lost on me on this patriotic holiday.

My dad jerks his head around, glaring at me in stunned offense. "JW is more than just an actor. He's an American institution. He's the quintessential cowboy. He's the epitome of what it means to be a man."

"Was. *Being a man is very different these days. Your beloved*

John Wayne would probably be canceled for his toxic masculinity."

He sits back in his seat, grumbling. "JW is the definition of masculinity."

I snort, bemused by his indignation.

The grumbling continues. "I still can't believe you've never seen one of his movies."

"Well, maybe if you had been around more, we could have watched one together."

"Touché." He settles back into his seat and gestures at a brown building with a bronze statue erected inside a circular stone courtyard. "That's his museum. Maybe we can go later."

"Okay," I mumble.

"Turn left here." We head down a quaint residential street and he points at a small white house sitting catty-corner from us on the curb. "There's the house where he was born. You can go in if you pay for the museum. I'd love to see inside."

"You've never been?"

"Never had the time."

"Well, we have the time today."

"After. I want to take you to City Park."

We get to the end of the road and turn into a beautifully kept span of green space. A covered red bridge sits grandly to the right, welcoming us to this showcase of Winterset's historical wonders.

"Pull over and let's explore," he directs me. I only slightly balk at his demanding tone, but I'm getting better. It is his final trip, after all.

We walk inside the bridge and read the milieu of messages: some sweet declarations of love, some poetic observations of silliness, some vandals' obtrusions of the space. We meander beneath the grand trees, untouched by civilization enough years to tease the sky's limits, and we tick off the boxes of the other must-see attractions:

stone bridge, old cabin, English hedge maze, Red Delicious apple dedication rock. And with it being Memorial Day weekend, we are able to walk the line of flags that border the drive, showcasing the town's pride and reverence for those who have died in service.

Winterset has really outdone itself.

After, we sit in the shade of giant ginkgo trees and I look over to my dad, whose eyes are half-open, his breaths labored from our prolonged walking. "You doing okay?"

"Oh yeah, I'll be fine. Just need a rest." We sit in silence, listening to the birds call to each other from the tall branches, the squeals of happy children and chatter of picnicking families interrupting the sounds of nature. He takes a deep breath and leans back into the bench. "You know, this takes me back to when I would take you to the playground."

"I don't remember that."

"Well, it happened. I'd take you to the playground in Ottumwa when I was in town, the one with the wooden hamster wheel, and you would beg me to get in with you and run as fast as I could until we fell down. Then I'd have to stop before you tumbled head over heels. You would just laugh and laugh..." His voice fades away with the memory, a moment of innocence and connection that we will never get back.

"Oh, yeah. I think I do remember that now." My chest swells, shocked yet pleased that he can vividly recall an instance I had doubted was real.

"I know I wasn't always around, but I always thought about you. I always wondered how you were doing. Always missed you. And I always loved you."

I hate my tear ducts for betraying me, so I just continue staring forward, focusing on a little girl swinging as her outline becomes blurry from the ensuing moisture in my eyes.

I feel Dad shift next to me, giving me space as he changes the topic. "You know, I always thought you would be a good mom. Figured you'd have had two kids of your own by now. Especially after getting married so young."

I blink away the tears and prepare for battle. "You and Mom were younger."

"Yes, but that was a different time."

"The time of John Wayne and toxic masculinity?"

He chuckles at my callback. "Sure. So why didn't you and what's-his-name have any kids?"

"Why? So we could have the same lovely predicament of child support and custody schedules as you?" My voice is sharp, a warning of an unwanted conversation if he would just pay attention. But First Sergeant McClarnon marches forward.

"Hey now. I never regretted having you. Sure, there might have been difficulties after the divorce—"

"Difficulties?"

"But I was always glad we had you. Kids are a blessing, even when it's not easy."

I cross my arms and settle back into the bench. "Well, from what I've heard, kids are never *easy."*

"There's still plenty of time. You could still meet someone, have kids. You're still young."

"Thanks for your permission, Dad." My tone is clipped, but I don't have it in me to fight. I check the time on my phone, officially ending the conversation. "You ready to head out? Want to grab something to eat, or maybe head to the museum?"

"Sure. We can go in a bit, but can we just sit for five more minutes? It's beautiful out here."

I force myself to turn my gaze on him, and my heart jumps into my throat. His eyes are closed, his face turned toward a sliver of sun shining through the shade. His chest rises and falls with the rhythm of his breathing, and a soft murmur follows every exhale. No matter how much I want to begrudge this man, my soul still grieves the loss of him: the past loss from when I was a child, and the future loss I'll experience as an adult. It infuriates me that I can't cut him out cleanly, that the roots of his attachment are deeply woven throughout my being. But another part of me is calmed by his presence, a salve to the burning ache of past injuries.

It hurt when he left the first time, and it's going to hurt when he leaves again.

I'm used to hurting, and I know I'll survive, but our time together now may make the hurt even worse. And that's what I'm dreading, the final stab into my previously shattered heart.

How will it ever recover?

14

What's worse than waking up with a hammering headache, thick cottony tongue, and shaking limbs, unable to remember anything that occurred the night before? Waking up with a hammering headache, thick cottony tongue, and shaking limbs, remembering EVERYTHING from the night before in perfect, excruciating detail.

Three heavy knocks on my door rouse me with the same sensation as having three nails driven into my skull. I want to holler at the offending visitor, but I can only manage to groan in pain. No, I think I'll stay under my mound of covers, a bear in hibernation as I wait out this hangover and hopefully slip into amnesia or dementia, whichever comes first.

"Logan, sugar, we're about to head to the bridge. Are you ready?" Rene's booming voice, no matter how much I enjoy it on a normal day, is a railroad spike in my cranium.

In response, I cover my head with my pillow.

"Logan I-don't-know-your-middle-name Sterling, you get your butt to this door right this minute or I am going to the front desk, getting a key, and letting myself in. And if I let myself in, I'm going to treat it as my own room, rummaging through all your belongings, rolling around in the bed naked, and taking my morning shit!"

The scene in the hallway along with the potential of an angry Rene making good on her word and vandalizing my room is finally enough for me to emerge from the covers. I set wobbly legs on the ground and make my way to the door, even though the ground feels like a funhouse floor, tipping up to meet my steps too soon, and sending me veering from side-to-side. I cling to the knob like I'm hanging off the side of a cliff and crack the door open.

"Now was that so—" Rene stops as she takes in the tragedy before her. "Oh, honey. You look like roadkill. Or worse, the stuff that comes out of roadkill when it's run over repeatedly."

I gag at the visual and hold the door open so Rene can come in.

As always, she's perfectly put together, her dark curls tamed into low pigtails, a grass-green summer jumpsuit hugging her curves perfectly. In contrast, I'm sure I'm a mess. My hand slowly rises to touch the top of my head and I feel a tangled, crusty nest. I stand there in my near nakedness, having managed to pull off my pants at one point in the night, and struggle to comprehend any further action now that I'm vertical. It feels as if the alcohol is flowing through my body again, renewed by my body's upended position, and I sway beneath Rene's pitiful gaze.

"What the hell happened to you?" Her voice punctuates the silence, causing me to wince with pain. I sit back on the edge of the bed, not trusting the sturdiness of my own legs.

"Football. And beer. Lots of beer." I tip over, curling into a fetal position.

"Deedee said you were doing great last night. What changed?"

"I puked. And puked and puked…after I kissed Tom." My voice is small as I admit my transgression.

"Kissing Tom made you puke?"

"No, drinking my weight in alcohol made me puke. Tom's rejection just added an extra sprinkle of bitterness to the cocktail." My word choice makes me burp, and my hand shoots up to my mouth, hoping to keep everything in. After last night, I don't think there's anything left to sacrifice to the porcelain god, but better safe than sorry.

The words start pouring out of me. "We had such a great time together yesterday, and he gave me a piggyback ride, and when he dropped me off at my room, it looked like he wanted to kiss me. So I stopped arguing with myself, finally gave in, and I did it. But then he pushed me away. Said we shouldn't. But really, he just doesn't want me. No one wants me." Tears sting my eyes and I choke down a sob.

Rene sets her hand on my back and starts rubbing in soothing circles. "Oh, sweetheart. That's not true. You're very want-able. If I was single and liked women, you would be top of my list."

"Thanks. But I doubt even that's true with Megan on set," I sniffle, and bury my face in the rumpled sheets.

"Why do you think it's about you? Maybe it's him. In fact, I'm sure it is. He's got a lot on his plate with this movie. I could see him not wanting to endanger the future of the production. You two are going to have a lot more time to spend together after filming wraps. I'm sure he'll want to bring you in for editing, and there will be a press tour, and hopefully other projects—"

"Oh God, I've ruined everything." I slap my hand over my face, mortified by my lack of forethought.

"Logan, if you think one unrequited kiss is going to ruin everything, then you haven't spent much time on film sets. It'll be fine. I'm sure Tom won't make it weird."

"But I'm not fine, and I'm sure *I'll* make it weird. I always do."

"Well, it's good to know your own strengths and weaknesses." She chuckles lightly, and I respond with a loud groan, the mattress muffling my sounds of agony. "Okay, enough wallowing. I'll get you some water and Advil, you'll take a shower, I'll do your hair and makeup today to cover up the green, and you'll hold your head high during filming. Tom will regret ever denying you."

"Pass."

"What do you mean 'pass'?"

"I pass. I don't want to leave this room. I don't want to go on set today. I don't want to see Tom. I *want* to wallow. Please, can I just wallow?" I turn my head to free my voice, whining with my plea.

"You're an adult, Logan. You can't just opt not to show up to work," Rene chastises me, but continues rubbing my back.

"What about a sick day?"

"Oh, you didn't know? Hollywood doesn't believe in sick days. Especially sick days due to hangovers. Otherwise, half the workforce would be out daily."

"I just want to disappear," I cry.

"Nope, no disappearing for you today. In fact, the opposite. I'm going to make you look so gorgeous that no one is going to be able to take their eyes off of you," Rene announces, and I stare up at her with wide doubtful eyes.

"Gorgeous" turns into "passably attractive" as Rene realizes how little time we have and has to rush the process. She weaves my damp hair into a French braid that wraps around my head like a maiden's halo and covers up my wan complexion with neutral makeup. After diving into my pile of clothes, largely composed of T-shirts and jean shorts, she emerges with a white scoop-neck tank and a flowy blue skirt with polka dots that hugs my hips and flares out just above my knees. I might look vibrant and alive, but I still feel like walking death.

Rene and I meet Kalina in one of the cars. She's anxious to get going as the filming's been moved up in an attempt to beat possible storms in the forecast. I mumble an apology and we all hop in.

I sit in the backseat and sip my bottled water, hoping no one else can hear it as it drops into my hollow stomach. Rene tried to get me to eat breakfast, but the sight of food still made me have the dry heaves, so I appeased her by grabbing a cereal bar and banana for later. The breakfast items rest on the seat next to me, taunting me with their ability to turn my insides with nothing more than a glance at them.

The drive out to Roseman Bridge doesn't help my stomach as Kalina takes the winding gravel roads at a California speed, trying to get us to the set location as soon as possible. We turn off of Roseman Bridge Road and are met with the iconic covered bridge stretching over the Middle River. Its barn-red exterior, white wooden fence, and lattice framework seem to transport us all to another time, a more romantic time of relying on horse-and-carriage, working the land, and appreciating nature for what it already provides rather than what can be ripped out of it.

Kalina parks and Rene nearly drags me out of the car. I shuffle my feet across the loose gravel feigning taking in the quaint gift shop, forested surroundings, and fresh air, but really, I'm doing my best to prolong the moment when I make eye contact with Tom. I'm being immature, I know, but I'm hurt. Forging a friendship and believing that Tom was beginning to see something more in me, something I didn't even see in myself, was more intoxicating than the liquid now poisoning my body. He's always acted like I'm special, like I have something to contribute to the world, to his life, and when I finally gave in to that little boost he gave my ego, he sent me catapulting back to the ground. I can't help it that I'm still bruised and sore from the experience.

My body betrays me, straightening up and leaning forward at the sight of Tom standing at the mouth of the bridge, his back toward me, framing different views within the rectangular eye of his outstretched hands. My heart swells at the sight of him leading as he always does, a Clint Eastwood of his own time directing his own movie featuring the famous bridges of Madison County. It takes my breath away, but it also pokes at the gaping hole in my gut, still too raw from rejection. I know now that I can't confront him. Maybe it's childish, but I'll be an adult tomorrow. Today, I just need to be alone and lick my wounds.

I turn to Rene who has been talking nonstop, to herself, to me, to whomever to try and ease me over this minefield of embarrassment. "So, this is the bridge from the movie, huh? Well, I guess it will be the bridge from your movie now, too. Eat your heart out, Meryl. Actually, I take that back. I've worked with Meryl a few times. She's pretty much the best human I've ever met. It's downright annoying how perfect she is—"

"Hey, Rene. I can't do this."

She stops abruptly, her feet kicking rock down the road. "You can't?"

"No, I'm sorry. You went through all this work to make me look presentable—"

"Girl, you look better than presentable. At least give me that."

"Okay, you did so much to help me this morning, but I just can't see him. I'm sorry. Tell Marnie she'll need to supervise the script today. She'll love it. She's been chomping at the bit ever since I took the official role. I think it's her favorite part of her job, and Tom took it away from her and gave it to me—" My voice catches, my thoughts always returning to Tom. I've let myself get so lost in my infatuation with him that I've lost sight of why we're really here. Sure, I've been an active part of the filming process, but would I have invested as much if it weren't for Tom? I look up to see Rene staring at me, her pity only strengthening my desire to fold in on myself and hide for as long as possible. "Just tell them this scene's too much for me." Phil and Megan are filming an argument, getting more into the details of their failed marriages. Even though I wrote it, seeing it is a much more visceral experience. It wouldn't surprise anyone if I bowed out of viewing it.

"Okay. Do you want me to drive you back?"

I look around, already aware of how late I've made her, and I shake my head. "No. Actually, I think I'm going to walk for a bit. Some fresh air will be good for me."

"Okay, but take water. And eat a snack!" She reaches out and squeezes my hand, then turns to join the gathering crew.

And that's how I end up walking alone on the gravel road eight miles south of Winterset, berating myself for every wrongdoing I've ever committed. There are a lot of them. This is going to be a long walk.

I've always tried to follow the rules, be the steady dock in the storm that has so often surrounded my life. The divorce, growing up with a single parent, taking care of my sick mother, all of it required me to drop anchor, tread water, anything to avoid rocking the boat. Then when Mom died, I lost the reason to follow the rules. I dipped my toe in deeper waters, and I was sucked beneath. It took a long time for me to resurface, to reclaim a sense of who I am as an individual instead of someone always tied to another person. But every time I try to venture out on my own, I feel as if I am drifting out into dangerous seas. Breaking the rules never works for me, it always pushes back against me, a white squall of karma and consequence. I've been living in a bubble, protected from the storm by the people who have unknowingly barricaded me from the truth. But one misstep could cause a breach, and then the whole dam could break.

I falter in the middle of my musings and stop next to a pasture, a hint of change in the air making the hair on my neck rise. I've been walking for at least an hour, maybe more, and the constant sounds of the birds trilling, the cows calling, the breeze whistling through the grass have been my companions, urging me forward in my angry march of self-flagellation. But now, there's an eerie stillness, an absence of anything living that chills my skin. A rumble of thunder echoes from the distance.

I look up, having been focused on my feet for the majority of my walk, and I take in the rolling hills of green with a winding gravel road carved between them. To the west, a dark front of blustering clouds loom on the horizon, tinging the once blue sky with an alarming green pallor.

I knew there was bad weather coming, but I overestimated how much time I had. My breath speeds up, and I spin around, trying desperately to locate the origin of my journey. Stray strands of hair escape from my braid to whip my face, and my skirt flutters precariously around my hips as the wind suddenly picks up. My stomach feels as if it has swallowed my entire being, hollow in the knowledge that I need to get moving. *Now.*

I head back the opposite way I was walking, praying that I didn't veer in direction or take an off-road turn in my walk of shame. The black clouds are on my heels as I start to jog, the forceful air pummeling my back and pushing me forward, making me stumble and fall. I wince, bending my knee to see a jagged gash right under my kneecap. I push myself up, my head dizzy with the fall, my fear, and my already weakened state. But I need to get back.

I look over my shoulder and see the sky start to swirl, the hair on my arms standing on end as I notice a feathery tail start to snake down from the wall of black plumes.

I scan the sides of the road and the surrounding pastures, searching for the deepest ditch or most protective covering. My heartbeat is a drum, quickly pounding out the percussion that it wants my feet to take me away from the danger. I look back toward the angry sky, my eyes widening at the violent cylinder taking shape. I force my gaze forward as I jog ahead, though I'm compelled to stand still and watch one of Mother Nature's most vengeful fabrications. The previous silence has been replaced by the gusting wind, screaming its siren song through the corn, trees, and grass. I could swear it's calling my name, luring me to certain death.

But it's not the air toying with me—I do hear my name carried on the breeze. I look down the road and squint to see a figure rising over the crest of the hilly rural road. My heart is buzzing with hope and fear, adrenaline rushing through my body with the force of a broken dam.

"Logan!" My name rips from the figure's throat, and I gasp out loud with recognition.

"Tom!" I scream, as we run toward each other, a roar like a train behind me. The world is in chaos, the storm doing its best to disorient me, but all I see is Tom as I continue running, his name slashing against the heavy air, trying to battle its way home. I focus on making my way to him as he leans into the punishing wind, his hair whipping across his brows and his T-shirt plastered against his chest. The clouds have split, releasing rain and hail that batters us both.

We collide, Tom's arms instantly wrapping around me, his body tense yet reassuring as he envelopes me. But we have no time to waste on a heartfelt reunion. He grabs me by the shoulders and pulls me away so he can look down at my face.

"We have to find shelter!" he shouts, our voices barely registering over the thunder of the oncoming tornado. I nod and we both look around frantically. I point to a culvert underneath the road from the direction I just came. Tom zeroes in on the drain pipe and begins running toward it, his hand tight around mine as he pulls me with him into the wind. It's pushing against us, trying its damndest to curb our escape, but Tom continues forward, his head tucked down, his body braced against the oncoming force. He jumps down into the ditch, puts his hands around my waist to secure my own descent, and we dive into the culvert. He pulls me into his body, covering me as we kneel in the water, soaked up to our waists, our heads fitting together like puzzle pieces as we listen to the world screaming above.

The only things I can hear are the howling of the wind as it blows past the opening of the culvert, Tom's rapid heartbeat, and our choral panicked breathing. My nose is pressed against Tom's neck, and I drown in his scent of sweat, rain, and soap. The lower half of my body is cold, shivering from the drain water, but the upper half is warmed as Tom and I knit ourselves together.

We continue holding each other even after the sky's banshee cries cease, soon replaced by the sound of dripping water, hesitant birds, and agitated livestock. Tom lifts his head slowly, and I follow his lead, our faces close enough to breathe each other's air. His eyes are huge, wandering my face as if looking for injury. But when he speaks, it is not with the gentle delicacy of concern.

"What the hell were you doing out here all alone?"

There are so many reasons: *I didn't want to see you after I kissed you and you pushed me away. I'm extremely hung over and can't hold my liquor like an adult. I can't bear to be around you anymore as just a friend*. But all that passes my lips is: "I just needed to be by myself."

"You can't just run off like that. You could have been killed." His chiding tone ignites my own resistance, and I begin extricating myself from his body and the culvert. My retreat is clumsy at best as I slosh through the water and stumble on the lip of the steel tube. Tom reaches out to steady me, which only fuels my anger.

"And you can't just come out here, save my life, and pretend that we're okay!"

Tom leans back as if I've smacked him, and he stammers for an answer. "I'm not—what are you talking about?"

"You know what I'm talking about!" I yell, disturbing the

post-storm peace with my piercing accusations. I start trudging up the ditch, back to the road, tripping on scattered branches and other debris deposited by the wind, throwing barbed words over my shoulder as Tom follows closely. “I needed to get away from you! After last night, when I kissed you, and you pushed me away. I just needed some space. How was I to know the storm of the century was going to interrupt my brooding!” I struggle to clear the ridge back to the road, and Tom pushes my butt, giving me a boost. “Thank you!” I snap, venom bristling at the edges of my words of gratitude.

He easily clears the rise and I start marching back to the bridge.

“It’s the other way.”

I turn on my heel, and start marching the other way, shoulder checking him as I pass. “God, you’re so aggravating!”

“I’m aggravating? You’re the aggravating one! We just survived a fucking tornado and yet you’re still mad at me? Just stop running away and talk to me!” I hear his feet pounding the gravel behind me, but I refuse to slow down. “Are you really going to ignore me after I came looking for you?”

I stop abruptly, spin back toward him, and jam a finger in his chest. “I want to. I want to ignore you, but you make it so fucking hard! All I want is to do my job, get paid, and move on to the next project. But instead, all I can think about is you!”

“All I think about is you, too!” Tom hollers back, leaning forward into my finger.

“Then why did you push me away?” My hand splays against his chest, but we continue with our shouting match.

“Because! You were drunk. I didn’t want to take advantage of you, especially after you stopped me from kissing you the other night!”

“Well, that’s just downright chivalrous of you!”

“Yeah, I know! I was raised right!”

“So you didn’t push me away because you don’t want me?”

"Of course not! I want you more than anything I've ever wanted before!"

"Then why are you still yelling at me?"

"Because! I'm mad!"

"Why are you mad?!"

He takes a deep breath, his face suddenly relaxing, and he answers with a strained whisper. "Because I thought I'd lost you." He grabs the side of my face, tilts my head up, and presses his lips to mine. The kiss holds everything: our companionship, our fear, our attraction, our relief. Kissing him feels like breathing. It's natural, easy, necessary. I wrap my arms around his neck, my nails pressing into his skin as he pulls my body into his. We were woven tightly together when tucked into the culvert, but that was for protection. This is all desire. Hot, death-defying desire. My skin burns as his hands roam to my back and sneak under the hem of my shirt. I moan against his mouth, and he answers with a more forceful grip. My own hands now tangle in his hair, gripping him for dear life, anchoring our kiss as our bodies begin to move against each other with a current of passion and need.

Suddenly, Tom rips his head up, pulling his lips from mine. He looks behind him, then meets my forehead with his, his whispered words teasing my swollen lips. "Someone's coming."

"Huh?" I angle my head around his and see the approaching truck, a trusty farm vehicle with a busted headlight and rusted frame.

An elderly man with gray stubble and a straw hat pulls up. He tips his hat as he leans out of his window. "You folks all right?"

Tom and I look at each other, bodies still pressed together, and we both burst into grins. Tom steps away, but his hand slides down my arm to grab mine, refusing to let me go completely. "Yeah, we're good. We were able to hide in that culvert over there. Did you get any damage?"

"That's what I'm checking. You need a ride somewhere?"

"Sure, that would be great. We don't smell the best, though."

"Just hop in the back." The farmer points a thumb to his truck bed, and Tom helps me up, asking the man to take us back to the bridge.

When we arrive, the cast and crew swarm us with questions. Rene, Atlas, and Deedee rush close, as if to inspect me for damage, but rear back, their noses in the air after being assaulted with the clinging smell of manure and sewer water. "Oh honey, I'm so glad you're alive. But you smell like a clogged toilet."

"Thanks, Rene."

"Whose hood are you going to hang onto during the drive back?" Atlas asks, laughing at the image of me clinging to the top of a sedan, and I chuckle with relief. Tom and I meet each other's gazes as our friends fawn over us. All I want is to be back in his arms, but I know this isn't the moment. For now, we need to assure our friends we are in fact unharmed. But a tremor of anticipation electrifies my skin. Thomas Price kissed me, upending my entire world and ruining me for any other man. Kissing Tom felt like being resurrected, and I'm thrumming with new life as he starts to give directions about filming, cleanup, and our return to the hotel.

As I watch him, animated and in control, a dark cloud, like a stubborn remnant of the storm, starts to fog the clarity of the kiss in my mind. What if it was just a moment of weakness, an impulsive act motivated by our ability to cheat death and best nature? I wish I could outrun my doubts, that the cloud would dissipate like its previous kin, but it's part of a larger storm that lives inside me, constantly raging against any potential joy or assuredness. It's a storm that will never settle, made by past actions and destructive thoughts. It's a storm that never ends, and all I can do is try my best to find shelter when it rages.

Excerpt from *Iowa Nice*

WINTERSET

"Did you see the movie? The Bridges of Madison County?*" My dad's accusing tone puts me on the defensive. He might know history, but I know film and fiction.*

"Of course I did. Did you read the book?" I throw him a challenge of my own, fairly certain of his answer as I walk up and down the bridge, my eyes scanning the penned names and notes left on the wooden skeleton of the Roseman Bridge.

"Uh…no. I didn't. I guess you're just more sophisticated and literary than I am." He tries to tamp down my quiet boasting, his hands patting the air with surrender. "Okay, so what did you think of them? The movie and the book?"

It's been years since I've seen or read either, but I furrow my brow in concentration, trying my best to glean important details from my memory.

"I mean, it's romantic. Usually the book is way better than the

resulting movie, but they were so different in structure and execution that I think they both stand on their own."

"But what do you think of the story? Of what happens?"

"Again, it's romantic, but it's also wrong, right? She's married. And it just taints the love affair. At least for me."

"I disagree. I think any love affair is worth it, as long as there is real love involved. Might not make it right, but it definitely makes it more understandable."

"Huh, I'm not sure how understandable adultery is. Sounds like a weak justification to me." I hug myself tightly and start walking away, pretending to read the various writings on the wall.

"What is with you today? Did I do something wrong? I thought we'd gotten over all of this!" He calls after me, his frustration echoing off the wooden pillars.

I spin on my heel. "That's the thing, Dad. I'll never get over it. Sure, I can squash it down, ignore it in order to be more amenable, to make it more convenient to be around me—because in the end I would rather have at least one parent in my life than none. But I'm still affected by it, I'm still damaged, still broken by the choices you made. Thanks to your love affair, my ability to love and be loved is fucked."

"You don't believe that." A note of doubt hangs on his statement.

"I do. In fact, I know it."

"Then you need to change it."

"How do you change a fact?"

"The same as you change anything. Just start working at it."

I go to offer a retort, but no words come to mind. Instead, I walk away, out of the opposite side of the bridge and down the road, my stomping feet leaving my father on the famous Roseman Bridge as I seek a moment by myself. No matter what, he refuses to see the lasting scars he caused that still crisscross my heart. Or maybe he's right, and they're only phantom scars that I can't seem to let go of. Either way, I'm damaged, and I don't know how to heal.

15

There was minimal damage from the storm, the resulting tornado registered as an F1 that touched down in farmland only. Some trees were lost from a few farm groves, but no people or livestock were injured or killed, and the Roseman Bridge was left unharmed, having experienced little more than forceful winds.

For obvious reasons, filming is postponed for the day. Atlas, Marnie, and Kalina plan to arrive early tomorrow morning and clean up the debris for continuity's sake, and in the meantime we all journey back to the hotel. Rene and Megan dramatically hold their noses, having drawn the short stick of riding with both Tom and me since we didn't want to ruin the olfactory experience for double the riders, but Deedee is kind as always, even sitting next to me in the backseat as Tom drove with all the windows open.

The drain water has dried, and my clothes are now stiff and dusted with silt. All I want to do is take a shower and eat something. I'm starting to feel weak, my hands shaking with the lack of food and the aftereffects of shock. Deedee notices and grabs my hand, squeezing my fingers.

"Oh, Logan! Your hands are freezing. Tom, can you turn on the heat?" I see his eyes meet mine in the rearview mirror, creased with concern. His face is spattered with dirty water, but the blue of his eyes cuts through, a clear sky surrounded by smog. They are a beacon, and it's difficult to look away.

"No, I'm okay," I assure everyone in the car. "Just cold. And hungry. And tired."

"Baby girl, you've got a lot going on." Rene whistles, and the entire car erupts in laughter at her obvious statement.

Tom regales the others with details of the storm for the rest of the ride while I lean my head against the back window. By the time I step into my room, it takes everything I have to turn on the shower, drag my body inside, scrub it clean, and emerge better smelling and better feeling. I wrap myself in a fluffy white towel and drop heavily onto the bed. Cocooned in the comforter and towel, the mattress cradling me gently, I drift off to sleep, the echo from the sounds of the storm still roaring in my head.

***

My head feels staticky, white noise having replaced the rumble in my ears. But something broke through the stasis of sleep, and I peer around, groggy and disoriented. A yellow hue marks my room with the light of the setting sun, and a glance at the clock radio confirms that I've been asleep for nearly four hours.

My ears perk up with the repetition of four soft knocks on my door. I roll up and out of bed, holding the towel tightly around me, figuring I'll crack the door just enough to see what's needed, then retreat back to my downy nest.

I look through the peephole, the fisheye lens distorting a darkened figure, but my breath catches as I recognize the shoulders and relaxed stance. The door clicks loudly as I turn the knob and open it, hiding my body behind it and sticking my head out enough to greet Tom accordingly.

"Hey," I manage to breathe as he grins sheepishly in greeting, his foot scuffing the floor absentmindedly while relegated to the hotel hallway.

"Hey. I was worried about you."

"Really? Why?" I shift from foot to foot, my craned neck starting to ache.

"Well, I texted. And called. And walked by your door multiple times before knocking. Nothing obsessive. Just a healthy amount of stalking to ensure your wellbeing."

His nervous grin disarms me enough that I can only fumble for an answer. "Oh, I was…I was sleeping. I passed out almost as soon as we got back."

"Okay, good. I'm glad you're okay." He pauses as our eyes finally match up, latching onto each other's gaze, undoubtedly both thinking of our earlier roadside rendezvous. "Can I come in?" he finally asks, his voice quiet despite the blaring meaning behind his words.

I glance down at my body and gulp, cringing as I look up. "Uhhh, now's not a good time." He glares at me, assessing what could be going on, before launching into negotiations.

"Why is that?"

"I'm sure my breath is horrible."

"I have mints."

"I'm still feeling nauseous."

"I can bring you some crackers."

"I'm just really tired."

"Didn't you just sleep for four hours?"

"Well, yeah…okay. But I'm only wearing a towel."

"Oh…well…that's fine." His resulting smirk finally shatters my apprehension, and I open the door, clutching the towel to my chest.

"Fine. You can come in." I stand off to the side and he passes by me, his arm brushing against mine. I close the door, then turn back, jolted by his nearness. He's freshly showered, his usual scent of sandalwood mingling with the complimentary lavender shampoo I also used to scrub my body clean of sewer water. A soft gray T-shirt clings to his shoulders and chest while black athletic shorts reveal his tanned calves. I wish I could say I was taking all this in discreetly, but due to my recent nap, still present hangover, and the overall trauma of the day, I'm slow to process and slow to react. Tom catches my eye, pulling my gaze back up to his face.

It seems he's been doing his own scan as his eyes dart downward and he says, "So, did you throw the towel on special for me, or was it more of an afterthought?"

"I took a shower, wrapped up in it, then fell asleep. Here, let me change so you're not distracted."

"I'm not distracted." A pointed look causes him to amend his statement. "Okay, I guess I'm a little distracted. But really, you don't need to—"

I place a hand on his chest as I walk by. "Just give me a second." I take a moment to grab some clothes, change in the bathroom, and still my shaky breathing, finally emerging to find Tom sitting on my bed. He's smoothed out the covers, his hand still toying with the fabric when I come out in a tank top and cotton shorts, my hair curled and fluffy from air-drying. He looks up, a glimpse of warmth passing over his face, his previous trance broken by my presence. I sit next to him on the bed, giving him enough space so our bare legs don't touch. We've sat on countless beds together, but now it seems dangerous, as though we're standing at a fork in the road and whatever way we choose will have an impact on the rest of the journey. These paths will not cross, so it's imperative we pick the right one.

"So?" I ask, extending the one-syllable word with an upward inflection.

"So," Tom responds, a small smile lifting the corner of his lips.

I widen my eyes with raised brows, silently urging him to speak, but he remains silently grinning at me.

A surge of irritation swells within me. Tom woke me up, pushed his way in here, made me get dressed, and now he can't even put two words together. "Great talk. Glad you could come by. Now if you don't mind, I could really use something to—" I go to rise, my knee bumping Tom's, and he reaches out and grabs my right arm, pulling me to him. I'm nestled between his legs, and both of his arms settle around me, his hand splayed at my lower back, pushing me closer against him as his other cups my face, his fingers dipping into my hairline.

"I never said I wanted to talk," he utters breathily, his eyes darting down to my lips. He angles his head so his mouth hovers over mine, his breath tickling the surface of my lips, and then there is only pressure, warmth, and want as he closes the small distance between us.

My mind is void of reason, the heady scent of sandalwood intoxicating me with his nearness, as I let myself sink more heavily into Tom's lap. He deftly maneuvers me, hoisting up my bottom and bringing my legs to wrap around his hips, and I gasp at the feel of him against me—the softness of his lips, the hardness of his growing need, and the clutch of his roaming hands are almost enough to strip me of any coherent thought. But my need for air does cause me to pull away, enough to breathe and voice the doubtful shadow looming in my mind. I start rambling as Tom continues kissing my neck and chest.

"Hey…I know what we said on the road…was fueled by fear…and adrenaline…and I understand if you didn't really mean any of that…if you aren't feeling it—"

"Are you insane?" he rasps as he brings his head back up, his lips on mine once again. "Of course, I'm feeling it." He emphasizes his point by rolling his hips against me and I throw my head back with the sensation, but he tilts it back down, capturing my face in his hands. "Logan, I meant what I said. I want you. Obviously." His lips curl devilishly and his eyes flash downward to where our bodies meet, but they sober instantly as he brings his gaze up, clinging to mine as he says, "I know you wanted to just stay friends, that you're worried about being professional, but the thought of losing you today…it terrified me…I don't want to feel that ever again." He reaches up to brush my hair out of my face, his hand lingering on my jaw. "I don't want to hide my feelings for you anymore. I don't think I could even if you asked me."

I smile, starting to ease back into his hold. "Your feelings? What type of feelings?"

He leans back and raises an eyebrow, dropping his hand so both cling to my hips. "Big feelings. Gooey feelings. Sexy feelings. Feelings people write books about."

"Are you thinking of writing a book?" I bite my lip, and he fingers the hem of my tank. I nod in consent, raising my arms as he lifts the shirt over my head.

"No, you're the expert there. I'll stick to my lane." He watches me hungrily as I shake out my hair and reach back to unclasp my bra.

"And what's your lane exactly?" I ask while watching Thomas Price soak in the sight of my released breasts, his body stilling beneath mine.

He reaches out and cups my right breast, his thumb circling my nipple. Without changing the direction of his glance, he replies, "Right now, my lane is right about here." He then takes his hand and slides it down my rib cage and hips, his fingers mapping out a roadway to the most sensitive areas of my being. "And here." His fingers swirl seductively as they dip beneath the waist of my shorts, and he looks up to see my reaction. I nod and exhale a breathy consent as his fingers make contact. "And finally here."

All I can do is moan with pleasure as he begins teasing me with light circles, his pressure increasing as I rock against him. Just as my body rises, the relief of my pent-up pleasure mere movements away, he pulls his hand back up to trace my belly button then raises it to settle on my sternum.

"Why did you stop?" I ask, unable to disguise the disappointment lacing my plea.

"Don't worry, I'm not done. There's just more I want to see before we reach our destination."

"Did you just quote one of your movies?"

"Huh? No, I don't think so. Maybe. So what if I did?"

"It's fine. Just don't stop touching me."

"Now that's a direction I will gladly take."

"Okay, enough talk—" I'm undone as he seals my mouth with his, our heartbeats syncing up as we start moving against each other. His hands snake to my back, supporting me as he holds my shoulder blades, my skin on fire with his touch. But impatience steers my own hands to his shirt, and we both help to free the burden of clothing from his muscled chest. I reach out to trace the ridges of his abs, abs I've seen oiled up on the big screen, but they're even better up close and personal. I bring my tongue down to lick the length of his collarbone, and his skin trembles beneath my touch. I lift my head up to meet his gaze, my bottom lip caught between my teeth.

"What are you thinking?" he whispers, his body gently rocking beneath mine as we sit wrapped in each other's arms, bared from the waist up.

"I'm thinking this can't be real."

"It is real. It's very real. Why can't you see that?"

"I guess I just don't know what you see in me."

"I see everything in you, Logan. Everything."

I'm speechless, gawking as he takes his thumb and trails it across my bottom lip. His touch glides down my jaw and beckons me forward to catch my mouth with his, a playful nip sending a shiver down my neck and spine. He looks as if he is ready to devour me, and I have no will to resist.

"Stand up," he commands, and I rise from his lap, his hands still on me. He holds my gaze as he slides my shorts and underwear slowly down my legs, drinking in the full sight of me when I step out and kick my apparel to the side. He stands, his body grazing the length of mine, and I repeat the actions on him, a sharp intake of breath marking the moment I release him from his boxers.

"You okay?"

"Yep. It's just…I've seen so much of you on the big screen. But I've never seen that."

"Yeah, I save it for special audiences. VIPs only." He smiles and pulls me close, our bodies searing with heat as they press together. He turns me and lays me down on the bed, his lips and fingers exploring the length of my body with boundless touches and kisses. I shiver as he nuzzles my inner thigh, gasping as his mouth comes down over me, his tongue evaporating all sensical thought. I am unbridled sensation, squirming and writhing beneath his hold as he presses me down with a wide palm on my stomach. I release a moan of pure pleasure as I reach the brink, even more powerful after almost breaching the precipice before, waves of ecstasy rolling through my core.

He comes up, his body resting atop mine and grabs my face with his hands. "I want to be inside you now. Can I?" I nod my forehead against him, but then falter.

"Wait, do you have a condom?"

His lips stretch up into a hesitant grin. "Don't hate me for this, but yes, in my pocket."

My eyebrows raise with jesting judgment. "Really?"

"I might have had some ideas of how this would go."

"Oh?"

"I told you not to bother getting dressed."

I laugh, "Well, thank goodness you came prepared."

"Yeah?"

"Oh yeah."

He pulls himself off me, the cold of his absence assaulting my skin, and I watch as he digs in his pocket for a condom and returns to me. Cocooned within his hold, I feel nothing short of wanted and protected. He kisses me deeply, and I open beneath him, hissing at the feel of him sliding in slowly. We move against each other, all need and desire building until we both reach a new height of pleasure. Afterwards, when we separate and are lying side by side, he leans over and kisses my shoulder.

"Was it worth it?"

"What?"

"Me waking you?"

"Thomas Sydney Price, you are always worth it."

"You are, too, Logan Alice Sterling."

I let him pull me in, and we drift into a light doze with our bodies intertwined, my mind unable to argue with Tom's assessment of my self-worth. In this moment, I actually believe him.

CELEBRITY
Daily Online

Actor and producer Thomas Price has been spending the past few weeks in Iowa filming the screen adaptation of Iowa author Logan Sterling's breakout literary debut *Iowa Nice*, set to be released sometime next year. Price, who is a first-time director on this project, brought Sterling in as the screenwriter and script supervisor to ensure the film preserves the heart of the book, which is a memoir of Sterling's journey through the state of Iowa's hidden treasures and roadside attractions with her dying father. Phil Grant, known for his work in television, film, and theater plays the role of Sterling's father, First Sergeant Malcolm McClarnon. Megan Marks, who used to date Price while costarring together in *Rocky Mountain High*, takes on the role of Sterling herself.

Price leads a crew of fifteen, but it hasn't been all work and no play for this crew. The entire cast and crew gathered at a Winterset bar where they viewed the ultimate college football rivalry game between the University of Iowa Hawkeyes and Iowa State University Cyclones. One patron reported that, "Tom and Logan apparently had a bet going about who would win. Logan ended up losing, since the refs had it in for the Cyclones, and she had to sing the 'Iowa Fight Song' wearing a Hawkeye shirt. Her voice isn't the greatest, but she did put on quite a show." A video of Sterling's performance has been circulating social media and various news outlets. Apparently, Sterling climbed on the bar to sing, then fell, with Price thankfully catching her. The unnamed patron continued, saying, "There were definite sparks between the two of them." Sterling and Price were seen leaving together later that evening along with other crew members who had partied late into the night.

Filming will continue in the eastern part of the state throughout the rest of September and into October.

16

My growling stomach wakes me up, and I lift my head off of Tom's chest, our legs tangled beneath the sheets.

"Hey," Tom murmurs, his hand deep in my hair, aimlessly playing with the strands.

"Hey," I respond, bringing my arms up to rest underneath my chin, my body lifting gently with the rise and fall of his breathing. "Have you been awake long?"

"Not too long," he answers, his eyes still transfixed on my blonde locks curled around his fingers.

"What have you been doing?"

"Oh, just watching you." His eyes shift to meet mine, his face soft and relaxed. His hair, long enough to grip, sticks up in various directions. In this moment, he seems younger, less the Hollywood hunk everyone else sees and more the Iowa farm boy, his origins running marrow-deep. My heart swells at the notion that I am getting to see this side of him, the private person that still lives at the core of his being.

"Not creepy at all." A smile tugs at the corner of my mouth, and he matches my smile, reaching down and tweaking my nose.

"Hey, so I have a very important question for you." His hand drifts to the side of my face, then my forearm, constantly moving and constantly touching.

"And what is that?" I ask, a hint of concern starting to invade my warm and fuzzy feelings.

"Are you hungry? Because I've been listening to your stomach, and I can feel it rumbling against me." I start laughing and Tom suddenly grabs my shoulders, rolling me over so he's poised above me. "Is that a yes?"

"Yes, I'm starving. I was starving when you first arrived, but then you distracted me—"

"Oh, I distracted you?" He starts tickling my hips and rib cage, and I fight for air between my laughter. "Is that what you're calling it? Not rocked your world? Changed your life? Gave you your first true glimpse of enlightenment?"

"Stop! Please, stop!" I sputter out, inhaling deeply when he finally relents. "Fine, you rocked my world. Are you happy?"

"That's it? You're the writer. Don't you have something more poetic for me?" He sticks his bottom lip out, and if I weren't desperately trying to regain my oxygen intake, I would desperately be tugging that lip with my teeth.

"I can't mentally grasp the words to describe you. Your body broke me," I answer, my focus still on his adorable pout.

He barks out an amused laugh and brings his forehead down to mine. My head dizzies with the scent of sandalwood and sex. "Actually, that's perfect. Exactly what I wanted to hear."

"And as I said, I'm so hungry I can't think."

He brings his hand to my chin and tilts my mouth toward his. "Okay, let's fix that." He places a tender kiss on my lips, pulling back just enough to utter the sexiest words I've ever heard: "Do you want me to order pizza?"

I nod vigorously, and he kisses me again before rising out of bed, pulling on his boxers, and placing the most important phone call of my life…or this hour. Hunger makes me hyperbolic.

Thirty minutes later, Tom and I have successfully demolished a pepperoni, pineapple, and jalapeño pizza.

"How in the world did you get hooked on this combination?" he asks, licking his fingers as we both lay across my bed, the empty pizza box between us.

"My ex."

"Well, I've got to hand it to the guy. He's got good taste." He winks and sticks his finger in his mouth, pulling it out slowly in a cringe-worthy parody of seduction, effectively lightening my moment of heavy reflection. "Maybe I can thank him in person someday."

"Oh God, I hope not." I roll my eyes at the thought, but can't help smiling at his affability. I love being with this man and am starting to feel myself lose some of the protective shielding I have erected over the past few years. But I still need to protect myself. I can't just jump into an affair with an internationally known celebrity. My sense of self-preservation battles with my desire for him, and I shove the box aside and reach over to grab his hand, pulling it from his mouth and into my grasp. "Hey, so what are we going to do?"

"What do you mean?" He starts rubbing my knuckles as I begin rambling.

"I mean…is this it? A quick bang to blow out the tension, then back to work—"

"Whoa, a bit offensive—"

"Or are we going to keep this secret—"

"What, are you ashamed of me?"

"Or do we just go on about our business, and damn it all. Let the crew talk, alert the tabloids, break thousands of hearts—"

"Only thousands?"

"I'm serious, Tom. Is this just a film set hookup or …"

"Or?"

"Or…you know what I'm getting at!"

"I know. But I love to make you squirm, as you may recall." He pulls me over and sits me on his lap. Straddling him already feels familiar, and I'm struck with the realization that this would not be a clean break if we chose to part. Luckily, it doesn't seem that Tom is swaying that direction as he captures my gaze, his hands resting beneath my shirt, gently tracing the inward curve of my waist between my rib cage. "I meant what I said. I have feelings for you, Logan. Feelings that I want to explore. I don't mind others knowing that, but if it makes you uncomfortable, I can play it cool."

"It doesn't make me uncomfortable…it just concerns me. You're a pretty big deal, Thomas Price." I let my hands wander the landscape of his body, my eyes following the path of my touch as I talk.

"Why thank you. Is there any way you can put that in writing?"

I pull my gaze away from his bicep to look at him in mock-warning. "You know what I mean. If this…whatever this is…gets released, there's going to be people wanting to know who I am, why you would waste your time with me…" My gaze drifts downward, pulled in the direction of my sinking gut.

"Hey," he interrupts me, reaching to cradle my face, pulling my focus back up. "You're a big deal, Logan."

"I wrote one book—"

"I'm not talking about that. I'm talking about you. You are beautiful, kind, considerate…" I try to look away, heat flooding my cheeks, but he steadies me with his grip. "I'm not done. Creative, funny, beautiful—"

"You said that already."

"Because it warrants repeating. You, Logan Sterling, are a big deal to me. This is a big deal to me."

"I'm not perfect, Tom." My breathing is starting to pick up in an attempt to match my racing heartbeat.

"I know. I don't want someone who's perfect. I want you." The ocean waves of his eyes threaten to surge forward and carry me out to sea, a fate I would gladly accept at this moment. "What's concerning you so much? Your name is already connected to mine, you've been interviewed with me, photographed with me. What's so different? What are you afraid of?"

I focus on the feel of his thumb on the corner of my mouth as I air the concerns swirling inside my chest. "It's different when it's professional. But if people start to sense a personal connection, then they start wanting to know more, start digging up dirt—"

"Is there something you're afraid they're going to find?" He says this as a whisper, providing a safe space where I can share my burdens.

I lock eyes with him, my heart pounding in my ears, and I answer, "No, not really. I just don't like being the center of attention."

His eyes crinkle with his smile, the serious turn of our conversation starting to bend. "Well, that's unfortunate. Because I plan on slathering you with nothing but attention for the rest of the night."

"I suppose I can handle that kind of attention." My body shivers as his hands dip down beneath my waistband to cup my butt and pull me in closer.

"Think you can handle me being such a big deal?" he says, evidence of his arousal brewing beneath me.

I can't help but grin at his innuendo. "Oh, I think I can. But maybe we should go slow. Like really slow."

He reaches up and cradles the back of my head, bringing my mouth to his in an unrushed kiss, a slow-burning ember that promises to ignite within me. We continue exploring the shape, feel, and movement of each other's lips, tongues, and teeth and when he pulls back, a protesting whine hums from my throat. He holds my face in both hands and looks at me as he says, "I need you to start believing in this, believing in yourself. Because I believe in you, in us. And I see you for all you are, Logan."

A small smile dances across my lips before he brings his mouth back over mine. We take our time, clothes shed in a prolonged seduction, feathery touches teasing the most sensitive skin until we can't hold ourselves back anymore. Our bodies unite in a powerful crash, and we both surrender to the sweeping waves of pleasure.

We fall asleep in the haven of my hotel room, isolated in our own private world, unworried about the potential fallout, the possible gossip, and the truths capable of upending our entire existence.

***

Tom sent out a group message yesterday, telling the cast and crew that we would finish filming at Roseman Bridge today, then take the rest of the day to discuss production and schedule needs.

When we arrive back at the bridge, I'm astonished by the work of Marnie, Kalina, and Atlas, who spent all morning cleaning up the debris from the storm along with a city cleanup crew. Megan and Phil jump into the scene fluidly, and I'm actually able to pry my hungry eyes away from Tom's backside long enough to appreciate their artistry. Megan has been able to capture her own version of me, seamlessly weaving in her own mannerisms with observations of my habits. But it's her easy ability to come to tears and Phil's command of a strained voice that effectively capture the emotion of the scene, and I find myself sucked in, my heart aching a bit until I look over and see Tom grinning in my direction.

"That's a wrap," he announces, and he strides over to my perch as the rest of the crew starts picking up. My eyes widen as he goes to touch me, and he pulls up short, letting his outreached hand float in the air before awkwardly returning to his side.

"So I'm going to be holed up for the rest of the day. Do you want to be part of the conversation, or do you just want a day of rest?"

Greedily, I wouldn't mind being near Tom all day, but it would be torture not to be able to touch him like I want to in front of the others. And I could use the downtime. I answer, "Well, for some reason I didn't get much sleep last night, so sure, I'll take your offer and let you handle the production meeting on your own. Is that okay?"

His eyes flash with the mention of our amorous activities from last night and this morning, having woken up naked in each other's arms and unable to resist the call of each other's bodies. He's able to hide any other response, but I notice his fingers twitch at his hip. "Sure. Can I come by this evening?"

"Hmmm, let me see if I'm free." I pretend to be searching my mental calendar before releasing him with a relaxed smirk. "Yes, of course. I'll wait with bated breath."

"Good. Much better than waiting with unbated breath."

I fail at stifling my laughter and feel eyes on us. I'm sure the crew wouldn't care; they'd probably expect it and may have even placed bets, but I still want to keep this just between us, a precious secret untouched by the outside world.

I ride back to the hotel with Rene, Deedee, and Megan and there's only one suspicious comment to field when Rene asks, "Are you fully recovered from yesterday, Logan? You seem a bit tired."

"I'm good," I answer perfunctorily.

"Oh. Great. Do you know if Tom is doing okay? He seemed tired, too. In a good mood, but still a bit distracted."

"Huh, don't know. I haven't talked to him much." *Not exactly a lie.*

Rene continues driving, an observational hum deep in her throat. Deedee catches my eye from the backseat, and I send her a quick smile before shifting the topic. "Hey Megan, I meant to tell you,

you're doing an amazing job. You nearly made me cry today."

Megan lights up with the compliment. "That's so sweet of you to say. Hopefully, it's not too painful reliving this all over again."

I take a breath and answer, "No, it's okay. I wrote it after all. Worked out most of the bad feelings."

"But I'm sure it's different seeing it in person. Seeing Phil as your dad."

"Yeah, it is different," I say, my voice fading with distance.

Deedee chimes in, changing the subject. "Well, I for one am looking forward to a free afternoon. What should we do?"

The rest of the ride is filled with planning the rest of the day. I look out the window and watch the rows of corn stalks file behind us as we speed by, my heart and head calmed by the beauty of the Iowa countryside.

***

That evening, the entire cast and crew gather in Tom's hotel room where he announces that we will sojourn to Iowa City tomorrow where his parents are awaiting our arrival.

"We'll get some driving and landscape shots, might stop for some roadside and location settings, but we should be at my family's acreage by lunch. So enjoy the rest of the night, and I'll see you all in the morning. We roll out at seven." A few groans follow this detail, but we all disperse in good spirits, ready for another night of relaxation. I file out as Tom continues talking with Marnie, but I catch his eye as I leave. Thirty minutes later, he knocks on my door. Then he closes the door behind him and heads straight for me…kisses my neck…lifts me up as I wrap my legs around his waist, and presses me down into the mattress where we spend the rest of our night of relaxation doing anything but relaxing.

WIO
Iowa News Source

The cast and crew of the film adaptation of *Iowa Nice* experienced a not-so-nice side of Iowa when filming was interrupted by an F1 tornado. All parties were uninjured and property damage was minimal, but filming has been halted for a few days. A Winterset citizen reports that filming concluded at the Roseman Bridge the day after the storm, and it is suspected that the crew is headed to the childhood home of Thomas Price, who grew up outside of Iowa City and is known to visit his family whenever in the state.

Price, who has graced the screen as a variety of heroes, proved himself a real-life hero when he went after Logan Sterling, Iowa native and author of *Iowa Nice*, who was walking on Roseman Bridge Road at the time of the isolated tornado. Both sought shelter in a culvert, where they were thankfully unharmed, though undoubtedly a bit shaken.

Various news sources have been speculating on the nature of Price and Sterling's relationship as the two have been photographed together on multiple occasions, whether working on the project or spending free time with one another. Either way, we here at WIO are glad everyone in Winterset is safe and we look forward to more news and updates about the filming of *Iowa Nice*.

17

The Price family farm sits at the top of a valley looking over a span of gentle hillsides northeast of Iowa City, an idyllic babbling creek carving through the eastern border of the property. Patches of corn, soybeans, vegetable gardens, and scattered wildflowers dot the undulating land as the white farmhouse overlooks its kingdom. I've seen pictures of the farm before, featured in lifestyle magazines while Tom was promoting an upcoming movie, but it's an entirely surreal experience getting to journey up the winding driveway and be greeted by his parents as they stand on the wraparound porch, two Golden Retrievers prancing happily in the yard as our team piles out of multiple vehicles.

My phone starts vibrating as Rene turns the car off, and a brief glance tells me that it's Niya. I haven't heard much from her lately, but I have been doing my duty and sending her updates every couple of days. I might have let too much time pass since the tornado, so I'm sure she's just calling to check up on me. I put it on silent, not wanting to meet Tom's parents while attached to my cellular device. We may not be announcing our relationship, or whatever it is we're doing, but I certainly don't want his mom and dad thinking I'm rude. I'm nothing if not a people pleaser.

Mr. and Mrs. Price rush forward, arms spread wide as Tom leads the crew to the house. Tom's mom wraps him in a hug, squeezing tightly and swaying him back and forth. I see her mouth moving next to his ear as she whispers greetings only meant for him to hear. She and Tom have the same brown hair, though hers is curly with strands of gray catching the gleam of the high sun. Her denim dress comes down just below her knees, and a woven brown belt cinches around her small waist. Mr. Price shakes hands with some of the crew members, a few shoulder claps revealing a previous meeting as he waits for his wife to release his son from her hold. It's as if Tom were poured from a mold cast from his father. They have the same build, same face shape, same smile that reaches their blue eyes. Mrs. Price finally lets Tom go, and his father hugs him, slapping his back as he chuckles at some exchange.

Megan and Phil are introduced—or reacquainted as in Megan's case. As Tom explained, he and Megan did indeed date, long enough for her to meet his parents and receive an enthusiastic reception. His parents are huggers, and I see them greet everyone with the same warmth doled out to their son. I hang back by the car, not always sure what to do in such functional family scenarios. But Tom looks back, tilts his head in question, and beckons me forward. My legs feel stiff as I make my way toward our beaming hosts.

"Mom, I think you know who this is. Logan, this is my mom, Camille."

"It's nice to meet you, Mrs. Price." I nod in greeting, a tense smile on my face.

"Oh please, call me Cami." She pulls me into a hug, then turns outward, her arm still hanging on my shoulder. "And this is my husband, Scott." I shake his hand, but am swept up in Cami's continuing whirl of conversation. “I’m so excited to meet you! I just loved your book! We read it in my book club and then I called Tom, told him to read it immediately.”

“So, I pretty much have you to thank for this?”

“Oh, sweetie, no. I’m sure I wasn’t the first one to think it would be a good movie, but if you feel like it, go ahead and dedicate your next book to me.” She laughs, and I release my own strained chuckle. It would be easier to join in on the merriment if I actually had an idea for a next book…and if I wasn’t so worried about impressing Tom’s parents. But my worried thoughts lose their momentum as Cami and Scott gesture for us all to follow them to the red barn next to the house, and we step into a room with polished wood and strung lights. Several large picnic tables have been placed together in the middle of the room, creating a banquet area laden with plates of sub sandwiches, bowls of various Midwestern salads, platters of fruit and cookies, and pitchers of lemonade, water, and iced tea.

Scott Price spreads his arms wide and announces, “We’re so honored to have all of you with us today. In our house, friends are family, so welcome to our family table. Eat, drink, and be merry.”

“Great speech, Dad.” Tom teases, but his affection outweighs any actual annoyance, and he grins as he repeats Scott’s sentiments. “Let’s eat! This one’s on my parents’ tab, so fill up!”

“Come sit next to me, Logan.” Cami materializes at my elbow and steers me toward one end of the table. My eyes search frantically for Tom, who catches my gaze with a small smile; he and his dad are gathered at the other end with the camera and light crew, Scott going on about how much he loves the technical side of Tom’s craft. I widen my eyes in faux terror, but he shakes his head slightly in reassurance as his mom proceeds to ask me questions about my book while loading my plate with food.

“Tom tells me you’re from Ottumwa. Do you go back there

often?" she asks as she plops a scoop of pastel-colored fluff on my plate between a heap of potato salad and a wedge of watermelon.

"Oh, that's plenty, thank you. Uh, no. Not really. I don't have any family there anymore, so no real reason to. I work in Des Moines, at least I did before the movie. I had to quit when I started having meetings about movie rights. They wouldn't give me the time off."

"Oh, well, you showed them, didn't you?" She winks as she fills a glass with lemonade. She's constantly serving me or someone next to her, but she never wavers in her focus on our conversation, a master in multitasking.

"I suppose. I mean, I hope the movie does well. And I'd like to write more, whether books or movies, but I don't really have any ideas yet. This project has sort of taken all my energy."

"Oh, I can only imagine. Tom is always telling me how stressful it can be bouncing from project to project. He likes to pour all of his energy into one task at a time. He's extremely dedicated that way, always has been. As a little boy, if we told him to snap peas or shuck corn, he would sit in the same spot without complaining for as long as it took. And I don't know if you saw our garden, but it's substantial. He'd be at it for hours at peak harvest times. Here, sweetie." She hands a saltshaker down the line to Pam.

"He is a hard worker, that's for sure," I fill the first small pause in the conversation, my eyes drifting to Tom as he talks animatedly with his dad and Jasper.

"He's a good boy. Pretty much a mother's dream. I mean, sure, he'd get into the normal hijinks around here: come home after curfew, get a tractor stuck in the ditch while playing chicken with friends—"

"Oh my."

Cami continues without missing a beat, her fork waving in the air as she illustrates her story. "But he's always had a strong moral compass. Those first few years in California, I think he let the fame get to his head. That was the first time I was really worried, but he pulled out of it, got back to the basics."

"What worried you?" I take a drink of lemonade, the perfect blend of tart and sweet tightening my cheeks.

"As a young man, all that attention inflated his ego. Dating supermodels, getting into any club he wanted, having tons of girls who were all sending him fan letters, photographs, marriage proposals—"

"Wow. That's a lot."

"Yeah, and just having his picture in every magazine and plastered on billboards. I mean, that's a lot for any person to handle, let alone a twenty-one-year-old man! But he grew out of it, started focusing his attention more on his career again rather than the glitz around it. I always told him and his sister, 'It doesn't matter what others think of you so much as what you think of yourself at the end of the day.' He just needed a simple reminder." She punctuates her declaration with a forkful of macaroni salad.

"That's good advice." I watch as she washes her food down with iced tea, then jumps back in.

"My own mother used to tell me that. Now I make sure to pass it on to everyone I think needs to hear it, though I'm sure you already have a good head on your shoulders. I bet you'll be just fine navigating the extra attention." She waves the air next to her, as if brushing off any floating concerns.

"What do you mean?" I freeze while bringing a scoop of potato salad up to my mouth, setting it back on the plate.

"Well, I just mean with how much you've been in the tabloids."

I blink. "In the tabloids?"

"You know, for the football game, and the tornado, and then just the random speculative articles with pictures of you and Tom. I wouldn't worry about it. They're always making up headlines for clickbait. I remember a story once saying that Tom was estranged from his sister. Couldn't be further from the truth. And then there was the story that said we threatened to disown him as a teenager when he moved to California."

"What are they saying now?"

"Who?" Cami looks at me, having forgotten what she was just talking about as she veers from topic to topic.

"The tabloids. What are they saying about me? About me and Tom?"

"Oh, just following the filming. There's been a few pictures of you two holding hands. One of you both swimming in the lake. I mean, I know you two have gotten close. Tom said you've become good friends, and he's always been an affectionate guy, just like his father. You know, when I first met Scott, I couldn't believe how sensitive he was. When he took me to the movie theater for our first date..."

She drones on and my mind is reeling with the notion that I could be featured in a tabloid. Sure, some peripheral notice while around Tom was to be expected, but by the way Camille is talking, I'm not just an anonymous figure in the background.

"Uh, excuse me, Cami. Is there a restroom nearby?" I ask, interrupting her story about how she found out she was pregnant with Tom's sister.

"Oh, of course! Just down on that end of the barn. Don't worry, it's a nice bathroom. We had it constructed a few years back when we decided to rent out this space for events."

"Thank you," I mumble as I get up from the table and make my way to the bathroom, my phone clutched tightly in my sweating palm. I need a moment to myself...and maybe a moment to see what the tabloids are reporting. I shut the door and lean against it, taking deep breaths in and out as I try to process the sheer amount of information which Cami Price has divulged in such a short amount of time.

Of course there would be stories out there. Tom is an A-list celebrity. Anyone he meets for lunch gets a photograph released within the hour. But it's even scarier now because I am romantically linked to him, and if it's discovered the tabloids are correct, then it's going to be like throwing chum to sharks. There are going to be people looking into my past and even trying to dictate my future. I blanch at the thought of them contacting Caleb for an interview. And would a reporter think to find my stepmom and stepsisters? I haven't spoken to them in years, and they weren't in contact with my dad, either. Surely they wouldn't be propositioned?

My mind is spiraling with all the consequences that could arise as I start typing in Tom's and my names. I should have been content to work my lame job and write books in my spare time. Why did I let Niya rope me into movie rights conversations? What made me think I could handle all this, that I deserve the attention of someone like Thomas Price? It's all going to blow up in my face, and unfortunately, I'm not going to be the only one impacted.

A search page of various news stories pops up on my phone screen just as persistent knocking makes the door vibrate against my back. I drop my phone on the floor while someone hollers, "Are you done in there? It's sort of an emergency."

I take a giant inhale, scoop up my phone, and open the door to see Leroy's eyes rolling dangerously. "Oh, thank God. Sorry, Logan, but I gotta go." He brushes past me, nearly slamming the door in my face, and I start walking dazedly back to my seat at the table. Before I can sit and start sneaking glances at my phone, Tom stands up, catching my eyes with a mischievous gleam.

"Hey, everyone. I know you've all been working so hard, and I'm impressed with how you've all been so flexible given the tight schedule, and the sudden storm—"

"That's our storm cowboy, right there!" Cole shouts and Tom

nods his head, politely fielding the playful taunt.

"Anyway, I'm impressed with this team and with all we've been able to accomplish so far. We still have a lot to do, but I really appreciate everyone's positive attitude and dedication. So I have a surprise for you. As my dad said, you're all considered family, but I know you all have family back home that you're missing. So I bought you all tickets to fly back to Los Angeles for the weekend. Then you'll return on Monday and we'll pick up where we left off with even more enthusiasm and energy for the final haul. Sound good?"

The crew instantly rises, applauding and rushing over to Tom to thank him, clapping him on the back. Pam and Dawson start typing on their phones, alerting friends and family of their plans. I hear Rene laugh about how she can't wait to surprise Benji.

"The plane leaves in three hours, so let's finish up lunch and start heading toward the airport." Tom extricates himself from the end of the table and makes his way toward me while everyone is bustling around excitedly.

"Hey," he says nonchalantly, brushing up against my shoulder as we both watch the happy chaos.

"This is really generous of you. What made you think of it?"

"Well, I think everyone needs a break, and I've heard moans of homesickness from the crew. Figured it wasn't fair for me to get some time at home if no one else does. Not to mention I'm a sucker for a grand gesture." He sends a wink my way, then looks back on the happy scene.

"Is it going to set us back in filming?" I turn to look at his profile, trying to curb the previous anxious thoughts that almost had me doomscrolling in the bathroom.

"Nah, we'll be fine. With the boost in morale, I think we'll actually be better for it." I tilt my head, drawing his attention as he turns to meet my gaze. "What?"

“If you’re sending everyone back to LA, where am I going?” I ask, my voice cautious as I do my best not to overstep or overthink.

He raises a brow and the side of his lip twitches as he reaches out to hook his pinky finger with mine. “You’re staying right here for the weekend. With me.”

I’m relieved—and terrified. I get to spend an entire weekend alone with Tom—well, with him and his family—but it’s certainly less human contact than we’ve experienced the past month as a group of fifteen. While I’m honored that Tom wants to be with me (not that he concocted this whole scheme just to be alone with me…no…certainly not), I also can’t help thinking that this is only going to add fuel to the fire that is already crackling among celebrity news outlets. And though we might be laying low, this might be the strike of the match that I’ve been trying to avoid.

Excerpt from *Iowa Nice*

WALCOTT

"I can't stand driving on interstates anymore. Everyone's so crazy," I complain as I pull into the massive parking lot of the Iowa 80 truck stop.

"Do you want me to drive?" my dad asks, groaning as he stretches his stiff joints.

"A world of no." We've gone over this multiple times. A main stipulation of this trip was that I would be the sole driver for many reasons: my car, his illness, my need to hold onto the one thing I can control and the one way I can protect him...but who's psychoanalyzing?

"What bothers you so much about interstate driving?"

"Well, the semi-trucks, for one. They act like they rule the road."

"They kind of do. The truckers make these runs several times. It's probably automatic for them. You can't fault them for wanting to get their job done quickly so they can get home."

"Yeah, but do they have to be such assholes?"

"You'd better keep that down. We're in their territory now," Dad announces as the automatic doors open, revealing the wide expanse of color, products, and amenities available in the world's largest truck stop. "I'm starving. What do you want?" he asks, leading me to the food court where multiple options of fast food await, complete with illuminated marquees and jaded cashiers.

"All of it looks like a promise of heartburn and nausea to me."

"Ah, the true marker of a good road trip."

I can't help but snort out a laugh. For some reason, this truck stop is bringing out an impish delight in my father, and I begin to soften, the white-knuckled tension of high-speed travel beginning to loosen its hold on me. We put in our orders—a Wendy's burger combo for Dad and an Einstein Bros. bagel sandwich for me—and we sit at one of the court tables, content to scan the store and people watch.

"Where to from here?" I ask, my arms steepled on the table in front of me.

"I don't know. I thought we would hang out here for today," he says while looking past me at the sliding doors where a constant stream of customers file in.

"What? Why?" This is news to me. We still have some planned destinations in the northeast, as well as the southeast corners of the state. A day at a truck stop was not on the itinerary.

"Well, there's lots to see. There's a showroom, a gift shop, and a museum across the parking lot. We don't have access to the drivers' amenities, but did you know they have a movie theater and workout room?" His enthusiasm begins to quell my prickling need for planning, and after picking up our orders, I dig into my sandwich and his motivation, too.

"Have you been here before?"

"Many times. When I was stationed at Rock Island, just east of

here, me and some of the boys would come here. Shop, eat, flirt. I used to think it would have been neat to be a truck driver, to spend my life on the road, see the country, hang out in truck stops, but…"

"But what?" I ask, seeing the gleam of reflective hindsight shimmering in his eyes.

"But I suppose I would have just been running." There's a grim set to his jaw as he struggles with regrets from a life near its ending.

"Dad, no offense, but I think you still ended up running," I say quietly, hoping the observation will be less accusatory if whispered.

He crosses his arms and leans back, contemplating my statement. "I suppose you're right. But today, I'd like to just stay still if that's okay."

I reach over and steal a fry. "That's okay, Dad."

"Then we can figure out where we're going from here." He sighs heavily as he does another scan of the store, soaking in his current surroundings, memories from the past, and fantasies of another life path.

18

That afternoon, Tom and I wave goodbye to our thirteen friends as they embark on a weekend journey home. As soon as we get back to our car, the other vehicles secured in long-term parking, Tom grabs my hand and holds it the entire trip back to the farm, a normally mundane action that feels like the best gift possible now that we are free from prying eyes. Tom even convinces me to shut off my phone, both of us agreeing to ignore the outside world for the rest of the day.

That evening, we sit in his parents' living room, curled up together on the couch, and visit with Cami and Scott while drinking wine and eating cheese, crackers, and fruit. Cami's eyes occasionally drift to our entangled hands, a fond smile dimpling her cheeks. Tom assured me they would be discreet, that they were loyal to him versus the paparazzi, and I relax into the couch, set at ease by stories of Tom's childhood, Cami's maternal musings, and Scott's farming fiascos.

Afterwards, Cami shows me to a guest bedroom with a four-poster queen bed, lavender walls, and a view of the back vegetable garden. Her lips turn up knowingly as Tom lingers by my side and we bid her goodnight. Then he leads me down the hall to his bedroom, stifling my wine-soaked giggles with silent kisses before we stumble into a shrine to his childhood.

"Uh, what is all this?"

"It's my bedroom." I scoff at Tom's simple answer, and he elaborates. "My mom never wanted to change it when I moved out. Said she always wanted me to have a place to come home and be myself."

"That's really sweet of her. She seems like a good mom."

"She's the best." He leans against the door jamb, arms crossed, watching me as I step farther inside. I slowly pan the room, soaking in the decor, pictures, and knick-knacks that scream teenage Tom. "I thought about updating, but just never got around to it. And now, the novelty of it, the timelessness is my favorite thing."

"It's better than your all-gray office," I tease, earning an amused snort from Tom as I take in every detail. White paneled walls are decked out in a hectic combination of posters, framed pictures of Iowa Hawkeye football, and memorabilia from the 90s and early 2000s. A bookcase of DVDs, books, Lego figurines, and die-cast cars sits in the corner next to a black bean bag chair that dares anyone over thirty to try to sit in it and manage to get out gracefully. I stop abruptly at the picture to the right of the door.

"You still have your ex-wife's picture in here!" I exclaim through my fingers, my hand placed lightly across my mouth in surprise.

"Well, yeah. As you said, she is a fox." He turns to look at the picture, his expression instantly turning from amused to concerned. "Why? Does it bother you?" Before I can answer, he reaches out and swipes the picture down, small rips of paper still stuck to the wall where the corners were adhered for years. "Gone."

I can't help but laugh at his eagerness to please me, and I reach out and graze his cheek with my hand, pulling it away despite his throaty protests as I continue my exploration of his room.

A closet with bifold doors is to my right, while a full-size bed is pushed against the left wall. The ceiling above slants down a bit toward the window, which looks out over the front of the house. It's too dark to see much outside, but I still walk over and peek out.

"What are you thinking?" Tom asks as he moves up behind me, his arms sliding around my waist and pulling me into his chest. He's closed the door, and I feel his body responding to mine as his hips press into the small of my back.

"I'm thinking you're never getting me in that bed as long as that blanket stays." We both swivel our heads to address the black comforter with Iowa Hawkeyes emblazoned across in gold lettering. Tom stares at the blanket, looks back at me, and then releases me to grab the bottom corners of the blanket, ripping it off the bed and throwing it to the other side of the room.

"Gone!" he announces, and I giggle at the flourish, falling into his embrace, my laughter reaching explosive levels as my eyes dip back to the bed.

"You have matching sheets!"

His eyes dart to the sheets as if he'd truly forgotten, then back to me. "You can get over it," he says, then covers my mouth with his.

I instantly respond, my tongue darting out to lick his lips, my body singing with his touch. Our legs are tangled as Tom stiffly leads me to the bed. "Okay," I concede. "Just this once."

"Don't worry, I'll make you forget all about the big bad Hawkeye sheets." His words tickle my lips and neck as he murmurs them into my skin. He guides me to the bed, his kisses traveling down my body, taking small detours along my collarbone, my rib cage, and my hip bone before reaching his destination between my thighs. I proceed to do what he says, forgetting everything except the pressure of his fingers on my skin, the softness of his hair in my grip, and the mind-numbing swipe of his tongue at my core.

After, we lay tangled in the dreaded sheets, Tom's head on my chest, his finger swirling lightly around my belly button.

"You have the deepest belly button I've ever seen. It's like a whirlpool, or a cave, or a portal to an underground world," he says, his fingers dipping lightly into the concave slope of my stomach. I giggle at both his teasing words and his tickling touch, his head bobbing up and down with the movement of my laughter. "Seriously, whoever cut your umbilical cord, I don't think they understood the assignment."

"That would have been my dad."

"Oh. Sorry. I'm sure he was a man of many other talents." He looks up to assess my mood, seemingly satisfied enough with my smile to return to his meditative stroking of my bare skin.

"Yeah, I suppose," I sigh, the words almost hidden in my exhale. This gets Tom's attention, and he rises and scoots up beside me, the absence of his body on top of mine leaving me instantly cold and yearning for him. The yearning is short-lived, as he drapes an arm across my chest and curls me toward him so we are lying on our sides looking at one another. His eyes are deep pools, the calm water pulling me in as his gaze caresses my face.

"Are you okay?"

"Of course! Why do you ask?"

"You just sound…sad, distant." His hand floats up to fiddle with my hair, his fingers weaving in and out of my messy blonde waves. "I don't mean to. I'm very happy…with you…with being here. I'm so glad we get this time together. It's just…" My words hit a wall and my eyes dip down to study our entwined hands.

"Tell me." He urges me on from my hesitation, and I oblige.

"Being here and seeing where you grew up, meeting your parents, it's all so charming, so quintessential, so…functional. It makes me a bit envious, that's all."

"I'm sorry."

"Don't be. I love that you have this. I love that I get to be a part of this, if only for the weekend. But it does make me wonder…what my life would have been like if my parents had stayed together…if my mom hadn't died…if my dad had wanted me."

The quiet hangs between us, Tom giving me time with the ghosts of my pasts, before he offers gently, "But he did in the end. Doesn't that make up for it, a little bit?"

I inhale, my lungs straining with the pull of oxygen, my chest aching with fuzzy memories and unobtained longings. "I guess."

"It's not like you have a bad life. I mean, look at you. You're a bestselling author, a burgeoning screenwriter, and you are currently enjoying naked time with a past recipient of *People* magazine's Sexiest Man Alive." His lips curl with a roguish flare, and I can't help but laugh.

"No, you're right. Life is good right now. But …"

"But what?" His hand reaches out to trace the corner of my mouth, my lips sensitive to his touch.

"I could have avoided so many mistakes, so many wasted years of aimless wandering, of not having the confidence to speak up and take what I want."

"And what do you want?"

My throat hums as I consider. "Well, I want this movie to do well. I want to have a consistent way of supporting myself by writing. I want you, of course—"

"You have me." He grabs my hand and brings it to his lips, kissing my knuckles.

"For now." My eyes glaze over as I take a moment to consider everything my life has turned out to be and all the wrong turns, bad choices, and stumbles that I've experienced along the way. My next words are wary, gentle in their footing as they've never journeyed past my lips. "I guess what I really want is freedom. Freedom from my constant doubts, freedom from my regrets, freedom from always feeling so…displaced."

We let my admission of pain linger in the tight space between our bodies until Tom finally speaks, his voice pulling me back into the protection of our bubble. "Instead of looking for that freedom in the past, look for it in the future. Even if you made mistakes, they brought you to this point, made you who you are…and I really like that person."

I match his gaze and try to soak in his words of wisdom, affection, and acceptance. He makes it sound so easy to move forward, to forget, to ease into a new life, but I'm still moored to the pier of my past, straining against the restraints, still unable to break the ties. I know I won't break free tonight, but as I look at Tom and feel his soft touch on my bare skin, it becomes easier to imagine that there's a possibility, a hint of release on the horizon. For now, that's enough to keep me grasping for what's in front of me, and I do just that as I place both hands on Tom's face and bring his lips to mine in a kiss that fuzzies my brain and calms my soul. He matches my energy willingly, pulling me against him, our bodies pressed tightly together until it's impossible to know where I end and he begins. At this moment, we are together, interwoven, one. And, at this moment, that is all I need.

***

The angry toss of gravel and insistent squeal of tires send me shooting upward, Tom merely stirring next to me, tremors of annoyance dancing across his muscled back. It takes a moment for me to remember where I am, a month of hotel wakings creating a precarious center of gravity each morning. The sight of Tom's teenage haven comes into focus, and I'm comforted by the grounding of an actual home rather than the slew of generic rooms to which I've grown accustomed. My head drops back onto the pillow and I close my eyes in an attempt to fall back asleep, but a consecutive slamming of car doors reminds me of the initial impetus for waking.

I do my best to extricate myself from bed without disturbing Tom, but the mattress is only full-size with our bodies clumped together, and he ends up rolling over and groaning as I hover above him. He instantly reaches out and grabs my hips, dropping me onto his lap, my squirming protests only making his drowsy smile spread more widely across his face.

"Let me go, just for a minute. I need to look outside."

"Why do you need to look outside? There's nothing for you outside. Stay in bed—with me." He arches up against me, his morning arousal tempting in its promise, but my curiosity wins out. I playfully yank his hands off my hips and hop off his lap, scrambling out of bed and over to the window.

"A car just pulled in. Are we expecting anyone today?"

Tom yawns and lifts his arms in a full-body stretch, his words distorted as he answers, "No, I don't think so." He places his arms under his head, watching me from his reclined position. "It wouldn't be my sister and brother-in-law. They took the kids to the Dells this weekend. Do you think it's a reporter? If so, we can kick them out. It is private property after all."

"No," I hold out the syllable as I peer through the window. "I don't think it's a reporter." My ears perk up as I hear banging on the front door followed by repeated uses of the doorbell.

Tom sits up and starts looking for clothes. "What time is it?" He asks while pulling on boxers.

"I don't know. We don't have our phones." I start looking around for my own clothing, disappointed when I realize my bag is in the guest bedroom. "What if they wake your parents? Do I need to hide or run down to the other bedroom?"

Tom breaks the hurried tension in the room by catching my gaze and soberly stating, "Logan, I'm thirty-six years old. I don't think we need to hide."

"Oh…yeah." The knocking and ringing continue, and Tom rushes out of his room. "Let's see if we can get to the door before whoever it is wakes up the whole damn house."

I follow Tom through the hallway and down the stairs, still not familiar with the layout of the house, and he almost throws the front door open, the force of his grip intensified by our mad dash downstairs.

"It's about goddamn time!" Landon hollers in lieu of a greeting, his arms spread wide with dramatic fervor as he marches in, squeezing between the two of us. But my shocked silence is more the result of seeing Niya following in his wake, her arms crossed, shoulders pushed back in tense irritation. She wears a navy-blue suit, the skirt slightly crumpled from travel, while Landon is in a white collared shirt paired with chinos and blinding white sneakers. They both turn on their heels to stand in the entryway, fiery glares sizing us up as Tom and I hover near the door.

"What are you doing here?" I manage to mumble at Niya, her dark-brown eyes glittering with a cold stare. But it's Landon who answers, loud enough for every living thing on the farm to hear.

"We've both been trying to get a hold of you since yesterday afternoon! Why the fuck haven't you been answering your phones?"

Tom steps forward to match Landon, his stance strong, yet on guard. "We turned our phones off so we could get some peace and quiet after we dropped everyone off at the airport. I don't see why the panic."

Landon and Niya look at each other with pointed gazes. The familiarity there piques my curiosity, but I'm not able to entertain speculation for long as Landon continues.

"The airport! That brings me to reason number one for our impromptu visit—"

"There're multiple reasons?" Tom asks, but Landon blows right past the interjection with his own question.

"Why the hell would you stop production for a weekend and not tell me? Do you have any idea how this impacts the film's budget?"

Tom's shoulders drop with the realization of his manager's main concern, and he sighs. "It won't, Landon. I personally paid for the tickets, and it's only for two days. The crew needed the break, needed to see their families, especially after the storm the other day."

"Reason number two!" Landon's declaration punches the air. "Why in God's name did you not call me after you survived a fucking tornado! I only got wind of the story when it was picked up by the Associated Press. You've got to tell me when these things happen!"

"Okay, Landon, next time I ride out a tornado in a storm drain, you'll be the first to know. Anyway, we're fine. I'm sorry I forgot to tell you. I got distracted by cleanup and schedule changes and other things." Tom's eyes blatantly flit to mine and my breath instantly stops. Niya narrows her eyes, then turns her attention to Landon who continues watching us as he holds up three fingers.

"Reason number three: you two." His hand sweeps the air between us. "You know you haven't been discreet, right? Everyone is talking about your on-set flirting and late-night hookups. Not to mention all the social media photos and the video that's gone viral."

"What video?" I find my voice, and it quavers with the fear of more attention.

"The one of you singing on top of a bar and being caught in Tom's arms." Landon's accusation steals my breath and I struggle to reply.

"How did a video get out?" I finally manage to stammer.

"That's how phones work, sweetheart. People take pictures and videos and post them online."

"Don't talk to her like that, Landon," Tom bristles, stepping slightly forward to block me from his mockery. "I don't know where the pictures would come from. Sure, we've been spending a lot of time together this month, but it didn't become more until recently." He gulps and looks at me apologetically. I just shrug. There's no use in denying it now.

"You know as well as I do that hand-holding is a criminal offense in your world. You might as well have just marked her with a scarlet *T* claiming her as your property."

"Hey!"

"Landon—"

"Anyway, the stories have really been pumping out since you sent the entire cast and crew home for a weekend minus your script supervisor. Word got out that she was still with you at the airport, and now a bunch of paparazzi have gathered in town to try and get a glimpse of you." His earlier anger has seemed to ease, but his words still have a warning bite to them.

"Okay, this all sounds easily manageable. Definitely not life-shattering news. So what if Logan and I are together? We're both single adults." Tom drapes an arm across my shoulder, bringing me into his side. My body is stiff, unable to melt into him, and he turns to look at me, concern etched across his face.

"Therein lies the problem," Niya takes a step forward, her hands on her hips, a pointed look waiting for me to jump in and explain.

Tom looks between the three of us, trying to sort through their knowing looks and my own frozen visage. "What are they talking about, Logan?"

The words are stuck in my throat, razor edges clinging to the soft tissue as I try to rip them up and out of my body. I can almost taste blood as they drag through my flesh and pierce the silence. "I'm not single…technically."

My confession hangs in the air until Landon interrupts with a flat, "And that brings us to reason number four."

***

"How was the divorce never finalized? You haven't been with him for, what, five years? And why did you never tell *me*?" Niya asks from across the kitchen table, the hurt in her voice slicing my heart. Niya is never hurt. In fact, Niya is known for her inability to feel any human emotions, but here she is, her eyes pleading and her mouth set in a grim line, dangerously close to a pout. I think I broke Niya.

"Your assets have undoubtedly increased since your separation: your book sales, the movie rights, your work contracts. That could be a messy deal to broker during divorce proceedings," Landon chimes in.

"Well, you need to make an official statement. Especially if this thing between you and Tom is serious. God forbid the press seeks out your ex and asks for his statement," Niya adds, smoothly picking up her half as part of this quickfire duo of crisis navigation.

My heart starts beating rapidly. "You don't think they would do that, do you? I mean, I'm nobody. Sure, I sold some books, but no one cares about me."

"Of course they do, Logan. Your life story is going to be a movie. The character in the movie is you. Your name is plastered on everything," Niya refutes, and my stomach flips.

"Then we'll change the name. It's not too late, right? Can't we have Phil and Megan dub over their lines?" My request is quickly reaching begging status, and I look to Tom who has so far kept quiet from his seat directly across from me. His lips are pulled thin, his hands drumming nervously on the table. He looks away from me just as Landon jumps in to answer.

"That would look even more suspicious. And even if no one cares about you, lots of people care about Thomas Price, making this a PR problem for the both of you."

I go to respond, but my mouth opens without a sound. Instead, I exhale loudly and raise my hands in defeat.

Landon sees my weakness and hits me with the knockout punch. "No, the only way to deal with this is to address it head-on. And you're going to need to talk to your ex."

I drop my head in my hands, wishing I could ignore the problem away just as I've done for the past five years. But apparently, my happy isolation with Tom was destined to be short-lived and now I need to be an adult and clean up my business.

Niya continues attacking the task-at-hand as she barks out directions. "Logan, I can drive you to Ottumwa. We can get this sorted out today. Why don't you get dressed and meet me at the car in thirty—"

"Can I speak with Logan alone, please?" Tom finally speaks, and a hush falls over the table. I lift my head and make eye contact with him, happy to finally hear his voice after his consuming silence since learning that I'm still married. Niya and Landon exchange a brief look and then both rise from their chairs and retreat to the living room. We hear the front door shut, and I assume they've decided to hang out on the front porch with Tom's parents who made coffee for all of us in the awkward silence immediately following the reveal of my dirty laundry before taking their own cups outside.

Once alone, I expect Tom to shout at me, punish me with his words, but instead, he stands up and starts pacing the length of the room. "Why didn't you tell me?"

"I just…it didn't come up…and this is all so new…we really

haven't had much time to…" I fumble with my words, trying my best to drum up the best excuses.

"We've had tons of time, Logan. Even before we slept together, we talked. A lot. We're friends. I just don't understand why you would have lied to me about this." He runs his hand down his face as he continues to pace.

I stand up and move into his path. "Tom, I haven't thought of myself as married in a long time. When I left Caleb, I wasn't in my right mind. I didn't know for sure if I was going back. And then I just didn't. He didn't call. I didn't call. It just…ended. Honestly, the legal proceedings were just an oversight."

"But they're not just an oversight. They're necessary. Without them, you're legally married. And this…between us…becomes much more complicated." He stares at me, his voice small as he asks, "Did you never go through with it because you still want to be married to him?"

I rush to explain. "Absolutely not. I'm completely over Caleb. I haven't even spoken to him in five years! As I said, I just became so absorbed in my writing, in trying to build a new life that I completely forgot we never signed any papers."

"And do you want to be with me? Is this something that you want to pursue further?" He gestures between the two of us, his hand landing on his chest as he unwittingly clenches at his heart.

I reach out and grab his hand in both of mine, moving closer so our fists are pressed between our bodies. "Of course I do. I want you, and I'm so, so sorry that I've gotten you into this mess."

He tilts his gaze to the side, as if considering my words, before turning back and looking into my eyes. "Would you be willing to sign divorce papers if we could get them procured and ready by tomorrow?"

"Uh…yes. Of course." I'm caught off guard by the swiftness of his plan, but I want to take action to show him that I'm in this.

"Okay. Well, it just so happens I know a guy." A small quirk of the lips signals a turn in tone, a lessening of tension, and I exhale my held breath.

"You're not mad at me?"

He reaches up to cup my head, smoothing the wild strands of my unbrushed hair. "Well, I'm not overly enthused, but I don't think you meant to hide this from me maliciously. Luckily, it's easy to fix."

"What about all the PR stuff Landon was talking about?"

Both his hands release my head to grip my shoulders, his fingers massaging my back. Seamlessly, he's become the one reassuring me. "Honestly, I don't give a shit about that. Most people won't believe it anyway. Half the stuff they write about me is usually made up. And even if they do believe it, any publicity is good publicity, right?" His smile is still strained, but I can tell he wants me to be okay with this, wants me to move forward with him. I want to do so as well, but the dirt has been stirred up, and it's getting more difficult to see through the dusty cloud of my past decisions.

"I'm not so sure in this case."

"Logan, don't worry about it. I'll have Landon reach out to my lawyers, we'll get the papers ready, then you and I can drive down to Ottumwa tomorrow. You'll have to call your ex and make sure he can meet, though."

I search his face as I imagine contacting Caleb, owning up to the injuries of our marriage, pleading for a clean break. The thought makes me feel hollow and weak. "You don't want to wait until we're down there for filming?"

"No, I'd rather handle this on our own, without thirteen other people milling about."

"I guess that's valid." Tom has already decided, and if I want any chance of keeping him, I'm going to need to be brave and confront the skeletons in my closet. I just hope they don't all come spilling out.

"Hey, we'll fix this. Now any other deep, dark secrets that you need to tell me?" His eyes glint playfully, but my own widen at his words.

"Well …" I start to say, but Tom places a finger on my lips, cutting me off.

"If so, please tell me later. I can only handle one scandal at a time." Shame colors my cheeks and I look down, but Tom lifts my chin and looks into my eyes. "Do not let this ruin our day. In fact, I'm making a rule. Once I tell Landon and Niya the plan, you and I are done talking about this for at least today. I have other plans for us. Can you give me this one day?"

I nod and let him place a hurried kiss on my mouth before he strides out of the room and to the porch. My legs feel wobbly, unable to hold me up, and I pull out a chair and collapse into it, my lips trembling as my eyes tear up.

That could have gone so many ways, but instead, I emerged unscathed and still wanted. It's an unknown feeling, to be cared for despite my flaws. Unfortunately, it leaves me feeling even more worried about losing it all as I realize losing this, even with how new it is, could easily destroy me.

Additional Script Scene for *Iowa Nice: Working Title*

INT. DIVE BAR - NIGHT

LOGAN sits at the bar of a moderately busy pub in Mount Pleasant. She has a drink in front of her but spends more time twirling the glass than actually drinking from it, preoccupied with the fight she just had with her father.

A handsome stranger TOM walks up to the bar and signals to the bartender for another drink. He notices Logan next to him.

TOM

In my world, what you're doing is called drink neglect. I could have you arrested.

LOGAN

Are you a cop?

TOM

No. It would be a citizen's arrest.

LOGAN

Charming.

TOM

Usually. You seem to be immune to my wiles.

LOGAN

Sorry. It's tough to charm me these days.

TOM

Oh yeah? Want to talk about it?

Tom takes a seat at the bar, pays for his drink, and angles himself toward Logan. She turns toward him, realizing he is not going away.

LOGAN

Sure. How far back should I go?

TOM

I'm in no hurry.

LOGAN

Okay. Well, buckle up. So my mom and dad divorce when I'm five, Mom and I move back to Iowa while my dad stays on the east coast where he marries a woman with two daughters, dragging me out there for the occasional awkward summer. He eventually divorces around the same time my mom dies of cancer. I refuse to change schools my senior year of high school, he gets pissed, I marry a musician, a struggling musician that is, and all of this results in my dad and me not talking for nearly ten years. Then, while my marriage is in shambles, my now-dying dad calls me, asking to go on a statewide trip so we can bond and build memories before he finally kicks the bucket. Today, we got into an argument about his estate and how I don't want to clean up his mess. Makes me feel like that's the only reason he reached out to me. Now logically, I know that's not the case, but years of abandonment and insecurity have made suspicion a knee-jerk reaction of mine. So now, I'm sitting here, knowing I can't drink too much because I have to drive tomorrow while my dad sleeps in our hotel room down the block. You up to speed?

TOM

Yeah, I think so. So you're single?

LOGAN

(laughing despite herself)

Yes, I am.

TOM

Can I buy you a fresh drink and then maybe we can make out in the parking lot?

LOGAN

(raises her drink in cheers)

Sounds like a solid plan.

19

With the increased number of reporters around the Iowa City metro, Tom adapts his plans to remain on the property. He sticks to his word, transferring the burden of my impending divorce onto Landon, who immediately disappears to bark orders into his phone after dropping off his bag in the second guest bedroom.

"Niya, I'm so sorry, but Landon took the last bedroom. I could ask Tom to use a couch or bunk with—" Cami struggles to find a solution while we stand in the upstairs hallway.

I quickly interrupt. "She can stay with me in the other guest bedroom. I don't mind." Niya cocks her head inquisitively, and I answer with a soft shoulder bump. Though Tom and I aren't keeping our relationship a secret, I still don't want Cami explicitly knowing that I'm shacking up with her son just down the hallway. Cami leaves Niya and me to freshen up, and I start rifling through my bag, locating an outfit before I hop in the shower.

"I'm assuming I have the bed to myself tonight?" Niya leans her hip against the headboard, her arms crossed. This may be the first time I have ever seen her in a relaxed position.

"I mean, I hope so. Tom doesn't seem too keen on kicking me out of his life—or his bed—just yet. Which pretty much makes him a saint in my book."

"Yeah. I have to admit, I'm impressed." Niya sits on the mattress, her arms reaching behind her to brace her seat.

"Impressed? That I lied to everyone about my marriage?"

"Okay, not about that in particular. More that you have it in you to lie. And that you bagged Thomas Price. My God, Logan, I always took you for a meek goody-goody."

"Niya! That's not nice."

"I never claimed I was." She shrugs as if discussing a mild change in the weather. "But seriously, you need to be forthright with me from now on, at least when it pertains to your career. I don't care if you lie about the personal stuff, unless it impacts me. Got it?"

I freeze and go to open my mouth, feeling the force of honesty start to rise within my throat. But before I can utter a syllable, Tom and Landon appear in the doorway.

"All taken care of. Landon has the papers being delivered today, then you and I will head to Ottumwa first thing tomorrow morning." I meet Tom's nod with my own and his face brightens. "Well, now that that's all sorted out, let's get out there and meet the day! Ladies, get your comfy shoes on. We're going for a hike!"

"Really?" Niya raises an eyebrow as she glares at Tom and his overflowing enthusiasm.

Tom rushes in, thrusting bags at us in an effort to get us moving. "Really. All of us. It's a team-bonding experience. Oh, and my parents are going to join. And the dogs, of course." He looks at me, a sheepish grin warming the iciness coursing through my nerves. It's hard to stay frustrated at a man so personable, enthusiastic, and forgiving. Every day I find myself falling for him even more deeply, so much so that I am actually looking forward to a hike with our business counterparts and his parents.

He claps at our static movement, urging us to action, and we all follow orders. We're in his house, he's solved the majority of this morning's problems, and now we must humor him with forced acquiescence. The fact that I would follow him willingly is both encouraging and alarming.

***

Tom sits on the end of his bed, rubbing my bare feet as I stretch out, moaning with the pressure of his fingers kneading my sore soles.

"If you want me to continue massaging your feet, you'd better stop making those sounds." Tom tilts his head to look up at me, a sly smile curving the corner of his lips. His hike ended up taking us on a four-hour jaunt through the surrounding fields and forests. Niya was surprisingly capable (not that I should be surprised, she's capable at everything she does), but Landon and I were definitely the weak links, Landon's suede shoes unable to find traction on the loose dirt and my legs just unwilling to do their job and carry me forward during the last and longest hour.

"I'm not extremely out of shape, I promise you. I do exercise. But it's the combination of terrain, weather, and bugs that does me in." I squeeze my eyes shut and wince as he presses a circle into a particularly sensitive spot.

"So it's the being outdoors part?"

"Essentially, yes."

He sets my foot down gently, then crawls up the mattress to sprawl out next to me, pulling me by my hips and turning me so we are face-to-face on our sides. He trails the tip of his nose along mine before angling his head and capturing my mouth in a tender kiss that sends rejuvenating tingles down to my toes. Even after breaking the kiss, he remains close, and I study the sweep of his lashes, the crease of his forehead, the arch of his hairline. All the tiny intimate details one can only notice when pressed tight and given time to meander, learn, and memorize them.

"Did you not like our day today? I wanted to do more, take you into the city, but obviously plans changed." My heart blooms at the anxiousness hanging on the edge of his initial question. It was actually a lovely day, filled with heartwarming exhibitions of Tom's love for his parents, impressive examples of Tom's patience with Landon, and no lack of physical affection between the two of us. Landon and Niya seemed to bond over their shared cynicism regarding romantic relationships, and I swear Niya's eyerolls became less dramatic as she began waiting for Landon's own snarky responses to what she deemed our "disgusting and cliched displays of human affection."

Their taunting didn't cause Tom to waver, and it's easy to see where he picked up his penchant for touch; Scott and Cami held hands the entire hike and were always finding ways to connect physically during the rest of the day, which included a lazy afternoon movie, a group effort tackling a spaghetti dinner, and an epic board game night. At first, I felt like I was intruding on their love story, not used to seeing such a devoted couple, but then I found myself smiling at their cute exchange of pet names, at the familiar choreography as they maneuvered around each other. Tom caught me staring at them during a cutthroat round of Sorry! and later asked if it bothered me, his parents' demonstration of their unwavering attraction toward one another. I answered, "I find it beautiful, but rare. Is it really possible to love someone that much for that long?" Instead of responding, Tom started rubbing my feet, and all doubtful thoughts evaporated from my brain.

Now, as Tom's gaze sears into my own, I answer with as much honesty as I've ever uttered. "It was an amazing day—because I got to spend it with you."

I'm rewarded with another kiss, Tom's teeth lightly tugging at my bottom lip as his hands explore the curve of my back and hips, landing on the punished muscles of my glutes. I moan at the pressure of his fingers, and he smiles against my mouth. "You want me to massage your ass, too?"

A laugh bubbles out of me, becoming frantic as Tom starts to dig in, his touch turning ticklish. After I threaten to scream, pushing him away with my hands pressed firmly against his chest, he finally relents and sits up against his wooden headboard. Still wary of his true intentions, I turn myself so my head is at the end of the bed, my legs stretched out next to him. His hand goes idly to my calf where he continues caressing my skin, always touching, always soothing.

"How are you feeling about tomorrow?"

I look up at the ceiling as I answer. "Oh, nervous to talk to Caleb. Bad that I have to put you through this. And scared."

"What are you scared of?"

"Losing everything. Losing you." I bring my gaze back to his after I admit this, his own eyes full of concern.

"Logan, what made you so afraid to want more for yourself?"

I swallow a lump in my throat as I dredge up the painful memories I've worked so hard to keep down. The only way I am able to even imagine talking about this is due to the pressure of Tom's hand on my leg, his anchoring my body while my mind drifts to darker times. My voice is a scratchy croak as I begin to speak, but I still manage to push the words out. "Not everything in the book is true."

"Well, I'm sure you had to take some creative liberty with your recollections."

I'm parched, my throat threatening to close as I dabble with speaking the truth. "Yeah, it's kind of like that."

"Don't believe everything you read, didn't I say that?" Tom

gives me a small smile of encouragement. "What are you wanting to tell me, Logan?"

"Well, for one thing. My dad never knew the real reason Caleb and I got married, and I didn't want to include it in the book."

"And what was that?"

"I got pregnant."

Tom continues to rub my shin, giving only a calm "Okay" as I look back to the ceiling, hoping the act of confessing my secrets to the sky will make them a little less stabbing, a little less real.

"Obviously, it was unplanned. We weren't even technically still together when it happened. I cried when I found out; I thought my future was ruined. Caleb told me it was my choice what to do, but I decided I wanted to keep it, so he stepped up and proposed. That's the real reason I transferred out of Iowa State. The plan was we would continue going to school and working on music while living in Caleb's mom's basement. She was going to help us with the baby." My voice catches on the last word, a fact not lost on Tom as he squeezes my calf. "We got married at the courthouse. I didn't want a wedding. My mom was gone, my relationship with my dad was tenuous, so we just went and did it. I called my dad a week later, told him we were married, but before I could tell him about the pregnancy, he blew up. Told me I was an immature child, that it was just another way for me to punish him after my mom's death. He said it was never going to last, that getting married so young was a huge mistake and I should have learned from him and Mom.

"The most hurtful part was that I felt like he was saying I was a mistake, that the baby I was carrying was a mistake. But even then, I stayed on the phone as he lectured and chastised me. Right before he hung up, he told me to call him when I came to my senses and got a divorce. He hadn't even met Caleb, didn't even know his son-in-law…the father of my baby. And yet, he was already condemning us. Five days later, I lost the baby."

I take a deep breath through my nose, willing myself to get through this disclosure. If I can do this, any other reveal should be less trying.

"I was ten weeks along when I miscarried, had already seen the baby in the ultrasound, had heard the heartbeat…I'd already fallen in love.

"It wasn't my dad's fault obviously, but at the time, I blamed him. Sure, the pregnancy had been an accident, but in the end, I wanted that baby, had already fantasized about holding him…or her. I felt like the miscarriage was proving my dad right, that I had made a mistake and was stuck. So I fought back by leaning further into marriage and my idea of motherhood. Caleb convinced me that we should wait until we graduated, and he was right, of course, but I resented him for it. After the miscarriage, I worried that I would never be able to get pregnant again. Waiting to try again felt like letting the train leave the station, my future traveling far away from me. And when we did start trying, right after graduation as promised, my fears came true. I'd gotten pregnant so easily the first time, without even trying, but when we were actually intentional about it, it wasn't happening. It took me almost two years to get pregnant a second time, then I miscarried at six weeks. Then another year with a miscarriage at seven weeks. Finally, I made it to the second trimester with the fourth pregnancy, but…well, the last one was pretty traumatic. It left me with some scarring and an official proclamation that I may never be able to get pregnant again or carry a child to term."

I bite the inside of my cheek and take another cleansing breath.

"I can't say if Caleb and I would have broken up anyway, but the years of infertility and failed pregnancies killed the joy of our relationship. By the end, I think it was less painful for both of us to just move on. So I left, moved to Des Moines, found a job, and focused on my writing. I'd always been a good writer in school, had even composed some songs with Caleb, but when I started writing longer works as a way to process all of my feelings, I began to wonder if I could actually create something others would want to read. I began to hope for more. So I started submitting my work to publishing contests, on Reddit, to literary agents. I was just so desperate to be seen, to be valued, to be good at something after having failed at so much else in life."

"Logan—" Tom, who's been quiet the entire time, watching me with sorrowful eyes, finally goes to speak, but I put my hands up.

"I'm telling you this not because I want you to feel sorry for me, but because I want you to understand why it's so hard for me to let go, to want things. Everything and everyone I've ever wanted has been ripped away from me, so I found it easier to stop wanting."

Instead of speaking, he holds his arms open, and I scramble up the bed, sinking into his hug, my face pressed against his chest. When he does speak, it's a soft rumble beneath my ear. "Didn't you want to be a published author, to make your story into a movie?"

"I never wanted that, not initially. Niya pushed for all of that. And I suppose I owe her, because that put me on the trajectory to meeting you and starting to want things again, starting to believe I deserved to want things again."

I pull my head up so I can look at him. His hand goes to cup my cheek as he asks, "What makes you think you could lose me?"

"Because. I want you so much, it's inevitable that I'll lose you, too. That's just how life goes for me. You see, I don't get happy endings. I have to make them up…in my writing. That's the only way." His thumb comes up to brush away a singular tear I didn't even know was there. He tilts my head down and kisses my forehead, his lips lingering on my skin. There's so much more I could tell him, that I should tell him. "Tom, I have—"

He silences me by bringing his mouth to mine. My lips tremble as we both sigh into the kiss, my mouth opening to allow his tongue to dart in and slide against the length of my own. I accept the gift of his touch as a distraction from my haunted thoughts, and I crawl on top of him as he places his hands firmly on my body. My skin sings with desire, itching beneath the veil of my clothing, begging to be free. I lift my shirt off and unclasp my bra, delighted by Tom's blown pupils as he gazes at my bared breasts. He takes one in his hand and bends down, capturing my nipple between his teeth. I flinch with the pleasure, the pain, and arch backward giving him full access to roam.

My hands blindly scramble for the hem of his shirt as I unburden him from the yoke of fabric. My fingers dance across the lines of his abs, tickle the hair below his navel before dipping beneath his waistband and enveloping him in my grip.

He gasps against my lips and utters, "God, I want you so much." His words undo me, and I begin moving, my hips beginning to rock with the pumping of my hand. Before he loses all control, he stops me, gently pulling my hand away, then lifting me up by my hips. I move to one side of his body, able to slide my shorts and underwear down my leg, before returning to my post, straddling him as he shimmies his own clothing down his hips.

I reach down once again to position him against me. We've had the discussion about birth control and STIs, both of us clean and protected, and the bare feel of him sliding into me sends tremors through my body.

As I move on top of him, his hands digging into my hips and thighs, I forget about the loss, forget about the hurt. All I see is a man who cares for me, wants me, has proven he will be there for me. We continue to move, our rhythm quickening, accompanied by his murmurings of lust and adoration and my own sounds of pleasure. We climax together, my body arching away, but his hands bring me back to smother my peaking cries with his mouth. We stay there, our sweat-flecked bodies clinging together, unable to move from the trembling force of our physical crescendo. We look into each other's eyes as our heartbeats slow and our breathing deepens, the pattern of our bodies syncing up, harmonizing, as the symphony of our love-making softens.

At this moment, all I see is him, all I feel is him. But as is the case in real life, this moment will end. Sleep will arrive—and then, a new day: a day of moments, possible revelations, and the potential to lose all future moments with him.

Excerpt from *Iowa Nice*

ELDON

"Why are you so crabby?"

My eyes widen and my nostrils flare as my dad accuses me of being anything other than bright, shiny, and amenable while hauling him across the state of Iowa. "I'm not crabby. I'm just…on edge."

"Why?" He throws the single-word question over his shoulder as he continues walking up the short path to the American Gothic House. Robust rows of wildflowers line the sidewalk in an array of orange, yellow, and white speckles against the green span of the lawn.

"Can't I just be on edge? Does there have to be a specific reason?" The fact that I'm trailing behind him should be enough of a sign, whether of his good mood or my not-so-good mood is unclear. Dad has become increasingly winded on our journeys, and I've found myself having to feign needed breaks to accommodate both his physical constraints and stubbornness. But since reaching the eastern side of the state, he's gained a skip in his step, a boost in energy and

positivity that should make me happy but instead is only dragging my own wary countenance down further.

"There's always a reason." He stops on the pebbled circle on the lawn in front of the modest white house, hands on his hips as he absorbs its details. The American Gothic House, iconic for being the background feature in Grant Wood's American Gothic *painting, is probably one of the most recognized subjects of American art. The pointed arch of the large Gothic window on the second story adds a flair of sophistication to the otherwise plain farmhouse from the late nineteenth century. It's like a monkey wearing a fancy hat; the novelty drew the eye of an observant artist and brought a source of life and fame to this small rural town. I've seen the house numerous times, have been to the visitor center, and taken the touristy pictures next to the concrete figures from the painting. This is not a roadside attraction for me. No, this is home. But not the home that welcomes one with open arms, a plate of cookies, and a warm bed. This home barely acknowledges me, sends me a stiff nod, tells me there's food in the refrigerator, and leaves me to find a clean set of sheets by myself and make up the couch.*

"Dad, why are we here? You've been here before. I've been here before. This was not a necessary stop." I plop down on the bench surrounding the paved viewing circle. I've sat on more benches the past few weeks than I've sat on my whole life, and my lip curls downward at the realization that I will have to get up soon enough.

He points at me, exclaiming as if he's made a long-sought-out discovery. "See! You are crabby! I knew it."

I throw my hands up, surrendering in hopes that we can move on. "Fine! I'm crabby. This is a tough place for me to be, Dad. There's too many memories here, too many reminders of Mom, my childhood, my marriage. It's painful to be here."

He comes to sit down beside me, lowering himself slowly enough to give away his still-weakened status. "You know, painful memories are just as valid, just as important as fond memories. In fact, I would say they are more important. They fuel us, teach us, leave an impression far more lasting than any good memory. Tell me, what have you learned from a good experience?"

I squint at my dad, trying to meet the challenge with furrowed brow as I sift through the storage cabinets of my psyche. It's hard to pinpoint specific instances, and even more difficult to identify any corresponding lessons.

"You're having trouble, aren't you? Now what about bad experiences? What have you learned?"

My mind sifts through memories of car mishaps and blown-out tires, high school parties busted by the cops, misguided crushes and broken hearts, hospital visits for Mom's treatments and the aftermath of those failed treatments. "Lots. I've learned lots." My tone indicates my disinterest in relaying any specific examples.

He settles into the back of the bench, draping his arm behind me and sighs. "Yeah, I've learned lots from my mistakes, too."

"Who says I was only thinking of mistakes I've made?"

"I didn't. But I figured some of your bad experiences were because of mistakes that I made."

"Oh." I'm surprised by his willingness to claim responsibility, but if this trip has shown me anything, it's that people are capable of change, even if it isn't at the most convenient time. Spurred by his apparent proximity with full-blown honesty, a thought strikes me, and I turn to look at my dad's profile. He seems settled in this moment, at peace, and I almost resist asking, afraid to disrupt his pleasant respite. But in the end, curiosity beats out conscientiousness. "Hey Dad, why exactly did you ask me on this trip? I've been trying to pinpoint the locations, to make sense of the road map you've chosen, but I can't. It's nonsensical. At least in my own head. Care to tell me

the sense it makes in yours?"

He bites a corner of his lip, his gaze trained on the tree-lined street ahead of us. I worry I've lost him, whether to deep thought or insult, but then his words pierce the silence, mingling with the outside ambience of birds, locusts, and breeze. "You know, this trip may have started out as being for me, something for me to accomplish before I die, a checklist to cross off…but it's become more than that. And I've realized it's for you. Something you can remember when I'm gone, something to cherish and cling to, the good and the bad."

I go to interject, to add in some careless additive to lighten the heaviness, but he holds up his hand, halting my intrusion. I close my mouth and continue to listen as he angles himself toward me. "This is the state in which we both were born. It's in your DNA just as much as I am. It's made you into the person you are today, probably more than I have, and I think it's important to acknowledge when something or someone has impacted you on such an intrinsic level.

"I know I've messed up, and I know we wasted years, but this is something you will always have, even after I'm gone: our home state and the memories we made exploring its hidden treasures. But what I want you to know, what I need you to know, is that for me, the biggest treasure is you. The most important item on my checklist, the biggest accomplishment. It's always been about you, Logie Bear. Even when I didn't realize it, my life has always been about you. I just wish I'd figured it out sooner."

I'm frozen in place, my eyes wide as they pool with the blur of unshed tears. I've waited so long to feel seen, to feel valued by my father. Now that it's happened, I don't know how to respond.

Instead of ruining the moment with impulsive words or defensive snark, I twist around to lift my dad's hand from the back of the bench, and grasp it with my own, settling our joined hands in my lap.

"Thank you," I say, and we continue sitting there, in front of the

American Gothic House, hands intertwined, until the sun sets behind us, our shadows mingling on the pebbled ground until they're one mass of wavering lines and shaded shapes.

20

"Are you ready?" Tom asks, pulling on a fresh shirt after returning to the room from his shower. I stare down at my open bag, unsure of what one should wear on the day their divorce is finalized. A dress, a collared shirt? Or do I downplay it with good ole shorts and a stained T-shirt? Granted, Tom is wearing a T-shirt, but it's probably designer, and it's not his divorce being finalized. I also have no intention of him interacting with my ex, so it really shouldn't matter what he wears. But, for me, the decision seems daunting.

Tom comes to stand beside me. He looks at my bag, looks at me, then places a kiss on my shoulder as he moves to locate socks and shoes. "Wear the yellow dress. It's supposed to be really hot today. And you look beautiful in it."

"Do I need to look beautiful today?"

"You don't need to, but you will no matter what." My heart skips a beat as Tom winks at me from across the room. I go ahead and grab the dress, pulling it over my body and smoothing out my hair.

Tom opens his bedroom door, holding it open for me as I step through. I stop abruptly when I'm met with the sight of Niya trying to quietly shut Landon's door while draped in an oversize collared shirt. Correct that: Landon's oversize collared shirt.

"Uh, Niya?"

She startles at my voice, then looks up at me, her body bent over and her face set in a clenched grimace.

"Whatcha doing there, Ms. Sanghvi? Having an early morning business meeting with Landon, are we?" Tom stands next to me, his hands stuffed into his pockets as he rocks on his heels.

She straightens up at his sarcastic jest, smoothing out the rumpled shirt as she starts walking toward us with her usual confident strides. She jabs the air with a pointed finger as she nears. "I blame you two and your annoying lovey-dovey parents. Makes a woman weak after a few too many glasses of Merlot."

"No judgment here," I say, biting back my smile.

"A little judgment from me." Tom smirks as Niya retreats into the bathroom. I slug him on the shoulder as she closes the door, and he looks at me innocently. "What? It *is* Landon we're talking about."

"He's your friend."

"He's my manager. Very different."

I roll my eyes and we continue on our way to the car.

"We should get there around ten. Where are we meeting him?" he asks as he settles into the driver's seat and turns the ignition.

"I told him I would stop by the house." I start shifting in my seat, organizing my purse and paperwork, repositioning my legs, trying to get comfortable for the trip ahead. I'm fairly certain that will not be achievable; my skin is already crawling with anxiety.

"And where am I supposed to be during all this?"

"The car?"

We've reached the end of the driveway, unsettling two photographers who have camped out on the road. They immediately rush our vehicle and start asking questions, their voices muted by the glass of our sealed windows. Lights from the cameras click as a series of rapid-fire photos are snapped. Tom pastes a tense smile across his face, lifts his hand in a polite wave, and tells me to just look down at my lap.

It's absurd. I'm not ashamed to be with Tom. If anything, it's the thing in my life that I am least ashamed about, that I wouldn't mind shouting from the rooftops and slapping across magazine covers, claiming him as mine. But I'm ashamed that I've brought this additional attention onto him. It shouldn't be big news that he's dating me; the fact that I'm still technically married makes it big news, the lens of legal infidelity tainting our story.

"You okay?" Tom looks over, having finally navigated us onto Highway 1. Eventually we will link up with 218, drive south until we hit Highway 34 in Mount Pleasant, then drive nearly one hour west until we're tossed into the belly of the beast. My palms are already sweating with anticipation. I should admit everything to Tom right now, let him drive, keep his eyes on the road and off of me as I reveal my secrets. But there's still a small part of me clinging to the hope that I will emerge from this unscathed, my transgressions undiscovered.

So instead, the coward I am, I merely nod and smile. Tom reaches over and takes my hand in his, squeezes it in reassurance, and proceeds to talk about landmarks that we pass, either trivial knowledge passed down to him or memories associated with them. I focus on my breathing and the pressure of his hand on mine, only half-listening as I'm hypnotized by the white lines of the shoulder whizzing by—leading me back to my past and onto a journey that will hopefully deliver me to a future where I can put all this behind me.

***

When I was young, Highway 34 carved through the towns surrounding the then-metropolis of Ottumwa. But now, the highway has been reconfigured to bypass those smatterings of small towns, and the new route further isolates these communities from the outside world, communities that used to thrive from the incoming travelers. The highway transports drivers to their destinations even faster, but leaves a trail of ghost towns in its wake.

Ottumwa, a once-bustling economic hub of the southeast corner of the state, has not proven immune to the phenomena of urban migration. Since I've moved, even more changes are visible: empty shells of vacated businesses with broken signs; blank facades of abandoned houses with windows boarded up and yards left to weeds; pothole-riddled roads that have been left to the elements, hardly traversed enough to justify fixing. A city I once explored and frolicked around, its lights and colors reflecting brightly off the sheen of teenage possibility, is now muted with a cloak of gray, harnessed beneath a weight of poverty and age. Sure, there are random pools of revitalization that pop up in a determined attempt to unearth what used to be, but it is definitely not the town I remember. Nor am I the same person that used to live here.

Per my directions, Tom steers us to the south side of town where small lots sit on crosshatched streets in the flat terrain south of the Des Moines River, which carves through the middle of the city. He pulls into the gravel driveway next to the small yellow house wedged between other modest, boxy houses and turns off the engine. I stare out the window, my heart pounding in my ears as I try to prepare myself to re-enter the house Caleb and I bought after he graduated with his associate's degree and started working at the Ford dealership in town.

It has only two bedrooms, a decent starter house that we planned to upgrade from after we had our first child. As it became less likely that day would arrive, Caleb started stamping more signs of permanence on the property: making a fenced-in backyard for the day I would let him get a dog, building a not-at-all-child-friendly deck and firepit right off the kitchen, and ripping up carpet to reveal the original wooden floors. The renovation that really stung was when he started hanging his guitars on the wall of the second bedroom, creating an official music room instead of a future nursery. He claimed we would have the baby sleep in our room for the first few months anyway, which would give us plenty of time to revert the bedroom to its original intent if needed, but his lack of belief in my ability to carry a child screamed between the lines of his words. He didn't think we were going to have children, and I didn't think he wanted to anymore…at least, not with me. At the end of our relationship, it didn't even feel as if we were married; it felt like we were playing house, taking on our assigned roles, looking for a way to move on to something else but too afraid to stop playing the game.

"Are you sure you don't want me to come in? I can dazzle him with my smile, offer him an autograph, then whisk you away while he's still counting his lucky stars he shared a lover with Thomas Price."

I turn slowly toward him, my nose scrunched up in disgust. "Ew," I say before breaking into a nervous laugh. Tom's raised brow and cheesy smile betray his real goal of lessening the tension, and I lean over to kiss him, my hand running over the stubble that's been free to grow this past week, the hint of a beard giving him a rustic edge, making him even more handsome—if that's even possible. "Thank you, but I don't think he's the type that will be dazzled."

The sudden sound of tapping on my passenger window causes me to jump and almost fall into Tom's lap. My hand flies to my chest as if to keep my startled heart contained, and I turn to see my ex squatting down and peering into the car. He makes a rolling gesture with his hand, and I acquiesce by lowering my window.

Caleb sticks his head into the car, his dark hair longer since I last saw him and the curve of his upper lip now rocking a thin mustache. As the window panel slides down all the way, he crosses his elbows and leans forward, his hazel eyes roaming first over me, then over Tom. “So it’s true. My wife really is cheating on me with Thomas Price.”

I roll my eyes and go to open the car door, Caleb stepping back to avoid getting hit. “I’m not cheating on you, Caleb. We’ve been separated for years. And yes, this is Tom.” I gesture to Tom, who remains seated, crooking his neck to see through my window, waving at my husband.

Caleb leans over, his hands on his hips, assessing the car. “I thought movie stars drove Lamborghinis or Ferraris, or at least those electric hybrid contraptions they’re calling cars nowadays.”

“It’s a rental,” Tom offers from inside the sleek sedan, and Caleb nods in understanding as he straightens up, his gaze landing on me once again.

“Hey, Logie Bear. You look good.”

“Thanks. You do, too.” I’m not just being polite. He does look healthier than the last time I saw him, like a plant that has been given adequate sun and water after being previously locked in a dark interior room. He’s always been tall and thin, but he’s filled out in the past few years, the bulk of his chest and shoulders straining nicely against his T-shirt. His nose, always crooked after getting it broken in a bar fight at the age of eighteen, has shifted even more, but is evened out by his thick eyebrows and shaggy hair. He squints at me, the sun shining in his eyes as he completes his own assessment of my physical changes, and I begin to relax. I tense up again, however, as he steps closer to me and opens his arms for a hug. I step into his hold and let him squeeze me in greeting, but back away once released.

"Are you ready to sign some papers?" I ask, charging past any small talk and reaching into the car to grab the legal documents from off of the dash.

"What, right here? Don't you want to come in, catch up?"

I shift nervously, my gaze flitting between Tom and Caleb.

"We weren't planning on staying long."

"You have time for a cup of coffee though, right? I have that creamer that you used to like. Oh, and my mom dropped off cookies the other day. The ones with cranberries and white chocolate chips."

"I do love those cookies."

"Then come in," insists Caleb as he begins stepping backward toward the front door.

I look from Caleb to Tom. "Tom, do you mind waiting here?"

"What? Of course not! Bring him in! I'm not leaving an American treasure like Thomas Price out here to be accosted by Mrs. Reed."

"Is she still nosing around?" My eyes dart to the house nestled next-door.

Caleb follows my focal point. "Oh, you know she is. Anytime a new car pulls into the drive, I see the corner of her blinds lift. In fact, I wouldn't be surprised if she's already posted on the neighborhood watch site about your arrival."

"She wouldn't!" I look at him, shocked by Mrs. Reed's potential disloyalty. I even helped shovel her drive one winter.

"Social media has turned her into an even bigger gossipmonger. We'd better go in. From what I've heard, you two are prime targets. She could have the local news here before we know it. Although I wouldn't mind meeting Penelope Winters. She's the newest reporter and is very easy on the eyes." Caleb raises his eyebrows, and I can't help but snort with slight amusement. By this time, Tom has joined us and Caleb reaches out to shake his hand. "Caleb Sterling. Nice to meet you."

"Tom Price. Nice to meet you, too." Tom looks up at Caleb who stands a couple inches taller. He smiles, then looks over at me and winks as Caleb starts leading us to the front door, gesturing for us to follow.

"Well, come on in. You like coffee, Tom?" He continues without listening for an answer. "And Logie, I can't wait for you to meet Suzie."

"Who's Suzie?" I pull up short as Caleb opens the door, a wriggling Cocker Spaniel with ruddy hair and a white stripe down her snout bounding out. Caleb catches her midair.

"*This* is Suzie." Tom and I both bend to pet the dog, her tongue lolling and tail wagging furiously. I'm glad that Caleb finally got a dog, something he always wanted but I always resisted, saying it would be tough to have both a puppy and a baby. I now realize my endless pursuit of motherhood blinded me to my husband's needs. Seeing how he lights up as he hauls Suzie's buzzing body into the house is reassuring, but it's also disheartening to realize I never made him light up like that. Just another man in my life that I let down. I walk into my old house and head toward the kitchen with the two men, one I already disappointed and one yet to feel the full wrath of my curse.

***

"Logan tells me you were in a band. Do you still play?" Tom asks, his hand wrapped around a green mug stamped with a cartoon pickle and the phrase, "Sort of a Big Dill." The three of us sit in the kitchen at the round table I bought from a garage sale over a decade ago. Suzie sits at Caleb's feet, her head jerking up to look at him adoringly every time he shifts next to her. Tom and Caleb have dominated the conversation, Caleb asking Tom for the inside dish on celebrities he's worked with, and Tom asking Caleb about his job in sales. So far, having my estranged husband meet my famous boyfriend is going swimmingly. But I don't want to push my luck, and I nudge the divorce filings toward Caleb as he finishes telling us about his lineup of regular gigs around the county.

"I'm glad you're doing so well, Caleb. So what do you think? Should we rip off the Band-Aid?" I fan the papers in his direction, and he purses his lips before snatching them away from me.

"I'm not sure ripping the Band-Aid is the correct metaphor here, Logie Bear. More like slowly exposing the skin pore by tiny pore. I mean, really, five years? How did we let it go this long?"

I shrug as he flips through the pages, signing on the lines that have been marked with a highlighted X. "I don't know. Life's sort of been a blur since then."

Tom tilts his head as he asks, "Logie Bear? Where does that come from?"

Caleb grins as he finishes signing. "Oh, I've always called her that."

Tom looks at me. "Didn't your dad call you that?"

I open my mouth to answer, but Caleb slaps the papers on the table, causing both of us to redirect our attention.

"Well, all I can say is that I'm really happy for you, what with your writing taking off and becoming a Hollywood bigwig." He looks at Tom. "Logan was always a good writer. She wrote a few songs for me. I still play them every now and then." He turns to look at me, his eyes shining with gracious pride. "But even I didn't know what you were capable of. I mean, that story about your dad, that was like reading the contents of your soul after watching you get hit by a semi-truck. It was heartbreaking to read the way you wished things could've been, but encouraging to know that you could create something positive from such a bitter ending."

Tom tilts his head, and my fingers start to tingle. I grab the papers and rise to go. "Thanks, Caleb. And if anyone contacts you about me—"

"It'll all be handled with the utmost discretion." He mimes zipping his lips and the tightness in my chest relaxes just a bit.

"I appreciate that. I really do." We exchange a knowing smile, and Tom looks between the both of us. That's my signal to get out of here. I search for the time, making a big deal once I locate the silver and white wall clock that's always hung next to the calendar and the pantry door. "Oh boy, Tom, we should probably get going. We have a lot to do before the crew returns tomorrow." The men stand as I've already started drifting toward the front door.

"What did you mean by all that, Caleb? By 'the way you wished things could've been'?'" Tom asks, but I refuse to look back, refuse to halt in my exit plan. If I just hurtle myself toward the sun, perhaps I'll burn up before I freeze beneath their stares.

"Well, it's just that Logan was having such a hard time, first with the miscarriages, and then with the news of her dad's death. I was worried she was depressed, which maybe she was. I don't know, because it was shortly after that when she went to clean up her dad's house, and then she never came back. I mean, we agreed to separate before she left, so I wasn't completely blindsided—"

I've reached the door, but I can tell that Tom and Caleb are standing in the front living room, no longer following me. I turn and see Tom looking up at Caleb, his eyes narrowed in thought. Caleb looks from me to him, his brow creased. He's guessing that he's said too much, and he tries to clear it up. "I suppose I shouldn't assume what you two have already discussed. It's just we had a lot of trouble trying to start a family, and I know that was tough on Logan. And then to not have either of her parents around. I never got to meet her dad, but I still felt horrible when we got the call about his aneurysm. I know Logan always regretted never making up with him before he died. But I told her it wasn't her fault. It was always his choice." He turns his gaze on me, his eyes large with emotion. "I'm glad you found a way to work through all those emotions, to give you two a better ending. And I'm sorry if I didn't do enough to help. But I always wanted you to be happy, Logan."

A tear slides slowly down my cheek as I stare at my official ex-husband, and my voice trembles as I say, "I want you to be happy, too, Caleb. I'm sorry." I look at Tom. "I'm sorry for everything."

Tom stares at me, then shakes his head, bringing him back to the moment. He shakes Caleb's hand and follows me out the door. Caleb stands by the passenger side, his arm bracing himself against the roof of the car as I turn to say our final goodbye. I step forward awkwardly, and he pulls me into a hug.

"No hard feelings, Logie Bear. I mean it, I'm happy for you. About all of it." He kisses the top of my head and I step back.

"Bye, Caleb. Thanks for the divorce." I hold up the paper and give him a small smile even though the ground beneath me is crumbling. I take my seat and shut the door, and Tom waves at Caleb as he backs out of the driveway, retracing our path as we begin the journey back to Iowa City. I'm afraid to look at him, but from the side, I can see his jaw is tense, his hands tight on the steering wheel. He stares at the road in front of him, his lips set in a fine line as he concentrates, whether on driving or on the newly revealed information in his head, I'm not sure. But I know I'll find out soon enough.

As we leave the town of Ottumwa behind and use the entrance ramp to return to the thruway of Highway 34, Tom finally speaks, his voice even as he continues looking forward. "Is what Caleb said true? Did your dad die while you two were still together?"

"Tom, I'm so sorry—" I try to say, but he holds up his palm.

"Don't apologize. Just tell me the truth."

I close my eyes and try to focus on the rhythm of my breathing. It's been so many years of lying, so many close calls that it's almost a relief to be free of the massive burden I've been carrying ever since I signed my publishing deal. Without opening my eyes, I exhale out the truth.

"It's true. I was still living with Caleb when the hospital in Omaha called me about my father's death."

"So how, and bear with me as I try to wrap my head around this, how did you and your dad ever go on this life-altering trip around the state of Iowa before he died of cancer?"

I open my eyes and turn to look at Tom's profile. His brows are furrowed, crinkling the bridge of his nose, and a hint of red creeps up around his cheeks. I steel myself to lose him, to lose everything, as I destroy the life I've created with lies and fabrications over the past few years.

"Because it never happened. I made it all up."

Four Years Prior

from: Niya Sanghvi <niyasanghvi@windycitywriting.com>

to: Logan Sterling <lasterling@gmail.com>

Mr. Sterling,

Thank you for your interest in representation. While I am intrigued by your writing sample, I am hesitant to proceed because the fiction market is currently flooded, and I cannot risk time and energy on a project that does not have high chances of obtaining a lucrative publishing deal. The writing industry, however, is very fluid, and I hope you find the agent and representation that is right for you.

Thank you and best of luck,

Niya Sanghvi

from: Logan Sterling <lasterling@gmail.com>

to: Niya Sanghvi <niyasanghvi@windycitywriting.com>

Ms. Sanghvi,

I completely understand. The story of my reunion with my dad after years of estrangement set with the backdrop of our home state is very niche, but I had hoped that others would be able to gain something from the lessons that I learned on this memorable journey. I'll continue to send queries and I appreciate your quick response.

Thank you,

Ms. Logan Sterling

from: Niya Sanghvi <niyasanghvi@windycitywriting.com>

to: Logan Sterling <lasterling@gmail.com>

Ms. Sterling,

Pardon me for the previous mistake regarding your title. I'm sure you get that all the time. I didn't realize this was a true story. That changes everything. Memoirs are highly coveted in the current market, and I would love for you to send me the entire manuscript.

Looking forward to reading more,

Ms. Niya Sanghvi

<<Deleted Message>>

from: Logan Sterling <lasterling@gmail.com>

to: Niya Sanghvi <niyasanghvi@windycitywriting.com>

Ms. Sanghvi,

I'm so sorry for the misunderstanding. This isn't a real story. It's a story I wish was real. My dad and I were estranged and he did die, but unfortunately, we were not able to reunite before his sudden passing. However, my reimagining of our reconciliation proved to be a valuable step in my healing journey. I would love to talk to you more about it and hope to find a way to continue on a path to publication while being honest about the origin of this story.

Thank You,

Ms. Logan Sterling

from: Logan Sterling <lasterling@gmail.com>

to: Niya Sanghvi <niyasanghvi@windycitywriting.com>

Ms. Sanghvi,

Thank you for the opportunity. You will find the entire manuscript attached. I look forward to hearing from you.

Ms. Logan Sterling

21

Tom and I have been pulled over on the shoulder of the highway for a good five minutes. He continues staring forward, clenching the steering wheel, his knuckles glaringly white from the force of his hold. His eyes are trained on an image in his mind rather than the real world, and I occasionally glance over, catching him in my peripheral vision while my head is dipped down.

I want to disappear, to free Tom of this mess, this burden that I've carried on my back ever since signing with Niya. If I'm being honest, however, I've always had some burden on my back: the burden of not being wanted by my father, the burden of losing my mother too young, the burden of an unwanted pregnancy and youthful marriage quickly followed by the burden of infertility and dashed dreams. It just so happens I took the wheel and started fabricating my own tales in an attempt to dig myself out of the trash pile of my past, though I ended up burying myself under even more burdens of my own making.

I've slipped into my own trance, trying to ignore the shake of the car every time a large vehicle races past us. I'm uncomfortable and nervous on the side of the road, but I've lost the right to complain. Instead, I must wait. My trance is broken when Tom suddenly bursts into motion, throwing his car door open, slamming it shut, and stalking to the grassy line at the edge of the asphalt. His back is to the car, and I see him reach his hands up and run his fingers through his hair, gripping the back of his head as he stares up at the cloudless sky. I'm nervous to approach him, but his obvious state of distress calls to me, and I unfold myself from the front seat and leave the car, my steps quiet except when my foot slides across loose pebbles.

"Tom?" It feels ominous to speak so quietly at the height of the day, the sun shining at its peak position, the brightness encouraging action and motion. But Tom remains still. I reach out to touch his shoulder, and he whips around, gripping both my shoulders.

"Logan! What have you done?" he hisses through clenched teeth, his eyes boring into mine as he searches my face for answers. "Tell me everything."

It's my turn to explode. My words steal the air from my lungs, my eyes blurring with tears, my body trembling with the release of the truth. "All I did was write what I wished would have happened. That's it. Dad died and I hadn't spoken to him in eight years, seven months, and fourteen days. There wasn't a day that passed during that time where I didn't consider calling him, didn't fantasize about him being the one to return to me, about opening the door and seeing him there, arms spread wide, ready to take me back and claim me as his daughter. It's all I ever wanted. But then he had to go and die. And he destroyed my dreams, Tom. He left me for good. He died without telling me that he still loved me; that I wasn't a complete disappointment. I wasn't the best daughter, I know that, but he should have still forgiven me. He should have still loved me."

A semi-truck blasts its horn as it surges by, and we both swing our heads to the road. By this time, tears are streaming down my cheeks and I swipe at them with a raised hand, dropping my head in shame. Tom turns his gaze back to me, shaking me slightly as he pleads, "But why? Why did you do it?"

My voice begins to rise in response to his tone of anger, fueled by my own indignation as I dive into the past. "After I got the call, I realized that I had worked so hard to justify a marriage he disapproved of, that even though I wasn't happy, I was trying to make it work, trying to build the family that I never had in order to prove him wrong, to prove everyone wrong. But with him gone, I just couldn't do it anymore. So I told Caleb it was over and then I went to Omaha to wrap up his estate, to clean up and sell the house. I did it thinking if I was a good daughter, even after his death, I'd have some chance of gaining his approval, of winning him back. That maybe it was all a sick test to see if I really loved him. But of course, he was dead, and I was serving out my penance, doing my part to further erase his mark on the world. It was torture, sifting through his belongings, staying in that house alone, seeing him in everything. When I finished and stood in that empty house for the last time, I realized that was it. I was never going to talk to Dad again. And then I started driving."

By this time, Tom has loosened his grip and straightened his stance, his eyes still pinned on me as my story unfurls. I disentangle myself from his hold and turn to stare at the ditch, the long grass swaying in the wind, whipped violently with a gust of air every time a car passes. I feel Tom come to stand beside me, studying the plants along with me as I continue.

"I drove around the whole state of Iowa. I visited all the places in my book and more. I didn't know what I was doing exactly, whether I was purging my past life, searching for my dad, or searching for a new version of myself. But on that trip, I imagined what Dad would have done, what he would have enjoyed, what he would have said to me. Then it became more than fantasy, it became catharsis. I *needed* to take this journey with him. I *needed* to hear him apologize, hear him tell me that he loved me, that he was proud of me. At first, the conversations stayed in my head, but then I started writing them down. Actually seeing the words made them more concrete, more permanent, and I began to feel like I was healing. Like I could actually continue on in this world, give it a second chance, give myself a second chance. So I moved to Des Moines, got a job, finished the book, and started querying agents."

My voice drifts off, swallowed by the deafening roar of a passing swine transport truck, newly emptied after leaving its previous passengers at the packing plant. My gaze follows the sound and I find myself locking gazes with Tom. His face no longer holds the same fiery disgust; instead, it's pulled down by the weight of pity, which tugs at my pride and leaves me feeling even emptier than the emptied wheeled cage speeding off into the distance.

Tom's voice is small, barely audible over the roadside sounds. "But how, Logan? How did it get this far? Why involve all of us in this mess of a lie?"

"I didn't mean to. In my exchanges with Niya, she somehow got the idea that it was a real story. It probably didn't help that I used my dad's real name—and mine—but that was only because I wanted the story to feel real to me. It wasn't a devious plan to trick everyone. I just wanted to share my story, to prove to the world that my father did love me, and to find some purpose, some success of my own after having failed to do so for so long."

My words catch in my throat, and I have to pause to swallow the stone of emotion blocking my airway. Once I can breathe again, I rush to the end of my explanation. "So when Niya showed renewed interest because she thought the story was a memoir rather than a novel, I went with it. And when sales started increasing, I began giving interviews, and then movie deals were being discussed—I just kept my mouth shut. I never added to the lie. I just never corrected anyone."

Tom crosses his torso with an arm, holding his other elbow as his head drops into his hand. "Oh, Logan…"

I rush to defend myself, scrambling for any control in this out-of-control situation. "You said it yourself that if you want something you need to make it happen. I was making it happen."

"But not by lying to everyone. Not by lying to me!" The disappointment in his tone pierces my heart, and my eyes refill with fresh tears.

"I didn't lie to you, Tom. I just didn't say otherwise. Doesn't that count for something?"

His head shoots up, shocking both of us with his sudden fury. "Logan, you've done nothing but lie to me since we met. You lied about the story, you lied about being married, and you lied about your feelings for me."

"I never lied about my feelings for you!"

"Yes, you did. Remember all that bullshit about wanting to remain friends, wanting to stay professional? Even then, the lies crossed your lips so easily. You lied to me and you lied to yourself. You're still lying to yourself. You need help, Logan. You need to talk to someone about all this, process your grief, make sense of what's real and what's not." His voice shakes as he teeters on the edge of losing his composure.

"Everything was real to me. The story, the end of my marriage. It all happened to me, even if it was just in my head," I say, my voice small with defeat.

"That's not good enough."

"I know, but I swear I wasn't trying to trick anyone, never wanted to hurt anybody. Especially you. The fact that I may have… it just kills me. I love—" I stop before I give away everything I have.

His own eyes widen, and he steps forward.

"Say it. What were you going to say?" His eyes light up, scorching me as they cross my skin. He takes another step forward and I instinctively move back. He repeats himself, each word slow and purposeful as it crosses his lips. "Logan, what were you going to say?"

"I don't…I'm sorry…" I stammer, the words tumbling over one another as they clammer out of my throat.

"Why can't you just tell me? Why can't you finally be honest with me? Or are you still just making everything up as you go? Writing some story you think will make you happy?" The light begins to dim as he stands there, his hands listless at his sides.

His words hit me like a slap, and I cross my arms, holding my stomach and protecting my underbelly. I could tell him that I love him, that I've suspected that this feeling that overtakes me whenever I am with him is more than a simple crush, more than lust. I love the man he is, love how he treats others, how he treats me. He's smart, funny, and hardworking. But even without all that, my body recognizes in him a missing part of the whole picture of my life, a torn-off piece that, when returned, completes the image and makes me whole. I love him more than I've loved anyone in my life.

But I can't say any of that. If I do, he's just going to think it's a ploy to keep him, a line to get him to stay after learning my darkest secrets. I've always known I don't deserve him, don't deserve to be this happy—and I'm realizing I don't want to bring him down with me just so I have company in the miserable hell I've created. So I tell Tom one last lie.

"I was going to say I love working on this movie. Being a part of this team. And I'm sorry if I jeopardized everything you've worked so hard for."

He stares at me with dull eyes, their flame blown out by my inability to open up and be honest about my feelings for him. His shoulders droop and he holds out his hands as if to tamp down the rising mess. "We need to get back to the farm and figure this all out. When this gets out—"

"It's not going to. Caleb won't say anything."

"He already did, Logan. He knows, and eventually, everyone will. And they should. No more lies. I told you how important honesty was to me…" his voice softens, the fight having left his body, now only a husk of sadness and disappointment. "But I guess that never mattered to you."

My lips quiver as I ask my next question. "Is the movie done, then? Does everyone lose their job? Do you…do you not get the directing debut you wanted?" I understand how important this movie is to everyone involved, and I dread the impact this could have on those I've come to know and love.

"I don't…I don't know. I need to talk to Landon. And you need to come clean with Niya. So we'll head back to the farm and meet with them, figure out what to do next." He starts to pace in front of the car, his eyes cast on the ground as he racks his brain for logical next steps. I want to go to him, to calm him with my touch, reassure him that it will all be all right, but my feet are cemented to the ground.

"Tom, I'm so sorry. I never meant to hurt you. It just…felt so good to feel wanted, to feel accomplished, to feel like I mattered…"

He stops short and turns to look at me, his gaze glassy. "You do matter, Logan. You always have."

"Do I still matter to you?" I take a timid step forward but stop when Tom shuffles backward.

"I need…I need time…to process." His eyes are dark, a storm of uncertainty raging within. He's barely keeping himself above water, and if I push him, we could both be lost to sea.

I nod slowly and bite the inside of my cheek, trying to stop myself from voicing any more foolish declarations and desperate explanations. Tom heads for the driver's side, and I look out at the distant line of trees, wishing I could walk into them and disappear rather than sit in a silent car for the next two hours next to the man I love, the man I just destroyed with the truth of who I really am and what I've done.

***

The trip home proves painful, but the conversation with Niya and Landon is even worse. We meet them on the driveway, the two of them walking hand in hand, Niya actually giggling like a lovestruck schoolgirl. But once Tom tells them what he's learned, the frozen exterior of professional coldness straightens her spine and silences her laughter. Niya drops Landon's hand and rushes toward me, dragging me to the barn, demanding a play-by-play of everything from our first email. As I reveal all to my agent, I wonder where Tom and Landon have gone off to, wonder what they are discussing, wonder if Tom is thinking of me. But that's all over. He's now just another man walking away from me after I've disappointed him. The sooner I accept that, the sooner I can move on.

"I still can't believe this fucking happened! How could you, Logan? How could you be so careless and ignorant?"

I wince at the stinging jab, but I don't retreat. I deserve every lash, every violent word spat my way. "I'm sorry. It was…a misunderstanding…at first. But then—"

I've been hiding behind my grief, behind the trauma of my past, but there was more motivating my actions than weakness and happenstance. There's strength to be found in my flaws, something Niya herself has taught me. I need to be honest and admit those, as well. I lift my head, locking eyes with Niya. "I wanted it, Niya. I wanted to be published so badly. To have a chance to put my words out there, to be heard, to be valued. I wanted to contribute to the literary world and impact others with my story. When you passed on it as a novel, I'd had twenty others pass on it, and I was just about to quit. But then you wrote back, enticed by it being a memoir, a real story we could lure people in with. And, yeah, I probably should have told you, but it was my only shot, and I took it. And then it became bigger than I ever dreamed. And now I've created this PR nightmare. But you know what? The book is still good. It's still relevant, and it still helped a lot of people. I've had so many readers reach out and tell me that the story helped give them the final push they needed to reconcile with a loved one, or helped them connect with a family member, or even showed them the power of an apology. I don't regret being able to help those people. I do regret lying to you, and I do owe you an apology for that. But I'm not sorry that you took me on as a client, and I'm definitely not sorry that we published my book."

I stop my rant, out of breath and readying myself for Niya's rebuttal. She peers at me through narrow eyes, her hands on her hips, her composure as rigid as ever. "It's about fucking time you spoke up for yourself. This business is not for the weak, Logan, and I've been waiting for you to get a goddamn spine. I just wish it wasn't such a fucking nightmare for your career. But we'll figure it out."

"What? You're not releasing me from my contract immediately?"

"No. Like you said, it's an awesome book. I should have realized that from the first sample, but I was so caught up with stats and trends. And I'm not without blame. I should have fact-checked the manuscript before we sent it off to publishers. But shit happens. And we'll recover. It's not the first time an author has lied about the origins of a story."

"Umm, okay."

"Did you get your divorce papers signed?"

"Yes."

"Good. We have a lot of image cleanup to do. Might as well attack the whole pile."

Niya instantly pulls out her phone and starts dialing numbers, telling me between calls that I need to pack up and get ready to leave immediately.

"What about the movie?"

She reads an incoming text message, then looks at me, a hint of remorse on her usually stoic face. "The movie will continue filming, but Landon and Tom have decided that you should no longer be a part of it."

My chest feels as if it has split open, the contents spilling out on the ground. Any glimmer of hope I had is extinguished with Niya's announcement, and a new coldness takes over my limbs, shards of ice shooting through my veins and plunging into my heart.

I've finally lifted the weight of dishonesty off of my shoulders and I'm moving forward with a renewed fervor, but I've officially lost Tom and all the friends I've made on set. I might still have a professional future, but I'm marching into it alone.

***

Less than an hour later, Niya and I are piling our bags into the car she and Landon rented while Scott and Cami stand on the porch to watch us depart. I doubt Tom has filled them in; their goodbyes are still friendly, but I can tell they sense something is wrong, their actions slow and muted, as if wading through water as each offers a hug for the road.

Landon walks Niya to the driver's side and kisses her against the door. I use their awkward make out session to turn back to Cami and Scott with one last act of hope as I ask, "Is Tom around? I'd like to say goodbye."

Cami sighs and reaches out to pat my cheek as Scott explains. "He, uh…he had a few errands to run in town. Said he wouldn't be back until late this evening. We'll let him know you got on the road safely."

"Okay. Thank you for your hospitality. And sorry for any trouble I caused." I turn around, their sympathy more agonizing than watching Niya and Landon exchange saliva. I walk to the car, feeling as if I am floating above my body, watching one life die, all attempts at resuscitation abandoned.

I wish Tom were here, even if I had to face the burn of his angry gaze, even if I knew he hated me—at least I would still have closure. But I'm used to the gaping hole of sudden loss, having suffered through it enough times. I'll never be the same after this, but I'll remain standing. And, for now, that truth is enough to help me slide into the car, close the door, and leave the Price family farm without falling apart completely.

Excerpt from *Iowa Nice*

BURLINGTON

"Can I drive?" My dad looks down at the winding brick curves of Snake Alley as we stand at the top of the bluff. We've left the car parked on Columbia Street so we can see the entirety of the undulating roadway first before we attempt to traverse it with wheels. Correction: before I attempt to traverse it with wheels.

"Absolutely not." I turn on my heel and start walking back to the car.

"Why? Because I'm old, decrepit, senile?" Dad hollers at my back.

"Yes to at least half of that entire statement." I turn around and answer, walking backward as I taunt him.

He stops with his hands on his hips. "Come on, are you really going to deny a dying man's last request?"

I stop and mirror his pose. "Your last request was for this trip. You never said anything about driving my car."

"Well, last requests can change. Now I'd like to drive down the world's most crooked street before I die." I look to my right at a brick monolith of a church, as if asking a higher power whether I should let my sick dad operate my only vehicle down the 1,100 degrees of turns. Dad stands firmly in place, his stubbornness becoming endearing on this leg of the trip. There will be a day when he won't be able to fight anymore, when I won't be able to verbally spar with him, a now common occurrence that has become a secret delight of mine, though still irritating at times.

Past Dad, down the street, I can see the Mississippi River peeking out from behind the buildings and trees. We'll follow this American artery up to the north corner of the state, signaling the end of our trip as my dad nears the end of his life. Really, what do I have to lose?

I exhale, any hint of resistance escaping with my breath of surrender, and I toss my keys to my dad. "Fine, you can drive. But take it slow. This isn't a thrill ride."

The glow of joy that lifts my father's pallid face instantly clears any doubts I have about giving in to his whim. It's a beautiful day and I get to share it with my dad. These days are numbered, so I'd better make them count. I lean into that thought even as I squeeze my eyes shut while he navigates the tight turns and steep grade of Snake Alley.

Iowa Nice Film Adaptation Still Underway Amid Author's Reveal

...The film version, spearheaded by Thomas Price who is acting as director and producer, will continue filming in the southeast corner of the state before moving north through the Mississippi Valley. Logan Sterling, author and screenwriter, was visibly absent from the first day of filming in Ottumwa, which is where the author grew up and lived for many years...

Author and Screenwriter Logan Sterling Released from Filming

...Price announced on his Instagram that though filming would continue, Logan Sterling will no longer serve as script supervisor after the shocking reveal of her story's origin. He is quoted as saying, "Even though the story was written after Malcolm McClarnon's death, the message and heart remain the same, and I am going to uphold my promise to give that same message and heart to the movie. This is my love song to the state of Iowa...'"

Too Little Too Late: Divorce Finalized for *Iowa Nice* Author Dating Thomas Price

...While separated for nearly five years, Caleb and Logan Sterling had never officially signed divorce papers. The legal handlings were finally wrapped up shortly after media speculation reached a frenzy regarding the author's relationship with actor Thomas Price. The signing coincided with the reveal of Sterling's memoir being fictional in nature, leading many to believe the reunion with her husband somehow facilitated the disclosure.

Caleb Sterling, who was approached by reporters at his place of employment, said, "Logan's a great person and a wonderful writer. I have no ill feelings toward her and want nothing but happiness for her. Honestly, I hope she and Tom [Price] can work it out. He seemed like a really nice guy." Apparently, Price and Sterling visited Mr. Sterling in order to...

Megan Marks Officially Comes Out with Instagram Reveal of Girlfriend

...The actress, who is known for mostly teen dramas and rom-coms, has also made headlines in the past due to her relationships with other Hollywood A-listers including her *Rocky Mountain High* co-star Thomas Price. While it is unknown if these relationships were real or fabricated in order to hide her sexuality, it is a sad reality, in this author's opinion, that she ever felt it necessary. Many other celebrities have come out in the past year with subtle outings or blatant social media posts. Marks went with the latter as she posted a selfie with identified girlfriend, Deedee Markowitz, renowned makeup artist that has worked...

Iowa Nice Tops New York Times Bestseller List Once Again

...Just this week, it was revealed that Logan Sterling penned the tale of her road trip with her dad across Iowa after the first sergeant's death. She claims she undertook the trip alone after hearing of her father's passing, later writing the story in her Des Moines apartment. After she was unable to find representation for the book as a fiction manuscript, a misunderstanding with current agent Niya Sanghvi led to it being branded a memoir…Despite the reveal of its fictional origin, both past and new readers are flocking to read the book with new eyes. Some have even said there is more substance to it now knowing that it was written from a place of regret and grief. There has been talk of a new edition being released with an updated ending…

22

Coming home feels like failure. However, I need to assure myself that my trip to Chicago with Niya was not a failure, and I'm lucky to be able to reenter my sparse downtown apartment with most of my professional credit intact.

After two weeks of meetings, press releases, and painful interviews, Niya and my publishing team are confident that I've actually drummed up more book sales and stirred up even more publicity around the filming and release of the movie. The possibility that I've profited from this whole fiasco leaves a bad taste in my mouth, a bitterness that persists despite any attempt at freshening my conscience.

Price Pictures has graciously agreed to keep my name on the credits (the deal obviously being lubricated by Niya's burgeoning relationship with Landon) but has severed the remainder of my filming contract. I'm not surprised, but I'm still forlorn. Even more painful than my euphemistic firing is the fact that I never had a chance to say goodbye to thc cast and crew. I've received several selfies from the Trendy Trifecta, Megan often squeezed in next to Deedee. Almost everyone else has sent me texts of encouragement or well wishes, while Rene has been my secret informant, updating me on the state of filming and the state of everyone on set. She was the first one to reach out when the team returned to Iowa the day after I hightailed it to Chicago. After the initial shock, she started texting me about the book: If it was made up, why didn't I include more salacious details, like sex with a stranger or a nasty heroin addiction? I know she was only trying to make me laugh and show me that she still supports me, but even though the interactions with my dad were concocted by my grief-stricken mind, the rest is all true. It is a story about my life; an honest depiction of my past, my deepest feelings, and actual thoughts flow through the fabricated pillars of plot depicting what I wish the end of my dad's life could have been.

This is essentially the spin being sold to the media, and I've become an expert at retelling it. While I usually hate talking about myself and my writing, now that the truth is out there, I'm finding it easier to do. And the majority of people's reactions have been positive, even sympathetic at times. Sure, a few internet trolls have called for my creative cancellation—comparing my work to that of James Frey's embellished memoir about addiction, or even to the counterfeit journals of Adolf Hitler—but overall, my readers have remained loyal and understanding.

I have to remind myself how well this all turned out and how much worse it could have been as I slip between the sheets of my cold and lonesome bed that night. I miss Tom. I miss the lightness he brought into my life, the safety I felt when wrapped in his arms, the confidence he was beginning to instill in me. But he's gone, trying to salvage the story that I manifested rather than lived out for real. My mistake has become his burden, and I need to focus on moving past all of this and instead work on myself and my writing.

He called me that first night in Chicago. My heart leapt when I saw his name cross my phone's screen but plummeted when I imagined all the reasons he could be calling. Whether it was to fight, cry, or release me from any further responsibility, I couldn't stand the thought of hearing his voice. So I let it ring. I did the same the next night, and the next, until he finally stopped calling. I know I wanted to see him back at the farm, but if I'm ever going to move on from him, I need a clean break.

But as I look at my clock radio and see that it is barely past ten, I can't help but wonder what he's doing right now. My arm shoots out and grabs my phone off the nightstand, hitting Rene's contact information before I even register my own actions.

"Logan! It's Logan, everyone!" she shouts out joyously, and I'm met with a muffled choir of greetings. I grimace at the possibility of Tom hearing this, but Rene seems to read my mind. "Don't worry, it's just me, Megan, Deedee, Atlas, and Bruno. Everyone else has already turned in for the night, but the five of us are living it up in Clinton, Iowa, raising hell in Applebee's!" Her spirited declaration is met with tipsy whoops and the clinking of glasses. "So what's going on, baby girl? We miss you!"

"I miss you all, too. I'm so sorry about everything."

"Hey, stop apologizing. We're good. None of us care about that. You had a broken heart and you needed to write something to heal. Doesn't take away from the merit of your work, and it certainly doesn't take away from the person you are."

I'm speechless, almost moved to tears as I lay in bed, my head sunken into my down pillow. "Thank you, Rene. That means a lot."

"I mean, you should still probably see a therapist."

"Yeah, I've been hearing that a lot."

"But don't worry, almost every celebrity has their own therapist on retainer, so really, it's a sign you're moving up in this business."

"Okay. Well, thanks."

The line quiets and I can sense that Rene has moved away from the table. I hear the background noises of the restaurant disappear and imagine her standing outside, perhaps to sneak a cigarette. I'm proven correct as I hear the snap of a lighter and the suck of air as she inhales.

"I know you didn't just call to apologize for the fiftieth time. Seriously, what's up?"

"It's just…well, I'm home. Just arrived from Chicago today, and it's the first time I've been completely alone since…it's just hard. I used to be fine with it, but now, it's like I know what I'm missing and…it's just quieter, lonelier than I remember."

I hear Rene blow out a plume of smoke, and I can envision it clouding her visage with a halo of silvery wisps, can imagine it stinging my eyes, closing my throat. Oddly enough, I wish I was there, suffocating smoke and all.

"I can tell he misses you, too."

"That's not…I wasn't just calling to…" I stammer, trying to save face, but give up any pretense when I ask, "You think so?"

"Oh. I know so. I would know anyway, because, well, I know things. But everyone else sees it, too. He's still good to work with, as respectful and considerate as ever, but he's just…mopey. He doesn't come out at the end of the day anymore. Just retreats to his room. Megan asked him to get drinks with us tonight, but he said he needed to review the dailies. You've taken the wind out of his sails, sweetheart."

"I didn't mean to."

"Oh, I know. I'm not saying it's your fault. Well, I guess it sort of is, but not purposefully. I mean, I figured you two were banging, but I didn't know how head over heels he was…is…not that I don't think you're worthy of his love. It's just, these film hookups are usually just that, short-lived hookups…but, what do I know? Megan and Deedee are seemingly in it for the long haul. Maybe there's something in the rural water of Iowa that makes everyone cuckoo with love. Sorry, I'm rambling. Those Applebee's margaritas ought to come with a warning label."

"Tom called me a few times, but I never answered."

"What?! Why?" I flinch as she hollers into the phone.

"Because I'm an idiot incapable of telling people how I feel. I almost told him…but I didn't want him to think I was only saying it to keep him around…or maybe I just chickened out. I don't know. I think there's something wrong with me."

"There's nothing wrong with you, sugar. You've just been through a lot in your life. If anything, there's something very right with you considering how good of a person you are despite all that." Her compliment curls around me, giving me the strength to continue this excavation of my true feelings.

"I'm not good at this, Rene."

"Good at what?"

"Being in love." There, I've said it, and it feels like I've finally surfaced for air after holding my breath underwater for way too long. And once I've gotten that first sip of air, I can't stop. "I love Tom so much. I should have told him. I need to tell him, even if it's too late."

"I knew it. I knew you were both loopy for each other." I can hear her smile over the phone, but am still surprised when she offers, "Well, what are we going to do then?"

"We?"

"Of course, we. I'm in this with you. Didn't you know I adopted you as my film set baby? I'm not going to abandon you now just because you're in your awkward teen years." I start to respond, not sure how I feel about being called a baby or a teen, but Rene suddenly shouts out in excitemcnt, my ear ringing with the splitting volume. "You have to come back!"

"I can't, Rene. I was fired…I think."

"That doesn't matter. We're doing this thing, this public event in Dyersville. You haven't heard? Maybe they haven't released it yet. Anyway, they do these Ghost Games on Saturdays at the Field of Dreams movie site. They've invited the whole team to stay for a game; Phil, Tom, and Megan are going to do…something…I don't know. Stand up there and look pretty? Maybe give a motivational speech? And then Tom is supposed to throw the opening pitch. It's going to be good marketing after…well, you know. Anyway, what if you come? You could find a way to talk to Tom, to tell him that you love him."

"You don't think I should just text him?"

"Absolutely not. This is Hollywood, baby girl. Has a text ever worked as a grand gesture of one's devotion?"

"I suppose not."

"Just think about it. We've got a couple days in Dubuque, then we head to Dyersville to wrap up the Iowa portion. And then we all head back to LA. This is your chance, cupcake."

I take a big breath and blubber through the exhale. Confronting Tom in public and possibly making a scene is the last thing I want to do, but I also can't let him leave the state without knowing how I really feel. "Thanks, Rene. Do you think you could send me the details tomorrow? When you're done partying at Applebee's?"

Rene laughs and I hear her reenter the restaurant, a cacophony of cheers greeting her as she returns to the table. "Of course. I'll talk to you later."

She hangs up and I throw the sheets back, knowing I won't be able to sleep after that conversation. I plop down onto my couch and start channel surfing, the act of hitting the channel button more occupying than what I'm actually seeing on the screen. As I flip through stations, my mind starts working, running through all of the possible scenarios: Tom could reject me, he could flat-out refuse to talk to me, but maybe, just maybe, he loves me, too…or at least doesn't hate me. And if there's any possibility of that, I have to take a chance. But how am I going to get him to listen to me after I shut him out, and even more vexing, how am I going to get him to believe me?

My credibility might be dented, but I've proven that I have writing chops, and that seems to be the best way to get my voice heard. Ever since my first publication, I've been worried about what to do next, what to write, what to publish. When everyone was so sure that *Iowa Nice* was a memoir, a journalistic rendering of a real journey, I was pushed to continue in that literary vein. But now that I've blown the lid on my fictional abilities, I feel free to write whatever I want. And what I want is a better ending, a happy ending for Tom and me.

As if fate is listening to me, plucking the strings of my very bruised heart, I come across an old episode of *Rocky Mountain High*. There's a young Thomas Price, arms wrapped protectively around a youthful Megan Marks, their eyes wide with fear. They both stare up past the camera, which swoops to the crumbling rocks of a cliff. Just as the first wave of rocks and boulders comes tumbling down toward the camera, sure to crush the beautiful couple, the screen turns to black and the credits start rolling.

I remember this storyline clearly. At the last minute Rooster, Tom's friend and sometimes romantic competition from the nearby reservation, pushes them out of the way. He'd been following Megan's character, Iris, jealous of her time spent with Tom's character, Jackson. Rooster ends up breaking a leg due to his courageous act, and Jackson has to carry him down the mountain. Iris nurses Rooster to health, the season ending with them falling into bed together, unwittingly seen by Jackson, who spends the next season hopping from woman to woman in some twisted attempt at revenge.

It's easy to lose myself in the comfort of the show, the predictability of a constant plotline. But I don't live in a show, and real life is not predictable. Life only proceeds if one takes action. And I need to get off my ass and do something. But what?

The next show cues up, and I laugh out loud from the sheer coincidence. *The First Order of Flight* begins with a close-up of Captain Altide's face as he stares out at an incoming asteroid shower. Dramatic music underscores the subtle furrowing of Phil Grant's brow as his character thinks through his next order to his crew. Suddenly, the screen explodes as he shouts his directions, "We've got to punch through! It's our only chance of survival!"

If I was looking for a sign, well, I've just been pummeled by one. I might not be one for big dramatic speeches and public appearances, but I can write a scene with powerful dialogue. And I happen to know a couple of talented actors. And now, I have the beginnings of a plan.

Excerpt from *Iowa Nice*

DUBUQUE

Standing on the bluff, overlooking the Mississippi and the downtown skyline, I'm overwhelmed by the beauty that accompanies the perfect marriage of land, sky, and water. The picturesque architecture of Dubuque seems frozen in time, a memorial to an era of horse and carriage, booming boat travel, and economic surplus. The wide span of the Mississippi's murky water serves as a natural division between our great state and Illinois and Wisconsin. All we have to do is cross a bridge and we are no longer in Iowa. A desperate part of me wonders if we were no longer in Iowa, if this trip was preemptively halted, if Dad's disease would somehow follow suit, frozen in time like the town below, unable to reach its end without the proper completion of our journey.

But those are the musings of a child, the sign of an immature understanding of the world. Because the world doesn't stop even if your heart is breaking. I should know that by now.

"Should we ride?" Dad asks, still looking ahead as we lean over the white wooden railing on the Fenelon Place Elevator's south deck. For the past half hour, we've been watching the two cable cars slide past each other on their alternating ascent and descent, the slow pace creating a meditative rhythm that has easily swallowed up the minutes and a majority of our worries.

"Sure. A round trip, right?"

"Unless you plan on giving me a piggyback ride up the hill." I laugh at the image of my dad clinging to my shoulders, his legs sticking out at my sides. He turns to look at me, his face softening under the glare of the shining sun. "I love making you laugh. Makes me think about how you would laugh as a baby. Your whole body would open up and pour out the most high-pitched squeal of pleasure. Nothing is as mesmerizing as a baby's joy."

"Mom said no one ever made me laugh as much as you."

The corner of his mouth lifts, and he raises one brow. "It's only because I'm so funny looking."

"No, I think it's because I just liked being with you." He looks away, trying to hide the swirl of emotion in his eyes, but he can't help but look back when I say. "I like being with you now."

"I like being with you, too."

23

The number of parked cars has already exceeded the limit of the gravel lots, requiring lines of vehicles to park in surprisingly straight rows in the grassy overflow area. One thing about Iowans: give us a field and we will figure out how to park in it. The Ghost Show isn't set to start for at least an hour, and the sun beats down on all of us bold enough to venture out for a game which takes place at the peak of the heat on this early October day.

It's been three weeks since I've seen Tom, and his absence still aches within me like a missing limb. If I have any hope of reattaching him to my life, I must swallow my pride and go through with this silly, possibly self-destructive plan.

I start walking with the steady stream of people heading toward the house and field. The entire property sits in a green valley cupped between rolling hills and yellowed corn fields ready for harvest. We cross a bridge over a creek, and then the gravel walk forks either to the dirt field or to the white house that sits on the hill like a sentinel. Next to the original film structures sit a gift shop and event center in the designs of an idyllic red barn and machine shed, erected to transform this movie site into a lucrative tourist attraction. While only two permanent wooden bleachers surround the field, other seating has been brought in to accommodate the large crowd lured by the novelty of meeting celebrities and being a part of Iowa history.

I go through the details in my head, remembering that the cast and crew are being housed in the event center before being pulled out to preen and prance in front of the audience. I need to get there, but don't know if my moxie will be enough to grant me access, and even if it is, I don't want to be seen by Tom before my plan unfurls. This is the part that Rene was leaving up in the air, waiting until we could see the locale to plan our next move.

Suddenly I'm attacked from the side, and all I can think is, *Oh shit, they have security!* But then I realize I'm being dragged behind the gift shop, my sight dominated by big hair, big boobs, and a white pinstripe baseball jersey.

"Rene! You didn't need to tackle me!" I hiss through clenched teeth as I wiggle out of her alarmingly tight grip.

"I'm just getting you primed for a day of baseball." She turns to look at me and instantly starts fixing my hair. I brush her hand away.

"That's football."

"Oh, well, whatever. Tom's in there, so you have to stay out here." She jabs a finger toward the event center, then points aggressively at the ground, indicating our current position hunkered behind a row of porta-potties.

"Okay, so how do I get to Megan and Phil?"

As if on cue, the door of the porta-potty to our right swings open, and Phil Grant steps out, wearing an identical jersey and relaxed gray pants. Instead of a belt, he wears a pair of navy-blue suspenders, which he adjusts as he exits the foul-smelling container.

"Took you long enough. I've been waiting in there for over twenty minutes." Phil pulls at his suspenders, then greets me with a nonchalant, “Hey, kid.”

“What are you both wearing?” I stare in wonder, my gaze flitting between their matching shirts and coming to rest on my own denim sundress.

“The organizers gave them to the entire team. Here, I was able to nab one for you.” Rene instantly starts dressing me, holding the sleeves open for me to slide my arms into, and tying the front of the shirt to cinch in around my waist. “There. Now you look legit. Not like a crazed stalker at all. I wish I had time to do your hair, though. Have you been conditioning?” I swat her hand away, but gently, grateful for her help and attention.

“Well, if I have it my way, no one except Tom will see my hair. And whichever way it goes, I doubt he’ll care what it looks like.” I start rummaging through my shoulder purse and find the folded papers, giving a crinkled copy to Phil. “Where’s Megan?”

Rene sucks her teeth and shakes her head. “Therein lies the one snafu in our plan. They’re announcing Tom and Megan together, capitalizing off the whole *Rocky Mountain* reunion. Tom has been glued to her side all day. So that part is a no-go.”

“What are we going to do?”

“You're going to have to read it,” Rene says casually, as if she hasn’t just dropped a live grenade in my lap. “See, don’t you wish I had time to do your hair now?”

“Me? I can’t! I’m not an actor!

“No, but they’re your words. Can’t you say them like you mean them? That’s all that’s required.” Rene sees someone in a crisp polo pass by, and she nods for the three of us to move further into concealment.

“Don’t worry, Logan. I’ll make it easy for you. I’ve been told I’m a very giving scene partner.” Rene and I both look at Phil for a beat as he continues staring down at his lines.

"You do it!" I suddenly burst, grabbing Rene's shoulders. "You've been around actors much longer than I have."

Rene reaches up and grabs my hands, bringing them down between us. I focus on her pink and purple eyeshadow, expertly blended from lash to brow, as she stares into my own terrified stare. "Logan, it should be you. It should've always been you. Your words, your voice. That's what he needs to hear. It's going to mean even more this way." I nod, unblinking, as she releases my grip. "Well, I have to get back. Phil is scheduled to appear first, so just say you're his personal assistant, then escort him to the mound and…well, then it's all you, babe." She reaches up and pats my cheek, pats Phil on the back as she passes, and leaves me and television royalty standing behind a plastic shit box.

As Phil looks over the script I've written, I stare out at the winding road that carried a string of headlights to the baseball field in the movie. Kevin Costner listened to the voice in his head, and everything worked out. Maybe it will for me, too. Unfortunately, I have multiple voices in my head, many of them with conflicting advice, which makes it more difficult to act on blind faith.

"This is good, Logan. You're a talented writer." Phil shifts, his feet shuffling across dirt and gravel. "Do you want to read through this aloud, or are you okay?"

"I'm okay," I respond listlessly, still shell-shocked by the change in plan. I continue staring off into the distance, the stream of patrons only pouring in thicker as we get closer to gametime.

"You know, I don't think you did anything wrong with your book. Did you conceal the truth in order to get a publishing deal? Sure. Have you lied about other things because it's easier to fabricate than to live with what's uncomfortable? Probably. But it's still your work. It's still your experience, and I still think you're a damn good writer and a good person."

I turn my head slowly to look at Phil who's preoccupied with adjusting his sliding suspender straps. "Thank you. That means a lot."

He looks up and I see the same calculating intellect, the same boldness and heart that defined Captain Smith Altide's character and made him such a beloved fixture in so many homes for so many years. "You know, you and I haven't spent much time together. At first, I thought maybe you were just so preoccupied with the movie, and then with Tom. Oh yeah, I saw it. Don't fool yourself. Everyone saw it." He laughs at my look of horror, then continues. "But I don't think that's it. I think you avoided me for other reasons. Deeper reasons that had to do with your dad."

I sigh, letting my shoulders slump in defeat. "You may be right. Whether it's because you're playing my dad or remind me of him… you know, he loved you and your show so much…it's been hard to be around you. I feel like he's watching me, judging me for lying about the book, angry at me for putting our lives on display…and disappointed that I never apologized before he died."

"What did you need to apologize for? Didn't you stop talking because he didn't approve of your marriage?"

"Yes—"

"Then the ball was in his court. He was the parent, he was the adult in the relationship. It was his job to model proper behavior, and he should have been the one to apologize. He's the one that let you down, Logan."

A sheen of tears begins to coat my eyes, and a tightness in my chest starts to loosen, unknotting itself at the wise words of Phil Grant.

"I have two children. They're grown now, thirty-eight and thirty-five. Married with kids. I have seven grandchildren. And even though my kids are parents now, I'm still their dad. I'm still responsible for being the type of parent they deserve. Sure, I've messed up, lost my temper, had my share of bad headlines, but I own up to my failures.

And they've done some stupid shit over the years, too, but we keep moving forward. We're family. There's nothing they could do that would ever make me not want to be in their lives."

Tears have escaped my eyes and are streaming down my cheeks. Phil reaches into his pocket and pulls out a handkerchief. He pats my face gently, then places the fabric in my hand. He steps closer, cradles my face and tilts his gaze to mine. "I don't know if hearing this helps or not, but Logan, I'm incredibly proud of who you are and I think you are an exceptional woman."

The leaden ball of regret, bitterness, anger, and despair melts at his words, and I gasp with renewed air. I lift the handkerchief to my mouth to stifle my sobs, and Phil opens his arms and lets me tuck into him. He holds me as a parent would hold a hurt child, and it's what I've needed for so long. To be cared for, to be vindicated, to be released.

Once I can breathe normally, I straighten up and Phil gives me the space I need, rocking on his heels as he checks his watch. "Oh, jeez. We have to get going. Ten minutes until we're on, kid." He grabs my arm and marches us toward the field where a tent has been erected to house sound equipment and the game commentator.

"This is my assistant. She's going to escort me onto the mound since my knee is giving me the fits today," Phil says convincingly, even though he is the one that just dragged me across the property. But, of course, he is a renowned actor. I just hope I can hold it together and keep up.

Excerpt from *Iowa Nice*

DYERSVILLE

"Dad, we shouldn't be doing this. You're not well enough to be frolicking around on a baseball diamond." I kick at the dirt, creating a cloud of tan dust as I trudge behind my father. He's selected a mitt from the chest of baseball supplies provided at the Field of Dreams movie site and ambles out into the field.

"You think I'd let us leave here without playing? Are you crazy?" He tosses the words over his shoulder as he mounts the pitcher's mound.

"I've been called worse things," I mumble. I'm not of the athletic variety, and I'm resistant to this forced participation in America's supposed favorite pastime. I myself have never passed time throwing a ball back and forth or trying to hit one with an aluminum stick. And yet here I am, being signaled to grab a bat and take my place at the plate.

My dad shouts out various corrections to my stance, hold, and overall state of being before he throws a ball directly across the plate. I miss, of course, and drop my arms, my mouth turned down with frustration.

"I can't do this." The whine of an insolent child has replaced my usually pleasant voice.

"Three-year-olds can do this, Logan. Of course you can."

"Well, it's not my fault. I was never in Little League."

"Is that another barbed accusation I detect?"

I hit the ground with my bat, then resume what I consider a batting position. I swing and miss again. "Ugh, I suck."

"You're fine. It's just practice. Just try again. You can always try again."

I roll my eyes and stand hip-width apart, the bat hovering over my right shoulder. My dad throws and I swing, the clang of the bat announcing contact with the ball which skitters across the dirt to the left of third base.

"I did it!" I shout, juvenile insolence quickly replaced by childlike joy.

"You did! It's a foul ball, but still, you hit it. See, I told you that you could do it. Now let's try again."

I take my position, more determined than ever to improve. A batting star I'll never be, but if I keep trying, I just might make it to where I can run the bases.

24

It's as horrible as I thought it would be to be on the pitcher's mound at the center of everyone's attention. No, I take that back. It's actually worse. There are people packed in on all sides of the baseball diamond and even crowds standing in the grass near the house who were unable to secure seats, but instead watch large screens that have been brought in to project images to those on the sidelines. It's a big deal, and I'm questioning everything that has brought me to consider going through with this desperate act.

After Phil introduced me as his assistant to the organizers, I walked him to the mound as his name was announced and met with a round of cheers. But instead of walking back, I stayed by his side, and I now drop his arm and grab the wireless microphone from him.

The audience quiets, looks of confusion passing across faces. Near the headquarters tent, I see a gathering of white jerseys, and my nervousness reaches an apocalyptic level as my gaze lands on a particular figure with swept-back brown hair, bronze skin, and strong shoulders. Tom lifts his hand above his eyes, squinting into the sun. Megan clings to his arm, Deedee on her other side, huge grins plastered on both their faces. My eyes travel over the other crew members, faces I feared I would never see again varying from bewilderment to amusement. Their presence gives me the courage to speak into the microphone, my voice cracking at first.

"Hi. Um, I know you are all here for some baseball, and to see Phil Grant, Megan Marks, and Thomas Price, of course. But I was hoping you would humor me for a bit." The echo of the sound system makes me feel like I am speaking over myself, and I stop, letting the fizzle of the mic settle in the deafening silence. A few coughs punctuate the air, and I rush back into my spiel. "I'm Logan Sterling. You might have heard of me. I wrote *Iowa Nice*, wrote the screenplay, worked on the film, and then made headlines for many other untoward reasons. I've learned a lot these past few months—about myself, about relationships, and about honesty. And I'd like to share those lessons, but because I am super uncomfortable speaking for myself, I thought I could use a little help.

"Phil has kindly agreed to play my father in this dialogue, as he does in the movie. While this conversation never actually occurred, similar to all the conversations I had with my dad in the book, writing it still helped me sort through my feelings…of which there are a lot.

"So here's Phil Grant reading the part of First Sergeant Malcolm McClarnon, and I'll be reading the part of…uh, me, Logan Sterling."

I look over to Phil, his eyes glittering with mirth, enjoying my flummoxed performance. I take a deep breath, hold up my script, and nod to signal the start of the scene.

"Hey, Dad." I'm hesitant as I say the scripted opening line, a real hook if I say so myself.

"Hey, Logie Bear." Phil winks, his lips curling up in an amused grin.

"So I don't know if you've heard, but our story has gained quite the attention."

"Our story?"

"The story I wrote after you died. The story I wish had been true. It's what I needed to write in order to work through your death, to move forward with my life after realizing I'd been living it only for other people, including you."

"How were you living it for me if we weren't even speaking?"

"Well, you see, I still did everything as if you were watching me. Tried to make the right choices, tried to make you proud. Even though you were mad at me, I always thought you would come back, that we would make up, and I'd have all these amazing things to tell you about. But there were no amazing things. I was trying to be a good daughter, a good wife…I wanted to be a good mother, but I couldn't even do that. So when you died, I didn't know what I was doing it all for anymore. And I overcorrected. I focused solely on what was inside me, and I barely batted an eye when an opportunity came to share that with the world. But, you see, I was still living for others. For my publishers, for my agent, for my readers."

"It's not so bad to live for others, is it?"

"It is if you no longer know who you are." We pause, and I'm lost in the moment. It's just me and my dad, talking in the middle of the Field of Dreams, having our first and last heart-to-heart. "But I know who I am now, or at least who I want to be. Which is why I'm here."

"To play baseball?" A lone whoop rings from the audience, followed by some aggressive shushes.

"No one would want to see that. No, I'm here because I need to apologize for what I've done."

"Haven't you already done that?"

"Well, sort of. But there's someone in particular that I need to apologize to. Someone I can't stop thinking about, who I want to spend every waking moment with. Someone who's brought me joy, shown me what it feels like to be cherished, someone with whom I have fallen deeply and irrevocably in love."

"You're making me blush, Logie Bear." A few chortles punctuate Phil's perfectly delivered line. "So go for it. Apologize and be with him."

"I would. But I'm not sure he wants me anymore. Not sure he loves me back."

Phil is supposed to recite my lines about the power of forgiveness, how love can grow among weeds, and other poetic metaphors I've poured over for the past few days. But in true Phil fashion, he drops his script and turns to look solely at me.

"Who wouldn't love you, Logan?"

"Well, you, Dad."

"I always loved you, no matter what was going on between us. Real love doesn't disappear just because you stop talking or life pulls you apart. Real love persists despite the distance, despite the silence, and despite the pain. And if you think you could have this type of love—real, powerful love spanning across space and time—then you should tell him. So start by telling me. What is it about this man?"

Phil's words dwarf anything I've written, but he's saying them for me, and I'm not the intended audience. I mouth a thank you, then turn to find Tom among the crowd. I find him standing at the backstop, his arms crossed as he stares at me.

"The first day we met, he saved me from falling in front of a fancy restaurant and flashing a flock of Kardashians." Pockets of laughter skip through the audience, and I proceed. "He took a chance on me, believed in me, and brought me into the filming process. Sure, I was fired, but still, it was nice while it lasted." More rippling chuckles from the crowd gives me the courage to continue, and I list more ways Tom has touched me and my life.

"He gave me his shirt when I was cold in Sioux City. He held my hand when we jumped off the boat in Clear Lake. He arranged a private carousel ride for me in Story City. He caught me when I fell off a bar while singing the 'Iowa Fight Song,' and then he saved me from a tornado in Winterset. He introduced me to his parents and showed me his home in Iowa City. He forgave me for being married, traveled with me to Ottumwa, and met my ex—" My voice catches as I reach the end of our adventures. "And then I broke his heart on the side of Highway 34. He saw magic in me and my story, but really, he's the one who brought the magic into my life. And I've ruined it all."

I firm my stance and find Tom in the crowd, my eyes locked on him and him alone.

"Thomas Price, you told me how important honesty is to you. I don't know if you consider this a grand gesture or just human decency, but this is me telling the truth: I love you. I know I've lied, and it might be hard for you to trust me, but here I am declaring myself publicly. Every day in this state, every small town we visited, and every single roadside stop has led me to fall deeper in love with you. And I hope you are in love with me, too."

I drop my hand that's holding the microphone and stand awkwardly. Tom doesn't move, and the crowd starts to stir. Intermittent hollers start ping-ponging through the stands, everything from "Don't do it, Tom. Marry me instead!" "I love you, too, Tom!" "Forgive her!" and "Kiss her already!" start assaulting my ears. My hyperfocus on Tom is interrupted, and my body suddenly remembers I'm standing in front of a very large gathering of strangers who have just witnessed the public flaying of my soul. My hands start to shake and I look toward Phil. I look back to where Tom was standing, but instead see Megan jogging across the field.

She hugs me and whispers in my ear, "Maybe he just needs time," before taking the microphone and directing the crowd to applaud me for my vulnerability. She starts spinning it into a marketing tactic to promote the upcoming movie, and I leave the mound, my legs leaden with humiliation. I veer toward the right side of the field, away from the congregated crew, my vision clouded with tears. I tried. I put myself out there. Declared my love and was denied. Now, there's nothing left but to go home with my tail between my legs and my heart ripped in half.

I'm about to cross the bridge over the creek when I see him standing in the center of the walk, his baseball jersey unbuttoned over a white T-shirt and a Hawkeye baseball cap shielding his eyes from the sun.

"He's right, you know." He starts walking toward me. My body trembles at his approach.

"Who?"

"Phil. When he said we could have that kind of love."

"How do you know that was Phil and not me?" My feet manage to propel me forward and we meet at the end of the bridge.

"I've been directing Phil for two months. I can tell when he goes off script."

I search his face, trying to read his motive, still unsure of what's happening, guarded after my lone retreat. "Why did you leave me up there?"

He holds out his hand and grabs mine, pulling me toward him. "For a moment, I thought I needed time, thought I needed to go somewhere and think. But the minute I tried to leave, I realized the only place I want to go is where you are. You are my destination, Logan Alice Sterling. I love you. Real-love you." His lips part to reveal his perfect teeth in a smile that illuminates his entire face.

I reach up to graze my fingers across the back of his neck and tilt my head up. "I real-love you, too, Thomas Sydney Price."

"Please, call me Tom." He smirks and I go to retort, but he brings his mouth to mine, his arms wrapping around my back and lifting me off my feet. The pressure of his lips is a breath of new life sending jolts of electricity through my body. Nothing else matters, nothing else exists in this moment as he kisses me under the blue Iowa sky. A whine of protest hums in my throat as he pulls away, but then I see him look up behind me.

"What is it?" I spin around and see that our image is being projected onto the two jumbo screens and that everyone is watching us.

"Now that's a grand gesture," Tom laughs as a loud roar erupts from the crowd.

Megan's voice carries across the sound system. "Could Thomas Price and Logan Sterling please proceed to the pitcher's mound to throw the opening pitch?"

He waves his hand and smiles. "Shall we?" He looks down at me, his hand encircling mine.

"You expect me to go back out there?"

"You mean, you haven't caught the acting bug?"

"I think I'm immune."

"Lucky for you, this isn't acting. Just baseball."

"I'm not good at that either."

"I'm not asking you to be good at it, just to be with me." His eyes drink me in and I'm helpless, forever unable to resist him.

"Always."

We walk out to the pitcher's mound and I look around at the smiling faces, strangers who have seen the most thrilling moment of my life, who are cheering me on, accepting me for who I am. And next to me is the man who has helped me see who that is more clearly than ever.

Tom throws the pitch, letting me go only as long as it takes to release the ball from his hand, and then we are walking off the field as the ghost players emerge from the cornfield to their own applause.

Tom and I take our place among the cast and crew of *Iowa Nice*, greeted with hugs, kisses, and the occasional butt slap. I'm suddenly overcome with a wave of exhaustion, my body and soul relaxing after finally obtaining what I've always wanted: a home, people who accept me for me, and unconditional love that can withstand bumps and curves in the road.

I used to wish life was easier. I wanted to treat milestones in life like pinpoints on a roadmap, to be able to check them off once a destination had been reached. But very rarely do we know we've reached a destination until we've passed it. Then it's just a ghost town made of unreliable memories and overpowering regrets. Or maybe it's haunted by the past versions of ourselves, the layers we shed as we drive forward, moving away but carrying the lessons we've learned with us. Instead of wishing life was easier, I'm now grateful for the road I've taken and looking forward to the next stops along the way.

Updated Ending from the Revised Publication of *Iowa Nice*

DYERSVILLE

I sit on the wooden bleachers, the iconic white farmhouse looming behind me as I stare out at the empty baseball field. My voice, barely a whisper, rides on the Iowa breeze, the particles of sound blown asunder among the shuddering cornfields, the yawning blue sky, and the dancing tree limbs. I am a product of this state, and every day I am here, I drop pieces of myself into it. My father was as much a piece of this state as I am, and I close my eyes, imagining him caressing my hair, running his fingers through the tangled strands like he used to do when I was a child.

"This journey with you has meant so much to me." I look next to me, where my father should be, but there's no one there. Nothing but sun-warmed wood and heat-laden air. "I just wish you could have taken it with me." He's never been here. It's always been me, alone on the road, traipsing through the countryside, absorbing the beauty

that is the essence of all of those who have traveled through this great state.

"But you were with me, and you always will be. Because real love doesn't just disappear. It's forever in me. In my memories of you, of times we laughed, cried, even fought. It all came from my love for you. And I'm ready to set it free."

I stand, inhale the scent of wildflowers, corn, and farmland, and I say goodbye.

"I love you, Dad." The words barely reach past my lips, but I know he hears them. I feel it in my soul, and finally, I feel whole.

EPILOGUE

"You doing okay?" Tom takes his seat next to me backstage as we wait for our segment to arrive. "I know you hate doing these interviews." He shoots me a reassuring smile, and I reach over to squeeze his hand.

"I do, but it's easier when I'm with you." I return his smile, mine wavering with nerves. I never dreamed I would be meeting with Georgia Mills, the lead anchor of America's top-ranking morning broadcast *The Morning Real*, but here I am, about to pee myself with anticipation. "Distract me. Let's talk about something else."

"Okay, how's the writing going?"

I sigh mournfully, wishing I could be writing now.

Last night, in our Manhattan hotel room, I showed him my outline and some of my randomly written excerpts. As he scanned the document, his reactions aglow with the light from my laptop screen, I studied his face.

I'm still taken aback by his movie star handsomeness, still overcome with butterflies when he flashes that poster boy smile at me; but he's become so much more in the past year we've been together, losing ourselves in post-production of the movie during the day and losing ourselves in each other's bodies at night. My fingers can trace the curve of his jawline, the bow of his top lip, the tiny scar at the tip of his left eyebrow, and recite the story of his life. He's told me all of his secrets from his past, regaling me with tales of follies and feats. He has shared all of his present feelings and plans, giving his all to the movie and thoroughly supporting me in my career endeavors. And he has whispered his hopes for the future into my skin, his breath tickling the hairs along my naked body as he murmurs sweet promises of our life together. He's mine, and there's not a day I'm not grateful for that fact. Therapy has helped me see all that I have, all that I've done, and all that I want to be, which is becoming more real to me every day, even as I devote myself to fictitious composition.

"Any notes?" I cautiously asked, his eyes having reached the blank page at the end of the document. For a while, I had gone back and forth, telling Tom I didn't know what to write about next, how nothing interesting had happened to me. That a year of happiness had proven disastrous to my usual creative inspiration of angst and insecurity. But I eventually realized something interesting *had* happened to me. I had fallen in love with a movie star and begun to love myself more in the process. So I wrote a story inspired by our story but have been completely upfront with my plans to market it as a fictional romance.

Tom narrowed his eyes, slowly releasing his words. "I think it needs a little more drama, some conflict."

"Oh really? There's not enough conflict?" I had felt the prickly heat of self-doubt start to moisten my brow and pits, had begun worrying that I was going to need to throw everything out and start over from scratch.

"Yeah, I'm thinking like…a brutish business manager." His gaze slid over to me, a sly smile lifting his lips. The anxious heat turned into a familiar warmth as I picked up on his playfulness. I left my perch on the bed and made my way to the recliner.

"Or how about a publicity scandal?" I lifted my laptop from his grip and set it on the desk next to him. Tom looked up at me, his pupils brimming with want, his hands reaching for me.

"Or maybe a secret marriage?" He pulled me onto his lap, my legs settling on each side of his hips.

"There could be a football rivalry. A division so strong even love can't conquer it." My hands dug into his hair and tugged his face up to mine.

"Or a tornado? That could really add some drama." He brought his mouth to mine in a quick peck, his teeth quickly skimming my bottom lip.

"Oh, that's good. That's just what I need." And that's when the notes stopped. After a crazed round of lovemaking in a hotel room—our specialty—I couldn't help but flip open my laptop and start writing. I hadn't gone to sleep until two in the morning, and we had to be up at five in order to leave for the studio and get to hair and makeup. I haven't been able to think clearly since waking up, finding myself lost in the smoky scenes of a story in progress, the tendrils of characters and plot coming together to form a concrete picture from the haze.

"Mr. Price, they're ready for you." An intern comes to take Tom onstage and he leans down to kiss my cheek. For this interview, they're going to talk to him alone first, and then bring me out. He's definitely a more practiced opener, and it helps me ease into a conversation once it's already started.

Niya appears from some hallway, taking Tom's spot, her head bent down toward her phone. She starts reading an email intended for me and my publishing team, derision thick in her voice. "Are you fucking kidding me? Who doesn't know Logan Sterling is a woman by now? Everyone knows you're shacking up with Thomas Price. This had better be a Nigerian prince asking for money or I'm coming for their fucking throats."

I laugh, entertained as always by the fiery persona of my agent, but all too aware of her gooey insides that have begun surfacing more and more as her relationship with Landon survives the distance from Chicago to LA. I'm happy for them, even though I walked in on them doing some kinky shit on Facetime. That's the last time I enter a room after Niya says, "I'm coming."

I turn my attention to the monitors and watch as Tom hugs Georgia. He looks as handsome as ever in a textured blue suit, matching vest, and cream shirt. I found myself wanting to rid him of his bothersome clothes as I was tying his silver tie, intoxicated by his scent of spiced orange and sandalwood. I've since learned the name of his cologne and have ordered a crate of it to ensure he never runs out.

"Oh, hey. Remember, we need to pick up wedding gifts while we're here. New York's Macy's is the best," Niya says as her fingers tap away on her phone, probably eviscerating whoever dared mistake me as a man.

"Sounds good. We have some time this afternoon. I can't believe the wedding is three weeks away!" Megan and Deedee are getting married in Spain, and I couldn't be happier. For them—and for myself, as I finally get to travel internationally and enjoy a well-needed week away with my boyfriend.

The intern suddenly materializes. "Ms. Sterling, please come with me." I push myself out of the chair, hoping the momentum will keep me from running in the opposite direction. As I hear my name announced, I step out of the sidelines and under the bright lights, Georgia and Tom both standing to greet me. I take a seat between the two of them and put on my most dazzling smile. It may not be as blinding as Tom's, but I've been practicing and am starting to wear it more easily.

Georgia is all personable warmth as we start talking about the upcoming release of *Iowa Nice*. We showed an early version at South by Southwest, and it was met with enthusiastic feedback. We're hoping a Chicago premiere will play off the Midwestern heart of the movie, followed by a tour across Iowa and the surrounding states.

Tom and I easily maneuver between the usual questions about the filming, a few carefully structured answers about the inherent scandals, and updates about our coupling since the hard launch of our relationship at the Dyersville baseball game. Then Georgia's voice softens, her look serious as she says, "Logan, I just have to ask. The years of lying, the near demise of the movie, the possible negative impact to your career, was it worth it?"

I look over to Tom, who is watching me, his face splitting into that charming smile of his, his hand resting on his thigh. I reach over and grab his hand, pull it between us, and squeeze. I think of how even though it was a painful road of loss, lies, and grief, it also led me to this moment, when I can hold the hand of the man I love, pay the bills doing the thing I love, and experience life in technicolor. I may still wish that my dad and I had reunited, that our ending could have been different, but I also realize the gift he has given me: a rich life full of love, worth, and value.

I might not have gotten everything I wanted in life, but I'm no longer suffering from the mistakes of the past. Life isn't simple, but my answer to Georgia's question is.

"Yes. It was worth it. Every bit."

ACKNOWLEDGMENTS

On Saturday, September 2, 2023, my sister called me crying. Our dad had passed away that morning. It had been over ten years since he and I had spoken. I had seen him once at a family wedding since then, but he had looked at me and my infant daughter, then turned away from me. He never did meet my children. I'd changed so much in the decade without him, as a mother, wife, teacher, and writer. I'd gained confidence in myself, learned to take professional and personal risks, and waded through the mess of childhood trauma that had left me so weak for so long. I always imagined I would get the chance to talk to my dad again, to show him the strong woman I had grown into, both because of him and in spite of him. Hearing that he had passed away without our ever having mended our relationship felt like the biggest betrayal ever and the saddest ending possible. There was so much that went unsaid between us. And that is how *Road Maps* was born. From the death of one comes the life of another; it was a chance for me to work through my grief and regrets while seeking some sense of closure.

There are many people to thank, not just for their support in my writing of this book, but also for the support they provided during the loss of my dad and the subsequent plodding through of my messy emotions.

Thank you to Dr. Anthony Paustian and the Bookpress Publishing team as they continue to support my publishing dreams.

Thank you to Ann Hanigan-Kotz for her help navigating writing, marketing, and event-attending. Those long events are more fun with you, and I've learned so much during our conversations and time together. Thank you for being such a wonderful mentor.

Thank you to my beta readers Phoebe Myers, Kari Fokken-Nattress, and Tara Rechkemmer. Writing is a process and stories take time to develop. Thank you for your feedback as I worked through the rewriting and revision process.

Thank you to my English department family. The love and support I feel at work has only helped me continue to strengthen my confidence as a teacher, author, and individual.

Thank you to all the readers of *Another Dance* who reached out and told me they enjoyed the book. Your kind words gave me the boost I needed to continue on this difficult road of publishing. Writing requires putting oneself out there, being vulnerable, accepting both criticism and praise. I don't know if I would be able to continue if it weren't for those willing to share their sentiments of support.

Thank you to my sister, Gina Sedore. Our time together remembering our dad and sharing in the ups and downs of life have helped me make peace with our loss and has allowed me to see all that I should be grateful for in life, including you. I'm lucky to have you as a big sister.

Thank you to my mother, Dixie Carder. As a single parent, you have never failed in your love and support. I never knew how tough it must have been for you until I had children of my own, and I have a supportive partner to share in the experience. You amaze me, and

I hope I've made you proud.

Thank you to my friends who let me vent and process the loss of my dad and the idea for this book. Whether it was listening to fond memories, letting me cry, or inducting me into the "dead dad club," your support has been invaluable.

Thank you to my husband, Jeremy. For a few years there, I thought all relationships were fraught with deceit, conflict, and pain. You have shown me what a partner and father should be. You are the most honest, loving, and supportive man I could ever dream of being with and seeing you with our children has shown me how important a stable father-figure is and how lucky Toby and Aubry are to have you as their daddy.

Thank you to my children, Toby and Aubry, who show me every day what real love is and what a parent's love should be: pure and unconditional. Through you, I have found my own strength as a mother, partner, and woman. I know I make mistakes, but you make me want to be better, and I will never abandon you or make you think you are undeserving of my love. There's nothing you could do that would ever make me not want to be in your lives.

Two weeks after my father's death, I had a dream from which I woke up crying. In the dream, I was in my front room, my children and some of their cousins running around while I sat on one end of the couch and my dad sat on the other end. We were both watching the children play, and then we turned toward each other and both said, "I'm sorry." We began crying, and I climbed into his lap as if I were a little girl again, both of us sobbing and repeatedly apologizing. When I woke up from the dream, I gasped, feeling as if something pivotal had just happened. I'd like to believe that this was my father's way of telling me he's sorry and that he loves me. And *Road Maps* is my way of telling him.

Dad, I'm sorry. I forgive you. I miss you. I love you.